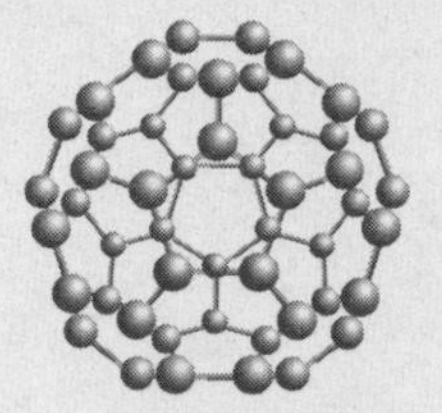

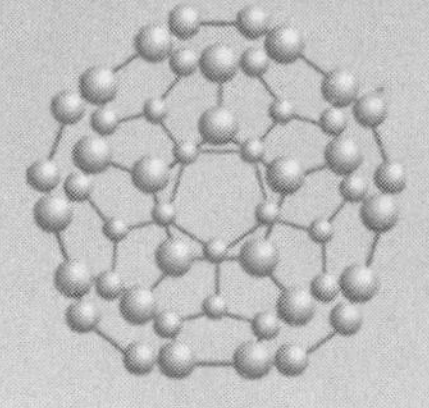

SHAITON'S FIRE

JAKE THOENE

Tyndale House Publishers, Inc.
WHEATON, ILLINOIS

Visit Tyndale's exciting Web site at www.tyndale.com

Buckminsterfullerene molecular structure illustrated by Alyssa Force

Edited by Ramona Cramer Tucker

Designed by Ron Kaufmann

Published in association with the literary agency of Alive Communications, Inc., 7680 Goddard Street, Suite 200, Colorado Springs, CO 80920.

Library of Congress Cataloging-in-Publication Data

Thoene, Jake.
Shaiton's fire / Jake Thoene.
p. cm.
ISBN 0-8423-5361-5 (sc)
1. Terrorism–Prevention–Fiction. 2. Undercover operations–Fiction. 3. Nuclear power plants–Fiction.
4. Middle East–Fiction. 5. California–Fiction. I. Title.
PS3570.H465 S53 2002
813′.54–dc21 2002004772

Printed in the United States of America

08 07 06 05 04 03
7 6 5 4 3 2

To Wendi,

My lovely wife, a wonderful mother, and my best friend:

Without you, I would never find the time

or have the peace of mind.

Thank you!

ACKNOWLEDGMENTS

For every moment of life, as well as the passion and opportunity to pursue truth diligently, I thank God.

I also wish to express great thanks to:

My parents, for their unending support and lifelong education in the field of writing.

My family and friends, for enduring the countless hours of busyness.

Rick Christian, for calling the right shots, and the Tyndale team, for their help in dialing in a direct hit!

Justin and all those at 2ndamendmentsports.com, for your intense interest in the discipline of tactical precision and the preservation of the Second Amendment.

The staff at Diablo, for the questions they answered, and those they wouldn't.

Those in law enforcement, as well as domestic and international security, who are committed to giving their lives for the safety and quality of others. All Americans owe you a debt of gratitude.

And to the rest, who remain unnamed but vital in my life, thank you.

The purpose of terrorism is to terrorize.

Sympathy in a revolutionary is as wrong as cowardice on the field of battle.

Paraphrased from V. I. Lenin

Terrorism is a crime by any civilized standard, committed against innocent people, away from the scene of political conflict, and must be dealt with as a crime. . . . Let us shrink the dark and dank areas of sanctuary until these cowardly marauders are held to answer . . . and receive the punishment they so richly deserve.

William Webster, Former FBI Director

Mercy toward evil is cruelty to the innocent.

Ancient Jewish Proverb

PREFACE

Dear Mr. President:

The purpose of this letter is to inform you personally that the interagency counterterrorism unit, as envisioned by the Homeland Security Act of 2001 and previously designated Chapter 16, is fully operational and ready for assignment as needed.

As you know, it is my fervent hope that Chapter 16 need never be deployed.

In the ongoing war on terrorism, the prospect that scenes of horror like those perpetrated on New York City and Washington, D.C., might be repeated causes all Americans (and freedom-loving people everywhere) understandable distress.

Rooting out and eliminating terrorist organizations internationally and preventing terrorist activity aimed at our citizens are obviously of paramount importance.

Nevertheless, prudence dictated the formation of a domestic, fast-response, streamlined unit

- able to draw on all law-enforcement and intelligence-community resources as accurately and rapidly as possible, without being hindered by traditional bureaucratic protocol and
- able to anticipate and prevent additional terrorist acts once such a threat is detected.

Chapter 16 is that team, composed of carefully selected, highly mobile, highly capable, quick-response, no-strings-attached people, the most elite in their fields.

As a believer yourself, you recognize the significance of the designation we've chosen. Clearly the threats to civilization posed by terrorists who have no regard for human life include all the apocalyptic perils envisioned by the author of the book of Revelation, whether they be weapons of mass destruction, biological agents, or some as yet unimagined tool of terror.

Thank you for the confidence you have expressed in me by designating me the first director of Chapter 16. I will do my best to fulfill that trust.

God bless you, sir, and God bless America.

Sincerely yours,

James A. Morrison
Executive Director, Chapter 16

ONE

Bay Area Rapid Transit (BART) Station
West Oakland, California
Friday, 20 April
6:16 A.M. Pacific Time

I LEFT MY HEART IN SAN FRANCISCO

The dawn air was cold, yet Rhamad was sweating profusely beneath his overcoat. He clutched the handle of the heavy sample case and gazed across the dark waters of the Bay toward the fog-shrouded silhouette of the San Francisco skyline.

Beautiful. Peaceful at the moment. This was the sort of ethereal image imprinted on a thousand postcards and labeled with the caption "I Left My Heart in San Francisco." Within the hour the old lyrics would take on a new and terrible meaning for those about to board the BART subway train. Some would indeed leave their hearts behind.

Rhamad glanced around at the passengers making their way into the subway station. Every race and color was represented among the early commuters.

A white husband and wife, tourists, with two boys.

A gaggle of four young women: white, black, Hispanic, Asian. Heading to work in the fashion district, perhaps? They juggled cups of Starbucks coffee and newspapers as they gossiped with one another.

Businesspeople, stockbrockers needing to catch the opening bell in the East, secretaries, and salesclerks all mingled with blue-collar workers who staffed the shops, restaurants, and hotels of San Francisco.

Who among these, Rhamad wondered, would be dead within the hour? *Death will be the great leveler,* he thought.

Stopping to pick up a newspaper, a gray-haired executive in a Giants baseball cap caught Rhamad's eye. Such a hat seemed out of place with the Armani business suit, expensive shoes, and Coach leather computer case. And dangling from the strap on the case was a catcher's mitt. A strange, incongruous combination. Pitiful somehow that this fellow could not guess what waited for him on the other side of the waters.

So this was it. Rhamad's cue to follow, to buy a ticket, to crowd into the subway car with all of them.

He could see his target plainly.

First light tipped the pyramid of the towering Trans-America Building looming in the heart of the city's financial district.

One brief look over his shoulder and Rhamad descended into the station. He stepped behind the Giants cap. The automated ticket kiosk was out of order. A longer line formed at a window where an irritated Asian-American transit worker sold rail passes and made change the old-fashioned way. It took much longer than Rhamad would have liked. Acutely aware of security cameras peering down, he slipped on his sunglasses and tugged the wide brim of his hat low over his brow.

Just another pimp or druggie getting on the train, he thought.

The Giants cap moved to the front of the queue. "Montgomery Street Station, please." The man shoved a handful of coins toward the ticket man.

"Return?"

"Yes."

So the baseball fan was getting off at Montgomery Street. Second stop on the San Francisco side. There would be no return for him!

Rhamad ducked his chin until his features were hidden by the shadow of the hat brim. He dug into his pockets for exact change. He could see his image reflected in the glass of a two-way mirror. Good. Little detail. The sunglasses and hat accomplished what he wanted.

He slid the coins across the stainless steel counter. "Montgomery. Return."

The tokens were issued.

Rhamad followed the Giants fan through the turnstile just as the sleek westbound train hummed into the station. Clusters of commuters took their places behind the yellow line. The doors hissed and slid open. No one got off. This meant there were more travelers on board who would never see the sun again.

It was interesting for Rhamad to consider how such a mundane act could make the difference between life and death. Ride to Montgomery Street in Rhamad's car and death was almost a certainty. Get off at the first stop and live. Ride to the second and die. Board a different car; miss this train. . . . Those who were lucky would be talking about such fateful decisions before this day was over.

As for those who would die? He had nothing personal against any of them. He was doing what he must do, and they would either escape or die. It was not in his hands.

He trailed the Giants fan onto the fourth car.

Rhamad sat two rows behind the executive. He placed the sample case on the floor in a way that discouraged anyone from sitting beside him.

Rhamad counted 26 passengers. The tourist family—mother, father, and two boys—found seats across from the Giants fan.

Over the PA, a woman's recorded voice announced, "Please stand clear of the doors."

From the words Rhamad overheard, the family was bound for a hotel near the Powell Street Station. Their fate was sealed now; the doors were shut. This train would never reach Powell Street.

The Giants fan struck up a conversation with the boys. Nine and seven years old, they were from Arizona. They played baseball. Right field. Shortstop. They liked the Diamondbacks better than the Giants.

The Giants fan was a kids' baseball coach. He was breaking in the catcher's mitt for his grandson. The grandson would be on his team this year.

And so it went. Pleasant conversation. The last words of the condemned.

"Are we under the Bay now?" the younger boy apprehensively asked the man in the cap.

"Yes."

"How deep?"

"Very deep."

"What if there's an earthquake?"

"This is the safest place to be if there's an earthquake. When I was a kid in London during the war, we used the underground stations as bomb shelters."

Other commuters sipped their coffee and raised newspapers in front of their faces so they wouldn't have to look at anyone else on their short journey into oblivion.

Rhamad's blood rushed in his ears. Involuntarily he reached down to touch the lever on the case. When the train moved into Embarcadero Station, Rhamad would release the false bottom and arm the bomb. He would step off at Embarcadero, leaving the device behind. A few minutes later it would explode . . . just as the train arrived at the Montgomery Street Station.

A small beginning only. A necessary prologue in a chain reaction that would soon change the world forever.

A dead baseball coach. Would this make a difference? A couple of kids. A family here and there. Secretaries. Bus drivers. Clerks. Bank tellers. It was all worth it for the sake of the ultimate goal, was it not?

The PA voice crooned, "Embarcadero Station. We are arriving at Embarcadero Station."

Rhamad looked out the window as the train emerged from the tunnel. Lights illuminated tiled art murals depicting the history of San Francisco on the curved walls of the station. He wondered what images were on the wall of the Montgomery Street terminal, where the bomb would explode. Perhaps that of the earthquake or the Great Fire of 1906?

Now he would provide the city's artists with a new disaster to immortalize in mosaic. Smoke and fire and death would take on deeper meaning in San Francisco.

An electronic bell signaled arrival. Rhamad pushed the button releasing the false bottom from the case. A duplicate case containing the seemingly innocuous cube of Semtex remained on the floor of the train. Rhamad nudged the container of explosives beneath the seat in front of him lest any passenger trip over it between Embarcadero and Montgomery.

Not that it would make any difference if they did.

Empty satchel significantly lighter now, Rhamad stood and moved toward the exit. The doors opened wide. The way of his escape was clear. Several lucky passengers waited to disembark with him.

He heard the Giants fan explain to the family, "Not yet. I get off at Montgomery Street. The stop for your hotel is one after that. You'll come up from the station and you'll be right by the cable cars! Sure. They're running now. They'll take you all the way to Fisherman's Wharf."

Old Mission Elementary School
San Luis Obispo, California
7:52 A.M. Pacific Time

THE ROOTS OF GRAY HAIR

The early morning fog of California's central coast swirled around the rugged volcanic outcropping known as Bishop's Peak. Traffic on Highway 101 was thick with college students bound for Cal Poly University.

Thirty-three-year-old Cindy Alstead tossed her tight, dark curls impatiently as she glanced in the rearview mirror of her dark blue GMC Yukon. A rusty old Ford pickup honked and blasted past her. She was going too slow.

Her radio blared with the recorded chaos of the San Francisco BART bombing. The oft-played screams of injured survivors mingling with the sirens of rescue vehicles nearly drowned out the voice of the newsman on the scene in the city's financial district.

". . . This morning's explosion on board a BART train rattled windows as far away as the Trans-America Building . . . number of dead and injured still uncertain . . . rescue workers digging through the rubble . . . so far forty-two brought up alive . . . burns . . . smoke inhalation . . . authorities have not ruled out terrorist . . ."

Images of the World Trade Center disaster replayed in Cindy's mind.

Strapped in his car seat behind her, four-year-old Tommy declared irri-tably, "Mom, you missed the turn. If you played a Wee Sing tape, I'd be at school."

Miffed at the precocious preschooler's accusation, Cindy snapped off the radio.

Beside her in the passenger seat, nine-year-old Matthew furrowed his brow in an expression that made him look so much like his father. He reached to turn on the radio again. "I wanna hear."

Cindy slapped away his hand. "Enough already."

"Mom!" the boy protested.

"I need a little quiet. I'm trying to drive here."

Matt brooded. "The guy said Trans-America Building! That's close to where Dad lives!"

She shrugged in a gesture she hoped conveyed a lack of concern. "It's miles away from Pier 39. Besides, your father never rides BART."

Matt muttered, "Yeah. He swings from building to building like Tarzan."

"What a guy," Cindy agreed, her blue eyes flashing.

Any other day she might have added caustically that Steve Alstead was too paranoid to ride San Francisco's public transportation system. While sensible people feared to ride the BART for fear of earthquakes, Cindy's estranged husband had proclaimed that lax security made it an open invitation to a terrorist bombing.

And now it seemed he had been right. He was always right somehow. But what if he had chosen that morning to ride the underground train? What if he had thrown his usual caution to the wind and picked yesterday to purchase a ticket and ride to Richmond? What if he was among those bleeding and dying on the sidewalk outside the station? or one of the uncounted dead trapped in the rubble of the tunnel?

And he had not called to put their minds at ease.

Typical.

She would try not to think about it. The same way she had tried not to imagine him dying every time he vanished on some top-secret assignment over the past 10 years.

Loving Steve Alstead had aged her. Only 33 years old and already she had enough gray to need a little Loving Care. Steve tried to blame it on the fact that Cindy taught fifth grade at Old Mission Elementary School. Indeed, parochial school could seem to be a hotbed of future terrorists, anarchists, and assassins. But Cindy knew better than to blame her students. Thirty fifth graders all deprived of Ritalin couldn't compare with the hyperactivity of Steve Alstead.

No. Loving Steve was the cause of Cindy's gray hair. Of sleepless nights. Of days and weeks and months and years living with the terror of possibly losing him. At five feet four inches tall she weighed under 100 pounds when she finally told him, "If you leave without telling me where you're going, don't bother coming home to me and the boys."

She still didn't know where he had gone for those seven weeks. It had been the last straw and the first stage of what was now seven months of separation.

So now Cindy weighed 110 pounds. Size six. She had gained something in his going. And the boys seemed more or less used to the idea that their father and mother couldn't live under the same roof. They enjoyed visits with Dad. The adventures, camping out. While other estranged or divorced fathers took their kids to Disneyland, Steve taught them how to play survivor. Kill a snake and fry it for supper. Cure the skin and make a loincloth. Useful skills for children, right?

"What a guy," Cindy muttered as she pulled up in front of Tommy's preschool.

Matt retrieved the cell phone. "Can I call him, Mom? Try him again?"

"Sure." She unloaded Tommy and escorted him to his schoolroom. The faces of the teachers were grim and worried. Everyone was listening to the news.

The entire staff was concerned. Preschool principal Carmen Daley was ashen and shaking as she hurried past Cindy and out the door. In low tones someone told Cindy that Carmen's father was in San Francisco on a business trip. Carmen had been trying to reach him ever since the first report on CNN. All the circuits were jammed. Now Carmen's mother had telephoned. She was in tears. Probably nothing to it. But from the distance of San Luis Obispo, mother and daughter should maybe watch the news and fret together.

No one asked about Steve.

Cindy left the building feeling queasy. This was too close to home. What if . . . ? She whispered a prayer and watched as Carmen Daley's silver Toyota tore out of the parking lot. It was going to be one of those days.

Matt was still on the phone when she got into the car. No need to ask him if he had reached his dad. Usually Steve didn't even bother to turn on an answer machine. The buzz of ringing was clear.

"He's not there," Cindy snapped, angry at Steve for worrying Matt. For worrying her too. Thoughtless. But what if he was hurt?

Matt kept the phone pressed to his ear. "Maybe he's at the marina. Taking a shower or something."

"He's not there," Cindy said. "Hang up. We'll try later. You hungry? Want an Egg McMuffin?" Her own appetite had vanished, but maybe Matt could eat.

He shook his head. "Not hungry."

"Shake it off, Matt. He's okay."

"You sure?"

"Sure." Her stomach churned as she lied to her son. She was never sure.

She tried to tune out the images she had seen on the news. Tried not to imagine Steve lying burned among the dying.

Cave Rock
Lake Tahoe, Nevada Side
9:17 P.M. Pacific Time

THE SERPENT IN THE GARDEN

There was a soft whirring noise from the electric motor as Dr. Timothy Turnow adjusted the focus of his telescope. The glowing fan of the Great Nebula in Orion filled the wide-field Panoptic eyepiece. Even in his distracted frame of mind, the sight gave him surprising pleasure, considering how many hundreds of times he'd viewed it before.

Raising his head from the LX200 scope Margaret had given him for their anniversary four months earlier, Turnow drank in the rich expanse of the night sky over Tahoe. It was still hard to believe that the fuzzy patch of light visible to the naked eye in Orion's sword contained so much glorious detail. In the crisp, crystalline atmosphere at 6,000 feet of altitude, the four stars of the Trapezium at the nebula's heart were easily resolved at the lowest magnification.

He was sorry now he'd watched the news after supper. He'd already seen the same clips of the bombing over and over. The inescapable tape loop displaying a somber lineup of black body bags being loaded aboard waiting ambulances was bad enough. The tearstained face of the San Francisco cop with the oh-so-small unmoving child in his arms was infinitely worse.

Turnow was grateful for the sharpness of the just-above-freezing air and the perfection of the night sky. Through the combination he could set the disturbing television images momentarily aside.

Orion was already dropping into the west. In a couple of weeks the lengthening hours of daylight would place Turnow's favorite stellar target behind Mount Tallac, gone for the season.

He experienced a twinge of nostalgia. Some people counted years by birthdays, others by holidays, but for Turnow, the passing of the calendar was inextricably linked to the night sky.

The vastness of space and the insignificance of planet Earth wasn't disturbing to the scientist either. In galaxies and globular clusters he saw the hand of God. The universe showcased the wonder of creation; only humans screwed it up.

He and Margaret were not avid skiers, though Turnow did some cross-country for the scenery and the exercise. They had moved to the Tahoe Basin to escape polluted skies and to give their adult children and grandchildren a mountaintop respite from the hustling world.

Remembering his grandchildren wrinkled Turnow's face with concern and compassion. Though a few inches of snow still lay in the permanent shadows under the pines, Turnow had already brought the swing set out of hibernation and installed it on the winter-browned lawn. They'd all been up for Easter, hunting the colored eggs Turnow delighted in hiding in the yard.

But in San Francisco there was one little girl who would never know she was world famous, who would never again dress up for Easter Sunday or exclaim over finding a colored egg.

The thought made him fiercely protective, angry, and sorrowful—all at once.

He heard the door open and shut and the slap of the screen door, though no light escaped from the darkened house. Margaret had learned years before that 20 seconds of inopportune porch light meant 20 minutes to a full recovery of night vision.

Wrapped in a parka, his wife of thirty years followed the gravel walk until her auburn-haired, five-foot-nine-inch frame stood close beside his six-foot-three-inch form. She tugged his arm around her shoulders and snuggled close.

Pinching the sleeve of his Gore-Tex lined jacket, she said, "Where's your heavy coat? It's freezing out here."

Turnow knew she was right but argued anyway. "It feels good," he contended. "I needed something to clear my head, Meg."

He knew she comprehended immediately what he meant. "You'll have to go, won't you?" she said.

He gave a hum of agreement.

"Will you be away long?"

"Can't tell," he asserted. "We've had it so good. In this country, I mean. Other nations live with terror all the time . . . then it caught up with us."

The sound of an engine on Highway 50 alerted them to the approach of an auto and both fell silent. An instant later the sweep of headlights glared off patches of snow as a heavy sedan pulled up outside their Cave Rock gate.

Instinctively Turnow squinted his eyes shut even as Margaret turned to look.

Both recognized what it meant: the official summons that Dr. Turnow was needed by Chapter 16.

"I hope you're back soon," she said, removing a mitten from her hand and pressing her palm against his cheek. "But, Tim . . . catch them. Catch whoever did it."

He nodded and kissed her hand, then bent to fold her in a tight embrace. "I will," he promised grimly. "I will."

Mojave, California
11:13 P.M. Pacific Time

SING-ALONG WITH MILES

Mounds of trash punctuated the wall of wrecked and dismantled cars that surrounded the rocky red plot of land. With the presence of a few dying cacti, the land where the faded, sky blue, single-wide mobile home sat was a B-grade moviemaker's version of a grim future world.

Playful children's music echoed up to the star-frosted sky from inside the trailer, completing the surreal Mad Max effect.

"I love you, you love me . . . "

A tall, lanky, honey-brown-haired man wearing a purple shirt slouched in front of a computer screen. The monitor was perched on top of a decrepit icebox that lay on its side as a makeshift desk. The refrigerator's door was open on the floor. The man's chair sat unevenly on the shelves, his feet resting where bottles of ketchup and pickles once stood.

Piles of computer equipment connected by a net of tangled wires covered the floor.

The man's knees were almost to his chest. "Miles Miller," he chuckled, "you are brilliant. They are gonna love this one."

". . . we're a happy family."

"Cut!" Miles exclaimed, hammering the space bar. He clicked a tiny icon on the screen of his Power Mac G4, dragging it down. An image of Barney, the singing dinosaur, popped up. With a goofy smile, Miles mouthed the words of an Asian child on the screen: *Oh, Barney, I love you so much.*

A rattling knock startled him. Miles craned his long neck around and scratched his fluffy curls. "What was that?" he wondered aloud, pausing only momentarily before continuing with glee, "I love you . . ."

The rapping came again, louder this time.

"Hello . . . ?" Miles said, confused. "Is that the door?"

A voice came from outside. "I don't know. You live here. Wouldn't you know?"

Miles never had company.

He scratched his head before attempting to stand up. The leg of the folding chair hung up on the egg tray of the icebox. He staggered, tripped, and fell backward. With a desperate grasp, he seized the mouse in a last attempt to keep himself afoot. As the cable stretched and then unplugged, the chair continued backward. Miles's long legs flew toward the ceiling, and the whole computer setup crashed down on the floor with him.

"Miles Miller," came the voice from outside, "this is Special Agent Anton Brown of the FBI."

Miles gazed sadly at the dying computer as it popped and fizzled. His face became serious. "Othelon, is that you? It sounds like you, Othelon, and I just want to say I'm not buying any more of your crummy computers. I don't care how legit you say they are."

"Miles Miller, I have special orders for you from the president of the United States of America."

"The president of the . . ." Miles scrambled to clear the knot of cables and plastic boxes from his lap.

The flimsy front door creaked open. The freshly shaven, cocoa-colored face of Anton Brown leaned in apprehensively. "Miles Miller?" Half a dozen cats charged in between Agent Brown's legs.

"Uh, yeah." Miles stood, tripping over one last power cord, which was yanked from the wall with an electric pop. The lightbulb over the entry went out. He staggered to the opening. "Yes sir, that's me."

"I have a special assignment for you from—"

"It's about time the general came through," Miles interrupted, snatching the letter from the agent's hand so quickly that Anton reached for his gun. "You know, I told him I wouldn't be the fall guy on the Pentagon's security leak, but he promised me . . ." He read the letter silently. "Is that what this is? The general has a job for me now, does he?"

"Sir," responded Agent Brown, "I don't know what you're talking about."

"Oh, playing dumb, huh? I've seen the movies. I know what you guys do."

"Read the letter, sir."

"San Francisco? 'Your presence is commanded immediately!' What?" Miles crumpled up the letter and threw it on the floor. "Well, you tell the general I'm not going! You tell him he's a little too late for that. I've got a pretty good thing going here for the Friends of Barney fan club."

Agent Brown bent carefully to pick up the letter. "I can see that. However, this isn't a request, sir. It's an order from the president."

"From the president, ha! The only president I answer to is the FOB president, and he wouldn't like it if I didn't finish the 'I Love Barney' project." Miles attempted to shut the door in Agent Brown's face.

In an instant the door was kicked off its rusted hinges. Miles was tackled and forced to lie facedown on the floor of the dingy single-wide trailer. Brown cuffed him. "I don't know what in the world the president wants with you, but you're coming with me. Like it or not!"

"Okay, okay," Miles panted. "All you had to do was tell me."

Brown dragged Miles to his feet. "Let's go. Move out."

"Don't I need my equipment?"

Brown scanned the wreckage of the computer, a stack of pizza containers, and a half-empty box of Cap'n Crunch cereal strewn around Miles's overturned chair. "I imagine your needs will be met."

"What about clothes?"

"Mr. Miller, do you even own a suit?"

"No."

"Doesn't matter. There isn't time for packing anyway."

"But what about my cats?"

Anton glanced up at the kitchen sink, where an entire litter of cats was drinking from old cereal bowls. "Don't worry. I'll leave the door open for them. Say, anyone ever tell you you look like Ryan Stiles from *Whose Line Is It Anyway?*"

Miles smiled reluctantly. "No, but hey . . . will you take me to McDonald's on the way to the airport?"

Agent Brown ushered him down into the backseat of a black Crown Vic. "Miles, sit down and keep your mouth shut, or I'll keep the cuffs on 'til we get to Frisco."

TWO

FBI Chapter 16 Offices
San Francisco
Saturday, 21 April
8:30 A.M. Pacific Time

THERE THE EAGLES GATHER . . .

A large, oval, cheap-looking conference table emphasized the plainness of the Russian Hill office. One window overlooked San Francisco Bay. An easel shrouded with canvas stood enigmatically beside a blank, wall- mounted white board. Though filled with state-of-the-art scientific equipment, illegal-for-export computer and communications gear, and enough brainpower to run a Fortune 500 company, the premises still managed to exude an aura of bureaucratic drab.

The Chapter 16 team members, three red-eyed from their overnight travels, waited in leather swivel chairs. Anton Brown stood quietly beside the single door like the sergeant at arms securing entry to a secret fraternity. His stern demeanor was deliberately put on to be the opposite of the general hysteria in the City by the Bay.

Was the explosion really a terrorist incident? Would there be more? Turnow's thoughts added another question: *Did any passengers remain alive in the twisted wreckage of the underground transit?*

But panicky thoughts were not allowed (or at least not permitted display) under the watchful eyes of Agent Brown.

Teresa Bouche, the lone female occupant of the room, checked her features in a mirror but applied no additional makeup.

Dr. Turnow observed her struggle to look dignified and composed while obviously struggling with jet lag and frustration. With an impatient snap of the lid, Bouche closed the compact and sighed. "When, Agent Brown?"

"Any minute," Brown replied quietly. The guard's facial muscles barely moved as he spoke and no other parts twitched at all. His no-nonsense manner offered no sympathy.

The team had been hustled into the briefing room 30 minutes before . . . and their executive director, former senator James Morrison, still had not appeared.

"I haven't slept or changed my clothes," Bouche complained.

Turnow wondered how either action could possibly have altered anything. Bouche's severely pulled back blonde hair was flawless and her tailored red-with-gold-buttons suit crisply pressed. Both bespoke unrelenting command of herself . . . and of others.

The assistant U.S. attorney general was a tough customer, no doubt. Turnow had seen her on the evening news, deftly handling questions about the prosecution's case in pursuing a major spy ring.

"Thought the summons was urgent," added Charles Downing.

Unlike the hard-as-nails Bouche, Downing was more of an enigma to Turnow. Up close the smartly dressed, black-haired Downing was older than he looked in society photographs. Turnow also suspected that he was not merely the champagne-swilling, diplomatic corps offshoot of a wealthy family his reputation suggested. *What will Downing's role be?* Turnow wondered.

The door opened at last and a tall, very slender man in a navy suit entered. His face was chiseled with deep lines.

Anton Brown stepped aside. "Lady and gentlemen, our Director, Senator Morrison."

Turnow had only met the sixtyish former senator on two earlier occasions, but Morrison was instantly recognizable. Once the Assistant Director in Charge of the FBI's Los Angeles field office, Morrison had built his career on moral uprightness and an absolute commitment to American national security. After serving a term as the first chief of the FBI's International Terrorism Section, Morrison had moved into the public eye with a landslide victory in a Missouri Senate race.

It was he who had formally suggested to the president the urgent need for Chapter 16 as a counterterrorist unit within the FBI. Morrison's Christian faith also provided the biblical allusion that became the new force's name. Huge strides were made in developing and implementing domestic counterterrorism measures during his first term. His supporters spilled over Missouri's borders, expanding his influence and popularity. He would have run again—and won again, Turnow suspected—but the unfortunate onset of his wife's cancer brought with it an unexpected retirement.

With the initiative for Chapter 16 having won presidential support, Morrison was the natural choice to act as the unit's first executive director and special advisor to the president. Morrison persistently resisted the notion until his wife's sudden death left him drifting and receptive to the president's entreaty.

"Miles, how are you?" Morrison said to the T-shirted computer geek.

"Fine, except . . . ," Miles began, rising from his chair.

Anton placed his hand on Miles's shoulder, causing the computer wizard to sink quietly back down.

"Let me first thank you all for coming on such short notice." Morrison greeted them warmly in his mild, faintly Southern accent. His deliberate gaze into Turnow's eyes made the doctor feel valued. Morrison took the time to repeat the gesture of respect with each team member.

The team was suddenly awake and interested. Morrison had a remarkable power, Turnow thought. He could sense nuances in a group, almost like reading minds. As for his speaking skills, reputedly he could motivate the dead.

The senator continued. "Further apologies for my own tardiness this morning. I was receiving the latest briefing of the facts as they are presently known. More on that in a moment. Let me first remind you of why you're here. Each one of you—after extensive interviews, evaluations, and your own indication of willingness to volunteer—is now part of the nation's elite, newly formed counterterrorist organization, Chapter 16."

Turnow heard Bouche cough and recognized that it covered a polite, ladylike but definitely derisive snort.

"Chapter 16, the nation's first exclusive internal terrorism unit, has a mission to detect, locate, and disarm terrorists on American soil. We are a streamlined counterterrorism unit, capable of fast response, that brings our nation's best under one roof. The president saw our inadequate security infrastructure and implemented the solution. By combining the research capabilities of America's corporations and government laboratories with intelligence and law enforcement resources, the U.S. is able to mount the optimum defense against domestic terrorism. You are our best. That's why you're here.

"We are currently at Threat Condition Orange, which, as you know, means there is a high risk of terrorist attacks in the U.S. The president has requested that Chapter 16 investigate the BART bombing, assess the threat of future attacks, and eliminate those dangers before we need to move to Threat Condition Red.

"Since you may not all know each other, let me briefly explain the backgrounds and roles of each." Morrison motioned to Bouche. "Teresa Bouche, our political liaison, is a former military protocol officer with ties and contacts all over the world. She served in Korea and Germany for a number of years. She has prosecuted terrorists for the United States government and is an advisor to the Homeland Security Council. She will handle all public statements and legal questions. Her presence reminds us that we are a civilian, not military, operation."

This was a polite way of saying that Bouche was a political watchdog, whose membership on the team was a sop to those who criticized the FBI in the wake of numerous scandals and misjudgments.

Turnow guessed that the president, and therefore Morrison, had been forced to accept her presence so the FBI operation could be clearly seen as subordinate to the Justice Department.

Turnow also imagined that now he understood her mocking grunt. Unlike the others, she probably was not a willing "volunteer."

Morrison's pivot caught Downing staring at Bouche. "Charles Downing, who actually helped me brainstorm this operation, is our profiler and intelligence analyst. He served with the CIA in Russia, the Middle East, and in Asia. He has personally rounded up more recruits and detected more moles than the whole of the agency. And most recently, he served the U.S. as a counterterrorist profiler with the FBI's Hostage Rescue Team. Don't let his casual dress fool you."

Downing tugged on his cuffs and straightened the knot in his tie.

Bouche coughed again. *What is at issue now?* Turnow wondered. Perhaps some unspoken tension existed between the attorney and the spy?

Then it was Turnow's own moment in the spotlight. "Dr. Timothy Turnow," Morrison explained, "is our resident expert on weapons of mass destruction. He is a former Associate Director of the Nonproliferation, Arms Control, and International Security program at the Lawrence Livermore National Laboratory. He's traveled the world and was actually one of the first foreign civilians ever to enter the secret Russian city of Oblinsk. He supervised converting the biological weapons plant into a pharmaceutical manufacturing facility. It was his invaluable information about certain rogue KGB agents and Russian mafia that enabled us to contain one of the world's most dangerous bioweapons."

While the others regarded him with interest, Turnow remembered how close to failing he had come. If the virulent, genetically altered bioagent—called VENOM for Vector Enhanced Necrotizing Osteo-Myelitis—had escaped into the grasp of terrorists, civilization would have been very different indeed.

Morrison's words were gentle, but his face serious. "He literally saved the world."

Turnow lowered his eyes and stared at the fake wood grain of the tabletop.

"I'm sure," Morrison said, "by now you've all met Miles Miller there. He's the genius who plugged a level-three security leak in the Pentagon's Electronic Information System. In less polite company he's known as a hacker. Make no mistake: we're very pleased he's on our side."

Indicating the massive frame of Anton Brown, Morrison continued, "Agent Brown is our security force, our bodyguard, a trained criminal investigator, and one of the two regular FBI personnel on the team."

For the first time since entering, Morrison frowned as he scanned the room. "The other FBI agent is not present. Steve Alstead is our physical point man and the tactical commander, should force be required. He served as a unit commander in SEAL Team 6 and, most recently, was Special Agent In Charge with the Hostage Rescue Team before his appointment to Chapter 16. If the team is required to infiltrate a terrorist-held area or take somebody down, he'll be the one to do it."

Morrison shot a pointed inquiry at Anton Brown, who gave the slightest of shrugs in reply.

The brief pause that followed allowed both Bouche and Downing to frame questions, but the attorney was a shade faster. "But *was* this a terrorist strike? Has it been confirmed that this was a bombing and not an accident?"

Turnow saw Morrison tighten his jaw as if bracing for a blow. It was one thing to be a prophet of doom, and another when your predictions of horror were actually fulfilled. "Two hundred seventy-three known dead . . . others still missing. The explosion obliterated the middle car of the train and heavily damaged all the rest. Yes, Ms. Bouche, this was a deliberate, cold- blooded act of terror."

Downing said quietly, "Any claim of responsibility yet?"

Morrison shook his head. "No credible ones. By this afternoon's meeting, I will have complete dossiers for each of you . . . including Mr. Alstead, who, I expect will be joining us then." Turnow watched as a look passed between Morrison and Anton Brown. The FBI agent offered a nod of compliance. Brown was security, but he was also there to ride herd on this strange assortment of strong-willed individuals.

"For the moment," Morrison suggested, "I know you're tired. Anton will escort you to your hotel. I have an expense card for each of you." He handed out gold credit cards to each. "You can get clothes or whatever you might need with these."

Morrison retrieved a box from under the table and removed four small bubble-wrapped items. "Secondly, and more importantly, these are called B-coms." He opened one, holding up a shirt-pocket-sized telephone. "Bureau communications cell phones. Specially secure for calls, but also electronically enhanced to enable updates to and downloads from the database."

"Be calm!" Miles mocked the grade-school approach Senator Morrison had taken with the acronym. He looked to the others for support in his humor, repeating the word again in a feeble attempt to coerce a laugh. No one even smiled. Under the weight of their blank stares, Miles sank quietly down, like a defeated class clown.

Morrison grasped at an edge of the phone, and it opened like an eyeglass case, revealing a tiny full-function keyboard. "Battery pack good for a thousand hours of stand-by. The signals they send and receive are encrypted and encoded. There is a highly durable, state-of-the-art fingerprint reader on the side. This allows only you or one of your team members to use your phone. Your prints are already encrypted in each. If someone else found it, it would make a nice fishing weight, but that will never happen because none of you will ever lose one." He handed one each to Bouche and Downing and another to Dr. Turnow.

Staring pointedly at Miles, Morrison said, "At no time are they to be forgotten, left behind, or turned off. You will keep them on you at all times, unless special circumstances require otherwise and a prior arrangement is made. They can be made to ring silently, but make sure you can feel it, as this little device is your lifeline to Chapter 16 and the sole means by which I can reach you at all times."

Anton opened his coat to show the group his B-com. Turnow decided it wasn't accidental that the same gesture revealed a hip-holstered pistol. Morrison and his partner, Brown, led the group to understand that the circumstances that brought them together were real—no drill, no Hollywood portrayal . . . real.

Morrison showed his approval. "Use them for FBI and Chapter 16 business only. And lastly, I ask that you not say a word about any Chapter 16 business outside of this group. Understood?"

Tired nods replied.

"I'll contact you by B-com for our afternoon meeting. Now go get some sleep, buy some clothes, or do whatever else you might need to do. Meeting adjourned. Anton, soon as you hear, give me the lock on Alstead."

"Sure thing, boss."

All had questions for him. However, before any could ask, the charming but elusive James Morrison was gone.

Turnow, the least tired of the group, stared out the window. At the bottom of his view was the Maritime Museum, housed in an odd, oblong box of a multilayered building meant to resemble the decks and superstructure of an ocean liner. Beyond were the blue, swirling, dangerous waters of San Francisco Bay, churning in a perfect likeness of Turnow's own troubled thoughts.

San Francisco Bay
10 A.M. Pacific Time

POINT MAN

Another swell hammered the gray Zodiac, which sat helpless in mid-bay. Steve Alstead pulled on the cord in another attempt to restart the outboard. It gurgled and sputtered but did not catch. He pulled again. The same result.

Nada.

It had been a long morning, wrapping up a self-imposed solo training exercise, or SISTEX, something Alstead required of himself. Living on Angel Island for days at a time with nothing but an ALICE pack full of gear and MREs, meals ready to eat. Hiding out; stalking tourists while hidden by green face paint and cammies; sleeping rough under a hide made of brush.

It kept his survival skills sharp. In a deeper reality the little four-day excursion had been planned to get away from the city sounds and petty annoyances. He needed the time and the solitude to think about his wife, Cindy, and his two boys, from whom he'd been absent for seven months. The last words Cindy had spoken to him were, "Don't call me. I'll call you!"

Last night he'd had a close encounter with a ranger after building a fire to stay warm. The fire had obviously been spotted by someone on the shore, who called it in to the Coast Guard. Out came the cutter, as well as a single-man inflatable raft from the national parks.

Years of service with the world's elite Special Operations, or Spec Ops, had taught him how to "make a good hide." His night lair was far from the fire. In case there was a need to evacuate, he could escape from the smoldering evidence. His own boat had been well camouflaged, flipped upside down in the water, and dragged up under the shore brush. A ranger in a Zodiac almost spotted it.

Steve missed the excitement of real danger and adventure. Since leaving active duty with the Hostage Rescue Team six months earlier, these little outings were the only thing keeping his mind sane.

He pulled on the starter cord again.

Burbles.

He realized that water must have saturated the air-intake sponge when the dingy was upside down. The engine had run fine for the first 10 minutes, long enough to get mid-bay, until too much moisture had built up in the cylinder for it to function.

A Spec Ops motor housing never would have leaked.

"Some people call this retirement," he mumbled to himself. "Civilian junk."

He removed the fiberglass cover and spark plug to let the engine breathe. This action did little good. The blowing mist and waves only made things worse. Steve glanced toward Alcatraz, considering the number of men who had been lost in the Bay while trying to escape the small island prison. There was a definite seaward set to the current.

Reassembling the cowling, he tugged at the starter again and again.

Nothing.

Frustration began to build in him. Steve, who still did his 500 push-ups and sit-ups every other day, was stronger than he sometimes realized. He yanked harder and harder until he ripped the cord out of the socket. A lesser man would have come unglued, but not Alstead.

Of course not.

He very calmly stood, gritted his teeth, and kicked the motor. The clamps broke loose, and before he could dive for it, the little five-horse Honda sank from sight.

Fortunately, Steve's luck had never been this bad as point on any of the six counterterrorist missions he'd been on with SEAL Team 6. Otherwise, he'd be dead.

He began to row.

An hour and a half later he rounded the concrete breakwater into the east end of the Pier 39 marina, a trendy place filled with tourists and tourist shops. It wouldn't have been his first choice of homes, but Cindy and the kids loved the carnival atmosphere and the clam chowder at the Boudin Bakery.

He turned around to peer ahead as he went, spotting an agent . . . a muscular frame poured into a suit . . . by his boat slip. Instantly classified by Steve as an MIB—man in black—the formally dressed man checked his watch impatiently and leaned against Steve's run-down trawler, *Hop 'n' Pop.*

It was Anton Brown, a friend of Steve's from the San Francisco FBI.

"Alstead," Anton called to him, "you honkie loser. Where you been?"

Already annoyed at the three-mile row and the loss of his outboard, Steve ignored the mock ghetto-speak banter. "Tie this up," he snarled, flinging the wet rope toward Anton. "And don't bug me. I'm not in the mood."

The tall, serious black man expertly knotted the cord to a dock cleat and shook the water from his hands. Taking out a letter, he dropped the dialect and intoned, "If it's an official greeting you want, Mr. Steven Alstead . . ."

"It's Tactical Commander Alstead. Here." Steve chucked his sopping- wet ALICE pack at Anton, hard enough to knock Anton backward into the water.

Anton stepped smoothly out of the way. The pack sailed over the dock, bounced off the forebrace of the neighbor's sailboat, and sank the way the motor had. Anton laughed. "Jujitsu. Use your attacker's force against him."

"You idiot! Can't you catch?" Steve said indignantly.

"Sorry, man," Anton apologized. "Ex-Spec-Ops officer having a bad day?"

Steve stripped off his boots, took a deep breath, and dove into the same spot the pack had disappeared. A moment later he came up with it, now slimy and tangled in a mass of fishing line.

He heaved the mess onto the rear deck of his 40-foot Californian trawler.

Anton extended a hand to help as Steve boarded.

Taking it, Steve thought about trying to hip-roll Anton into the water, then decided they'd both end up there. He was content to shake his friend's hand, sliming the suit sleeve with bottom scum as he joked, "Checkmate."

"You got me." Anton laughed. "But look, I've got a serious message for you." He began reading the letter as Steve unlocked his boat hatch.

"Summarize it," Steve suggested, ripping off the wet olive-drab pants and shirt and flinging them over a faded, broken-zippered cabin cushion.

Anton interrupted himself. “You live here?” he asked incredulously as he scanned the sloppy, disheveled living quarters.

Steve paused to look around. “Yeah. Bought it on a tip before an auction. It was seized in a drug bust.” He stared at the gouges and tears in walls, ceiling, and seats. “Needs a little work. The DEA boys were real thorough. Twenty keys of coke in the upholstery.”

Anton chuckled, then sneered at the dripping clothes that reeked of fish guts. “That’s nasty.”

The phone, mounted on the bulkhead near the helm station, rang. Steve continued to change.

“Want me to answer that?”

“No! Why don’t you just throw it in the Bay? Everything else I own wound up there today.”

“I’ll answer it.” Anton reached for the handset. “Brown answering for Alstead.” He paused. “Yes sir. I’ll put him on.”

“Who is it?” Steve queried.

“James Morrison, Chapter 16. Been trying to locate you.”

Steve took the phone call while still half dressed. “Sir. No sir, I’ve been camping. No, I don’t have voice mail. Then I’d have to return calls.” He listened for a minute. “Yes sir. Twenty minutes, max. Agent Brown? Yes sir.”

Hanging up, Steve demanded, “Anton, you thug, why didn’t you tell me terrorists had blown up half the BART system?”

“Tried to. Where were you? Everybody in the city heard the explosion. Didn’t you see the smoke? hear the sirens? Were you hiding under a rock again?”

Steve stared at Anton with amazement, then scratched his soggy brown hair as he sat down. “In a bush, actually. I just can’t believe it.” Anton started his official spiel again but was cut off. “Save your breath. The brass told me everything.”

Pulling on black jeans, black crewneck shirt, and cross-trainers, Steve stuffed a Glock 27 pistol into his waistband holster. He left a white button- up shirt untucked over the top. “Let’s go,” he said, previous irritations and distractions already forgotten.

FBI, Chapter 16 Conference Room
San Francisco
2 P.M. Pacific Time

. . . AND ALL THE MEN AND WOMEN MERELY PLAYERS

"This is Chapter 16's first Plan of Action meeting," Senator Morrison intoned as he opened the team's second gathering.

Motioning toward Steve, Morrison added, "I trust by now all of you have met Steve Alstead, our director of SCOT—Special Circumstances Operational Tactics."

Steve glanced up from staring at the closed, red-taped file folder lying on the table in front of him and shot a look around the room. Identical folders rested in front of each team member.

In return he received a goofy grin from Miles Miller, cool appraisals from Downing and Turnow, and a scowl from Teresa Bouche. As usual, Anton Brown, back to the door, wore a poker-faced expression.

Steve recognized his own shortcomings in concealing his emotions. One always knew how he felt just by looking at him. However, as a Spec Ops, telegraphing one's thoughts was critical and priceless when the moment depended entirely on another's ability to understand and respond to the leader's intention. "Leave the playacting to the negotiators," Steve always said. "And me and my boys will clean up whatever's left."

Morrison flipped open his own copy of the file and motioned for the others to do the same. "To begin," he said, "let me briefly review our mission statement. While we are privy to all levels of classified information from every source—local law enforcement, regular FBI, NSA, thousands of agents and detectives—we are not here to duplicate any of their efforts. Rather, we are a clearinghouse for data and a fast-response unit dedicated to quick analysis and the prevention of *additional* terrorist activities, in order to save lives and promote public confidence in the government's ability to protect against such threats." Morrison moved to a laptop computer. "Anton, would you dim the lights?"

Anton turned a dial on the wall. The lights softened and the windows polarized.

Continuing, Morrison motioned to a screen on the wall, where a projector on the ceiling shot out the PowerPoint slide from his computer screen. The strange jumble of shapes appeared to Steve like one of those futuristic metal sculptures he refused to call art.

Then he sorted out what he was seeing: the remains of a subway car ripped open and turned almost inside out along its length, like a Coke can burst in a freezer.

Steve heard Teresa's sharp intake of breath and turned just in time to see Turnow's jaw clench.

"I want to review the up-to-the-moment critical findings with you," Morrison said, "as well as delegate responsibilities to each of you. We need to find out who carried out the BART bomb and why, and stop them before any more attacks are carried out. We'll call it Operation BB Gun."

Teresa interrupted. "Do we have any more parties who have claimed responsibility for the attack?"

"In fact, we do. As of this morning, we had two confirmed groups taking credit. FBI researchers are investigating both, though neither was as credible as the one we got from the *San Francisco Chronicle* just an hour ago." Morrison clicked an icon on the screen and a box opened to a file. "This is a transcript of the phone call received by a senior editor," Morrison summarized as the team read silently. "This third claim, containing extremely violent language against the various cultures and sexual preferences of the people of San Francisco—'sending the spawn of Satan to hell'—was allegedly made by a representative of an organization calling itself the North Aryan Knights. Most notably, it's the only one of the three to make accurate reference to specific details of the attack, making them the most likely party responsible. The editor's secretary managed to ID the caller's number. The trace came up with a pay phone in Oakland when we ran it. We've looked in the FBI databases, and there's no previous record for this NAK group."

"But it fits," Steve asserted, doodling a row of swastikas interspersed with question marks on his yellow pad. "Sounds like a Bubba job."

Morrison agreed. "It could be . . ."

"What's a Bubba job?" queried Miles.

Morrison motioned for Steve to explain.

"A terrorist act carried out by a redneck racist group. Bubba groups usually don't have a clear political agenda, though most believe the government is Big Brother. Two things they do well: hate and kill."

Downing joined in. "And what with the date, April 20, being so close to the April 19 anniversary of Oklahoma City and Ruby Ridge, it may be a revenge attack."

"And Waco," Teresa Bouche volunteered. "Don't forget that Waco was also April 19."

Steve studied the woman for whom he had already conceived an unreasonable dislike. It wasn't that he disliked authoritative women, but he hated political-watchdog outsiders . . . especially those who looked over his shoulder and jeopardized his missions.

"A probability profile study would be part of your first report, Charles," Morrison noted.

Downing nodded and used a stainless-steel stylus to tick a row of boxes on his Bureau-issued PDA. "Construct a possible profile of this terrorist group, based on the type of weapon used, the target, timing, motivations, and so on."

Morrison nodded.

"Don't Bubba groups, since they are Americans operating within their own country, usually conceal their identity rather than announce it?" Bouche asked.

Steve toned his dislike down one notch. The woman was sharp. "True," he concurred. "Which may explain why this NAK has no priors. It's a phony dreamed up to match their agenda of hate but not reveal their actual connections."

"Or it could be a radical splinter group flexing its muscle?" Downing put in.

"All points to be considered," Morrison instructed. "Now, Dr. Turnow. My assignment for you . . ."

So far Turnow had neither asked questions nor made comments. Yet Steve knew the scientist had an uncanny ability to pull together threads of evidence. Of those in the room, only Steve and Senator Morrison knew the full story of what Turnow had prevented in the Russian caper.

Turnow raised his bushy eyebrows in response to Morrison's address. "Yes, sir?"

"Review the data that the lab has thus far on explosives, materials, detonation devices, and method of containment and transportation of the bomb. Compile your findings in a report circularized in the Operation BB Gun database file. Then you'll coordinate with Teresa and myself as to how much we make public."

Turnow studied the acoustic ceiling tiles. "Will do." It was clear he was already working silently on the case as he continued making mental notes.

Steve appreciated Turnow's quietly confident response and decided he would get along well with the man. Turnow reminded Steve a little of his own father—a smart, self-assured guy who never flaunted his stuff, unlike what he'd already guessed about Teresa Bouche.

Morrison clicked another computer file labeled "BB, Summary of Event." "We know that of the approximately 300 people onboard the Red Line train—it was early morning, remember—headed for Colma, over 270 of them were killed instantly, and another 40 or so remain critically wounded. Field agents have spoken to the only ones able to respond. Their disjointed stories have not helped at this time."

"Could they be suspects?" Teresa wondered aloud.

"None fit the Preliminary Profile. At least, that is, the PP at this time. However, we're not ruling anyone out, so the Bureau is running their phone records. In the meantime, Miles, you follow up. See if you can tie in to PacBell's database. We've made an urgent request, but maybe you can get a list of all calls made in the last six months from that number a little quicker."

"Hack in, Senator?"

Teresa Bouche looked shocked.

Morrison sighed and chuckled. "Use all of your abilities, Miles—within the bounds of the law."

"I can do that," Miles said, seemingly disappointed, "but it may take more time."

"And Steve," Morrison continued, "you're probably wondering what your assignment is."

Jabbing his thumb toward the white board, Steve suggested, "Thought maybe you'd make me stand in the corner and write sentences for playing hooky this morning." He joked to cover the dread he felt at hearing the others' assignments: building a computer database, or producing a written or verbal report to be reviewed by the high-and-mighty Ms. Bouche.

"What you deserve," Morrison offered, playing along. "But actually, you probably won't object to what I have in mind. I need you to meet with the Hostage Rescue Team members. If a lead is generated from Chapter 16's efforts and the HRT is needed, you'll be the one in charge of tactical planning."

Steve's "Yes sir!" was louder than necessary, given the size of the room.

Bouche shot him a librarian's glance, as if to say, *Quiet, you noisy child!*

He ignored her.

Morrison, seeming to sense the tension, demonstrated his grandfatherly ability to dissolve conflict. "I believe they're doing a live-hostage, live-firing drill today at the Shoot House," he said smoothly. "Get reacquainted with the team, prepare a briefing on current HRT tactics and weapons, including possible scenarios we might encounter." Then to the entire team Morrison stated, "I'm grateful all of you are acknowledged to be tops in your respective fields. But I warn you: such a reputation comes with a price. Expectations will be correspondingly high as well!"

It was a gentlemanly way of suggesting there was no place for prima donnas or glory hounds or philosophical differences if they imperiled the team's performance.

Steve believed he'd been handed a perfect assignment: a little bang-bang time, play with a few of the FBI's best toys, and then hit the frat file, which was tactical info on a computer that he and the other Bureau boys used to cut and paste their reports from as needed.

"As for you, Ms. Bouche, besides keeping watch over legalities, you'll be reporting new developments on the case to the press. A five-minute briefing in one hour, in the Bureau's Blue Room. Remember, generalizations only. And don't report the latest claim of responsibility. We want to see if we can draw the culprit out by not giving them the coverage they seem to want."

For an instant Steve spotted a glimmer of concern in Teresa Bouche's eyes. Inwardly he smiled at the thought that he'd be playing while she'd have to sweat out the next hour preparing. It must have been torture for her to be told by Morrison how to do her job.

The team edged off their seats as Morrison concluded, "I know you heard me the first time, but keep your B-coms with you in case there are developments. Frequently—at least every two hours—check the BB database. We are facing considerable pressure to show results . . . fast! Pressure from the *highest* level. I'll notify you when it's time for our next meeting. Any questions?"

Morrison scanned the room and evidently found none. "Meeting adjourned."

Disneyland
Anaheim, California
3 P.M. Pacific Time

BIG THUNDER RAILROADED

The salty smell of popcorn filled the air. The weather was a cool 74 degrees, the crowds had been small, the lines short, and everybody was happy. Maybe yesterday's explosion in San Francisco kept some people from coming out to big public gatherings like amusement parks, but in Southern California, no one spoke of it.

It had been a perfect day for the Middle Eastern man and his family.

He stood outside the Big Thunder Mountain Railroad roller-coaster entrance, holding a *churro* in one hand, a pirate hat in the other, and wearing a silly grin.

It was Disneyland, after all. Even the most cynical couldn't deny the warm, happy feeling every father gets when a day is this good.

He stood by as his wife and ten-year-old son boarded the bright orange- and-brown train. He was glad to have his hands full. Ocean waves and roller coasters, among other wild things, made him sick.

It was scary enough to watch.

His kid waved to him as the safety bar was pulled down. His wife, a Caucasian woman with gray-streaked black hair, pale skin, and those beautiful brown eyes that had so captivated him, shook her head with humorous apprehension.

Her husband grinned back in exaggerated disbelief.

"Dad, Dad!" the boy called. "Take a picture."

The man, juggling food and hat, motioned toward the first big drop on the roller coaster. The boy held up his thumb and grinned a crooked- toothed smile. The father nodded, lifting a camera. He snapped the shutter. A blast of compressed air sounded and the coaster car dropped down on the track. The woman stiffened and stared straight ahead.

"Hey, Dad!" mocked a heavily accented, Middle Eastern voice. "Take my picture." A hand reaching from behind snatched the pirate hat out of the father's hand, causing the *churro* to fall to the ground.

The father swiveled around, accidentally snapping the shutter in the newcomer's face. He lowered the camera.

He was afraid.

Placing the too-small hat atop his balding head, the father's assailant inquired, "Does it suit me? Death? Skull and crossbones?" Then, leaning closer, he hissed, "You know my voice, yes? You have always obeyed me before and this time again Shadir says: Allah, your god, needs you. . . . The party of god needs you."

"Not here," responded the father, glancing around nervously.

The implacable, alarming man called Shadir gripped the father's arm. "Do not worry. None of these people care anything about what we are saying."

"But my family. We're on vacation."

"You may be at play, but you are never on vacation from service."

"I've given you plans, dates, maps. What more could you want? I've shown you shipping supply routes, even codes. What more, I ask? What?"

"Did you think in that tiny little *American-tainted* mind that you were done?" Shadir gritted his teeth, searching the eyes of the father. "You are done when god is done with you!"

The roller coaster rounded the top of the big drop overlooking the park. Mother and son waved as the father attempted to raise the camera.

Shadir yanked it down. "Look, Dad! Take a picture of Rhamad. See, Dad? The one in the blue Dodger hat just behind Mommy?"

The father's stomach lurched when a ball-capped figure seated just two rows behind his wife grinned and waved.

Shadir angrily slammed the pirate hat over the sharpened spike of a wooden fence post, recalling the father's attention. "We are that close all the time."

"What do you want?"

"Do not ask what I want. Instead, ask the party of god, 'How may I serve?' "

The father was frozen with fear. Pleading, he said, "Okay, okay! I will give Hezbollah whatever they want. Just don't hurt my family."

"We will contact you soon." Shadir smiled and began to laugh. "Naturally, you will not mention this to anyone." He slapped and squeezed the father's cheek before sauntering away.

The family man stood with his mouth open for a moment, thinking the whole thing through. He stared at the crushed *churro* on the ground and the ruined pirate hat on the fence post. The roller coaster rolled into its landing bay, and he jogged around to the exit to meet his family.

Dodger Cap was nowhere to be seen.

Somehow that was even more chilling.

"Dad, what's wrong?" the boy asked. "Where's my hat?"

"Paul, honey, what's the matter?" his wife inquired.

Paul searched for an excuse. "Sick . . . I'm not feeling well. I dropped the things. Maybe we should go back to the hotel."

Marriott Hotel
Anaheim, California
8:33 P.M. Pacific Time

THE VIEW

Khalil, a thin man in a light-charcoal suit, stood in front of a mirror next to a broad expanse of sliding door. His long, coarse hair, streaked silver, was braided. Running his hand over his bony face and well-groomed beard, he nodded to himself with firm resolve and turned toward the scene outside.

His gaze from the upper-floor suite fell on the smoggy city of Anaheim. From where Khalil stood, Southern California's buildings, asphalt freeways, and concrete overpasses stretched seemingly to the ends of the earth.

In the near distance was Disneyland, tinted a fuzzy silver and orange by the interplay of haze and extravagant illumination. The white peak of the Matterhorn stood out, along with the bulky mass of Space Mountain, all of them false idols dedicated to natural wonder and human inventiveness. A place of joy and imagination.

Khalil hated it all.

Throughout Khalil's grooming and meditating, the other occupant of the room had not spoken. But now he did.

"I still do not understand why we do not let the Americans know who has struck the blow against the subway train," he complained. "When many of our people live under the boot of Zionism all their lives, is it not right that we, in their name, proclaim what we have done?"

"Rhamad," Khalil said in a cautionary tone.

But the BART bomber wasn't ready to relent. "I understand that more blows are to come! Yes! But why not give our people opportunity to rejoice now? A simple phone call and the American government will know that by supporting the Jewish oppressors, they have brought the plague on their own heads."

A knock at the door interrupted the tirade.

Rhamad's right hand slipped inside his jacket to grasp the butt of a Colt Python .357 revolver.

When a pair of knocks in quick succession followed, Khalil angrily signaled for Rhamad to stop.

Khalil opened the door to admit Shadir. "All is done here?" he demanded.

"As you ordered," Shadir responded.

Casually, Khalil said, "Rhamad thinks we are wrong to wait for the bigger plan to unfold."

"Oh?" Shadir replied blankly in the face of Rhamad's emphatic nods.

"It is worth thinking on," Khalil said with a shrug. "Rhamad, go and see to the car. We leave within the hour."

Both Khalil and Shadir listened as Rhamad's steps retreated down the hall. After the hum of the elevator had come and gone, Shadir cracked the entry door to confirm Rhamad's departure.

"I'm afraid it is his pride," Shadir stated flatly. "He endangers our work."

"Yes," Khalil said. "He still lives to drop mortar shells on Israeli settlements and blow up car bombs beside bus stops. But he thinks too small. For him the subway was the coup of a lifetime. Such efforts are too easy here! Unworthy. The Americans are still totally unprepared. Much more is possible!"

"It is as if he is infected too," Shadir complained.

"This place infects everyone," Khalil confirmed. "But soon it will creep to a halt. Soon this once-great cart horse will want for energy. It will die, and nothing will pull this grand carriage that brings such unholy things to the world. . . ." He faced Shadir. "I too have seen this change in Rhamad and will tell you Allah's will for him. But first, what of Salim? Did you see him today?"

Shadir searched the room for his thoughts. "I believe he will obey us, but he is reluctant. He . . . is becoming one with this place. His wife is American. His child. . . . they do American things. Like this Disneyland."

Khalil gritted his teeth. "I hate. I . . ." He raised his voice, then lowered it again to a growling whisper. "I hate this place. All that it does. That it stands for. Look at this vast waste of money." He motioned out toward the sprawling lights of the theme park. "It is a façade, a fake temple. People come from all over the world to worship these false cartoon idols that some man invented. I hate the masses and their filth, coming by the millions, even our own people standing in lines, pushing and shoving, taking pictures. I hate . . . but soon, soon it will be dark. I have heard from the Russian. All the money I have spent . . . the plans we have made . . . the tree is blossoming and ready to bear fruit greater than any previous effort. Nothing must interfere. Nothing!" He fell silent.

Shadir did not speak or interrupt his thoughts.

At last Khalil said, "What you will do . . ."

"Yes, Khalil?"

"You will invite Rhamad for a boat ride to my home."

Shadir replied again, as if hypnotized. "Yes, Khalil."

"And the ocean tides will cleanse his sins."

"When?"

"Return to the north. Then call him for an urgent meeting with me. I will be along with Mehdi and Mahmoud. Now go, say nothing further to Rhamad, but do Allah's will."

The first of the evening's fireworks burst over the fairy-tale castle, showering sparkling fake stars over an energy-ravenous, light-polluted city that could no longer see the real ones.

THREE

Chapter 16 Forensics Lab
San Francisco
Sunday, 22 April
4:40 P.M. Pacific Time

WEAVING THE THREADS

Charles Downing leaned over Dr. Turnow's shoulder as the scientist, wearing latex gloves, handled a scorched fragment of material.

"Could you turn on that other light there, please?" Dr. Turnow requested, motioning to the bright exam light on a long arm.

"Sure," Downing replied, swinging it around where it further lit up the lab counter. "What is it?"

Turnow held the small piece closer under the lens, moving to examine every angle. "Crime Scene Investigations did a thorough job. Preliminary findings suggest this is part of the bomb container. Lab tests conclude it's made of a certain type of advanced aramid polymer bonded with a woven nylon. It makes a very sturdy yet lightweight material."

"So maybe this is part of a case or satchel . . . ?" Downing guessed.

"Right, that is the belief, but . . ." Turnow lifted the lid to a flat glass case, fitting the scrap of fabric into what looked to be a patchy rectangular puzzle. "As you can see, this very sparse reconstruction is composed of all the recovered fragments of this material. Some of them had actually been blown through the floor of the No. 3 car and were found on the track. As you can imagine, when a force as great as that acts directly on a material such as this, it's very unlikely all the pieces can be recovered. But so far it's not a bad reconstruction job." He gently pushed the glass case away. "Let's cross-check the composition with cases and satchels known to use this exact formulation."

Downing slid a stack of binders in front of Turnow and pulled up a high-backed lab chair. "What's the Chem Code?"

Turnow flipped through the file. "Either NV36 or NV2-42." He laid the report down and opened one of the binders to a section marked NV36.

"I'll check the other," Downing volunteered. "What was it? NV . . ."

"NV2-42."

Downing scanned the index for the right number before flipping to it. An entire 20-page section was devoted to tiny photographs of various cases and handbags with their descriptions that matched CC NV2-42.

Turnow found CC NV36 to be about the same. "Now what we want to do is get a feel for as many of these items as we can. Then we'll go back and review the security photos of all the cases and handbags that were carried onto the train. There was a floor sweep at Richmond . . . the end-of-the-line station prior to this run . . . and hopefully maintenance actually did the sweep their records claim. Then we'll know the bomb wasn't left by someone from a previous journey. If we get lucky, the case is in one of these photos."

Downing gnawed his lower lip. "From what I understand so far, the date—April 20—and the blast site—near the financial center—make me think Alstead is right. The profile looks like a Bubba job . . . what with the racial slurs given to the *Chronicle.* And it probably was intended to go off where it did."

"But April 20 is one day after the Ruby Ridge anniversary."

"So what if they were late?" Downing asserted. "Something typical of sloppy, Bubba job planning. Maybe they couldn't get the explosives in time, or some test fell through, or someone was delayed or arrested. Any number of causes could exist for the job to have been held up."

"True," Turnow responded as he picked up a stack of still photographs culled from security cameras.

"And when we find a suspect," Downing continued, "if a cross-check links them with someone else who was arrested or delayed in some way, even if the two are connected only by a thread, we come that much closer to a conclusion."

"All the guessing you profilers do." Turnow closed his eyes. "Hunches are legitimate, but I'd much rather start from hard facts."

Downing smiled. "It's just another way of looking at the puzzle . . . like playing hide-and-seek or that old board game Clue."

Turnow thumbed through the stack of photographs. How fortunate there weren't more people aboard, he thought. The Highly Unlikelies, a term used to identify the people who were probably not involved in the attack, had been removed from the stack by the Prelim guys.

As Turnow flipped past the images, he found it strangely disturbing that these mug shots would be the last recorded images of the BART bombing victims. And the people hadn't even been aware that the photos had been taken! He wondered again how the family members had reacted when they were shown the pictures to identify their deceased loved ones.

No matter how many years he worked on these sorts of cases, the thought of those left behind never stopped bothering him. He'd seen too much pain, too much sorrow, and it had made its deep mark on him. Although he'd been a Christian for many years, it was still difficult for him to understand why God sometimes allowed evil to cause such suffering.

A photograph marked "Highly Possible" caught his eye. It was a man in an overcoat, holding a large satchel. "Look at this one."

Downing leaned in close. "He's certainly suspicious-looking enough. Hat and sunglasses at six in the morning. Has some kind of tattoo on his left hand. See it? Ring finger. A scorpion?"

Turnow grunted, then examined another photo tagged with a

matching ID number. "Nope. Wouldn't be him. Look here. There he is, leaving the station with his case."

"What station was that?"

"T-minus one."

"One station before the explosion." Downing paused to consider. "That would fit the profile. Rarely will you find a Bubba who blows himself up. Especially in a racially motivated attack. They usually want more room in the world for themselves."

"Right." Turnow flipped to a picture of a case he'd seen in the book. "His case matches this NV36, case No. 22 perfectly."

Downing respectfully disagreed. "But you said it yourself. There he is, leaving with the case and everything."

"He could have unloaded the bomb in the car," Turnow proposed. "Though that would not explain the reason for all this." He motioned to the glass display where the fragments lay in a shattered but suggestive rectangle.

"True, and others might have seen him unloading the device. What did Bureau pyrotechnics people determine the charge to be?"

Turnow glanced at the report again. ". . . trace elements . . . Semtex . . . estimates 10 pounds of Semtex."

Downing looked shocked. "Ten pounds! Wow! Why was this fabric not totally destroyed?"

Turnow read the description of NV36. "It says here, 'Originally developed for commercial airliners, NV36 is highly resistant to heat due to a chemical bonding process of the advanced vinyl formula and modern nylon structure.' It has a maximum shrink factor of 50 percent."

"Almost like a firefighter's Nomex suit," Downing mused. "So it may be ripped to shreds and it may melt, but it won't burn or shrink beyond half its original size. Bet the perp didn't know he was being so helpful when he chose this particular satchel . . . probably thought there'd be nothing left at all. So what was the original size?"

Turnow was already checking. "Let's see. I have two adjacent corners and one opposite. According to the layout of this rectangle, 15 by 25 centimeters. That would make the pre-exploded size somewhere around 30 by 50 centimeters, by however tall it was. . . . But CSI found nothing more. No top. No handle."

Downing grabbed the binder. "Look at that." He pointed to the dimensions of the suspect case as carried by the overcoated man. "That fits. Eleven by 19 ½ by 14 inches high."

"Yes, but we still have a major problem," Turnow reminded him. "There is photographic evidence that this man and his satchel got off one stop before the explosion." Dr. Turnow knew that a terrorist wouldn't have handled 10 pounds of Semtex and a timer in the open. Then it came to him. "He used a false-bottom case!"

"Precisely!" Downing exclaimed, grabbing the binder from Turnow. "That's it! The reason CSI didn't find a top to the case is because the guy didn't leave one."

"And see here, in the earlier photo, how the case sags near the handle when the man entered. His shoulder even drooped a bit from the weight of it."

"Yes," Downing agreed, pointing to another photograph. "Look how light the case appears on his way out."

"We'll need to do more research, enhancing the photos and video surveillance, but I'll bet we've found our man," Turnow concluded, hopping up from his chair and moving toward the door.

"Where are you going?" Downing quizzed.

Turnow barely heard him. His mind was already on to the next phase. "I need to find out if the lab has determined the type of detonation device used. It may point to where our terrorist got the elements. You buzz the senator and tell him what we have so far. But caution him that this is very preliminary. Political pressure or not, it's more important to get it right!"

FBI Shoot House
SOMA (South Of Market Street district)
San Francisco
5:02 P.M. Pacific Time

HONING THE BLADE

The establishment of a "Shoot House" in San Francisco was an important development in the FBI's training and preparedness on the West Coast. Prior to the creation of a western regional Hostage Rescue Team, all training exercises had been conducted at headquarters in Quantico, Virginia. The facilities at Quantico were vastly more complete, but they had one major drawback: their location on the East Coast was three time zones and six hours' flight time from the Pacific region. The creation of Chapter 16 and its associated SWAT unit as a highly mobile elite tactical squad established a West Coast counterbalance for the concentration of special forces back East.

Every Spec Ops assault team—whether it's Delta, the SEALs, or HRT—must train continually in order to keep their skills sharp and their minds in a state of constant readiness. The acquisition of the San Francisco Shoot House made this level of preparedness possible.

The building itself was suitably nondescript, a burned-out former hotel surrounded by a cyclone security fence. To passersby it was nothing more than a derelict eyesore, and only a few key personnel within the FBI and members of the West Coast HRT knew the property was even in use.

Inside a converted basement ballroom, the floor had been stripped back to polished concrete, and the walls and high ceilings were reinforced with heavy steel plates. In the center of the dimly lit room stood what appeared to be a homemade jungle gym. Stacks of truck tires 10 feet tall composed the walls of a maze laid out in the form of a large house. The tires were filled with dense rubber shavings, an effective means of stopping even high-caliber bullets.

Steve Alstead climbed the observation scaffolding to a point well above the action. His attendance was unexpected, which would allow him to make an accurate assessment of the West Coast HRT's state of readiness.

Steve adjusted the volume on his Tactical 7 stereo-amplifying/reducing ear gear. During the drill he would hear only the dull thuds of pistol and submachine-gun fire. When it was quiet, and with the volume turned all the way up, he could hear the men whisper from across the floor on the stage. There, two Observer-Snipers lay very still, almost invisible in the shadows.

Steve patched into the master control radio. He could hear his good friend and HRT commander, Dan Debusse, calling out a radio check. "Observer-Snipers . . . Oz 1, Oz 2, report."

Oz 1 and Oz 2 were the primary and secondary Observer-Sniper Teams. Each OS Team was made up of a pair of men who would alternate in shifts. One lay in wait with his firearm, usually a Remington 700, .308 caliber, equipped with a Leupold M1 long-range tactical scope. The other member of the team, equipped with a high-power spotting scope, watched for Tangos—targets or suspects—who might be moving around. Contrary to the public's perception of the word, the first job of a sniper was to observe. In the event of deployment, OS Teams would be the most valuable eyes, gathering as much exterior intelligence—intel—as possible. The second job, of course, was precision shooting.

"Oz 1 to command, two Tangos, stage side windows. They appear to be holding one of the Hostages, a small teddy bear. Over. . . ."

Aside from sniper teams, there were three other basic elements to Spec Ops. All were given names based on the phonetic alphabet. Command/control was referred to as Charlie. The Perimeter Team included those responsible for controlling the flow of traffic into and out of a given area, as well as securing any escape routes that might be used by the Tangos. The fourth and most dangerous element was Echo, standing for the Entry Team.

Oz 2 reported as Steve switched his radio net control module over to the Echo Team frequency. He could hear their voices, low, as the two five-man teams of Echo 1 and Echo 2 prepared a forced entry.

Steve remembered the lull between waves—the silence before the storm. It was a vacuum of movement and sound. As if everything ceased to exist for an instant. No one breathed.

Then the basement of the Shoot House erupted with sound and movement. Oz 2 fired a shot through the large front-window opening. The simmunition round, a paint-filled bullet, hit Tango 1 in the chest. He dropped the Hostage.

Echo 1 chucked in a flash-bang grenade. A burst of white, arcing light, like a welding machine exploding, lit up the room in a blinding burst. The five-man team charged the front door.

It was as if someone had plugged in a pinball game. The points of contact bounced around the house. Tango 1 was down. Tango 2 charged with a pistol down the main hallway, hoping to escape.

Echo 2 plunged in through the side windows just in front of him. Before Tango 1 had even raised his pistol, Echo 2 planted a controlled pair of bullets three inches apart, center chest.

Before Steve's eyes had even recovered from the brilliant flare of the grenade, the drill was over. He smiled as he saw Echo 1 leader holding the Hostage like a baby.

Steve knew the adrenaline rush that accompanied such a well-executed drill. He wished he'd been down on the floor with all the HRT guys he'd worked with before—Mooneyham, Chaz, Alpha, Willie, and Jim Sorveno—shooting up the bad guys and saving the day.

And, paradoxically mixed with all the simulated and real violence, the teddy bear had reminded him of his boys. He wished he were with them.

"Oh! Shoot! Cindy!" Steve said aloud, remembering he hadn't talked to her in way too long. He had planned to call her when he returned from his camp-out, but then Anton had been there and for the last many hours he'd done nothing but study and refresh with Chapter 16.

Steve thought about ringing her right then, but now he'd have a real firefight on his hands. He knew he'd better be somewhere quiet with a lot of time and a fully charged cell-phone battery before he made that call.

Dan Debusse's voice clicked into Steve's radio. "That's a wrap, everyone. Meeting in the video review room in 10 for a debriefing."

Steve glanced across the empty space where Dan sat in his control post van.

Dan made eye contact with Steve. Steve flipped to the Command Only channel on his radio. "Well done, Danny. I'm glad to see you haven't suffered from my absence." Steve pantomimed applause.

"Not bad, not bad. Glad you could join us," Dan said, grinning at Steve. Dan was one of the world's greatest small-arms instructors and a personal mentor of Steve's. He was a man of few words at times. At other moments he was full of jokes, though even then his face appeared apprehensive. It was as if he were always prepared to respond to an attack, whether from a thug, the ice-cream man, or space aliens.

"You better believe I'm ready to get back in there. There's no cure for a headache that comes from doing too much thinkin', except a bit of action," Steve quipped. "So, anyway. Who is Echo 1 Alpha these days?"

Dan hopped down from the van's sliding door. "Ol' Hang Fire," he said, and chuckled.

"Hang Fire!" Steve laughed heartily. Hang Fire was the nickname for Darjit Shaikh, a Pakistani-born naturalized American notorious for accidentally loading up dud ammunition in the biggest and hottest handgun calibers. Steve remembered a time when they were out at the range and Darjit was demonstrating his three-hundred-yard shot with a .454 Casul revolver. It was a pistol with the power of a large rifle. About every other shot the guy fired would either barely spit the bullet out, so that it lodged in the barrel, or he'd pull the trigger and the gun wouldn't go off until 10 seconds later. "You crazy, man? Hang Fire at the point? What's the second rule of a gunfight?"

Dan supplied the answer: "It's gotta go *bang* every time!"

Steve felt himself relaxing. It was good to be here. Steve's lateral move from HRT into Intel/SCOT Director at Chapter 16 was a challenging and interesting career move, but there was no one Steve enjoyed working with more than the HRT guys. They were like a second family to him.

Ruefully, he admitted to himself that in many ways they were even closer than his own family.

His B-com vibrated.

"You gonna come watch the films with us?" Dan invited.

"Hang on a second, Dan. I've got a call from the senator." He removed his headgear to answer the phone. "Alstead."

It was indeed Morrison. "Steve, I've got Anton Brown on the line, along with Charles Downing."

"What's up?"

"Miles made a breakthrough on the phone list. We've done a cross-check of the numbers called from the same phone that called the *Chronicle* and found a call was made right before the blast to a known drug dealer, rap sheet long as your arm, who is under light DEA surveillance. Known to deal *weapons* as well as narcotics. We need you to roll the other guys out there in street clothes. See what you can find."

"No problem. ETA is 10 minutes. Downing, Anton?" Steve listened for their acknowledgments. "I'll pick you guys up by the alley gate entrance."

"Ten-four," Morrison responded, clicking off.

"Downing, ten-four."

"Brown, ten-four."

Steve knew at that minute Downing and Anton would be hustling toward their point of rendezvous. He picked up the headset again. "Dan, these guys have me off and running again. I'll have to take a rain check on the films."

"Hey, you got it, buddy. Don't let 'em push you too hard."

"Thanks, man." Steve smiled at Debusse. Dan had been like a father to him at times. He was a pretty understanding guy. In the middle of the night, on weekends, when some nothing blow-up with Cindy turned into WWIII, Dan was always there.

"Next time," Debusse agreed.

"Roger that."

San Francisco
6 P.M. Pacific Time

TALKIN' TRASH

Steve Alstead turned up the radio in his white '67 Ford Mustang fastback with the blue skunk stripes. "From NPR News in Washington, I'm Diego Torre with a special report. The death toll from the BART bombing rose to 311 today when another of the critically injured survivors, a 42-year-old man, died. For more on the continuing investigation into the bombing, we take you now to an FBI press conference just underway in San Francisco. The FBI's Teresa Bouche is at the podium."

Her voice was faint at first. Steve turned up the radio again and adjusted the tuning. ". . . this time the FBI, as well as other law-enforcement and intelligence-gathering agencies, are following up on several leads."

A reporter's question was barely audible. "Who and what are those leads?"

Teresa responded vaguely, "At this time we can't say."

"Ms. Bouche, what about the claim received by the *San Francisco Chronicle* connecting the attack to a white supremacist group? Can you confirm or deny this?"

"As I said, I'm not going to make specific comments on leads the investigation is following, to either confirm or deny."

The voice of another reporter cut in. "Is this the beginning of a campaign of terror? Is there reason to expect that more attacks such as these will occur?"

Bouche ducked the question. "We have uncovered valuable forensic evidence and expect to . . . make substantial progress soon."

Steve sighed. "I hope she's right," he said to the light post at the corner of Columbus and Chestnut.

The broadcast continued. "What is the FBI doing to ensure that more of these attacks don't happen?" CNN's Rita Bradford queried.

"With me," Bouche said smoothly, "is San Francisco police chief Edward Solomon. He can comment more on security precautions being taken about the city. Thank you."

The sound of voices turned to a clamor, punctuated by the snapping of camera shutters. A man cleared his throat. "Let me first say that the BART Red Line is already undergoing restoration and will be back in full operation soon. As for additional precautions, there will be greater surveillance and a much stronger police presence, along with bomb-sniffing K-9 units in every station."

"Chief! Chief . . ."

Steve turned the radio volume down as he pulled up alongside the alleyway gate at the side entrance of the Chapter 16 building. "I wouldn't take that nasty train now if they paid me," he said to himself. "Hey, guys. What's up?"

Anton Brown was dressed in a Raiders shirt and raggedy blue jeans. Downing wore a ratty blue high-water sweat suit and Nikes. For a guy who didn't look right when not in Hugo Boss, this was ridiculous. And Anton . . .

"Anton, you're the scariest thing I've ever seen!"

Brown laughed, then flexed his biceps and displayed a mean face. "Glad you know it! Better unlock the door 'fore I whoop on yo' white self."

Steve blew out a breath of exaggerated disbelief. "And look at you," he said to Downing as he climbed in back. "You look like you got yours at Goodwill."

"Don't remind me," Downing said in disgust. "It's the only duds Undercover could find. They stink like the stairwell at the Union Square parking garage."

Anton chimed in. His whole attitude and demeanor had been transformed into his street persona. "Don't surprise me none. They probably got 'em off some street scum."

Downing frowned, almost gagging.

Steve harassed him too. "Ah, don't worry about it, Downing. This is no social call . . . at least not anybody you're likely to meet again socially."

Downing tried to scratch between his shoulder blades and then his ankles and then both at once. "Just shut up, will you?" He shook his head.

Eventually, on the ride across the Bay Bridge, everyone fell silent. Once in a while the stillness was broken by Anton, looking at Downing and laughing.

The other interruption to the quiet was the occasional stutter of Alstead's '67 Mustang. The engine's "missing" sound was followed by some comment from Anton like, "Man, look at all the money you make, and you still haven't fixed this piece of garbage."

It slightly annoyed Steve, though he knew Anton was right. He did do pretty well for himself. It was sheer procrastination that he hadn't redone the ignition system in the car, or whatever it was that was wrong with it. He thought about getting a new one, but even as old and beat-up as this one was, a brand-new plastic Mustang just wouldn't have the same feel.

But Steve wasn't going to let Anton think he'd gotten the best of him. Instead, Steve harassed him back. "Listen to your ghetto mouth. Get you outta that suit, and you go straight back to yo' roots."

Steve knew well that Anton, once a poor boy from Oakland, not far from where they were going, despised the drug dealers and pimps he'd grown up around in his neighborhood. When Anton wanted to, he could fit right in. In this line of work, it wasn't a bad thing to blend in with the thugs when you really needed to.

"Now you don't wanna go there, Mr. White Man Can't Jump," Anton teased.

Steve realized exactly what he was referring to. Anton would never let Steve forget the time a suspect had broken through the perimeter and jumped a wall near Steve's post. In hot pursuit, Steve bounded after him. Then at a 10-foot block wall he'd found it impossible to leap up and grasp the ledge of the barricade, as the guy he was chasing had so easily done.

Of course the perpetrator landed a foot away from Anton on the other side and was quickly and quietly subdued. It would have been out of character for Anton to let Steve know this immediately though.

Instead Anton had laughed silently for a minute or so, listening to the grunting and scraping as Steve attempted again and again to reach the top edge of the wall. Finally, Anton had called out, "Steve, have you got the suspect?"

Steve had replied, "I didn't see which way he went." Which, while true enough, was not the whole story.

Steve had been even more embarrassed after he dragged a pallet up to the wall, only to look over and find the suspect unconscious at Anton's feet.

Now, defending his honor, Steve maintained, "I never did like basketball. Now wrestling—that's something that comes in handy in this line of work."

"Well, from the looks of it, hoops would have done yo' lead feet some good," Anton retorted.

This kind of bickering between them could go on for hours. It was a kind of brotherly slang that helped them get into character, adapt to how people on the street talked.

They carried on as they crossed onto solid ground again, while Downing snored away with his mouth open in the backseat.

"Steve, Steve, look at him. He be droolin' like a kid."

By now Steve's smile began to hurt. He glanced back for a look.

"Mouth open in that greasy blue sweatshirt like he been drinkin' Thunderbird in the park!"

Uncontrollable laughter followed.

"Hey, lush!" Anton reached behind the seat and slapped Downing's leg. "Wake up, alky! We here!"

"Already?" Downing yawned. "That was quick."

Steve parked the car in front of the Oakland Freeport AM/PM Mini-Mart, where the phone call to the newspaper had been made. The three of them got out, all horseplay left behind in the Mustang.

FOUR

Sammy's Neighborhood
Oakland, California
7:08 P.M. Pacific Time

WHOSE SIDE ARE YOU ON?

Charles Downing rubbed his eyes. Steve and Anton scanned the streets in all directions. Had they been dressed in dark blue, they would have looked like cops on a beat. In their undercover gear, they were more like thugs on a mission to knock over the grocery, aside from Downing, who appeared so out of place he might have been a bystander forced to go along on a crime unwillingly.

Steve eyed the mom-and-pop store carefully. He half expected the store's proprietor to burst out the front door with a sawed-off double-barrel in response to their presence in his parking lot . . . except that they resembled the other customers.

The neighborhood was bad, as Steve expected. Dirt planters were filled with weeds and cigarette butts. The clientele in and out of the parking lot made it seem like a low-rider show had just let out nearby. No one seemed to notice them, Steve realized. It was the benefit of having someone as big and scary as Anton along. For all the civilians around him knew, a guy like Anton probably had a gun under the baggy Oakland jersey.

Ironically enough, he did, but he was one of the good guys.

Steve caught sight of a pay phone near a broken-down, crumbling, white cinder-block wall at the back of the lot. "That's it," he said with a jerk of his chin.

The three moved toward it. Steve spun around to see what the view was like. "Look there." He pointed toward the distance. "You can see the bomb site, all the way across the Bay."

From the pay phone there was a perfect view of the financial district buildings surrounding the center of the underground blast, though it was 10 miles away.

"Intel that I picked up right before we left says the guy whose house was called has a brother who was recently sentenced to life in prison for drug trafficking and conspiracy to murder. This evidence establishes a motive. . . ." Downing ran his hands over his head. Closing his eyes, he must have been getting into character. "Profile points toward a Bubba job, but still . . ."

Steve and Anton, quietly listening, imagined the scenario.

"Let's say it's a revenge hit. Get-even-with-whitey justice. The brother knows somebody who sets the thing up. They arrange it, maybe two guys total. And when the hit is made, the second guy calls to let him know. . . ."

Steve interjected, "But is he really stupid enough to then go make a call to the paper from the pay phone where he originally confirmed?"

"Steve, keep in mind, these are murdering drug dealers. How much of a corner on smart do you think they have?" Downing argued.

"This just feels bigger to me," Steve objected. "Than a revenge hit, I mean. Some planning went into this. What with the cost and difficulty of locating such a large amount of explosives, I'm just not sure."

Anton considered. "Maybe we take a walk up to the address we got and check it out from there."

Downing nodded. "You guys go ahead. I'll see what else I can come up with around here. Keep in mind there are already agents watching the house. Be careful. If you show iron, they may come out of the woods with guns blazing like rednecks after ducks."

"You just watch your own backside," Steve told him.

Anton added, "Yeah, you be pretty enough to get mugged in these parts."

Downing shook his head. "I'm going to take a walk. I'll see you back at the car."

Anton followed Steve up the street. Both of the men had a little more swing in their step—kings of the concrete jungle. It was an attitude for survival that made them fit in that much more. Up a side street and at the top of a hill, they came to a rickety three-story house with a cracked and crumbling concrete porch.

Steve spotted the surveillance. Forty yards ahead and behind the suspect's address, undercover guys waited. Steve actually winked at one as he passed by, barely showing a little corner of his badge from his pocket. The agent looked confused, and Steve saw him mouth to his partner, *Just who is* that?

"Let's cross and take a closer look," Steve said, motioning.

"Where are you going, Alstead?" Anton asked in a panic. "Don't get too close. You'll blow it!"

"Nah," Steve insisted. "Just follow me. Pretend like we're buyers."

"What?"

"Be cool, man. You know how word gets around out here."

At that point Anton was along for the ride, like a passenger in the tandem seat of a biplane. *You don't like my flyin'? It's a long way down to get out now,* Steve thought. He was fairly confident anyway. At least he had a plan.

The two walked right up to the front door.

The wooden door was open, and a screen door, missing its bottom panel, sagged. Steve couldn't see anyone, though he could smell the sticky-sweet scent of cannabis burning. "Yo, Sammy!" He called out the suspect's name. "I need a sack!"

"What, uh? Who is it?" a congested, smoky voice replied.

"It's J and Dr. Dre," Steve responded.

Anton snickered, getting into the role.

A sickly looking, sunken-chested black man appeared in the room. "Who? I don't know no J or Dr. Dre."

Black, Steve confirmed. *Blows the Bubba-job theory.*

"Come on, man," Steve insisted. "We know your brother. Used to run with him before he got sent up."

Anton cut in. "Just fill us a dime and we be on our way."

Sammy stopped face-to-face in front of the screen door, taking a long sober look. "I'm out. And the feds be watchin' me."

"Who? Like them cats down the street in that white Crown Vic?" Anton said, flicking his thumb over his shoulder.

"Now don't go pointin' to no cops," Sammy protested. "Don't be out there drawin' attention. Come in real quick." He opened the door and invited them in.

Steve could just imagine what the cops in wait were thinking by now. He knew the rules: once a guy invited you in, the house was your oyster. Anything you saw there might not be admissible in court, but it could be good enough to haul a guy in.

"What's that smell, man?" Anton pressed.

"Roaches," Sammy squawked. "I just burned the last one."

Steve peered around. The front room was small and square. It smelled of sour laundry and trash.

Sammy leaned forward, digging around in a full ashtray, spilling the gray contents all over the smeared, crumb-ridden table. "Here," he said, producing an inch of dope-filled cigarette. "Saw you all come up and buried it in the ashtray. Can't be too careful."

Shocked at how easy it had been, Steve reached for it, held on to it with the tips of his fingers. "Thanks, man . . ."

"Man," Anton interrupted, "did you see the bomb go off the other day?"

Sammy burst into laughter. "Sure did. Serves 'em right. You know sometimes they got it comin'."

Steve glanced at Anton as if to say, *You want to take this guy in?*

Sammy continued, "I hear a couple cops got took down on that train." He chuckled. "Heard the explosion all the way over here in Oakland."

Steve interrupted seriously, "You wouldn't know nothin' about that, would you, Sammy? I figure it would even things up for your brother."

"Shoot," Sammy exclaimed. "Way karma comes around, I wouldn't deny it. 'Course, sometimes you gotta help karma along, don't you? I did," he bragged.

Ignoring Anton's signal to slow down, Steve stood up. "FBI," he said. "You're under arrest." His hand emerged from his back pocket with handcuffs.

Sammy kicked and bellowed, but Anton had no trouble subduing the suspect. With his knee in Sammy's back, he ground the drug dealer's face into the filthy carpet and cuffed him with Steve's cuffs.

Steve read him his rights while Anton searched the house. "Steve, you sure we got probable cause here?"

Waving off the objection, Steve commented, "*Now* you ask? We got the phone call, we got the dope, and we got the assertion of conspiracy."

Steve led Sammy outside, just as Downing, who must have been wondering what was going on, turned up the driveway. An unmarked police car pulled up slowly, having sensed something.

The uniformed officer got out defensively. "What's going on here?"

"Special Agent Alstead, FBI," Steve said, flashing his badge. "We've placed this guy Sammy under arrest for possession and offering to sell cannabis to an officer of the law." Steve showed him the remains of the marijuana cigarette.

"You idiot! There was supposed to be a big shipment coming in tonight!" the enraged officer berated him. "This op has been under way for weeks!"

Steve had obviously blown the cover, though from talking to Sammy, the supposed cover didn't really exist.

"Yeah?" Anton said. "Well, you better tell your UC boys to go work some white-bread neighborhood. They don't cut it here."

Still angry, the officer placed Sammy in his car. By that time another unit had rolled up—this one containing a watch commander arriving in response to a yelp from his troops.

Steve explained again that the arrest was part of a federal investigation, though he couldn't say more.

That explanation didn't seem to matter to the officers whose case had been blown. Steve could understand their frustration. Sammy would prob-ably get off completely now on drug charges. It was doubtful he'd ever be nailed, even for trafficking. Steve found it ironic the way the system worked.

But at least Chapter 16 had gained some leverage. *If* Sammy really knew anything about the bombing. And Chapter 16 was short on solid leads so far.

Anton emerged, having found nothing. The police unit secured the house.

Steve asked for his handcuffs back.

"You made the collar," the officer snapped. "You can come down to the jail and get them!"

Steve, Anton, and Downing regrouped as they made their way back to the Mustang. "Guess I trashed their party," Steve commented wryly.

Downing didn't seem surprised. "Oh, you think so, do you?"

"Oops."

"And nothing tangible for the arrest other than a few antigovernment threats?" Downing sighed.

Steve imagined Downing was writing him off as a macho, use-your-head-as-a-battering-ram, leap-without-looking hard case.

Maybe Downing was right.

"Well, it may not matter." Downing abruptly changed the subject. "I may just have a new lead."

"And what would that be, Prince Downing?" Steve asked sarcastically.

"I got to thinking. If I was a terrorist living in the area, even a Bubba, I surely wouldn't make a call from the same pay phone more than once. So when I found another pay phone in the area with a perfect view of the bombing site, I called the Chief to get Miles working on records for the rest of the pay phones in this area."

"Now that's good thinking," Anton complimented.

"I hope so," Downing replied grimly. "If your friend Sammy turns up zip, we're going to need some good news when Morrison finds out what we spoiled."

Steve hated that Anton agreed with Downing. He knew a major investigation had just been compromised, and the results had better be worth it.

FBI Headquarters
San Francisco
8:58 P.M. Pacific Time

FUZZY LOGIC

Senator Morrison had passed the tip on area phone booths from Downing to Miles Miller.

Morrison accompanied the computer genius to the FBI's high-tech, state-of-the-art computer research lab. En route Miles was briefed on the workings of the National Crime Information Center database.

The NCIC was an incredibly powerful device. It could do everything from linking names and records of criminals to cross-checking profiles of potential suspects and running IDs of missing persons. Its lightning speed enabled it to compare evidence, such as fingerprints or DNA from skin samples, with any other previously processed records, of which the NCIC contained over one hundred million.

What was required was a talented operator who knew how to finesse the semiconductors. Asking the right questions, framing the optimal inquiries, was still the key to getting the full benefit of the machinery.

Morrison had informed Miles that the FBI computer lab would be his office, never dreaming Miles would take that to mean his *exclusively.* When Morrison left to attend to other business, Miles was busily hacking away at one of the terminals connected to the numerous racks of hard drives and other data storage devices.

But evidently Miles had failed to realize that the lab was also shared with dozens of other agents, who had been moved out while he was working on this sensitive project. By the time Miles had called Senator Morrison with urgent news, wires lay everywhere. The previously neatly organized components were stacked in high towers and circled around Miles like a sandbagged bunker.

The facility was in complete disarray. Racks were empty. There was a pile of deck screws on the counter and a bundle of cables in the middle of the floor.

Morrison entered the room. "What on earth?" He threw his arms in the air.

Miles grinned innocently. "Since I'll be working here, I thought I'd do a little rearranging." But his smile quickly disappeared under the weight of Morrison's disapproving glare. "I wanted to move things so they were at arm's length."

Morrison was speechless. The mess looked like the entire control room of a nuclear submarine had been cut out and dropped into an otherwise empty computer lab.

Miles ducked his head with the expression of a charming but inept pooch who had just been caught chewing a shoe. "I needed to layer the cross-checks, and things were just a little too far away. I . . . I got tired of getting up. Since this will be my office . . ."

"Miles! This is a shared lab! The entire San Francisco FBI uses this facility. When I said this was your office, I meant you would be spending a lot of time here—not that it was yours to dismantle and rearrange as you like."

Staring blankly back at him with his mouth open, Miles cringed as reality set in. "Oh," he replied stupidly.

"You'll put it back exactly as it was," the senator insisted.

Miles, whose already receding chin was tucked even farther into his chest, stared frightfully up at Morrison with one eye open and his face scrunched up like a prune. "Yes sir."

Sighing, Morrison gathered his thoughts, in search of the thread that could redeem the situation. "Okay. With that tiny clarification made and out of the way, what of the calls made from the surrounding area pay phones?"

Miles shuffled through some printouts. "One link came up." He flipped the pages. "Here it is. Let's see, it says . . . call made at 10:55 A.M., April 20, to . . ." He skipped over some detail. "Ah, yes, AMT, American Militia Training, known as antigovernment white supremacist group in Idaho."

"Now this is worth calling me for!" praised Morrison.

Miles read further. "Currently under surveillance by Boise FBI for weapons violations."

"Bingo!" Morrison exclaimed. "That fits the profile! Was the phone that the call was made from in line with the bomb site across the water?"

Miles checked. "Yep."

"That's it!" Morrison cried out. "We've got to act fast if we are to prove that Chapter 16 is the sharpest edge on the blade." He spun around. "Put this place back together, Miles. Don't worry about passing on the intel. I'll relay it on to the other divisions. You just have all of your necessary equipment for research and broadcast ready, as well as any other personal things you might need for an extended stay in the hills. We leave in two hours!"

The Alstead Condo
Morro Bay, California
10:12 P.M. Pacific Time

THE THINGS YOU CAN THINK

Still no word from Steve. Cindy kept her cell phone on and by her all day. It had rung twice while a local news story about the energy crisis, high electricity bills, and brownouts scrolled across Channel 6. The newscaster seemed to associate an energy crisis with laziness. At least that was the attempted humor.

Cindy had stared at the phone in terror for an instant and then scrambled to answer the ring. A pleasant female voice inquired if she would like to try a subscription to the San Luis newspaper delivered daily to her home.

Cindy snapped furiously, "Are you people nuts? Everything I need to know I learn from *Weekly Reader!* You called me last week! Just last week! I'm expecting an urgent call! Now bug off!"

It was a rare and entertaining thing when Cindy cracked and spilled her guts in front of her kids. They stared at her in silent fascination as she fumbled to hang up the little phone and regain her composure.

It had been a long and exhausting two days.

Was she worried?

How could she be worried about a guy who made his living facing bullets and machine-gun fire? What was the point? How could she spend even one more anxious thought on a clod who thought of no one but himself?

Why didn't he call? Hadn't she spent the best years of her life pacing the floor over him?

Was he still in San Francisco? Or had his occupation called him to confront something terrible in South America? or Iran? or Russia? What irony it would be if he were killed in a subway explosion! When he left her for the last time, she'd vowed she would never worry about him again.

Worried? About Steve? What a waste of her time and energy.

Of course she was worried.

Tommy and Matthew, sensing their mother's anxiety, had exacerbated her tension by fighting in the backseat all the way home from church this morning.

The early evening in their cramped Morro Bay condo had been miserable. She fixed a pathetic supper of macaroni and cheese for both of the boys. Mint chip ice cream for dessert. Homework, VeggieTales, and Wallace and Gromit rounded out the evening.

Her mom had called. Cindy had been short-tempered and impatient. The conversation went something like this: "Of course I haven't heard from him! What else is new? He probably doesn't even know a BART train blew up two miles from where he lives. Probably he's off in Timbuktu chasing hijackers. Probably he won't think to call us 'til Christmas! Don't defend him, Mother! Don't! Of course I knew when I married him but . . . don't take his side! There's a reason we're not living together, Mother."

She had slammed down the receiver, then immediately felt guilty.

Matthew leaned close to Tommy. "Don't mess with Mom tonight if you want to live."

"That's right," Cindy warned.

Thus the day and evening had passed.

Now Matthew was downstairs playing math games on the computer. All was quiet at last.

Cindy adjusted the pillow behind her back as she finished reading a battered Dr. Seuss book to Tommy. "'Oh, the THINKS you can Think!'"

Tommy screwed up his face and squeezed his eyes tightly shut. "I'm thinking."

"What are you thinking?" Cindy asked the four-year-old.

"About Daddy," Tommy said.

She repressed the urge to groan. Poor kid. Tommy was still too young to comprehend what a jerk his father was. "Okay. You want to tell me?"

"Thinking . . . about when we went camping. We forgot the pots, but it was okay because Dad cooked in the bucket."

"Clever man." She suspected that Steve had forgotten the pots and pans so he could show off his survival skills.

"It was fun."

"Yes, it was."

Last summer. One week together as a family without interruption. Steve had left his cell phone beside the frying pan on the kitchen counter. The boys had a tent of their own. Steve and Cindy shared a week of bliss on an air mattress. Tarzan and Jane. Romance blossomed. While the boys slept, she and Steve had gone skinny-dipping in Alder Creek. They made out like a couple of teenagers under the starlight. Talked about what they wanted for their boys. What they wanted out of life. Another baby? Promises had been made. Steve would leave HRT and start his own consulting firm. Soon. Yes. Soon they would have a normal, quiet life together.

How soon?

It had been perfect . . . almost. And then they had returned to the real world. To the frying pan and the cell phone.

"I miss him." Tommy turned his face toward the wall.

Cindy ran her fingers through Tommy's hair. A wave of pity swept over her. "Sometimes . . . me too," she admitted.

"Is he okay, you think?" Tommy asked.

"I think . . . sure. You know your dad."

"Sure."

"Let's pray and then you go to sleep."

"I wish he'd call," the child whispered.

"Me too." Now the steel trap of anger and resentment clamped down on her heart again. How dare Steve not call! Had he forgotten his boys? Never mind her. She was used to it. But how dare he leave them all wondering if he was alive or dead! How could he see the images on the news and not think about a couple of kids—nine and four—waiting for the phone to ring?

If Steve was alive—*if*—she would let him have it with both barrels when they finally connected!

FIVE

San Francisco International Airport
Monday, 23 April
12:01 A.M. Pacific Time

WHAT ARE WE FACING?

As the twin Pratt & Whitney turboprop engines wound up, Steve wondered if his gear had been properly gathered from his locker at Chapter 16 headquarters.

He remembered several intrigue/action writers who had a Special Forces Operator who had not packed his own gear. No way would a guy who was about to do a HALO (High Altitude Low Opening) jump from 25,000 feet into a hostage rescue situation not load, check, and recheck his own gear.

The agent would pack his own parachute, three times if he was superstitious. The alternate kind of scenario was a lame device authors used in cheesy stories in order to set up future conflicts. The unrealistic idea had always irritated him. Steve had put down or thrown away several books when a character did something stupid like that.

And so he found it ironic now that there had not been enough time to go to 16 HQ. Someone else was handling the very gear his life depended on. What if a magazine was dented and it didn't feed? What if the gun jammed at the worst possible moment? He hoped the pack job was supervised by Dan Debusse, though the thought of *anyone* handling Steve's stuff made him paranoid.

By now 50 of the sharpest HRT guys from the West and East Coasts would be close behind with Dan and all the needed gear aboard a C-130. It would do Steve no good to worry about equipment until they arrived.

Since Steve couldn't physically put his hands on the very things that would save his life, he mentally went over the exercise of gear prepping. Would the Federal Premium Nozler Ballistic Tip .223 rounds be correctly loaded into his nine AR-15 magazines? Would his tac vest have all the essentials needed for a forced entry: flash-bang grenades, flashlights, Mad Dog tactical fighting knife, half a dozen high-cap magazines for his Glock 22? *And what about a med kit?* he wondered. *Who would the medic be? I wonder if we'll need one.* "My vest!" he said aloud, hoping someone at HRT had grabbed the right size Second Chance ballistic level 4/5 bullet-resistant vest. It would stop virtually all pistol rounds and some light rifle bullets. Steve had considered going with a lighter vest, such as a level 2. Doing so would make it much easier to move about and reduce his overall weight slightly, but anything less would be a hazard—at least where they were headed.

Steve knew their opponents would have the big guns: Armalite AR-10s shooting the heavy-duty .308 rounds, or else the Belgian-made FN-FAL of the same caliber, frequently referred to as the world's battle rifle.

Steve reconsidered his choice of vest once again. Level 4 and 5 ballistics-wear would stop a .308 round, though wearing one was like running around with a 55-gallon steel drum around your belly.

Trade-offs.

His thoughts were interrupted when Anton closed and latched the fuselage door. A quick sucking sound *whoosh*ed and whistled as the cabin pressurized. Steve's ears popped. He emerged from the internal checklist, making eye contact with Anton.

Anton gave him an understanding look. "I know where you been, Saul."

Saul. The name sent chills down his back. In the Academy, his locker had a piece of tape strapped across it that said "S. Alstead." At some point, partway through training, half of the tape had been torn off in some locker-room wrestling match. Half remained. From then on he was known as Saul, partly because he beat up those who tried to tag him *Sal.*

It felt like the world was on his shoulders. He had a weak feeling in his stomach. The mission's success, if negotiations should fail, would fall largely on his planning and execution as Echo 1 leader. He could have gotten out of handling the Echo Team command a long time ago, though he relied on and trusted no one's instincts more than his own. If the mission was going to fall apart, he'd die trying. Death was a preferable alternative to watching his men and others get slaughtered through his own miscalculations.

Steve nodded resolutely to Anton, the only one present who could possibly begin to grasp what he was feeling. "Lock and load," he whispered.

"Lock and load," Anton replied. He passed the U-shaped, taupe leather sofa, where Bouche and Downing were talking, and took a seat in the back of the plane near the rest room.

Morrison and Turnow remained in San Francisco, following up other evidence, looking for ways to strengthen the connection to AMT or to disprove it if it was in error. They would be in constant touch by B-com and satellite link.

Steve breathed in the fresh, leathery smell of the new plane, taking a look around. Miles hacked away on his laptop at a small workstation near the cockpit door. His knees were up to his chest and his long neck craned over the keyboard like a stork's.

The copilot's voice, crisp and clear over the speaker, hailed the cabin. "The time, ladies and gentlemen, is approximately 10 minutes past 12. We'll be up in the air in a matter of minutes and should be touching down at Idaho's Boise Airport just around 3 A.M. local. I'll notify you if there's any change. For now, please be comfortable and know that we'll help you in any way we can."

The speaker clicked out.

Steve thought about Cindy.

"Don't call me. I'll call you!"

So he hadn't. Instead he had waited.

And waited.

It was unlike Cindy not to call. Maybe she really had been brainwashed while Steve was in the Sudan for seven weeks. From the moment he had returned, it seemed, her whole attitude toward him had soured after a woman in their church so generously counseled her. Only minor interrogation had been required to extract the information: While Steve had been toting a hundred-pound pack through the desert by night and sleeping in the sand by day, half the congregation, led by the one busybody, had been undertaking their own covert operation. "Operation Leave Steve," as he imagined they titled it, was a subtle indoctrination designed to help Cindy exercise "tough love." The goal was to cut Steve loose since he couldn't be there for her and the boys.

"Hypocrites!" he muttered scornfully. "So I should've dumped my rifle pack, abandoned my men, and swum home in order to satisfy their idea of what a godly father and loving husband should be?" Cindy and the kids *were* second only to God in his life, he reminded himself.

"Miles," Steve called out across the cabin, "when will you have the physical intel?"

"I have it now. I'm just printing it."

Seconds later three sheets of paper emerged into a plastic tray from a printer mounted behind a cabinet door. Steve walked forward and removed them. He returned to a swivel chair across the aisle from the rest. He handed one sheet titled "Talking Points" to Teresa, and another titled "Background & Profile" to Downing. He kept the other: "Terrain, Buildings, & Weapons."

Each of them read over the sheets silently.

Downing cleared his throat. "Let me just brief both you and Teresa,

Steve, on the background of these guys. It may help as you begin to develop the Tactical Plan, and as Teresa and I try to come up with the negotiation strategy." Charles Downing scanned the document. "The group is called AMT, American Militia Training. In spite of the name North Aryan Knights, given to the *Chronicle,* there is, at this time, no record anywhere of a group called NAK connected to AMT, or anywhere else, for that matter. However, based on the findings of a cross-check of calls made from other pay phones in the area of the first, when the numbers called were compared with those in the NCIC database, phone records show that a call *was* made to this AMT that fits the time frame and observation point of the bombing. A profile of this group, compiled two and a half years ago, after the FBI interviewed a young, disgruntled dropout, doesn't suggest that these guys are radical (meaning violent) racists, or that they are actively pursuing anti-government operations. Many militias are genuinely interested in safeguarding American rights. Not all are racists, but—"

Steve interrupted. "They don't have to have shown themselves to be extremists to be a threat."

"Exactly what I'm saying," Downing continued. "They have the equipment, and phone records prove there was a call made from a location that provided a distant view of the bomb site. It's a textbook confirmation call, made to alert the masterminds of their success."

Downing delved deeper into the AMT profile.

"AMT was founded by Andrew Adams, a brilliant Yale dropout who didn't like the politics of real-world military operations and law enforcement. He was an avid supporter of the Second Amendment, believing there was growing corruption in the United States government that needed to be held in check by pressure groups like his own. And here's something that might be either important or just coincidence: the AMT headquarters is near Hell's Canyon, Idaho." The profiler alluded to the words used by the NAK caller when claiming responsibility for the blast.

Downing continued by noting that Adams had studied the modern tactics of warfare. After reading Napoleon and Von Clausewitz, he refined his own small-arms training exercises from what he believed were the very best sources, like the Chuck Taylor School of Modern Technique and Gun Sight, among others.

Adams trained civilians in the art of self-defense at a gun store in Utah for a number of years. As his skills and abilities grew, so too did his notoriety. When his uncle died and left him more than a thousand acres in Idaho, the time was right for him to make his move.

According to the account, things were slow for Adams at first. He took up political causes, lobbying for the National Rifle Association and the like. Eventually his views became too extreme for the NRA. By that time, he was so well-known that a quarter-page ad in *Soldier of Fortune* magazine was enough to generate a hundred or so applications for what Adams called a Live Aboard. The ad presented his well-known views, offering the opportunity for others of like mind to come to Idaho, where specially selected applicants would train on a one-year commitment. Young men (women were strictly excluded) worked the ranch, raising cattle and harvesting timber, and forfeiting all claim to wages in exchange for training.

The first squad of 10 was a success. According to AMT's federal tax returns, more than a million dollars gross was offset by an operating cost of $983,000 the first year.

Adams was very careful with business, hiring the best tax attorneys money could buy. He was able to write off the guns and ammo—virtually his entire arsenal—against the money generated from logging and cattle ranching. Unconfirmed reports said that the only questionable thing Adams ever did was trade livestock for Class-3 weapons from another militia. It was still legal to own them in 48 states, though Adams didn't make a record of or amortize them on AMT taxes, as it was alleged that he wanted the Class-3s to be secret. And even more on point was new, unconfirmed intel: Adams had purchased weapons just two years before from an Egyptian arms dealer with ties to Islamic Jihad.

Very few members of AMT ever left unhappy with their experiences at the AMT compound. Many of them stayed on from year to year as the organization grew.

Of those who did leave, many remained under close watch by the government. Nearly all former AMT members were unsuccessful in finding work in law enforcement or military, due to antiestablishment views. Confirming this analysis, six of the 93 members tracked by the NCIC committed violent crimes against peace officers, including three separate murders.

But not Adams. He had managed to stay clean—a businessman in the sense of running a technically legit operation, behind which lurked a sort of backwoods mafia. Five former members, thought to have been disgruntled, mysteriously turned up dead in widely separated parts of the U.S. The crimes had never been linked to AMT.

The AMT organization, with 29 current members, rarely took new applicants anymore—maybe one or two per year. The thousand-acre inheritance had grown into a 100,000-acre empire, with land all over the North- west, the Rockies, and the Pacific Coast.

Adams had grown even more careful in recent times, surrendering weapons that were questioned by the U.S. government. Sources said he did this to appease the government and to ward off any cause for a search warrant that might be obtained against the AMT premises.

So why go ballistic now? Steve wondered. What would make AMT take the chance of losing everything? If the BART bomb was AMT's work, what was the motive that boiled over now?

Downing concluded the profile discussion. "This guy Adams could be dangerous. His people have the ability to hold out for a year, fight it out to the death, or send people out to kill us and our families if they want to find out who we are."

Steve took a deep breath as he thought of his kids and Cindy. In a way, in this line of work, it was better she lived distant from him. Maybe she could remain anonymous that way. On the other hand, he realized with a chill of helplessness, he could never protect them.

Teresa furthered Downing's point. "You know, these guys have enough resources that if we screw this one up, they may take the FBI to court."

We all know the negative ramifications, Steve thought. She didn't have to rub it in everyone's face.

Surprisingly, Downing agreed with her. "You know, Andrew Adams is smart enough and has adapted enough that it wouldn't surprise me if he somehow staged a mishap just so he could take on the government and win, thereby making his point."

Miles spun around from his workstation. Staring at Steve, he said, "Yeah, like Waco Bar B Q, except there was nobody left to sue."

"That's the most offensive thing I've ever heard!" Teresa said emphatically.

The other three team members also looked shocked. Didn't Miles know that Steve and Anton had been part of HRT, the group used to infiltrate the Branch Davidian cult?

Steve shot Miles a threatening look and stood up.

Miles backpedaled. "I meant, we don't want any more flaming compounds—I mean, we keep it together, right?"

Teresa pointed at Miles. "This man is to have duct tape over his mouth at all times he's in public. Agreed?"

Steve was ready to carry out the threat and it showed.

Miles cowered. "Uh, forget it. I don't know what I meant." Awkwardly spinning back around to his computer, he hunched his shoulders and bent over the workstation.

The temperature in the cabin cooled, slowly.

Steve realized his aggression wasn't so much directed toward Miles as it was part of prepping for a role, a frame of mind he psyched himself into. Having someone to be mad at calmed his nerves and made his queasy stomach feel better. All the same, he ignored Miles thereafter.

A little fear would do the guy some good, Steve decided, taking a seat by Anton in the back, where he began making notes for a Plan of Entry.

No one said a word the rest of the flight. There was time to sleep, but no one did that either. This sort of tension was perhaps the downside of having a tight team with members from entirely different backgrounds. None of them really understood what the other one was about, and yet each knew they faced a situation requiring complete trust and confidence in another's judgment.

Boise Municipal Airport
3:05 A.M. Mountain Time

GOOD OL' BOYS

From the air few lights were on in Boise, Idaho. At least fewer than expected for a city of about 170,000.

The Beech King Air 350 touched down right on schedule at Gowen Field on the southern side of the city. Anton lowered the stairs and the tired team emerged. Except for the passing of several distant automobiles, everything seemed extremely quiet.

Steve inhaled deeply. The cool northern breeze energized him. He felt light on his toes as he bounced on the tarmac, blowing out a couple of hard breaths. With the exception of himself and Anton, the rest of the crew looked long overdue for bed.

A thick, heavyset man walked out to meet them. The wind parted his thinning, slicked-back black hair. "How are you?" He extended his hand to Teresa Bouche. "Chuck Maines, Boise FBI, Criminal Investigation Division."

"Chuck, hi," Teresa said, feeling her face as if making certain her jaw muscles still worked. "Yes, we spoke on the phone."

Chuck greeted the rest.

Downing, though tired, appeared the same as always. His tie was straight; his suit still looked pressed. "Charles Downing, profiling specialist."

"Good, good," Chuck replied in an excited, good ol' boy tone of voice. "Nice to meet you, Charlie. We had a profiler on loan to us, but we don't have anything like you on call."

Steve swung his arms, trying to get the blood back into them. "Hey, Chuck!"

Chuck gripped Steve's hand firmly and squeezed his triceps to boot. "Look at them arms. You must be our Special Operations man."

Steve immediately felt like he knew the guy. "Steve Alstead."

Chuck had an earthy, ranch-hand way about him—the kind of guy who would suck rattlesnake poison from your leg and spit it out without thinking twice. He led them all inside, through a small hangar with maroon rubber carpets that smelled of shop grease.

"Come on out here," Chuck instructed as he exited via the front door.

Miles was the last one through. He gawked at the equipment in the building.

"We ain't got a limo for you," Chuck said, once they were outside, "but this baby's got four-wheel drive." He opened the sliding door on an oversized white Ford van. "It's about a three-hour drive to Council. I figure you'll be needin' as much room as we can get, but a school bus woulda been kinda suspicious."

Steve laughed. Teresa slid onto the front bench. Downing climbed in beside her. Miles opted for the very back, lay down, and immediately began to snore. Anton closed the door and took the second seat back, while Steve rode shotgun.

Chuck gave a little history on the way. The town of Boise was founded on the Oregon Trail in about 1863. Southern-central Idaho is a rocky, desolate high desert. When French Canadian fur trappers came along and saw the expanse of cottonwoods, birches, and willows that crowded along the banks of the Snake River, they exclaimed "*Les bois!* The trees!" And so Boise became known as the City of Trees. It was an oasis to travelers on the Oregon Trail and a centrally located place where nineteenth-century miners could pick up supplies.

It was a 10-minute ride up Vista Avenue to Capital Boulevard. The capitol building was a slightly smaller stone version of the U.S. Capitol, still massive at 200,000 square feet and complete with two wings, topped by a 208-foot dome in the center. It impressed Steve that a state with little more than a million people had such a grand capitol building.

The van headed eastward on Highway 44 for a few miles. Outside of town they joined Interstate 84, which they followed a short while until heading north on Highway 95 for another 65 miles.

Some of the team nodded off to sleep as they passed the small town of Payette, named after the Canadian Frenchman who ran Old Fort Boise in the 1830s and '40s. The road began to wind a bit more, and conversation between those still awake shifted onto the subject of AMT.

Chuck asked Steve if he'd seen the intel on the AMT organization that the resident agency in Boise had sent out.

"Yeah, we talked it over," Steve replied. "This Adams guy sounds pretty heavily armed."

"He is that," Chuck agreed. "Word has it that they've even got a LAW rocket launcher."

"I saw that."

"Me and a couple of the guys from Intel have done some flyovers. And we make a point to slip into the compound from time to time to get a feel for any changes that have been made."

"What's the terrain like?"

"Just about everything. The AMT land backs up against the Seven Devils mountain range to the west and north. Rocky and thick with white pines. Things open up a bit to the south and east, where there's dirt road access. It's down in the flatter land where they do most of their small-arms training. In all, the immediate property is about 100,000 acres, spread over the hills and plains. In the valley there, beyond the range, is where the Adams Family, as we like to call 'em, have cleared away timber and now grow potatoes."

Steve chuckled. "Name's right on for a group of paranoid freaks."

"You got that."

"What about their fortifications?"

Chuck rubbed his whiskers thoughtfully. "The fortified compound sits on a slight hill. Sorta right in the nest of rocky hills at the back of the land. There are two-foot-thick, 10-foot-tall stone walls that surround about an acre of the stronghold. Inside the compound there are three reinforced buildings in a triangle. All of them are connected by tunnels. The buildings have armor-plated roofs to guard against small-arms fire from the rocky hills or from the walls. Each strong house has what look like arrow slits, sealed off by heavy plate. They could hold out for quite a while, if need be. They've even got an artesian well inside the strong house. Hot spring, no less. The water comes out of the ground at 175 degrees, I hear."

"Geothermal heat."

"Yep."

"Long as they got food, they could survive the winter."

Steve visualized the compound. It was a macho fantasy for any survivalist. How funny, he thought, that if Adams had remained at Yale, he might have ended up in a life similar to Steve's. Instead he'd gone the opposite direction and was now a potential enemy.

Highway 95 took the group as far as the village of Council, with its 950 residents. On the edge of town was a convoy of campers and what looked like brown construction trailers.

The Chapter 16 group camped there for the night.

Old Mission Elementary School
San Luis Obispo, California
10:55 A.M. Pacific Time

RUNNING LAPS

The clock at the back of the classroom ticked toward 11 o'clock recess.

"All right," Cindy Alstead commanded two offending fifth-grade boys. "Aaron Daley and Michael Salim! Ten laps!"

Red-haired Aaron, a cross between Howdy Doody and Ronald McDonald, shrugged as if running laps was what he'd intended to do during recess anyway. Usually a quiet, easygoing kid, Aaron had been pushing her buttons all morning, Cindy thought. Uncharacteristically hyper. Loud. Hadn't followed one instruction. Cindy would have put him outside on a bench long before, except she knew he was vibrating from worry about his grandfather in San Francisco.

As for Michael Salim, there was no excuse. With his temperament he'd grow up to be president of the United States—or a computer hacker who stole a billion dollars from the Treasury. Either way he'd remember his fifth-grade teacher as the woman who taught him how to run.

The bell rang.

Wisps of clouds swirled, concealing the summit of Bishop's Peak as students of Old Mission Elementary School burst onto the playground for recess.

Ten minutes' break between classes isn't enough, Cindy thought as she grabbed her coffee mug and followed her students outside.

It was her turn for yard duty. She took her place on the edge of the asphalt basketball court as kids swarmed around her in a frantic effort to release as much energy as possible in one-sixth of an hour. As the force on the playground reached critical mass, shouts and squeals echoed against the green hills surrounding San Luis Obispo.

Beautiful day. Ordinary. The air smelled fresh and clean after an hour of dissecting frogs in science lab. The cool breeze against Cindy's face was a welcome relief. She filled her lungs with the sweet scent of blooming flowers. She had a headache: one part formaldehyde, one part pre-periodic, one part worry about Steve.

Why didn't he answer his phone?

Because he was the most inconsiderate human being on the face of the earth or . . . something. She didn't want to think about the something. So why didn't he even turn his answering machine on so she could leave him a piece of her mind?

Where was he?

She spotted her son Matthew coming out of his fourth-grade classroom after all his schoolmates. His face was a mask of surly resentment. Trouble. Joining Michael and Aaron, he jogged lazily onto the track. He didn't look up at Cindy. He had learned early about attending the school where Mom taught: it was best not to acknowledge the relationship publicly. This was one of those moments when Cindy didn't wish to claim her son, either.

Matthew's teacher, Sharon Bliss, stuck her head out of the door and rolled her eyes at Cindy in a gesture that proclaimed, *Such a day your kid is having!* So the worry about Steve had affected Matthew as well.

Cindy shrugged and grimaced. *Whatever,* she mouthed.

Michael and Aaron slowly and awkwardly rounded the backstop as Matthew caught up with them. Michael was teaching Aaron and Matthew to take their own sweet time; to put no real effort into penance but be sure to look miserable: *Lazy jog, please. Stumble once or twice. Look unhappy. Give our tormentors the idea we're suffering here.*

Lap five. The playground was certain proof that there was order in chaos. Kids were like electrons and neutrons whizzing around without any recognizable pattern. Amazing—some unseen order kept them from slamming into one another, from falling with broken arms and cracked skulls into heaps on the basketball court! Cindy would use this as an example in the upcoming section about atoms.

Lap six.

Mrs. O'Connor, the 70-year-old principal of Old Mission Elementary School, bustled from the office. An ex-nun who had discovered true love after 20 years in her vocation, Mrs. O'Connor had given up the convent and married her childhood sweetheart, Mr. O'Connor, at the age of 40. Seventeen years later he died, and she filled in as a temporary administrator at the school. There she had remained ever after.

Cheerful and pragmatic, the ex-nun was decidedly un-nunlike in her sense of humor. It was rare not to see a smile on her lips. Even when she counseled Cindy about the sacredness of her marriage vows, she teased, "Nowadays women outlive men by 10 years. Don't divorce him, honey. Just be patient. Eventually it'll all work out. Either way, you'll miss him when he's gone."

Cindy had laughed and retorted, "That's what I'm worried about."

Mrs. O'Connor had pounced. "So you love him then!"

Cindy could not argue. But neither could she deny that she also hated him.

Today Mrs. O'Connor's deeply lined face was crumpled with concern as she headed toward Cindy's post. Her serious expression betrayed some burden of terrible news. Was it Steve? Cindy's heartbeat quickened with a rush of fear.

The old woman cut a swath through the hordes of children. Yes. It was Cindy she was coming for.

Lap seven.

Without preamble Mrs. O'Connor announced, "It's official. He was on the subway. Dead."

Cindy drew her breath in sharply and reached out to grasp the basketball pole. "Oh . . . oh . . ."

Mrs. O'Connor scanned the track where the trio jogged. "There's the boy. I'll wait until the bell rings to tell him. You won't have to."

Cindy felt the earth spin around her. "No . . . I've been trying to reach . . . telephone . . . so worried . . ."

"What?"

"He didn't leave his answering machine on. . . . I've been calling him. . . ."

"Who?"

"Steve."

Mrs. O'Connor blinked at her through her thick lenses. "Steve?"

"In San Francisco . . . I've had the most terrible feeling ever since . . ."

Lap eight.

The information was processed. "No. No, my dear!" The old woman embraced Cindy in reassurance. Children paused to look at the women curiously. It was plain something had happened. "No, Cindy! Not your Steve. Well, I guess this leaves no doubt about what you feel for him. Good heavens, what a scare! Well, this is bad enough. Aaron Daley's grandfather. Christ have mercy. It's Frank Daley. Oh, my dear! He was on the very train car. They've made positive identification . . . security photos. Word is already out. Everyone has heard it. Aaron's mother called. She's on her way so she can tell Aaron herself. The whole city is shook up. The families from the plant are shocked to the core. No pun intended."

Relief left Cindy's knees quaking. "I thought you meant . . ."

Gently Mrs. O'Connor whispered, "Dear girl. I didn't know you were worried. I'll pray for your Steve. I had no idea. And he hasn't picked up his phone to let you know he's well? Shame on him! Have you tried the Red Cross emergency number? Inquiries for missing persons? Well, he'll need prayer once you get your little fingers round his neck for not calling, eh? The course of true love ne'er did run straight."

Lap eight-and-a-half.

The bell rang. The guilty trio of boys slowed to a weary walk and eyed Mrs. O'Connor warily. She came alongside Aaron, who considered her presence with alarm. His look seemed to ask if there was more than just running laps in his future. The old woman linked her arm in his and guided him back toward the office.

SIX

Bay Area Rapid Transit Underground
San Francisco
2:09 P.M. Pacific Time

READY OR NOT . . .

Market Street from First to Fourth was still cordoned off. Utility and transportation workers had replaced firefighters. Terrorism and investigation aside, the task of clearing the tracks and reopening the Bay Area Rapid Transit underground Red Line continued.

The blockish personnel transport in which Dr. Turnow and Senator Morrison changed into their protective coveralls was parked up the street from Moscone Center. A football-field-sized convention hall had been requisitioned for debris reconstruction and analysis.

They were two blocks from the demolished BART station at the foot of Montgomery in the financial district.

"I don't know what you expect to find," SFPD Deputy Chief Flannery remarked. "The FBI Crime Scene Unit has already combed the area. Samples of every substance, together with coordinates for location found, are on your Chapter 16 database. You can call up digicam recordings and overlay them with a grid of every item. Gives a 3-D view without the necessity of going in person."

Turnow had already viewed the tapes but wasn't satisfied.

How could he explain that part of science was intuition? Especially when many of his scientific colleagues still openly scoffed, saying God was a figment of less intelligent people's imaginations and needs? A completely rationalist approach to the universe was publicly championed by many researchers. But privately even they acknowledged how much "good science" depended on hunches, educated guesses, and leaps of faith. Turnow was glad that his own leaps of faith were based upon a lot more than just guesses.

Turnow wasn't even certain himself why he had requested this descent into the aftermath of the bombing; he only knew it was required. "Tell you afterward," he said, zipping the suit up to his neck and settling the hard hat on his head. He let the face mask/respirator hang loosely on his chest. The coveralls were less restrictive than those required in biological contaminant protocol, a potential terrorist threat Turnow was grateful didn't apply here. Senator Morrison was also suited up. The two men exited the van to walk to the entry point.

Down Market to the west, Turnow caught fleeting glimpses through the temporary chain-link barricade. Some normalcy was being restored to the city, though commuting was still a nightmare and tourism was off by a reported 95 percent. The few shoppers headed into the San Francisco Shopping Center averted their eyes from the tragedy.

It must have been in all their minds that some of the killed had been en route to Nordstrom's or Victoria's Secret or Foot Locker when they were snuffed out, Turnow thought. The victims had begun their day with no more consequential errands or greater anticipation of disaster than any of today's customers.

No wonder the buyers turned away their gaze. Who wanted to think that something as commonplace as a shopping expedition could end so violently?

This attitude of denial didn't exist in those hanging on the fence, however. A crowd of onlookers, mostly poor and many homeless by their dress, witnessed the cleanup efforts. A tall black man, dressed in a threadbare but neatly pressed dark blue suit, carried a sign: *Repent! The End of the World Is Near!*

Turnow reflected that whatever the self-styled prophet's position on Armageddon, he was still correct in a very real way. For anyone dying at that given instant, tragically or after a long illness, by bomb or car wreck, that moment *was* the end of the world for them personally. How many of those killed by the blast had been ready to meet their Maker?

In the early hours after the explosion, heavy equipment had ripped out chunks of Market Street to provide an alternate route to the underground scene. At first emergency scaling ladders had snaked into the pit and jury-rigged slings dangling from hydrocranes had lifted out blocks of concrete and bodies.

Now sturdy aluminum frames, complete with handrails, reached into depths illuminated by halogen lamps. It was like freeway construction carried out after dark—very orderly and methodical. Very businesslike and unemotional . . . except for the black, rubberized body bag toted by two masked Coroner's Office deputies.

"Fewer of those now," Morrison remarked. "The passengers on the train have been accounted for, but there's still the exact number on the platform to be tallied. It's all compounded by missing person inquiries: was Uncle Fred in the way of the blast, or did he wander off and get lost because of Alzheimer's?"

Track clearance activities proceeded from opposite ends of the line, leaving the central blast area the most time for investigation.

The part of hell into which Turnow and Morrison descended, though well lit, remained a jumble of twisted metal and hanging cables. High-intensity bulbs cast fierce shadows, turning jagged debris into the forms of malevolent spirits. A pervasive stench, compounded of acrid smoke, oil, ruptured sewer lines, and the malignant reek of charred flesh, made Turnow reach toward his respirator.

Turnow knew that Morrison, though too polite and reserved to interfere, had the same question as Deputy Chief Flannery: What could be gained by an expedition into this charnel house?

Impressed by the senator's commitment to the team as demonstrated by his presence on the scene, Turnow opted to answer the unspoken query: "Some things don't add up," he said. "I know that because of the date, backed up by the claim of responsibility, we all jumped to the same conclusion. This horror is the act of some radical American paramilitary group, like the Oklahoma City case. But 10 pounds of Semtex? A militia op would more likely be a truckload of fertilizer mixed with diesel fuel. And why the 20th of April? If it was meant to be symbolic, why not actually on the 19th?"

"Could have failed to put it all together for the 19th," Morrison argued. "Having the blast go off in the financial district is a strong political statement. You know the tirade: 'Big Money conspires with Big Government and Big Business to oppress the common man'—that sort of thing."

Turnow shrugged. "I admit I don't know the cause of my dissatisfaction. But something else about timing: why not strike during rush hour? Intentionally killing fewer victims argues a tenderheartedness I don't buy. Besides, the explanation seems too pat somehow. It was too easy for us to trace the phone lead. I hope we haven't been set up."

"Tactical disinformation . . ." Morrison mused, apparently quoting from his Senate Armed Services committee lingo. "Deliberately misled?"

Agreeing, Turnow asked, "Any success locating the suspect figure from the security camera? My studies confirm that the chemical signature of the explosives found in the briefcase material is pre-blast and not solely a result of the explosion."

"Nothing yet," Morrison admitted. "Law-enforcement agencies in six Western states all have a photo and the suspect's height and weight estimate, but it's really not much to go on. Have you seen enough here?"

"Soon," Turnow said. "Soon. I want to think about where the bomb was placed and why. I don't want to assume a motive related to the financial district and then argue circularly toward a Bubba job. If some other explanation might fit, I don't want to miss it. Even if Steve and the others already have the perps in the bag, we still have to know enough to convict them."

Seven Devils Mountains, Idaho
8:22 P.M. Mountain Time

ON YOUR BELLY

Twenty-eight miles from Council, an hour and a half up the winding, gravel-surfaced Hornet Creek Road, was the old copper-mining town of Bear. Farther on was a lookout point called Sheep Rock, which gave a glorious view over a stretch of Hell's Canyon—much narrower and deeper than even the much more famous Grand Canyon. At the bottom of the wide crevasse, the Snake River flowed more than 6,000 feet below.

Before any tactical operation could begin, intel had to be gathered. As much data as possible had to be collected in order to design perimeter and entry action plans, in case such actions were needed. In an instance such as a botched bank holdup resulting in a hostage standoff, the intel would be easy and quick to gather: check out the parking lot, streets, and nearby buildings. Then get a map of the bank, its doors, windows. . . .

But this one, a job with a privately built fortified compound that was guarded by highly trained armed men, was apt to prove a little more difficult. Just getting a view of the place was impossible without either an aerial reconnaissance plane or "sneakin' in on the sly," as Chuck had told Steve and Dan Debusse.

At that moment all three were exploring Hell's Canyon: slogging uphill, occasionally crawling on their bellies, anticipating being shot at in the black of night, where the next bush might conceal an ambush, where an innocent vine might be a trip wire to an explosive charge.

Steve loved it.

It was what he was trained to do—and to do better than anyone else. He loved it more than anything. Well, almost anything. He couldn't get

Cindy and the boys out of his mind. And how in all the craziness of the past days, he hadn't even had time to talk with them, to tell them how much he loved them. And here he was, crawling on his belly in another dangerous situation, when some crazy could shoot at him and end his life. He turned on his PVS-5 night-vision binoculars.

Chuck reached for the optics. His breath hung dense in the frigid mountain air. "Look at *that."* He whistled a note of admiring appreciation.

Dan handed his PVS-5 over. "We get the good toys in HRT."

"Yes, you do," Chuck replied, fondling the goggles. He handed them back to Dan and looked sadly down at his PVS-4 night-vision monocular. "I guess we get the hand-me-downs."

Jealousy between agencies was something that needed to be avoided and yet was almost impossible to prevent. And envy among divisions of the same organization could be worse. But as Steve listened to the banter, he recognized the tone of good-natured rivalry that had no shadow of ill will. After bragging, Dan must have felt guilty because he promised he'd see that Chuck got a pair of the newer PVS-5s, pronto.

Steve wasn't surprised that Chuck, being the cowboy he was, refused the offer, insisting that the old monocular was better because it would leave his other eye free to do other things.

A light rain began to fall. Its pattering on the sodden leaves and the gravel sounded like milk on a bowl of breakfast cereal.

In the oddest way possible, at the most unexpected time and place, Steve felt suddenly wistful for Saturday morning with his kids . . . and for Cindy.

He still hadn't called her.

She'd never forgive him.

Shake it off, he told himself. This was no time for self-recrimination.

Chuck stuck out his tongue, catching a few of the drops. "Well, thank God for that answered prayer. It'll be an easy night after all."

This elicited nods of agreement from Steve and Dan, though the mud on the sides of the trail was already the consistency of oatmeal and headed toward worse.

As much as every sane man—the definition could be stretched to include FBI, HRT, and Chapter 16 agents—hated to be cold and wet, on a black op recon, rain was good. The patter covered their sounds, scents, and tracks. The rain quieted the ground. Best of all, it made the opposing guards cold and uncomfortable, less alert, and more apt to shelter up somewhere.

In reality, Steve knew rain and cold were miseries worth thanking God for on a recon patrol.

The three men ducked off the side of the gravel road. Feeling their way along a narrow corridor in the elderberry bushes, it was a silent couple of minutes until they got to the southeastern AMT fence line.

Five-strand barbed wire stretched taut. There were 10 inches of clearance between the bottom strand and the mud.

Chuck went first. Steve checked his field holster before bellying out. As much as a holster with two protective flaps and three latches slowed down the presentation of a firearm, it sure helped to keep the mud off the rear sights in conditions just like these. With an MP-5 .40 caliber submachine gun on his chest, Dan slid through faceup. "It's a lot easier seeing what's above you when you're lookin' up," he always said.

Four miles down one valley and up another hill. No shots, no guards, no sign of life. Steve sang to himself: *Over the river and through the woods, to Grandmother's house we go. The horse knows the way to da, da, da, da . . .* He didn't know any more and so the two lines played over and over for about an hour.

About that time Chuck hushed up Steve's mental melody. "Over the next hill," Chuck said, "there's a listening post on the rocky point." He motioned toward a long slender ridge that dropped off abruptly.

Their brisk walk slowed to a crawl. Steve's senses became more acute. He could hear his heart beating in his ears as he scanned the hillside, glowing green in his night-vision scope. "One!" Steve hissed, indicating a sentry who was huddled on the opposite hillside under a rocky overhang.

"A lotta good he's doin', eh?" Dan whispered.

It was often a joke, this kind of Bubba group. They claimed to train as hard as any soldiers, though many of them never served in the armed forces, or if they did, were armed forces dropouts. Like this guy, they considered themselves every bit as tough as Delta or the SEALs.

Wanna-be mercenaries. Professional killing machines. These guys with their potbellies and their illegally converted fully automatic weapons. *What a joke,* Steve thought as he turned up his amplifying ear gear. The listening- post man was snoring.

There was just one problem with this brand of humor: incompetent or not, spray enough bullets and someone got killed. Set off a big enough bomb and innocent people were vaporized.

Chuck motioned for the recon team to cross the ridge about 75 yards west of where the man was sleeping. "Here on we gotta be real careful," he cautioned. "The compound is just down the other side."

Steve turned his Tac-7 electronic ears all the way up as they neared the top. Creeping on their bellies, the three men slithered under a row of fir trees at the edge of a high embankment. It was a perfect vantage point. From the sharp cliff they could see the lit compound 50 feet or so below and no more than 50 yards away. The stone walls, three fortified buildings, as well as other less-armored shelters, appeared much as expected.

The lights of the compound were too much for the night-vision goggles, so Steve removed them, placing them on the ground where he lay. He scanned the U-shaped natural cutout of the mountain that surrounded the compound. *If we can get in this close,* he realized, *real perimeter containment will be a cinch.* Four Sierra—sniper—teams well hidden around the edge of the cliff would be all it took for *black,* a term used for the back side of an operation. A good sniper could hit a hubcap at 500-plus yards. The longest shot, to the farthest eastern end of the compound, was probably 250 yards. "Piece of cake," Steve said.

The rain fell harder, which normally would have been a good thing—except it woke up the sleeping guard.

Dan signaled Steve frantically. "Movement down the path."

Steve hastily reached for his eye gear and, in the process, knocked them over the edge of the drop. He slid quietly after them, realizing he couldn't leave such obvious evidence of their intrusion into AMT space.

Leaning over the side of the cliff, he spotted the PVS-5s hanging on a projecting tree root about three feet down. He would have to get them, but for now they were out of reach. Dan and Chuck were able to slink back across the path.

"Steve, cover, cover," Dan warned in a frantic whisper.

Steve jerked the rest of his body under the line of plump, wet fir trees an instant before a spotlight lit up the path. He hardly breathed as the footsteps came near. He was facing away and couldn't see the guard's approach, but his Tac-7s amplified every sound for him. The man stopped, turning in a circle inches from where Steve lay. The guard even pushed through the trees for a view of the compound below.

What had the guard heard? What had tipped him off to the patrol? Did he know where Steve was? Why was he waiting to sound the alarm?

Steve lay in silent horror when the man's steel-toed boot knocked against Steve's head.

Should I move my head? A meteor shower of conflicting thoughts hammered Steve's brain. Should I stiffen it, or relax? he wondered. Will he think I'm a rock? or a stray limb?

As thousands of hours of training washed back to him, he realized he was safe, at least for now. Dan probably had a bead on the guy. At least he hoped that was true.

But if shots were fired, then what?

The real problem would be getting back out over the four miles of terrain if they were discovered. The real problem would be blowing the op before it had even begun.

What was the sentry doing? Why didn't he move?

Steve held deathly still. This could be it, he thought. The end of life. I wonder what Cindy and the boys . . .

Then he heard it.

It wasn't the sound of a slide racking or a hammer being pulled back. It was the sound of a zipper. He held his breath in silent disgust. Steve tried uncertainly to pretend the drops hitting his face were from the rain on the tree. He tried not to think about it. In a moment, he knew, it would be over, and the man would go on his way.

In total reversal of how war stories described things, this time it was a zipper making a noise like a machine gun, instead of the other way around.

Steve couldn't help flinching when the sole of a boot again nudged his head, but once more there was no discovery, no startled exclamation.

Even after the footsteps were gone, Steve waited for the all-clear from his two partners before moving. As soon as he was able to stand, Steve scrambled for his goggles, then grabbed a handful of mud to rub on his face and head.

It was a fast mile or so of retreat before anyone made a sound. The three weren't quite out of danger yet, though for two of them, it soon became impossible to hold in the mirth. Snickering led to muffled giggling, but the real fun began when they hit the gravel road again.

"Did you see the stream?" Dan broke out laughing. "Oh, man, you get a shower there, buddy?"

"Yuck," Steve shivered, rubbing more mud on his face.

Chuck snorted. "Guess you got to see more on this recon than you planned for, ah?"

"Very funny, guys." Steve spat. "You better not say a word about this to anyone!"

"Hey, Steve," Chuck teased, "did you get the name of your mud brother?"

Steve's silence must have said it all—that he found little humor in it. First of all, he'd almost been killed, almost ruined the mission, and to top it off . . .

"I'm sorry, Steve," Dan apologized. "I'm glad you're okay. And, you know, it was a good initial recon. We got everything we came for. I was really scared for you, buddy."

Steve had to give his friend credit for attempting self-control, but soon the laugh crept into his voice again. "And I knew . . . as soon as I saw that guy hit the trees, I said to myself, 'Steve, urine trouble!' "

"Yeah, man," Chuck agreed. "The mission went fine, but I gotta tell ya," he howled, "for a minute I really thought you were gonna blow it!"

The two men roared like children. Steve wondered if they'd start an avalanche with all the noise.

Steve rubbed his face and spat all the way back to the car, every once in a while convulsing with disgust. He refused to speak again until after he'd reached—and used—the shower back at Council.

Daly City
A Suburb of San Francisco
11:27 P.M. Pacific Time

X-MAN

The dingy teal walls, shadowed with dirt, were decorated with strange symbols embroidered on tapestries. Concealed within loops, swirls, and curlicues were slogans of hatred and unquenchable animosity.

Shadir leaned over the kitchen counter, waiting for an answer, with the old, brown telephone receiver to his ear.

A deep voice inquired, "Your business?"

Shadir responded, "I need to speak with X-Man."

The line crackled and the voice asked, "Who is this?"

"S. I need something."

"He's out by the pool," came the reply. "Hang on."

The sound of the phone being set down clunked in Shadir's ear. A moment later a second receiver was picked up. A smoke-thickened, confidently authoritative voice said, "I've got it."

After another click, the new speaker greeted Shadir. "My friend, S. How are you?"

Shadir smiled at the charismatic way of the X-Man. "I am well," he lied, glancing resentfully around the dingy apartment. "Very well."

"Making loads of money and fighting off the women, I imagine," X-Man chuckled.

Shadir laughed. "Not like I used to, but Allah has been good to me."

"Excellent. Excellent. How can I help you?"

"I'm looking for some *X* and the rest of the tools."

The man hummed. It was a thrumming, deep in the throat, like an old-style electric adding machine warming up. "You *are* busy. What kind, how much?"

Shadir cleared his throat. "Play-Doh. A lot." There was a pause, then he emphasized. "A big amount."

The man was quiet for a minute. "It is difficult. There are so many risks these days."

Shadir recognized the bartering patter of the souks. You want to pay how much? But this rug is purest silk! You insult me. It cost many times that sum.

Shadir waited, knowing Khalil was prepared to pay whatever was required.

Finally X-Man admitted, "I know of a man. He lives . . . it does not matter where. A shadow who runs a bit for me. In fact, I just spoke with him the other day. Anyway, he mentioned that he knows a source. An American, but one with already too much guilt . . . too much fear of prison for other deals . . . to refuse me."

"Really? Where?"

X-Man informed him, "An ugly place. Near Bakersfield, and he works on a rig out there . . . of the sort you need. He's a horse trader. My man has done business with him before."

"When can I meet this horse trader?"

"I'll get hold of him. I will arrange for next Monday?"

"It is well," Shadir agreed.

"Off the I-5 . . ."

"Yes."

". . . is a road called Seventh Standard. A hundred and twenty miles or so north of L.A."

"I can find it."

"Right," the X-Man confirmed. "A few miles east and you come to some huge white tanks. I'll set it up."

"Thank you," Shadir said gratefully. "Allah will bless you."

"Oh, he already has." The deep voice broke into an unseemly cackle. "Your patron will bless me very much more. I'll have the price when next we speak."

"Certainly." Shadir gritted his teeth.

"And now I've got to go. I have warm bodies in the pool."

X-Man hung up without saying good-bye.

Shadir looked around again at his shabby apartment. He lifted his head in prayer. Sighing, he cursed, *"Lahm chanzir."* Arabic for swine. "Money has consumed your soul. When it is time, you too can roast with the American pigs."

SEVEN

Council Town, Idaho
Tuesday, 24 April
9:45 A.M. Mountain Time

MINER'S MOTHER LODE

Warm sun had been shining through the blinds of his hotel room almost from the time Steve had lain down. He had slept deeply for an hour only and then tossed and turned all morning. He sat on the edge of the bed in shorts, rubbing his tired face, yawning and stretching. This was one side of what he did that wasn't glorious, or even a rainy, dark-night misery for which to thank God.

It was just another sleepless night without his family. He loved what he did and felt called to do it. Sometimes, though, he wondered if he was doing the right thing . . .

He looked at the clock.

Late.

Steve stood up and thought about hanging a blanket from the blinds to blot out the glare. Then, since he was up anyway, he decided maybe a run would be a better choice.

On the road, the pavement felt hard through his shoes. His legs were stiff. Steve concentrated on relaxing his body. *Let the oxygen and blood do their thing,* he thought. The town's elevation was significantly lower than the vista of Heaven's Gate above Hell's Canyon, but lately all Steve's exercise had been at sea level. While running, even this moderate altitude was something with which to contend.

Steve considered quitting early. After all, he had traveled eight miles or more on the night's recon only hours earlier. But the jumbled thoughts in his mind wouldn't let him quit.

He jogged through the center of town, past stores called the Joy of Junk and Cabin Fever. Eating establishments designated The Devil's Café and The Grub Steak confronted each other across Illinois Avenue. But the place that drew Steve's attention was a diner claiming to have the world's best biscuits and gravy: Madge's Eatery.

Such was the power of the air on his appetite that the advertising worked: it was all the convincing he needed. Trotting toward it, Steve reached inside his waistband where a tiny apron holster concealed a lightweight titanium five-shot .38. It also held his money clip.

He seated himself at the counter. Bacon, hotcakes, perking black coffee—the aromas in the little diner made his mouth water. A few glances from local farmer types told him he didn't quite fit in. Steve ignored them, instead picking up the menu proclaiming the same as the sign outside: *World's Best Biscuits and Gravy!*

He lowered the menu to the sound of bacon sizzling on the grill in front of him.

The cook/proprietor was a slightly gray-haired, slightly crooked-backed older woman, more than slightly overweight. Her hair was pulled back with pins. She turned around. "What can I get ya?"

Steve smiled at her. He could see a kind soul, despite her deeply etched lines and tired eyes. She reminded him a bit of his great-aunt from Arkansas. "You Madge?" A big nod of the beaming face. "It all smells great. Guess I'll have to have one of everything," he joked.

"Miner's Mother Lode," Madge said agreeably, writing on a pad before raising a pot of fresh-brewed coffee and waving it significantly.

She had taken him seriously. He turned his mug over for a fill, then glanced at the back of the menu. Miner's Mother Lode: Two scrambled eggs on two dynamite hotcakes, two jumbo biscuits with gravy, and four strips of bacon. Fruit, add $.75.

"Okay," he said. "But I think I'll skip the fruit."

Madge poured the batter on the grill, cracked two eggs into a bowl, and handed him the biscuits and warm gravy. "You here workin' on the Bear Lodge too?"

"Yeah," he replied, going along with the cover story put out for all the FBI agents.

"Big group of your guys come in this mornin' already," she pointed out.

Maybe he could get a little local perspective on the AMT compound. "We were up there yesterday scoutin' trailer placement. Heard a bit of shootin' over the hill."

Madge's back was toward him. "Them's the AMT boys. We don't see mucha them, but every once in a while a few of them'll come down for breakfast and supplies. A nice guy, that Adams, in spite of what you hear."

Steve played dumb. "Who's that?"

"Guy that runs that militia training camp up there where you heard the shootin'." She flipped the pancakes and faced him. "He ain't all that bad. Ask Harry over to Quality Power Tools. Some no-good punk passing through from California tried to stick up the place. Adams happened to be there and whipped out his pistol. He held the robber at gunpoint until the sheriff came." She paused, deftly scooped the griddlecakes onto a plate, and continued, "But I wouldn't be caught on his property. No sir. They say he's got patrols that'll shoot a man for steppin' over the fence. Reason that lodge you guys are workin' on never got finished in the first place. People say he ran 'em off."

Steve nodded thoughtfully. "I'll keep that in mind."

While Steve focused on his breakfast, Madge left him alone to eat. All the while he considered Andrew Adams. Good citizen, nice guy. It didn't add up to the profile he'd been given. This was getting harder to predict.

Domestic terrorists and psychopaths were often loners—social misfits remembered as unapproachable. Of course, at the other extreme were the demagogues who could recruit the more overtly violent to do their bidding.

Was that the key here?

Steve finished, paid, and trotted back up the street. He heard a car slow down behind him. It was Chuck in the van. "Hey, stranger. Want a lift?"

"You bet," Steve replied, grateful he didn't have to walk far after eating a miner's share.

"I was just on my way to roust you," Chuck said. "Dan mentioned they tried to reach you on your phone, but couldn't. Figured you were still sleepin'."

Steve realized he had forgotten his B-com, the one thing he was never supposed to do. "I forgot it. Better swing by and get it."

The van pulled away. When Chuck grinned at him, the climax of the previous evening came back to Steve. He hoped Chuck wouldn't bring it up.

It was a quick stop at the hotel. On his way out the door, Steve thought to call Cindy and the kids. He glanced at his G-Shock watch. 10:55. She was at work and the kids were in school. Could try her mobile, but she probably wouldn't answer it. *Better not anyway,* he decided. The rest of the team was already in camp. It wouldn't be good to keep everyone waiting any longer for the morning's intel briefing. *Later,* Steve resolved. *I'll call her later.*

A mile or so up the road, by the Hornet Creek turnoff, half a dozen big rigs loaded with lumber, roof trusses, and shingles angled onto the gravel road and ground up the slope.

Chuck cut out ahead of the convoy and raced ahead. "We don't want to breathe their dust all the way to camp."

Steve recalled the conversation with Madge. "So what do the locals think about this Adams guy?"

Chuck closed one eye. "Well, I'll tell you. Adams, in spite of him not likin' American politics, is quite a politician. He keeps the community thinkin' he's there for them. Makes himself look good, all the while promoting his trade. The townfolk around here like him, though they're a little afraid. They respect him. That's the reason we've had to go about this thing so cautiously. Council has a sheriff, but Adams and AMT are a local legend of sorts. If the world should ever fall apart, Adams claims he'll lead 'em out of it."

"But he's dangerous," Steve reiterated, realizing that he and the rest of the FBI were probably thought of as the enemy around these parts.

At the top of 25 miles of dirt road, in the ghost town of Bear, the brown single-wide mobile trailers were being blocked up. Behind them Steve could see the remnants of the old mining camp. A leaning water tower and a flume half hung in shambles on the side of a steep slope. Several other miner's shacks sagged into the earth.

The fifth-wheel trailers were strung with heavy black cable to a generator truck, which chugged away. Set back against the trees, facing it all, was the dilapidated framework of the lodge that the entire team was pretending to revive.

Undercover operations of this scale always seemed a little strange. One of the toughest difficulties to overcome was finding a cover story for this many guys. In this case it would be about 200 construction workers. To anyone watching, they would be 200 of the laziest, most physically fit men who accomplished less than anyone had ever seen.

The supplies were part of the cover. Most of the stuff would never be unloaded. The excuse to the public would be that the crew was waiting for some clearance that had, at the last minute, fallen though. That way no one would wonder why nothing was being done. The plan would buy them at least a week, which Steve hoped would be enough time to gather the needed intel about the AMT compound. Then they'd be ready to set a perimeter and start negotiations. It wouldn't matter then that people knew what was going on. Police roadblocks would keep out the curious. Until that time there were still quite a few preparations to be made.

Steve and Chuck ventured to the Command Center, masquerading as the construction foreman's trailer, for a briefing. The six two-man

Sierra/Sniper teams exited with their logbooks. Waiting at the bottom of the stairs, Steve heard snickering as they passed.

That jerk, Steve thought as he entered. *I'll bet Dan told them what happened to me last night.* Steve saw Dan leaning over a giant, aerial photo-map of the compound.

"Morning," Steve said, glaring at him.

"Steve." Dan smiled. "Can I get you something to drink? A soda or water? Maybe a glass of lemonade?"

"All right, Dan," Steve scolded. "Enough already."

"No, I'm serious," Dan replied, pointing to a cold, perspiring pitcher and some glasses.

Steve declined tersely. "No, thanks."

Chuck spoke up in his loud, country-twanged voice. "I'll have a glass, if you don't mind."

Dan poured Chuck a glass, then gestured toward the chart. "Just went over some details with Sierras 1 through 6."

The map presented a perfect top view of the compound they had been to the previous night. Steve recognized the walls and the three hardened buildings. Each had been perfectly placed so that the long outside walls could defend the interior perimeter. The narrow side walls also had cutouts that should allow men inside to defend against attack from the blind spots at angles, as well as guard the passage into the center of the compound.

Steve pointed to a round object in the center of the triangle. "What's that?"

"Remember last night," Chuck answered, "when you couldn't see because of the lights? Well, that's a round, probably 40-foot-tall stone tower that looks like a lighthouse. The searchlights are mounted around the roof in such a way that it probably appeared to be a radio tower to you. On top, there *is* a radio antenna that's another 20 or so feet higher. It isn't that big inside, but there appear to be slits where several sharpshooters can hang out."

Well designed, Steve realized. "What're the buildings like inside?"

Dan looked to Chuck.

"That's the missing piece of the pie," Chuck said defeatedly. "We got rumors, but no maps and no sketches. Because of the heavy activity in the daytime, we've got no daylight intel of the compound, other than aerial. And what with the steep angle of the mountains surrounding the compound and the close trees in front, the angles aren't even that good from the sky."

Steve shook his head. "This won't do. The Entry Team needs hard facts of the inside: tunnels, rooms, weapons caches, and the rest in order to proceed. Who can I talk to that knows this stuff?"

Chuck thought a minute. "I didn't want to say anything, 'cause I know you boys would be pressing. I guess there's no other choice but to—"

"What?" Steve demanded. "Give."

Chuck continued. "There's a real bad boy, a former AMT guy, been brought in on murder charges recently. Robert Nietcher. He's one of the ones in the background study I think your man Downing has. A cop killer down in Texas. Anyway, Nietcher won't say nothin' unless the DA, a good ol' boy, agrees to work on a plea bargain. And he won't."

Steve considered the options. If this was the only choice, they would have to get something out of him. "Wait," he said aloud. "Sixteen's boss man worked closely with the secretary of defense back in the early Texan White House years."

Dan chimed in. "Senator Morrison!"

"Affirmative," Steve said. "I'll bet he knows someone who'll have a thing or two to say to this DA . . . what's his name?"

"José Alvarez," Chuck replied. "Straight-arrow and hard-nosed, just like they like 'em down Texas way. Wouldn't offer a deal for anything, but he'll sure tell you a story about growin' up poor and pickin' oranges."

Steve contacted James Morrison on the B-com and explained the situation. Steve said he was sure the former senator knew people with influence over this Alvarez.

Morrison assured Steve that by nightfall he'd have some news for

Chapter 16 and the rest of the team. Until then it was a waiting game. In the meantime, maybe one of the two OS teams in the field rotation would come up with something better.

Pier 41, Adjacent to the Blue and Gold Ferry Slips
San Francisco
1 P.M. Pacific Time

THE CLEANSING

The wharf at San Francisco was a wonderful place. Restaurants, art galleries, markets, and new and old shops crowded the waterfront among the huge, now mostly empty, dock buildings.

The air was filled with the smell of fresh steamed crab, hot sourdough bread, clam chowder, and the blended drone of ship engines. Wandering people ate ice cream.

Shadir bought a ticket from the Blue and Gold Fleet ferry service. The woman at the counter had looked at him funny when he said he wanted a return only from Sausalito. After some convincing, she handed it over.

He bought himself a seafood chowder in a bread bowl and a Coke and returned to Khalil's power craft, moored nearby. Now Shadir sat lazily on the deck of the long, bright yellow-and-white cigarette boat, dipping hunks of the warm loaf into the chowder. Seagulls circled the deck, hoping for a piece.

In the distance a foghorn interrupted the incessant barking and snorting of a score of sea lions also enjoying the afternoon sun just 100 yards away. The crest of the wave of a fogbank poised above the Golden Gate and shortly after cascaded into the Bay.

The sky turned a chilled, smoky blue, and Shadir tucked the remainder of his lunch back into the paper bag. He pulled on his sweatshirt, and then looked up when he heard the pounding of feet coming down the dock. "Greetings, Rhamad," he said casually.

"Shadir!" Rhamad responded in his heavy Arabic accent.

"Are you ready?"

"As I will ever be. This city still swarms like an anthill stomped on by my boot," he exulted. "Where is Khalil?"

"Oh, something came up," Shadir replied. "He will meet us on the other side."

Rhamad boarded the 36 ½-foot Donzi. Looking in the paper bag on the bench seat, he asked, "Lunch?"

"Help yourself. There will be much to do after the crossing." Shadir fired up the beefy 485-horsepower engine, which responded with a thunderous roar. "You must be well fed and prepared."

Rhamad began munching away. Then a worried look came over him. "This isn't clam, is it? I wish to eat no unclean things in the midst of a holy war."

"No." Shadir laughed as he guided the painted flame-emblazoned *Fool's Paradise* away from the dock. "I would never."

Rhamad gratefully shoved another spoonful into his mouth.

In a moment they were around the breakwater and roaring across the Bay toward the Golden Gate Bridge. That the direction of their travel was not a direct route toward their destination was of no interest to Rhamad, his mouth full of bread.

There was a west-to-east swell running, but the wind chop remained less than whitecap strength. Besides, the knifelike prow of the cigarette boat cleaving the waves at 75 miles per hour was only using half its available power. The seaward set of the tidal race added another four knots to their speed. In just minutes they were in the middle of the Bay, well past Alcatraz Island, and Shadir corrected his course northward toward Sausalito.

Shadir took a look around. They were out of the active traffic lanes, between the inbound and outbound commercial channels. There were no other boats in sight. Shadir powered down the yacht. "I almost forgot," he said, handing the ferry ticket to Rhamad. "Put it in your pocket."

"What is it for?" Rhamad said, examining it. "A ferry ticket from Sausalito to San Francisco?"

"You will need it," Shadir replied, locking the throttle lever at idle.

Rhamad wiped his mouth, then shoved the rest of the food in the bag. "Thank you for lunch. It was wonderful. So what is the plan, eh? Have you convinced Khalil that we should trumpet our success to all the world?"

"Are you ready for what is next?" questioned Shadir.

"Entirely ready! When we announce what we have done, thousands will rally to our cause! Only tell me what we are to do and you will find me eager to comply!"

"Very well then," Shadir agreed. "I will tell you. But I must say, this may be the hardest thing either of us has to do."

"So long as it wounds these arrogant Americans, I embrace it! In their homes they will fear for their lives because of Rhamad. What is it?"

The boat glided to a stop. Shadir glanced quickly around. It seemed they were the only ones on the water. Rhamad picked at his teeth, not looking up as Shadir explained. "It has been the will of Allah, since before your birth, since the beginning of time, that you, one day, would sacrifice all you have for him. . . ."

"Yes, I know," replied Rhamad curtly. His response overflowed with impatience.

Shadir grasped an oar, which hung from a pair of hooks beside the helm station. "You have dedicated your whole life in service to him, even if it meant one day dying for him."

"Shadir, I know these things. Why do you bore me with such ceremony?" Rhamad retorted in annoyance.

"Because ceremony is required when a life must be given."

Concern filled Rhamad's face, though he recognized the implications behind the remark too late. "What?"

Shadir swung the oar with all his force. Rhamad flinched, but not soon enough to avoid the blow as the flat blade of the fiberglass paddle struck him on the forehead.

A splitting crack rang out and Rhamad tumbled over backwards, down two steps, onto the rear deck. Still clinging to consciousness, he pleaded with Shadir, "Why? Why?"

Shadir struck him again, this time with the edge of the oar's blade. A wide gash opened up, and blood began to flow.

The wounded man pushed up on only one arm. "Why?" His speech gurgled.

Shadir answered him with no remorse. "Because you chose glory over duty. And it is Allah's will that you die to receive it."

"No!" the barely living Rhamad cried.

"You want people to know how wonderful you are. Go and tell the dead!"

Shadir raised the oar for a final blow, then swung it like an ax. A soft, muddy thud rang out, like a melon splitting.

Searching the Bay first for any boats that might have come near, Shadir opened the back gate to the swim step. Grasping Rhamad's wrists, he dragged the body two paces forward, then stopped as a thought struck him.

From his trouser pocket he removed a lock-blade knife and flicked it open with his thumb. Bending over the body, he sawed clumsily at the tattoo on Rhamad's left ring finger. Grunting with satisfaction, he rolled the body off the fiberglass ledge into the Bay. Shadir then turned on the sea-water wash pump and hosed the blood off the deck.

"Stupid man." Shadir squirted Rhamad's battered head as he floated away. "You had to talk about the bombing. To boast. You stupid man."

When all was once again sparkling white, Shadir returned to his food. Leisurely he ate the chowder until the body sank from sight in the dark blue chop to seaward. Then he revved up the motor and sped away.

EIGHT

HRT Command Center, Bear Mining Camp
Hell's Canyon, Idaho
Wednesday, 25 April
3:38 P.M. Mountain Time

THE SOURCE

"You guys do own the red carpet!" Chuck Maines had exclaimed when Senator Morrison phoned back by 9:45 P.M. the previous night. Morrison had informed the team that District Attorney Alvarez had bowed to political pressure and Robert Nietcher had cut a deal with the Texas DA.

Nietcher had agreed to anonymously help Chapter 16 in every way possible, in exchange for life without parole. If at any time he refused to cooperate, the deal would be terminated. Only that could not happen. Once he agreed, he would have to remain 100 percent committed or risk losing the secrecy part of the bargain.

Missing only Dr. Turnow and James Morrison, the entire team waited with a few others. Anton, Dan, and Chuck sat with them at a cramped table in the command trailer. Miles fooled with the satellite uplink terminal that was supposed to establish a live, one-way-video/two-way-audio feed with the Fort Worth FBI office.

The image of a pale-faced man with thin lips, dark eyes, and heavy brows bounced up on the monitor. It was Robert Nietcher. His nose was elongated and upturned. His shaved-bald head sprouted black stubble.

Miles positioned the microphone in the center of the table. "Testing one, two . . . can you hear me? Fort Worth?"

There was no sign Nietcher heard.

Teresa sighed. "Miles?"

Miles messed with the wires, pulling plugs and reinserting them. "Hello . . . hello . . ." His face became serious and contorted. "We have a major malfunction."

Downing swallowed hard.

Steve's head drooped. Miles was such a dork. In other circumstances the HRT guys would have grinned at the sheer idiocy with which he conducted his life. But not now. Too much was at stake.

"You know, Miles?" Teresa spoke up again. "Where is your tape? Guys, I remember giving strict orders that he was not to be in public without that shiny-side—"

"Duct tape!" Downing intoned.

The words must have triggered a warning bell in Miles's pea-sized control center. He stood up so fast he banged his head on a swinging engineer's lamp. Thinking someone must have hit him, he searched the room, in hopes that no one would tackle him the way Anton had.

Steve knew that Miles wasn't lacking in intelligence. On the contrary, Miles was brilliant—but more like a watch with way too many features. Confused, confusing, tedious, and often difficult to understand.

Miles frowned expressively with pursed lips and went back to work. An instant later a test tone sounded.

Teresa called out this time. "Fort Worth?"

The tone stopped. A nondescript fellow in a dark blue pin-striped suit and mismatched tartan-plaid tie leaned in front of the camera. "Bear? We can hear you loud and clear."

Teresa cleared her throat. "Go ahead, Fort Worth."

The man appearing on the monitor spoke. "I am B. J. Harding, Mr. Nietcher's attorney."

"Thanks for joining us," Teresa responded, as if announcing the guests on an afternoon talk show. Steve waited for her to say, "and I'll be your host."

She continued. "I'm Teresa Bouche, Justice Department."

Steve growled at Miles.

"One moment, Fort Worth." Teresa clicked the mike on and off again. "Steve, if you're going to be present for this—"

He didn't wait for her to finish. "If I'm going to risk my life and the lives of my men in there, I want to talk with him myself—not have you talk to him through his attorney!"

She couldn't argue with him. Half of the men in the room were involved with the assault plan. All seemed in support of Steve.

Teresa collected herself. "Mr. Harding, there has been a change in plans."

The lawyer suddenly appeared suspicious and uncooperative. "What change is that?"

"Mr. . . . uh . . ." Teresa looked at Steve, who shook his head and gestured for the mike.

Steve took over. "Mr. Harding, this is Echo 1 leader. As Ms. Bouche said, there will be a change in plans. I will be speaking with Robert directly."

Mr. Harding shook his head. "No, I'm afraid I can't allow that."

Steve's temper flared. "Now you listen to me, Mr. Harding. My life is on the line, so I'm not fooling around. If your cop-killing client isn't straight—"

"Excuse me! That is a false statement." Mr. Harding attempted to protect the now-squirming Nietcher. "You could be held liable for—"

"Shut up, Harding. We aren't in court," Steve hotly retorted. "If your client wants to go to the Texas seat warmer for a good old country barbecue, both you and he can switch off right now. The fact that you're even talking to us tells me he's guilty! You switch off now, and I'll guarantee he goes down!"

It was clear the faceless, all-knowing voice was getting to Nietcher. Harding tried to interrupt but was overpowered.

"Furthermore," Steve hammered, "if we don't have a deal, then there's no such thing as 'strict anonymity.' That means if in negotiations with AMT Robert Nietcher's name happens to come up when I'm talking to Andrew Adams, it's really no skin off my back! In fact, we'll just tell him *you* guys called *us.* Nietcher, now's your chance. Either you spill it all 'cause you wanna be queen for a day and get off with life, or else you're gonna ride the lightning!"

Steve could tell Nietcher was near to jumping out of his seat and begging the camera for mercy. His hard face broke. "No, man, no! I'll tell you whatever you want to know."

Harding tried to stop him. "Robert, I can't allow this to happen!"

"I don't care, man," Nietcher argued. "If Adams finds out, then I'm dead meat anyway!"

Steve calmed down. Watching his adversary lose was like taking a muscle relaxant. It put him in the driver's seat, back in control. And that's where Steve liked to be. That facet of his nature was one of the many things that had made him the perfect point man on numerous operations, and why he'd been chosen for Chapter 16. "Good thinking, Robert. That's the right thing to do."

Most of the team had to bite their tongues or sit on their hands to keep from cheering and applauding. Teresa, bitterly composed, didn't look up or around. Her spotlight had been completely stolen, it seemed. It was clear she sternly disapproved of Steve's methods.

During the two-hour interview that followed, Steve, Dan, and Chuck spoke directly with Nietcher.

Nietcher drew detailed maps of bunkers and tunnels, described weapons caches and their whereabouts, and explained underground corridors that connected the central stockade with other buildings. He informed the team of AMT's tactical response plans in case of invasion and told where remote land mines were and how they could be shut off. Nietcher even knew what kind of locks were used on certain doors, which would allow the entry specialists quicker access.

But by far the most valuable piece of Nietcher's testimony was his explanation of Adams's suspected but undiscovered escape tunnel. A trench almost 120 yards in length had been dug. Then four-feet-diameter, black plastic sewer pipe had been laid and covered with dirt. The route led to an opening hidden in an overgrown embankment by a stream. A spot that might have been outside the perimeter containment could now be blocked but might also serve as a valuable point of entry for Echo Teams 1 and 2.

When the meeting closed, it was agreed that Nietcher would remain on call at the Fort Worth FBI facility for at least the next 48 hours.

The abundance of intelligence gathered from Nietcher was a green light, a signal from God, Steve felt. The invasion of the AMT compound had a chance, and Steve was the hero. All the men confirmed it. Slapping his back, they applauded loudly. Teresa congratulated him through gritted teeth, he noticed.

Smiling apprehensively, Steve both thanked her and apologized, for he suspected that now she'd be out for blood.

His.

Morro Bay, California
5:30 P.M. Pacific Time

DON'T CALL ME "BABE"!

MSNBC blared the evening newscast in the front room as Cindy flipped over the chicken pieces in the frying pan. Matthew was glued to the screen. Each time the phone rang, the boy rushed to answer it. "Dad?"

There was still no word from Steve. Calls to FBI headquarters and the Red Cross emergency hot line had come up empty. No one knew where Steve was.

Tommy, still too young to understand fully what was going on, was downstairs watching a VeggieTales video, *Larry-Boy and the Fib from Outer Space.*

Somehow, Cindy thought, the title of the video seemed more appropriate for the news coverage of the terrorist bombing:

"Today government sources said they are following up strong leads to the terrorist cell claiming responsibility for the bombing that took the lives of 311 people. They expect a breakthrough within days. We'll be back with Tom Kaufman, expert in international terrorism, after this commercial break. . . ."

And so it went. Hour after hour of talking heads, pundits who decried the lax security and vulnerability of American cities. And yet no one knew what could be done to make it better. After all, who could say when, where, or how tragedy would strike? Hijacked airliners were not required. It was bad enough that a couple guys in a rubber dinghy could blow up an American warship. Or run a car full of explosives into an American embassy somewhere. But what about Oklahoma City? or kids at Columbine? or ordinary people taken hostage and slaughtered on a rampage in a shopping mall?

The San Francisco tragedy was but one more reminder that no one in America really felt safe anymore. A mother could say good-bye to her child at the bus stop and not be sure she'd see that child again this side of heaven. Cindy understood enough about what Steve had been trained to do that she felt certain he was somewhere in the world trying to put a stop to such horrendous uncertainties. Making the world a safer place and all that.

But what about her own nightmares? What about Matthew and Tommy? Couldn't Steve think about his own family once in a while? Long enough to inform them he was still breathing?

The oil in the frying pan popped and sizzled. Fried chicken, Steve's favorite. She had cooked it tonight as though she expected him to walk through the door and sit down with her and the boys at the supper table. Like a real husband and father was supposed to do.

But Steve was too busy saving the world to come home for supper.

Tears of frustration and anger filled in Cindy's eyes. Most likely she'd never know. Steve's work was top secret, so he didn't talk about his missions, even to her. She never knew where he was, and that had never been easy. Many nights she had lain in bed, pleading with God to keep him safe. Somehow, before she'd met Steve Alstead, trusting in God had seemed so easy. Now, every time he left to go on another mission, she struggled. How much more could she take?

She sighed deeply and, for the millionth time, prayed for this man whom she both loved and hated. God knew where he was, even if no one else seemed to know. It would be nice, she thought, if God would let her know.

Now that the last of the grisly remains had been pulled from the BART wreckage, Cindy had begun to trust that Steve Alstead had not been among the victims. But where was he? How could he not think to telephone?

To dedicate himself to saving the world yet give so little thought to his own family seemed like *The Fib from Outer Space.* And so, Cindy thought, tomorrow she was going to get a lawyer. They would make it official. After all, this had never been a marriage. It was too hard for "two to become one" when one was running all over the world and hardly came home. Why should she expect it to be different—ever?

Matthew changed the channel to CNN, then ABC, then CBS, PBS, and then back to MSNBC.

"What are you doing?" Cindy asked from the kitchen.

"Looking for . . . news . . ."

Cindy realized he was really looking for his dad.

"Settle on one," she instructed, as the surfing began again.

"They're talking about the energy crisis now."

"Turn it off. You want to know about the energy crisis? Ask. You should see the electric bill."

And then the phone rang. Mother and son froze.

One ring.

Two.

Tommy piped up from below. "You gonna get it?"

Bob the Tomato was singing.

Three.

Matthew scrambled into action. Breathless, he grabbed the receiver. "Dad? Dad?" His eyes grew wide. He nodded and said quietly, "I'm okay. We're okay where are you?"

So it really was Steve. Finally! Cindy felt the room spin around her. She groped for a chair and sat down.

Matthew was disappointed, resentful. He replied sullenly to mundane questions about school, sports, and how life in general was going. Two minutes passed with answers coming in monosyllables.

"Where have you been?" the child demanded at last. "Don't you know we've been worried? Mr. Daley got killed on the BART! . . . My baseball coach, that's who! And if you were ever around, you'd know!"

And then Matthew passed the phone to Cindy and ran to his room, slamming the door behind him.

Cindy held the receiver to her ear.

"Matthew? Hey! Matthew!" Steve's words were tinged with remorse.

She replied coldly, "No, it's Cindy—in case you didn't recognize my voice. It's been three weeks since you called."

"Two."

"Two and a half."

"You told me not to call you. Not ever, you said."

Well, yes, she had said that. They'd argued and she'd told him she never wanted to hear his voice again. Her words had echoed constantly in her head ever since the BART bombing.

"You didn't think your boys would be worried about you? You, in San Francisco? With the news blatting night and day about the bombing? Pictures of the dead?"

"You don't let them watch that stuff."

"Nobody can get away from it! Especially not since one of the guys killed is somebody we all know!"

"I'm sorry about that," Steve replied quietly. "Daley. The coach. Yes. A nice guy."

"How would you know?" she responded angrily. "You only were

around to see a half-dozen of Matthew's ball games last season. How could you know anything about what we've all been going through—the worry!"

"Look, Cindy, I didn't think. You told me not to call you. I figured—"

"Do you always believe everything I say?"

"No."

"What?"

"I mean . . ." The very tone of his voice announced his defeat.

"Never mind."

"I should have phoned, Cindy," he said regretfully. "I'm sorry. I've been working."

"Right. What else is new? Where are you?"

"I can't say. I mean . . ."

"I'm getting a lawyer, Steve."

"No, Cindy. Don't do that. We need to talk."

"I'm getting an attorney. What's the point?"

"I want to see you. We can talk this through, babe."

"Babe is a talking pig in Tommy's favorite movie. You'd know that if you knew anything about Tommy. Don't call me 'babe.' "

"When I get time off here . . . finish . . . I want to come down. Want to see you and the kids. Talk about our future."

"Our future, Steve? Well, here it is. *Hon. Babe. Sweetie.* You want to see me? talk to me? Here's the deal. Your son has a home game. That's Matthew, in case you forgot *his* name. Old Mission Elementary School. Monday at 3:45. And a party at Avila Beach for the team's families afterward. If you love me and them, be there."

"I do love you—"

She cut off his declaration by slamming down the phone.

Okay. So Steve Alstead was alive. The creep. The chicken was almost cooked.

Tonight she would finally sleep.

NINE

AMT Compound
Hell's Canyon, Idaho
Thursday, 26 April
2:47 A.M. Mountain Time

COONSKIN SCOUT

In reviewing Robert Nietcher's recorded interview, Charles Downing assessed that most of the information given was likely true. In fact, there was only one reply given by Nietcher that concerned Downing.

The tunnel.

Nietcher didn't seem to know if the tunnel was booby-trapped. That would have been a valid answer, except there was a little twinkle in his eye. It looked like the glimmer of a second thought. Maybe the tunnel *was* booby-trapped, and Nietcher decided to play it down in hopes that his old friends would not be successfully raided. There was, after all, reasonable motivation for a man facing a life sentence to be bitter and vengeful. Nietcher could scarcely be charged as an accessory for saying he didn't know. How could anyone prove otherwise?

It was that one piece of evidence that now had to be reconned.

Steve and Chuck tiptoed along the creek to the place where Nietcher had described the exit hole of the escape route. April's heavy snowmelt had been generous to what would otherwise have been a dry creek bed six months of the year. The gully walls were steep and slick with slippery mud.

Anton Brown walked the opposite side of the canyon, scanning atop the bank for any patrolling guards or listening posts.

Dan's voice whispered over the three men's headsets. "Echo 1, this is Control. Do you copy?"

Steve paused, touching his earpiece. "This is Echo 1, reading you loud and clear. We are almost in position. Over."

"Echo 1, Night Stalker is in the air. ETA five minutes."

Night Stalker was the FBI's secret weapon. Though it had been speculated on in the press after several successful FBI covert operations, its existence still wasn't officially acknowledged. The presence of a stealthily quiet reconnaissance plane with a high-resolution, thermal-imaging system was rarely noticed by anyone when used at night.

Steve checked his watch. A lot of good the hundred-million-dollar plane did them right then. Night Stalker was 23 minutes late. The aerial recon should have been complete a long time ago. It set him on edge to think that contact with a lookout who might be feet away could have been easily avoided if they were on schedule.

In answer Steve said, "We will hold steady until notified of potential threats."

"Command to One: at this time, we'd like to test the FM jamming system."

Steve removed a small device that looked like a '60s transistor radio from his pocket. It resembled a handheld CB radio that received local civilian frequencies. This unit, however, wasn't a radio. Instead, it had a lighted number readout. Chuck, who stood close by, watched in amazement.

"Jamming now," Dan informed them.

Almost at that same moment the numbers flicked from 100 percent, representing the clear, usable civilian frequencies in the area, down to nearly zero.

Steve read the gauge. "Command, jamming successful. I'm reading less than 5 percent."

From that time until Dan turned off the jamming signal anyone within five miles of the beam of his directional broadcast would receive nothing but static on their TVs and radios. This jammer was useful not only for cutting off any suspects' communications with their command and knocking out any signals sent from remote-surveillance cameras, but also for another purpose.

Diversion.

A sentry walking along in dead silence might be startled by the sudden loud buzz of static from his walkie-talkie. Ironically, nine times out of ten, after a couple minutes of solid electronic whining, the patrol or listening post would go in to find out who the idiot was who was sitting on their radio's talk switch.

Opponents had been known to get suspicious after long periods of time, so the technique worked best at short intervals and was generally limited to night, up until a full invasion was underway. At that point jamming served to knock out any scanners that might somehow pick up police or other frequencies not encoded on the radio net.

Steve put the signal reader away. It amused him to think that the AMT guys were probably missing their favorite TV show, while his radio worked perfectly.

His tiny earpiece fell silent again.

Anton pulled a highly accurate, laser-based range finder from his vest. Even the *civilian* models had the capability to accurately assess distances out to about 1000 yards. The FBI's latest recon toy had the ability to penetrate a solid wall, yet still give an accurate distance reading beyond it. Not quite, but almost. It could perform its function through brush.

Anton squatted down and began to scan the embankment. Green numbers illuminated the night-vision screen. He set the device to read through the heaviest overgrowth. As he panned the hillside the numbers increased until the angle was too long and the readout stopped. "Nothing," he said over the local radio net.

Steve motioned *two, five* with his hands and gave the roll out signal by making circles with his hand and pointing in the direction of travel. Anton picked up and moved another 25 yards upstream.

"Echo 1, this is Control. Night Stalker is nearing low orbit. What's your position?"

Steve looked to Anton for an answer.

Anton shook his head and cut into the net. "Still looking." He scanned again. The yardage numbers flicked down. "Twenty-two yards, 21 yards, 20 yards . . ." Soon the handheld unit was pointed right at Steve. Anton continued to pan to the right and the numbers began to climb. "Twenty-four yards, 25 yards." Then the displayed yardage reading jumped way up. "Thirty-nine yards, 38 yards, 39 . . ."

Anton held there. "Command, I have a dramatic increase in yardage on the riverbank, north side, ahead 20 paces."

A dense patch of foliage was on Steve's side.

The concealed tunnel entry?

"Echo 1, wait for a reading," Dan instructed.

Steve paused five steps short of the section of the embankment that was covered in heavy ivy. Anton moved up parallel with him, raising another optic gadget to his eye.

Probably the most expensive and useful piece of night-time recon equipment they had, the Thorn EMI handheld thermal imager literally *could* see through walls. The device translated the heat signature of whatever it was pointed at into a positive image. The unit was so sensitive that it would even reveal a place where someone had been minutes before. The degree of an object's temperature determined the brightness of the image in the tiny screen. As time passed, the faint-glowing ghost where a person had been would fade away.

Anton used the EMI to determine if there was anyone inside the place where they believed the tunnel to be. He pointed the unit directly at the thickest patch of vines, not seeing the green shadow of a human, but he looked again carefully. Small green spots seemed to lead into the side of the solid mountain. "Echo 1, this is Echo 2. We've definitely found the tunnel. It looks as if someone had their boots up by the fire and walked down only minutes ago. However, the tunnel seems to be empty now."

Anton scooted farther upstream for a better angle up the long tube. The thermal imager showed the glowing footprints. The smallest, most distant spots were brightest, indicating that whoever had been in the escape tunnel had just left. "Echo 2 to Command. Tunnel is clear."

Dan cut in. "Well done, Echo Team. Hold for aerial data. Night Stalker, you're on the net. Go ahead."

"Echo Team, this is Night Stalker," the plane's electronic warfare technician announced in what Steve thought of as a weather forecaster's carefully modulated voice. "We have a visual of you three by the dark line, which would be the stream. Up the embankment toward the compound, I can see one patrol. A single individual. I think the jamming worked. It appears he's headed in."

Yes! Steve silently exclaimed.

"Echo 1, Echo 3, proceed with caution."

"Understood, Command." Steve tiptoed toward the entry.

Chuck, known as Echo 3, removed a bulky backpack and unzipped it.

Steve poked around in the bushes. His hand felt something cold and hard. "A metal grate," he whispered.

Chuck lifted something tiny and furry from the pack. Feeling around in the dark, he flipped a switch. A low electronic whistling sounded as the contraption powered up.

Steve rubbed the gizmo, as if patting a dog's head. "Well done," he complimented Chuck. Pulling out a laptop computer, Steve disappeared with it under a camouflage ghillie blanket.

Since Nietcher couldn't guarantee that the tunnel didn't have cameras or booby-traps, it had been Steve's decision to send a nonhuman scout instead of going in themselves. A dog would have been entirely too conspicuous, and a bomb-sniffing robot even worse. If there were cameras inside, infrared or not, such a ploy would surely be noticed. So Chuck had come up with the winning idea. Using the fur of a raccoon purchased from a local Indian trapper, the remote-operated, bomb-investigating, night-vision-equipped ROBI the Robot was instantly transformed into the Coonskin Scout.

Now ROBI glided toward the tunnel on small tank tracks. From under the blackout ghillie blanket, Steve controlled the robot, acting as its eyes and ears. He stopped the beast several feet from the opening, looked around, and then guided ROBI into the tunnel.

Chuck leaned against the bank to keep watch, while Anton stood guard across the creek.

Craning the robot's head up and back, Steve caught a glimpse of the tunnel's first overhead light. Then he zoomed ROBI's optics to the end of the tunnel, searching for cameras or explosives.

Steve knew it would have been unlikely for Adams to rig bombs around the outside of the plastic pipe. They would be very difficult to access and maintain and be less effective. Nor were there any obvious projections that appeared out of place. However, a remote-operated explosive device could very easily be installed in a light box and connected to a control switch using the same metal electrical conduit as the lights.

Scanning, Steve realized Nietcher had apparently been straight about the booby-traps. But what about cameras? Wait . . .

"Echo 1 to Command, we have a camera in the tunnel," reported Steve urgently.

Dan answered. "Does the camera appear to be remote or hardwired?"

Steve zoomed in on the image and refocused. "Command, it's definitely hardwired, but doesn't appear to be infrared or have night-vision capabilities."

"Echo 1, very well. Proceed and hope for the best."

Steve steered the ratlike ROBI farther in. When the "animal" was just beneath the camera, out of sight of surveillance, he engaged ROBI's next trick.

Using a toggle switch mounted on the keyboard, Steve raised ROBI's head toward the first light box. Inside the mechanical cranium of the robot were several nitrate-sensing, bomb-sniffing sensors.

Inches from the light, Steve held for a reading. "One to Command, No. 1 is clear."

A tremendous weight had been lifted. Usually in a setting like this one, in order to keep intruders as far out as possible, a booby-trap was set close to the outside. Having the first box clean was a good sign, though the other most common placement for a remote mine was at the deepest interior point. Called stovepiping, this technique allowed an entire group of men to get deep within. At that point the charge would be blown. Progress would instantly be halted by either killing the intruders or at least causing extreme chaos. In theory those who survived would turn around and retreat. It was then that a second charge, either near the middle or the first third of the tunnel, would be set off.

Steve could only grin as he imagined how the seemingly floating raccoon must have looked to a surveillance camera. He lowered the robot's sensor and continued to the next suspect area. It was also clear. And the next, clear as well. The tracked device ran perfectly to within 20 feet of the end of the shaft.

Glaring at the blue monitor, Steve tried to interpret the image ahead. It seemed as though there was a drop or maybe a corner. He edged ROBI closer before finally realizing what it was—a foxhole sunk below the level of the tunnel floor. A perfect place from which to snipe with a Remington 700 or other precision rifle, Steve knew. "Command, are you getting this image?"

Clicking in, Dan replied, "Perfectly, Echo 1. These guys thought it all through."

"Sure did," replied Steve.

"One, what is to the left of the pit?"

Rotating the joystick, Steve caused the animal to face slightly left. "It's definitely a corner," he commented.

"Look beyond it," Dan added. "It looks like a ladder and a . . . fireman's pole?"

It surely was. Steve was admiring Adams's work when he heard a noise picked up by ROBI's microphone.

"Footsteps!" Steve exclaimed frantically.

"Get out of there, One!" Dan ordered.

The image on the screen went completely white.

"What's happened, One?"

Steve scrambled to punch in commands on the keyboard. "Someone turned on the tunnel lights. Night vision is overpowered."

"Switch visual to natural light setting."

"I'm trying!" Steve argued. "This thing wasn't designed for a quick change."

Voices resonated down the concrete shaft and were picked up by the mechanical raccoon.

Finally the robot switched lenses. Steve could now see the brightly illuminated, corrugated black tunnel walls. He rotated the joystick, setting ROBI off at full speed down the tube. Unfortunately the tiny tracks of the robot were made for steady travel over any terrain, not scrambling like a bat out of Hell's Canyon.

Steve heard the squeak of hands and shoes going down the fireman's pole.

The voices grew louder. "I told you it's a raccoon in here again!"

"I get to shoot this one," another voice responded.

"Oh no!" Steve moaned. "Come on, ROBI."

The robot was nearing the exit now. Almost to the grate. Chuck readied the travel bag, but the raccoon got hung up.

Steve heard the voices cry out. "It's stuck! Grab my AR." Hitting forward and reverse over and over, Steve attempted to free it. The hide had become stuck on the sharp edge of the bars. Steve considered grabbing it with his bare hands. A moment later a shot rang out. The bullet grazed the deck and ricocheted, shredding vines. It hit dirt only inches from Anton, whose first instinct was to grab his weapon.

Another shot sounded. Anton's second instinct was to grab his gear and scramble up the bank and under cover. Still fighting with the robot's controls, Steve grew frantic.

The two voices in the tunnel argued. "Don't shoot in here, man! Adams is gonna come unglued!"

"He told me next one I see, to get it and make a cap for his kid."

In the midst of the bickering, Steve slid up to the tunnel's opening. Grabbing the mechanical beast by its nose, he yanked it out. The hide tore, leaving a shred of evidence behind.

"Look, it's getting away," one of the men called.

"One, this is Night Stalker. We have movement. Three armed men running toward you!"

The moment was too tense for Steve to reply. He tossed ROBI across the entrance to Chuck, who quickly stuffed it in the bag. Steve didn't even stop to repack the computer. With it under his arm he was up the bank and over the tunnel in half a second.

The hurried sound of running feet, crunching sticks, and gravel grew close.

Steve scrambled but realized he'd have to find a hide pronto. "Command, this is One. Cut the jamming signal!"

Dan must have read Steve's mind, because an instant later, Night Stalker cut in. "One, it appears to have worked. The parties pursuing above ground have stopped running. They are walking . . . no wait . . . they are standing in a circle. It looks as though they're talking. Okay, the men are turning around and moving toward the compound. Above ground is clear."

Voices echoed down the tunnel. It was the man who had been shooting. "No, it was just a raccoon. . . . I promise you. . . ." The shooter attempted to convince someone at the other end of a walkie-talkie contact.

But Steve, Chuck, and Anton didn't stick around to see how the argument ended.

Once safely away from the scene, Chuck started to laugh.

"What?" Steve demanded.

"I was just thinking what the reaction would have been if ROBI got clear, but not his coon hide," Chuck said. "Shot, skinned, and tanned all in one go . . . now that would make campfire yarns for a hundred years!"

HRT Command Center, Bear Mining Camp
Hell's Canyon, Idaho
11:02 A.M. Mountain Time

THE WEEK OF CREATION

Long nights had run into long days. Steve had lost track of how many days it had been since the BART bombing. Had it been two weeks? a month? In reality, only six days had elapsed.

At six days, Chapter 16 was still younger than the earth on the day God rested. And like the Genesis account, a whole lot had been accomplished.

Steve blocked out the forced-entry plan with Echo Teams 1 and 2. Always before a dynamic entry, where doors are blown off hinges and men clad in black suits fast-rope from choppers like hungry spiders looking for flies, a detailed layout of the building or facility is made.

Often a high school gym or an empty warehouse is requisitioned for such use. Miles of tape are stretched on the floor to represent walls, doors, and other features of the subject building's actual size. In the event a suitable practice building can't be found, HRT will block it out on a parking lot, or failing even that, a deserted lot.

In this case, the command trailers had been circled like frontier wagons to guard against lookie-loos who might be in the forest. In the center of Bear's abandoned mining camp, chalk sketched the boundaries of the AMT compound in the yellow-tinged dirt. For one who had not first studied a map of the target area, the entire mess would seem like an infield groundskeeper had gone crazy.

Snipers hung from trailer rooftops and perched in trees to represent the rocky walls surrounding the AMT facility. Their weapons were unloaded. These guys had fired many thousands of rounds in previous training. Accuracy was not in question. There was little more than a need for full-speed movements and the *click, click* of empty weapons control-pairing make-believe bad guys with the two well-aimed shots required.

Steve had been at it all morning. Chalking from first light to 7:46 A.M. There was a review of obstacle timing, used to calculate the time it would take to accomplish a specific task, such as blowing a door or climbing a ladder, from 8 to 9:15 A.M. These details were added to the blocking plan in order to more accurately stage the entry, as well as to coordinate other aspects of Echo, Sierra, and Command teams.

The initial blocking-out of the entry took place from 9:17 to 11:02. As blocking went, first the team would walk and talk through the plan several times slowly with dry practice, no bullets. The men had to have memories like actors, having only a very short time to learn ballet-like movements and the complexities of the layout.

Next came the full-speed dry fire. Once a consistent OT, or overall time, was achieved, and if there was a shoot house, the men graduated to slow-motion live fire.

Last was full-speed live fire. It was an incredibly dangerous process. Men might be entering rooms from opposite walls and firing simultaneously. Every member of the Entry Team had to know where every other member was at a given instant in order to avoid shooting a team member on the opposite side of a wall.

Over and over it went.

By the time they finished, Echo members, though they had never before been inside, would know the compound as well as any AMT member.

TEN

San Francisco Bay
12:30 P.M. Pacific Time

REALITY CROWDS IN

It was a typical Bay Area spring day.

The morning had been chilly but warmed up by noon. Heavy coats were abandoned in favor of sweatshirts and windbreakers. Just about that time the obscuring overhead haze departed, content merely to color outside the lines. The murky gray retreated as the wind picked up, tossing tiny whitecaps from the tops of choppy swells.

It was at this time that Mark and his fiancée, Tina, were sailing just a little too far out in the Bay. It was his first time aboard a wind-powered craft. He had read all the manuals but still knew little about riding in a 16-foot sailboat and much less about piloting one. He struggled with tangled lines and sheets and braces, not even sure what they were all for.

The craft had been a spur-of-the-moment purchase. Mark had taken Tina, his soon-to-be trophy wife, to Fisherman's Wharf the previous Sunday for a stroll. It was then that Mark had noticed: Tina's eye seemed to be more on a young shirtless hunk who hung from the stern of a 32-footer than on him. The tanned man had sent her a sparkling smile. Tina had batted her lashes and smiled back, snaring a wave.

Mark could hardly control himself. Grabbing her by the arm, he asked what she was smiling at.

"Sailboats," she'd replied quickly. "I like sailboats."

Mark was an intellectual, not a jock. There hadn't been time for working out, surfing all day, and lounging bare-chested in UV rays. Instead he had gotten heavy while making "serious money" as a phone broker for a popular stock-trading firm.

So Mark had pulled Tina away from the rail. "Would you like it if *I* bought a sailboat?"

Her squeal and embrace were diverting enough to be convincing, whether the sailboat was the object of her attention or not. It was then Mark had resolved to buy himself a sailboat, which he did within 24 hours.

He should have known better.

A guy doesn't buy every stock that is pumped on The Financial News Network, nor does a serious investor buy the first stock to cross the ticker. But despite Mark's proven ability to pick stock-market winners, he had sprung for the first crummy little sailboat he'd seen.

He didn't know until later that there were reasons why the Com-Pac 16 was for sale and so cheap. First, it never should have been on San Francisco Bay at all since it was too small for the big afternoon waves. And second, $1400 was already twice as much as it was worth. So the rigging was rusty and the sails moldy. Didn't matter, knock off 50 bucks. So it was a little leaky and the battery was dead.

Mark had been convinced he'd gotten a $5,000 boat for $1350. Not a bad buy, he'd congratulated himself. So what if the hunk's boat was *slightly* larger? *Close enough* was the decision. A wanna-be trophy wife would never know the difference.

After a day of cleaning and two more reading up on sailing, Mark had been ready for the big day. Midmorning Tina had arrived dockside in a red miniskirt and matching top. Mark had to smile. She looked great. But it hadn't taken long for her to become bored; 30 minutes or so and she was tired of sailing.

Now, unknown to her, Mark himself was struggling to keep his composure. He didn't dare tell her that the only sail he knew how to raise kept pulling them closer and closer to the dangerous deep waters and the mouth of the Bay.

Every time Mark attempted to swing the helm over, the sail flapped like a dying seagull and the *Sassy Lassy,* the name they'd christened her with that morning, swung sideways to the swell, threatening to swamp them. Having sensed that Tina's interest was slipping away, Mark had poured more wine on the fire.

Now she was feeling queasy.

As they neared the Golden Gate, something Mark regarded as the point of no return, he wondered how he would turn the boat around. He couldn't bring himself to admit to Tina that they were in trouble.

"Mark." Tina slurred her words. "I'm feeling sick."

"Had too much to drink, honey?" he replied, attempting to assure her that her well-being was his only concern.

By then her face was the color of the algae sprouting from the boat's bottom, her hair windblown beyond repair, and her outfit soaked with spray from the boat. "Mark, I think I'm gonna be sick."

"Why don't you go below and lie down for a while?" Mark answered. After all, the ad for the boat had stated that it actually "slept two."

Big mistake.

The lack of a horizon and the close mustiness of the coffinlike cabin must have instantly driven Tina's nausea to overwhelming proportions. A moment after she went downstairs, she scrambled topside, gagging. At the same instant Mark was scanning the Bay for someone to signal for help, Tina vomited over the rail. Two or three heaves was all it took.

Mark let the sail flap, and they coasted for a minute. Dragging her hand in the water, Tina rested her chin on the deck, barely raising it up to spit into the ocean.

Then something strange passed by, directly under her gaze. It looked like the open-eyed face of a man, reproaching her for puking on him.

"Mark!" Tina screamed when her hand touched the floating body.

Mark spotted the form immediately. Not realizing the man was dead and had been for some time, he grasped the blue coat and heaved the lifeless form onto the deck. Tina ran to the prow of the boat, sober and sobbing. Mark turned away from the horrific sight.

Now, he realized, he had the perfect excuse to use his cell phone to call for help.

HRT Command Center, Bear Mining Camp
Hell's Canyon, Idaho
Friday, 27 April
7:16 A.M. Mountain Time

A HAT FOR WHOM?

Dan lifted a stack of manila folders, passing them to Steve, who had just arrived. "More intel for you."

From Dan's tone, Steve realized there was something else his friend held back from saying. He opened the first file and flipped through the pictures.

"These are photos from Night Stalker last night," explained Dan. "As you can see here, there are listening posts on these four points." He pointed to the green night-vision shadows of men on the infrared pictures. "Look there: even one pretty close on the hill, where you were two nights ago."

Steve studied them. "And what about these other guys?"

"Patrols," Dan answered. "I have a map, constructed on an aerial photo, which shows their routes in detail."

One image struck Steve as strange. "This looks like a woman with two kids!"

"I've got bad news for you," Dan commented sternly. "It is. Taken last night. It seems they came out to look for the raccoon."

Steve dropped the photos. "But I thought there weren't any women or kids! Didn't reports say that Adams didn't allow them in the compound?"

"A small word was missing from that report . . . *other,"* commented

Dan. "According to the interview with Nietcher, Adams's wife and two kids, ten and eight, used to live there two, three years ago, something like that. She'd been gone, so we didn't even know about her. It wasn't until we saw this image that we searched her records. They indicated she moved out of her apartment in Arizona and probably came straight back up here two months ago."

Steve's memory flashed back to something that had bothered him ever since the ROBI recon. "The guard! He said something about a coonskin cap for Adams's kid."

"Bingo."

"This is a problem."

Dan exhaled. "I know."

"It isn't just about a shootout, Dan. This thing could become a hostage situation, or the kids could be hurt. That 10-year-old is now what, 12? 13? He might come out with a gun the way the kid did at Ruby Ridge. What if he starts shooting?"

Dan rubbed his eyes. "Believe me, I know, buddy."

Steve was concerned. This little complication changed everything. "We can't shoot a kid—not even if he's shooting at us."

Dan had a way of bringing things back together. "Listen, good cover, good concealment. It's the best preventive measure. They can't shoot what they can't see, right? We haven't even made with the powwow yet. Maybe Adams'll be reasonable."

Nothing Dan had said so far seemed to make any difference. As chief of the shooters, Steve found it impossible to stop worrying. His kids were not much different in ages from Adams's. What if it were Matt out there?

What if, what if, what if! Still unconvinced, Steve argued, "But what about our planned entry? What about Echo 1? If I find this kid, or both of them, in the tunnel, what am I supposed to do? Let 'em shoot me? I've got kids, man."

Dan placed his hand on Steve's back. "We'll take care of it. Teresa will talk them out in negotiations. There's nothing we can change until we get that far."

"But—"

Dan cut him off. "Look, we've got some guys with less-than-lethal ammo. You know that. We'll equip the No. 3 guy on every entry team with 12-gauge rubber projectiles and OC grenades."

Less-than-lethal force was a relatively new aspect of dynamic entry, created to reduce fatalities. OC (Oleoresin Capsicum) pepper spray and rubber slugs could injure or temporarily incapacitate a threat without killing the suspect. These special weapons were invaluable for protecting some people from themselves . . . like kids who were old enough to use a weapon, dumb enough not to know better, and still too young to die.

Steve was speechless. There was always at least one moment in every crisis situation when things seemed hopeless. He shook the thoughts from his head. He was a professional. It was just one more obstacle to be overcome.

"It's okay," Dan reassured him. "We know where they stay, and according to Nietcher, where they will go in an event like we're planning. Barring some unpredictable move of the family to another location, it's highly likely we'll be able to isolate and contain them."

"All right," Steve said. "You're right. It's not worth worrying about, beyond planning for, until we're there."

"That's the way, good buddy," Dan consoled. "Oh, by the way, I found this interesting. When Downing, Bouche, and I interviewed Nietcher again just a couple hours ago, he said Adams never had anything but dynamite."

"Only dynamite?" Steve exclaimed in surprise. "No plastique?"

"No." Then Dan added, "Adams may be antigovernment, but he's cautious about laying in things to get arrested for. I thought you might find that interesting."

"You bet," replied Steve, concerned. "It worries me. You know why we're here?"

"To arrest Suspect No. 1 for the BART bombing . . ."

"Yeah, but if Nietcher is telling the truth, we may be going in after some guy who had nothing to do with it."

Dan emphatically denied the idea. "No way. Evidence points toward this guy. He's heavily armed and antigovernment. Besides, he could have gotten the Semtex after Nietcher left."

"Right," Steve agreed. "And maybe Adams was only a part of it. He could have financed the BB and let someone else do all the work."

"Exactly."

Silence followed as both men mentally summed up all that had been said.

Dan finally broke in. "Hey, chow time!"

"No, thanks," Steve answered. "I'm going to stick around and go over some more of these intel reports."

"Suit yourself, man. Eight hundred breakfast burritos from Taco Bell just got flown in on the Chinook." The Chinook, a large double-rotor chopper, was used for lifting out large groups of personnel or heavy equipment.

Steve laughed as he considered a chopper going to Boise for an eight hundred-burrito run for the border. "They *would* need a Chinook to carry breakfast for this mob, wouldn't they?"

After Dan left, Steve viewed stack after stack of pictures, hoping to gain the little edge that might change the entire outcome. It was in the last folder that he discovered the most disturbing photos he'd ever seen.

Shocking, the pictures of the aftermath of the BART bombing. He wasn't meant to see them. They weren't part of his area of control and, for his own sanity, he shouldn't have looked. But they were too much to put down.

An old woman, a beautiful young girl—both killed, mangled, burned. By far the most devastating photo he viewed, however, was of a pair of little boys. One was about five; the other, dressed like a cowboy the way his son sometimes did, maybe nine, ten. Their bodies were crumpled.

At that moment Steve knew without a shadow of a doubt why God wanted him here—to make the world better. To catch guys who killed kids like the ones in the picture.

Tears flooded his eyes as he concentrated on the sweet, innocent face of the younger one. He was so quiet, so still. Steve felt sick, too weak even to hold up his arms. Shallow breaths warned him he would be sick. He couldn't shake the image from his mind that they could have been his kids. Or that tomorrow it might be the Adams boys.

Chapter 16 Forensics Lab
San Francisco
9 P.M. Pacific Time

THE BODY IN THE BAY

Dr. Turnow removed his glasses and rubbed his eyes. Hours in his lab space at headquarters, staring at information summaries, had wearied his vision. Printouts of blast characteristics and point-of-detonation estimates mingled with the National Crime Information Center reports of who was suspected of possessing Semtex explosives for sale. Leaning back in his chair, Turnow interlaced his fingers behind his head and arched his spine. Long experience had taught him to give himself frequent mental breaks. Fatigue led to faulty reasoning and erroneous conclusions.

If nothing substantive was settled within the hour, he'd go to the next stage of his work/rest regimen—walking around the block. For the moment he was refreshed enough to resume his analysis.

Turnow's job was to reconstruct the evidence trail. If everything clicked and the Idaho lead held up, then Chapter 16's job would be done for this crisis. He would turn his results over to the Justice Department for prosecutions and go home to Tahoe.

The links seemed solid enough. A revenge bombing for Waco tied in with the April date. The claim of responsibility in the name of a previously unknown white supremacist group was not surprising, if the perpetrators were a radical splinter faction of some other organization. Semtex was an unusual choice of weapon for a militia group, but not unthinkable. The type of detonator employed was readily available near mining operations, which certainly squared with the Idaho site and a militiaman's degree of expertise.

Most recently the use of the suspect briefcase as the delivery device for the weapon was reconfirmed: a piece of floor panel bore the imprint of the case's brass fittings where the detonation had driven them downward. That and other clues from the blast inquiry pinpointed ground zero.

Turnow's thoughts turned to the suspect individual. No remaining scraps of briefcase material were large enough to contain entire fingerprints, but there were no partial prints either. That fact argued for a carefully planned and executed operation . . . and led Turnow to again doubt the seemingly stupid use of a public phone to make a potentially damning contact.

Turnow made a mental note to see if it was possible to determine who else had been in the subway car with the bomb. None of them had survived, of course, but his innate attention to detail suggested the question.

The suspect was known to have exited the doomed train one stop before the explosion, which meant he got off at Embarcadero Station.

Where had he gone from there? The simplest escape would have been to reverse direction and take the next BART back under the Bay. But that was probably too hazardous to count on. If there had been any delay in the Oakland-bound cars, the bomber might have been in the way of the blast. With the tunnel acting as a gun barrel, pieces of rail car were transformed into bullets that rocketed down the track in both directions. Even if uninjured, the suspect would have faced the risk of automatic safety measures kicking in, shutting down all travel on the line and trapping him under the Bay.

So that scenario could probably be ruled out.

But exiting via Embarcadero Station still left myriad choices of escape routes. A waiting confederate could have sped him away by car. He could have grabbed a taxi or even headed straight for a waiting boat by the ferry building just two blocks down and escaped by water.

The San Francisco Police Department appealed for anyone near Embarcadero Station at the time of the blast who might have seen the suspect to come forward, but so far there was nothing promising. Men in hats and overcoats were uncommon in many American cities but not in San Francisco, especially not in the changeable weather of this wet April.

Turnow's B-com rang. While most of the team members didn't bother to customize their B-com rings, the scientist had altered his. Though not a techno-geek in Miles's class, Turnow had allowed the computer wizard to demonstrate not only a user-defined ring but how to make the device provide a unique audio-identifier for each caller.

The opening bars of Beethoven's *Fifth* signaled that Senator Morrison was on the line.

"Turnow?" Morrison's gentlemanly Southern accent inquired. "Sorry to interrupt, but SFPD's got something I think you should know about."

"Yes?"

"Body found in the Bay matches the description of our suspect, and he had a tattoo on the first knuckle of his left ring finger."

County Coroner's Office
San Francisco
9:36 P.M. Pacific Time

PLUCKING THE STING

The morgue reeked of formaldehyde and disinfectant. Like every autopsy room Turnow had ever entered, it was maintained at a constant 12 degrees Celsius.

And like all the rest, the presence of death—unarguable, unassailable death—and the unemotional reduction of human life to something approaching meat-locker status lowered the apparent temperature still further, till it hovered just above freezing.

Because the corpse on the stainless steel table had at first been believed to be either a suicide by drowning or the victim of a boating accident, the inquest was under the authority of the medical examiner and at his facility. But the sharp eyes of assistant ME Lee Fong noted a skull fracture not consistent with a steel propeller. The possibility of a murder led him to be extremely thorough with the rest of his exam. A skinned knuckle on the ring finger of the victim's left hand and what he observed there led him to call the FBI.

"You see where part of the tattoo remains," Dr. Lee said, pointing toward a pair of thin blue lines that stood out sharply against the waterlogged pallor of the hand. "Dull pocketknife used in the attempt to eliminate the tattoo. First a hack downward and then a rip back toward the wrist. Scorpion, you say?"

Turnow shrugged. "Fuzzy, partial video frame only. It looked like a scorpion."

Dr. Lee concurred. "Could be stinger and one leg intact here."

Turnow added, "Anyway, that's what we're running as a search, but so far no known matches. Cause of death?"

"Folks in the sailboat who found him thought at first they'd run over him, but he'd been in the water a day, maybe two. Not drowned. Near dead when he went in." Dr. Lee gestured toward an area of the skull about the size and shape of the fountain pen. "Hit with the edge of an oar. Fiberglass fibers in the wound. Whoever did this struck him hard enough to splinter the paddle, then almost succeeded in getting rid of the tattoo before dumping him in the Bay."

"Any ID on him?"

Dr. Lee grimaced, holding out a specimen tray. On it lay a scrap of soggy ticket stub reading *Blue and . . . Sausa. . . .* The rest was either blurred or missing. "That's all there is," the medical examiner said. "Ferry ticket for the Blue and Gold Fleet, one way from Sausalito to San Francisco."

"Unless 200 other passengers missed seeing this attack, it's all a setup to suggest that he jumped or fell," Turnow mused. "The lack of a round-trip ticket hints at suicide."

Lee agreed. "Not expected to be found at all. Pure luck that the body wasn't carried out to sea by the tide—or shredded by a great white—before our unhappy sailors made his acquaintance. But if he was found, suicide or accident would probably fit. Slicing off the dye mark was an extra precaution."

"Any idea who he is . . . was?"

"If he's your bomber, you don't expect him to be reported missing, do you?"

Turnow studied the black hair, Semitic appearance, and swarthy complexion of the corpse. "Well, Doctor," he said. "In your best clinical judgment, would you say this man was likely to have belonged to a white supremacist group?"

"Not unless he was their arms dealer," Lee said. "Maybe the deal went sour."

Turnow frowned, pondering where this new evidence pointed, then thought of Steve and the rest of the team preparing to assault a heavily defended compound in Idaho. "Thank you, Doctor," he said. "I need a private office to use my phone. But before I go, know this: your quick thinking may have saved lives."

Dr. Lee's face split into a grin. "In my line of work," he said, "that happy result does not happen very often."

ELEVEN

AMT Compound
Hell's Canyon, Idaho
Saturday, 28 April
6:07 A.M. Mountain Time

OPENING THE BALL

In the mountains of west central Idaho it had been light almost an hour before the FBI attempted to contact Andrew Adams. There was no response on the phone. Instead an answering machine instructed them to call back during business hours. The bitter smell of wood smoke hung like a patchy fog in thick pockets in the cool air.

It was hard for Steve to get a full breath. It felt as though he'd eaten too much the night before, though he knew that wasn't the problem. His stomach churned. It was just his nerves, he realized while lying inside an artificial bush in the gully near the escape pipe.

Half a mile away a local HQ trailer was being set up. Over the mountain, two Huey choppers waited to bring in aerial assault entry teams on wires.

From 3:15 A.M. on, the team had been playing a silent, one-sided game of chess with the AMT boys. Every time AMT sent out a patrol or changed their listening posts, with the aid of Night Stalker a corresponding countermove was played out by HRT, even though those in the compound were still unaware.

Intel reports showed that the compound patrols were divided into two teams covering three eight-hour shifts. The first team, who covered the top west side of the compound, normally changed at 3:30 A.M.

It was always a gamble when a surrounding perimeter team tried to time their arrival with an enemy patrol change. The oncoming shift might be late. The first patrol would be tired and impatient. In some cases, a first patrol would leave the perimeter uncovered and pass their replacements on the way in. Instances like those were ideal for a sniper to move into position by climbing into a hide on the side of a hill, in a bush, or at the bottom of a gully.

The flip side of timing was that a good guy might inadvertently end up in the midst of a change where there were twice the number of enemy guards present.

Maybe the radio jamming had tipped Adams off, because that night the AMT routine was completely different from what had been observed. According to Night Stalker, the patrol made its first change around midnight. The next change came at 4:30 A.M. The HRT perimeter boys were restless but ready when Night Stalker guided them in.

The compound guards seemed ready too, though. That night the four outlying listening posts were comprised of two-man teams instead of one. Steve decided that was probably due to the radio outage. Adams must have sent a second man out as a runner, in case his communications went down again.

Having a double guard was a mixed blessing as well. A second man at each enemy outpost would mean that twice the HRT coverage was needed, at the usual five-to-one HRT-to-Tango ratio. Five good guys to every one bad guy was Standard Op.

The good side was the enemy chatter: two people talk more than one. And talking people were less likely to be as observant of their surroundings. A less-observant guard was a good thing for Steve, who was pretending to be a bush near the stream. In fact, there were 10 new bushes in the area of the escape tunnel that morning.

Steve checked his watch. Another hour had passed. He clicked into the net. "Command, what's the status on contact?"

Dan responded, "Command to One. The phone is ringing now . . . They've answered. They're getting Adams." A long pause followed.

There was a lot on Steve's mind. At that moment, it was the alteration that the Strategic Operations Information Command had made to the FBI deadly force policy, as explained again in full by Teresa Bouche at the last pre-contact briefing.

Normally, a threat (meaning an armed opponent) would be ordered to halt. If, after a warning, he failed to comply, a flash-bang stun grenade would be used to thwart an attack. If the threat persisted or danger was imminent, then deadly force could be used to protect FBI lives. The FBI Deadly Force Policy had been written before the world had become so politically correct. Today there was only one change made to it, but it was a critical one: no one fired a shot until ordered to do so.

Asinine! It made Steve's blood boil. It took a vital decision out of the hands of those on the scene and gave it to faceless entities thousands of miles away.

Steve had argued with the boneheads in SOIC. "So some backwoods maniac attacks me or my guys with a fully automatic weapon and I'm supposed to order him to stop, then throw a flash-bang, but my men and I aren't allowed to shoot! What do we have guns for?"

"We don't want another Ruby Ridge, Mr. Alstead," had been their response.

Neither did Steve. In his opinion, the Ruby Ridge disaster could easily have been avoided, and Randy Weaver's wife and son, along with a federal marshal, would still be alive. The entire situation had been handled so badly that Weaver, the man the Bureau of Alcohol, Tobacco, and Firearms was seeking to arrest, was the only one unhurt. The incident had been such a black mark on U.S. law enforcement services that it had caused a knee-jerk reaction on both sides. The bad guys were mad and wanted revenge, and the good guys weren't allowed to defend themselves!

The good guys had blown it, and now Steve was paying for it. Steve could explain the entire scenario with the six *P*s: "Proper Planning Prevents Pretty Poor Performance."

End of conversation.

He understood where SOIC was coming from, though. The whole AMT case did have the potential to go bad, like a Waco or a Ruby Ridge. First of all, a woman and kids were the key ingredients for disaster in *any* armed confrontation. The boys might shoot. In this case the agent wouldn't shoot to kill but might lose his life trying to do his job gently.

Secondly, the woman and children might be taken hostage by someone in the compound who wanted to use them as human shields.

But the last possibility, one that plagued Steve with nightmares, was accidentally killing a woman the way the Observer-Sniper had done at Ruby Ridge. But again Steve reminded himself that the situation was not going to recur. The fourth basic rule of firearm safety was *Know your target and what is beyond it.* The Observer-Sniper at Ruby had fired at a door, hoping to hit a Tango running inside. Instead he had hit Vicky Weaver while she was holding their child.

Shivering with empathy, Steve recited to himself again. *"Know your target and what is beyond it."*

Experience and discipline were what Steve and all the other HRT operatives were getting paid for. Inside the compound might be a crazed megalomaniac who had already blown total strangers to bits to make some political point and who would fight to the death when trapped . . .

. . . or he might be a grumpy eccentric who playacted a lot and shot his mouth off more than was smart but who had done nothing worthy of a fiery death.

How to tell in a split-second decision?

Dan signaled him in his earpiece. "Echo 1. We've made contact. It appears Adams doesn't believe us. He may be sending out a scout. Hold at ready."

"Ten-four," Steve replied. His heart was pounding in his ears. If anyone exited the tunnel, the plan was to wait. Sierra teams across the bank would order the men to drop their weapons and surrender.

Compliance to this order was the question. Would AMT drop, or would they open fire, possibly hitting one of the 10 stray bushes that were to wait all of it out?

Steve cocked his head to get a better view.

"Command to Echo Teams 1 and 2. Sierra 6 has just reported the heat signatures of two individuals approaching your position via the tunnel."

"Understood, Command."

Anton shot him a wink from under a nearby clump of shrubbery.

On the embankment, in perfect view of the exit, the two snipers of Sierra Team 6 waited under a log, thumbs resting on safeties. Sierra 5 was behind a rock about 20 paces upstream.

Dan warned, "Hold tight, Echo 1 and 2. . . . Guards reported 20 yards from opening . . . nearing grate . . . exiting . . ."

Steve could hear their boots crunching on the brush. He grasped a flash- bang in his vest pocket. If one of the men saw them and raised a weapon, he would have just enough time to throw the thing and tackle one of them.

Dan's voice was a mere whisper in the earpiece, though it seemed like a megaphone. Steve feared the two bad guys, only feet from him now, would hear his radio.

The AMT men, dressed in hardwoods camouflage and military-style caps, stopped about a foot from Steve's head. Neither said a word, but he could see one of their boots as the men rotated around, scanning the gully and the woods beyond.

A bead of sweat ran down Steve's right eyebrow, hanging just above his eye. He was forced to ignore the irritation and the urge to scratch his nose. His thumb slid the pin of the flash-bang to a halfway-out ready position.

Dan's voice spoke softly over the net. "Sierra 6. Instruct the men to lay down their arms."

An instant later Sierra 6 called out, "FBI! Lay down your weapons! Get on your faces!"

The AMT members spun wildly around, trying to figure out where the voice had come from.

As soon as they seemed to pinpoint it, Sierra 5 called out, "FBI! Do it. Now!"

The AMT men turned frantically, trying to spot the men giving them orders. They shuffled slowly backward, still holding their weapons in a Rhodesian-ready position, muzzles level, about waist high.

The No. 5 man on Echo 2, who was hiding even farther upstream, yelled, "Surrender your weapons!"

The AMT guards acted as though completely surrounded by ghosts. They twirled away from the latest command and ran for the tunnel. Steve rolled a stun grenade right into their path.

It exploded with a deafening roar and a brilliant flash. The men were blinded. Both tried to flee back into the compound. One belatedly attempted to cover his eyes, then tripped over a rock. As he hit the ground, he rolled to his back, firing a burst of shots blindly into the air.

Steve sprang toward him as the rifle barrel swung toward his face. Steve yanked the gun away and kicked the man in the head. The other ran toward a bush . . . or what he thought was a bush.

It was Anton.

For the AMTer it was like hitting a slab of granite, or like a 160-pound running back colliding with a 300-pound nose guard for the San Francisco 49ers. A crunching noise resounded and the man crumpled unconscious. His weapon fell at his side.

Sight returned to the still-conscious guard under Steve's foot. He hardly breathed when 14 HRT men appeared, seemingly out of thin air. All had their rifles leveled.

Dan's voice was frantic for a reply. "One! Report on shots fired."

Panting, Steve backed away from the man, speaking between gasps of air. "Suspect accidentally fired shots . . . no injuries . . . two scouts . . . stunned with a flash-bang . . . one unconscious. Both have been disarmed . . . and taken into custody."

"Good work, Echo 1 and 2! Replacements are on the way. Secure prisoners until Teams 7 and 8 arrive."

Steve considered the tunnel. Now might be a good time to exploit it as a surprise entry. "Echo Leader to Command. Is tunnel still clear and should we take it? Over."

"Negative, Echo 1. Tunnel is clear, but we do not want to shrink the perimeter at this time."

The sound of booted feet tromping up the creek caught Steve's attention. Two lines of five men, all dressed in camouflage, appeared. The two AMTers, both awake but groggy, were handcuffed and hauled to their feet.

A salt-and-pepper-haired, blue-eyed buck with a jaw like an alligator trotted up to Steve. "Echo 7 Actual, reporting in relief."

"Thanks, Echo 7. Echo 1 Actual, accepting relief," Steve replied, stepping down from command.

Echo 1 and 2 escorted the prisoners back to the local field headquarters that had been set up just around the bend near the entrance to the Adams property. Dan had reported that once the shots were heard, two of the listening posts ran like greyhounds for the compound.

The prisoners were taken to the Prison Picnic Paddywagon, a van with bars on all the windows like the ones usually used to transport convict labor gangs.

Dan filled Steve in on the other details. "At the moment the stun grenade went off, the whole compound came alive. The guys inside knew we were here, but without a working radio, none of the guards or listening posts outside had any idea what was going on. Two of them, the ones by the stream, ran back to tell Adams. We got three of the other patrols. One more got away, and ran inside. The outside of the compound is clear now, and we're starting to shrink the perimeter."

Steve scratched his scruffy chin. "Why didn't we secure the tunnel from the inside?"

"Strategic Command thinks it would be too aggressive to penetrate that deeply this soon. They don't want to upset the AMT guys. And from a command point of view, I agree. I have concerns about things ROBI may have missed, or somebody tossing a frag grenade down the chute."

"Sure, I understand," Steve replied, though he knew the impatience in his tone conflicted with his words. He knew these sieges could and did go on for weeks, even months, when suspects were allowed to hole up inside their little Bubba forts. Waco had gone on for 51 days. "What's up with Adams?"

"Latest is he knows we're here."

Steve laughed. "When you tell him he's surrounded, and shots are fired, and five of his guys don't come back, that's understandable."

Dan jokingly replied, "Well, you know these Bubbas can be a little slow. They don't always get it the first time. Anyway, moments after Adams told us to get lost, smoke began to pour from his workshop furnace. It looks like he may be cooking up something."

"Or destroying something," Steve interjected.

"The same thought crossed our minds," Dan agreed. "As soon as the intel reached Teresa she instructed him, under order of the FBI, to put out the fire."

"And what did he say?"

"Told her to go to Hell's Canyon and us to get another negotiator 'cause he doesn't deal with women!"

"No?" Steve denied in disbelief. "He won't talk to her?"

"No. He made some crack about Janet Reno, too, so Charles Downing and Chuck Maines are gonna deal with him until we get some big shot in."

Steve could hardly believe his ears. Teresa's duties were being yanked away from her. "You've got to wonder what she's thinking," he pondered, surprised at his own sympathetic response.

"Yeah, first you and now Adams. She's liable to kill you both."

The two men laughed.

Then Steve's face grew serious again. "So now what?"

"We wait," Dan replied. "We can't raid the place based on suspicion that he was involved with the BB, so officially it's a standoff until he surrenders and lets us come in."

Steve considered all the supplies and the naturally flowing well Adams had inside the compound. "That could be years."

"True, but it's better to camp out here for years than risk the life of Adams's wife or kids."

That point of view did put everything in perspective. A slightly crazy man who built a fortified compound and was ready for war, if pressed, might do something stupid. The No. 1 rule of hostage negotiations: *play for time.* More often than not the threatened one would mentally wear down and eventually give up or at least let hostages go in the process. Steve knew that a raid might escalate things beyond repair—and end in a bloodbath. Heaven forbid something might happen to the kids. *"Servare Vitas,"* he quoted the HRT's Latin motto.

"To Save Lives," Dan agreed. "Go get some rest, buddy. You'll be on again before you know it."

The cot in the back of the mobile bungalow felt nice. After lying curled up in the dirt, pretending to be a bush for seven hours, anything else seemed a feather bed in comparison.

He nodded off to sleep, dreaming of Cindy and his boys.

San Luis Obispo, California
11:01 A.M. Pacific Time

TO EVERYTHING THERE IS A PURPOSE

Closed casket. Not a surprise. There was barely enough left of Frank Daley to be called a corpse. Enclosed in the deep mahogany coffin was the reality of the impersonal CNN newscast. But those at the service felt grief beyond measure.

The enormous sanctuary of the old adobe mission was packed with hundreds of friends and coworkers from the plant he had managed. Was there anyone who had known him who hadn't loved the man? This man who had seemed to give his all for others?

The overflow crowd spilled onto the steps and into the outdoor mission plaza where news cameras recorded this final farewell for 15 seconds on the evening broadcast.

His family filled eight front pews. *How many sisters, brothers, children, and grandchildren are here?* Cindy wondered as she took her seat near the back of the church. She recognized Frank Daley's daughter, Carmen, the principal of Tommy's preschool. Beside Carmen was the bowed red head of her son, Aaron. Behind them sat all Aaron's classmates, many of them members of the baseball team. Cindy caught sight of Matthew next to Michael Salim. The two were directly behind Aaron.

Aaron had not been back to school since the day his grandfather's death had been confirmed. After that, the entire school had been unusually somber. Everyone knew Mr. Daley. He and Paul Salim coached the middle- school baseball team together. His joy and enthusiasm had made up for Paul Salim's too-serious attitude. Frank Daley was the guy at pancake breakfasts who always made whipped-cream happy faces on the pancakes for preschoolers. The man who marched in pro-life candlelight vigils and donated a baby crib every month to the home for unwed mothers. He quietly paid tuition to educate dozens of underprivileged kids. Every year he personally led Cindy's fifth-grade students on a tour of the plant for science day. The annual field trip had been scheduled for next week. Permission slips had already been returned. The fire pits at Avila Beach had been reserved for the class barbecue.

Cindy would cancel the event, of course. What else could she do?

There were few flowers around Daley's bier. Contributions were to be made in his name to families of victims of the BART bombing. He would have expected that, approved of it.

Today in the ancient church building, the somber realization that everyone had been injured by this senseless act descended on the citizens of San Luis.

How could the life of Frank Daley be weighed against the political aims of some terrorist organization? Had they accomplished anything by slaughtering so many innocent victims? By cutting short the life of someone so loved?

But this was not what Father Jerry spoke about when he reviewed Frank Daley's life. No. Frank would not have wished the tragedy of his death to be discussed—only the victory of his life, his personal belief in Jesus, his hope in the resurrection and the world to come. He would have wanted everyone he left behind to believe that he had died for a reason. Someday, Father Jerry explained, the reason would be known, even if it could not now be understood. While in the chaos of despair, there seemed to be no purpose. But even in the darkness, God would be there. And for everyone left behind, God gave the mercy of discovering his great love through their great grief. "Blessed are they who mourn, for they shall be comforted. . . ."

In the meantime, there was the coffin. And the family, the friends, and the entire city wondered what on earth God had been thinking to let such a good man die in such a terrible way. What good could be gained from this? Each mourner would have to come to terms with the horror and sadness in his or her own way.

The hymns were sung, the prayers recited. Six strong, grown-up veterans of Frank Daley's baseball team carried what little remained of their beloved coach out to the hearse.

So it ended.

Cindy moved slowly through the crowd to embrace Carmen Daley and give Aaron's arm a friendly squeeze. Her eyes expressed her sorrow. "The kids loved your father," Cindy said to Carmen.

"He lived for them." Carmen's voice was husky with emotion. "He was so looking forward to the field trip. Showing off his little world. Inspiring little physicists."

"We'll be sorry to miss it," Cindy agreed. "A high point in the year."

"Oh, but you can't cancel it! We'll ask Paul Salim! He's interim manager of the plant now. Dad would want Paul to take them around."

Cindy knew Mr. Salim best through parent-teacher conferences about Michael. He was a quiet, introverted man who lacked people skills and parenting skills. Cindy had often thought it was no surprise that Michael was always vying for attention. Paul Salim had all the personality of a stone. How would he ever fill Frank Daley's shoes?

At that Cindy caught sight of Salim's dark, brooding form. His normally contemplative expression had taken on a haunted aspect.

Carmen motioned to Salim. "Paul! Paul! Come here!"

Clasping his hands, he joined the two women. He looked uncomfortable in his suit. The knot of his green paisley tie was crooked. He barely acknowledged Cindy. Perhaps he was also suffering acutely from the loss of his friend.

Carmen said, "You know Daddy had this annual trip for the fifth graders coming up. Did Michael tell you? So, I was saying to Cindy, you'll lead the group, won't you, Paul?"

The small man seemed alarmed at the prospect. He hesitated, then agreed. "Sure. Yeah, sure." His Persian accent was slurred. "Frank would like this if I should do it."

Cindy added, "We'll call it Frank Daley Day. Every year from now on."

"Yes." Carmen's face clouded. "Daddy would like that."

HRT Command Center, Bear Mining Camp
Hell's Canyon, Idaho
1:35 P.M. Mountain Time

MURPHY'S LAW

There was no such thing as a perfect mission—only those whose problems had not yet appeared and still waited to be confronted.

No plan survives first contact with the enemy. Or, to put it in Murphy's inimitable way: If something can go wrong, it will, and at the worst possible time, in the worst possible way.

Bingo.

That summary of despair was mild compared to how things were going for HRT when Steve was rousted from his cot. Still in his tactical assault vest, he hauled himself up like a sunken ship being raised from a waterlogged depth. A brisk jog to headquarters behind the messenger made him aware that suddenly everything was fouled up beyond all repair.

Chapter 16's Downing and Teresa Bouche, along with Dan and Chuck, huddled around the conference table.

"The satellite link's down!" reported Downing. "Talks with Adams broke off two hours ago, even though he called his attorneys and the FBI, confirming that we are in fact FBI and we do in fact have a search warrant."

"Why?"

"Why does a guy hole up in the woods with ticks and mosquitoes for company and teach other guys to hate everyone with a different skin color? Does his reasoning have to make sense?" Downing challenged.

"But what's different now from our point of view? Why the sense of urgency?"

Downing avoided looking at Teresa, as if he were hoping Chuck or Dan would take the lead. When neither did, he continued, "Because CNN broadcast a story about our being here and linked it to the BART bomb."

"What?!" Steve bellowed, staring at Dan. "True?" he demanded.

Dan grimaced. "Somebody leaked it. Adams has heard the whole nation being told that he is suspect *numero uno* in the latest domestic terrorism and—get this—that we have orders to shoot to kill."

With the circumstance that precipitated the crisis now detailed, Downing took over again. "Now he's afraid to come out. And there's more. Intel suggests the smoke coming from his furnace, well, destroying evidence is everybody's read on it. Which is why we've got to step things up to code red. Everybody's ready to go in."

This had all the earmarks of a total disaster. "What has Strategic Command said about this?" Steve asked, worried.

Teresa informed him, "We're waiting for their answer after a consult with the attorney general, but the Satellite Communications System is down."

They all stared at Steve.

"What? I can't make this decision. You've all seen the orders. No one shoots unless given permission. And I won't order my guys into a firefight without Weapons Free. What about the B-com?"

Downing shook his head. "They're not working in the woods any farther than our local com net does. We've sent a team to get a landline open, then strung a relay of radio contacts between here and there."

"Great," Steve muttered. "Who's got the tin cans and the string?"

With that, the team broke apart to review tactical plans and other talking points.

Dan and Steve sat down together over new intel. "Night Stalker is grounded during the day; however, we have information from Sierra teams." Dan showed Steve on a map. "There are armed sentries in every window of the three hardened buildings. It's believed that the woman and the kids are in the west wing, underground. On the south building is the furnace. This is our greatest area of concern, where all the work is being done. The eastern house is suspected to be the armory, where Adams's men may fall back."

Three AMT snipers were in the central tower. Their guns were visible from the ground, forcing all to keep to heavy cover. Under normal conditions the FBI would have deemed the visual display of weapons after their identity had been confirmed to be a reasonable cause for using deadly force.

But the present conditions were far from normal. In the present haze of orders, countersniping was out of the question. Without the permission of higher authority, any unauthorized shooting would be a plan for an early retirement, at the very least.

The AMT men were bold in their actions. It was almost as if they knew HRT's hands were tied, or were so guilty that they were preparing to go down fighting rather than give up.

Something wasn't right. Steve could tell there was a disconnect somewhere. But as the tactical chief, his duties forced him to deal with the present confrontation. "We can't sit around waiting for them to start something," he argued. "Suppose they come out shooting? What about the tunnel?"

"Should have taken it earlier," Dan replied sadly. "ROBI went for another visit and, as far as we can tell, the top of the shaft above the ladder is now sealed shut with some pretty heavy-duty plate."

"Jim Sorveno, explosives . . ."

"Already working on a design with Semtex ribbon. He's planning to line the frame with a directed blast and blow the thing in. But it's going to be slow going and unpredictable, deep in the tunnel, and at the top of the ladder. . . ."

HRT Command Center, Bear Mining Camp
Hell's Canyon, Idaho
2:22 P.M. Mountain Time

SHAITON'S FIRE

As the sun exchanged the eastern half of the Idaho sky for the west, so too did the mountain winds back into the opposite quarter and gain intensity.

By one o'clock a breeze had kicked up. By 2:22 it had become a gale force that howled around the command trailer, rattling the slender radio mast as if it were a buggy whip being cracked by an invisible coachman.

In the sparsely decorated but cluttered communications center, Miles Miller ran his fingers over his matted curls. Leaning back in his chair in front of several computers, he spoke with Dr. Turnow on the video-conferencing monitor. "Yeah, I got the info you sent. I've done a little bit of the digital layering you requested with Adobe Photoshop. It should be coming now."

Through a mild blizzard of video noise the image of Dr. Turnow responded, "As I said before, it strikes me as entirely too coincidental that this man would turn up with the remains of a tattoo so much like the one the bombing suspect displayed."

Miles agreed, tapping away on a keyboard. "And dead, too."

"Yes, Miles," Turnow noted, "that too. Okay, here it comes." Turnow's image bowed oddly as he leaned slightly away from the video camera's focus. "Yes, the image is coming up on my monitor now."

Miles explained, "I'm sending you an animation in real time. It documents the process of layering 12 individual images that were shifted and adjusted for size so they are flat." Turnow's face flickered. "Let's just hope the wind doesn't knock out the link before you get them."

On the monitor in front of Miles, a slow, slightly stuttering animation began with a close-up of the dead man's hand. Over the top of this a blurry, partial image of the tattoo glimpsed by the subway ticket agent's camera appeared. Step by step its resolution was enhanced. The fraction of the black-and-white image rotated and shifted as it became clearer.

Miles continued his explanation. "The reshaped, resized, flattened images were then laid on in order to build a high-res picture of the tattoo."

Dr. Turnow looked to the side as the construct appeared on his monitor. "Well done, Miles! See how exactly the lines connect, even including the little bobble where something made the tattoo artist jerk slightly. The enhanced photo looks like a definite match with the dead man's tattoo."

"I know," Miles noted with uncharacteristic simplicity. "But what I couldn't do was find any matches in the NCIC database with the squiggly scorpion. Scrawls and half loops. It looks like some Arabic tattooist was drunk when he did it."

Turnow, who continued to view the animated reconstruction process, was distracted by what Miles had said. "Arabic," he responded in astonishment. "Miles, you may be on to something. It does look like Arabic writing."

Miles acted surprised at his own comment. "It does?"

Dr. Turnow jumped with excitement. "Can you see the break in the squiggles, right where the tail turns up and curls back around?"

Miles nodded.

"Pull up the image in Photoshop again."

"All right." Miles hacked away until the image popped up on a white screen in front of him. "Got it."

Turnow squinted as he leaned forward. "See the break there, where the tail starts, as distinct from the body? I want you to separate those into two parts. . . ."

"Right," was Miles's succinct reply. "I think I know where you're going." On the monitor he clicked the dotted box outline tool in Photoshop. Very carefully Miles outlined the scorpion's tail as Dr. Turnow instructed. He lifted half of the image away, separating it into two parts. Moving the mouse to the toolbar, he scrolled down, selecting *Rotate.* "What do you think? Should I rotate it 90 degrees?"

After studying the image on his end, Dr. Turnow responded. "Try 270."

Miles's eyes opened wide. The result was what looked for all the world like two pieces of Arabic script. Miles paired them back again, close together, but side by side instead of crossing each other.

"Believe it!" Turnow exclaimed. "We're on to something. Miles, can you get into the NCIC database?"

"You want me to cross-check the squiggles?"

"Exactly."

Miles glanced at the third computer next to him. "It's right here. I'll just have to transport the image over to that network and paste it into the search engine."

Dr. Turnow had the look of a determined but impatient scientist on the verge of discovering a cure for a rare disease, bogged down by slow growth in the petri dish. "Have you done it?"

Tersely Miles announced, "I'm gettin' there." He piped the image through from one computer to the next and pasted it into the inquiry box.

Turnow leaned close to the camera, as if listening for a clue from 600 miles away. "What's it saying?"

Miles clicked *Search.* "It's looking . . ."

Another gust of wind shook the trailer. The video feed of Dr. Turnow temporarily faded to only static.

Miles slapped the top of the monitor, as if that would help. "Are you there?"

Barely audible, Dr. Turnow replied, "What's that? I couldn't—"

An alarming crash rattled the trailer. Miles leaned toward the window to see what had struck it. "Not again!" he moaned. "The local net antenna is down!"

"I'm sorry?"

Mumbling to himself, Miles said, "One more thing I'll have to fix."

"Say again," Dr. Turnow called.

"It's searching!" Miles snapped.

Words flashed across the inquiry box. Miles read aloud. "One match found . . . two matches . . ." The number of cross-check hits suddenly racked up. "Three hundred, four hundred . . . 437 hits found."

Dr. Turnow could hardly wait. "What do they say?"

Miles acted baffled. "All 437? I can't read that fast."

Turnow shook his head and rubbed his face with frustration.

Miles opened the first entry. He read it aloud. "It says Shaiton. This program suggests English equivalents . . . for that word it reads 'Satan.' The second word is 'Nar.' Translated, it means 'Satan's Fire.' "

Turnow lifted his head. "Go on."

"According to NCIC, Shaiton's Fire is a small, radical wing of Hezbollah, responsible for violence in Lebanon and northern Israel, bombings and the murder of hostages, and violence against Americans, thought to be partially responsible for the bombing of the American Embassy in Zaire, as well as—"

"Wait, Miles!" Turnow interrupted as a terrible thought came to him. "What's happening at the AMT compound?"

Miles paused to consider the question. "The standoff. Steve and the guys have orders to go in."

"Do you know what this means?" Turnow stood up and, in his agitation, disappeared from Miles's view.

"Yeah, it means this dead guy had a tattoo that said something about Satan, and I bet it's not because he's a heavy-metal freak."

Turnow leaned close to his camera. His face loomed large on the screen. "And this means we've been hoodwinked. AMT isn't responsible for the BART bombing. But somebody else wants us to think so." Then, in a rush, "You've got to get hold of them. Tell Steve! Stop them before they make an irreparable mistake."

The weight of what Turnow said hit Miles at once, for he shot out of his seat to grab the dangling radio mike. "Command! Command! This is Bear HQ. Do you read me? Command?"

The antenna was down!

Miles's jaw fell open and his eyes were wide. "Communications are out. I'm gonna have to drive down to AMT."

"Go!" Turnow exclaimed. "Tell them to hold and do not attack! I'll get Morrison! Go!"

In an instant Miles was out the door, roaring down the dusty gravel road in a Jeep.

AMT Compound
Hell's Canyon, Idaho
3:11 P.M. Mountain Time

POINT OF ENTRY

The entire situation had become way too tense, way too soon.

There would be no shooting until a green light was given from Strategic Command. But contact couldn't be made because communications were down. Yet there was reasonable cause and an urgent reason to go in. And Adams still maintained a stony silence. What were his intentions? Would he negotiate further, or would the next exchange be of bullets?

Against all his instincts, Steve prepared to assault the tunnel.

Jim Sorveno, FBI demolitions expert, spread out all of his needed supplies on a shiny blue tarp. Even at a full run it would take Echo 1 at least 15 seconds to escort him to the back of the tunnel. It was obviously a requirement to prepare as much as possible outside.

A large loop of Semtex ribbon was rigged to be pressed around the frame of the defensive plate. Sorveno explained, "I'll tie the ribbon in with the detonator. There'll be a small charge placed behind it, set to go off a millisecond after the ribbon. The door frame will be cut loose and an instant later blown inward."

Steve was impressed. "Sounds like a good plan."

"If we're lucky," Sorveno continued, "we won't lose the ladder."

"Good thinking," Steve complimented, thinking of one more consideration. "One to Command. What of the camera in the tunnel?"

Dan clicked in. "Sierra 6 took it out with a sound-suppressed round an hour ago. AMT is blind in the tunnel. Status on explosives?"

Steve looked to Sorveno, who gave him a thumbs-up. "Ready."

"Okay now, here is the plan," Dan explained. "We want you guys to place the charge and then get out of there. Understood?"

Steve made individual eye contact with the other 19 entry men, who each nodded. "Everyone understands, Command."

"Go when ready."

Sorveno carefully picked up his gear. As point man Steve led the charge up the tunnel. Two more men followed, then Sorveno, who was protected by two more guys from the Echo 1 Team. Steve prayed ROBI had been accurate in his findings. The thought of a booby-trap going off overhead reminded Steve of when he was little, playing hide-and-seek in the dark. He had feared the devil was behind him. And the faster he had run, the more he was afraid and the faster he would run.

He cringed at each light box. Every one he passed sent a shiver down his spine. Soon they were at the back of the tunnel. Steve cleared the foxhole and the left turn. No. 2 sighted in on the ladder. The others panned their guns back and forth with their fingers above their triggers as Sorveno climbed the ladder with what looked like a long Play-Doh rope connected to a small digital alarm clock.

"It's remote," he explained as he installed it, "in case someone from inside acquires it and tries to use it."

"Good," Steve responded hastily. "Get on with it and let's get out of here!"

Sorveno leaned against the fireman's pole for balance. He squished the soft ribbon around the outline of the door. The radio detonator was pressed onto the center and connected with wires to each corner. Multiple points of detonation would ensure an even explosion.

"All set," Sorveno called out, sliding down the pole.

"Roll out!" Steve commanded the men.

Anywhere within the tunnel the shock wave from that amount of Semtex would be enough to crush a man's skull. The blast would go two directions—in and out. Steve knew that in-between was not a good place to be. "Move it! Move it!" he yelled as they charged out. Steve was the last in line. "Command," he said to Dan, "this is Echo 1. Charges are in place."

"Command to One. Exit tunnel to safe location. Still awaiting contact from Comlink. Over."

Steve waited with his head in the dirt, along with the other guys. It seemed now that a dynamic entry was imminent. There was no time to wonder if they were doing the right thing, if Adams was guilty or innocent of the BART bombing. There was no time left to fret over his wife and kids.

"Word relayed from SOIC," Dan's voice came over the radio. "Permission has been given to raid, but not to shoot perimeter Tangos. Repeat, Sierra units hold fast."

Steve knew that meant his team could get inside; however, the AMT snipers in their central tower would still be alive and able to fire down into the compound. There would be no preliminary strike to take them out. For a split second after they emerged from the tunnel, he and his men would be sitting ducks.

"Arm explosive. . . ."

Sorveno turned a key on a tiny black box. A red switch glowed from beneath a clear protective lid.

"Stand by to blow door. . . ."

Sorveno lifted the tiny cover. His thumb was poised above the button.

There was a disturbance on the command circuit.

Steve pressed the earpiece tighter in place, trying to make out what was going on. "I didn't copy that. Say again."

It sounded like Miles Miller. But he had no business in the command center. What was he playing at?

"Have you got a link to Adams?" Steve heard Miles demand.

"Miller, get out of here," Dan retorted.

"Urgent from Morrison. Is that the phone link? Give it to me!"

A fraction of a second, the tiniest portion of an inch, separated Sorveno's thumb from the button, the fire from the explosives, and the planned attack from the reality.

"Adams!" Miles's voice quavered with nervousness. "You've been set up! We know you didn't do the bombing. Tell your people not to shoot!"

Suddenly it was Dan's voice, frantic and urgent, "Stand down! Hold charge! Hold charge! Disarm door. We have a restored link to Morrison. Nobody move."

Steve held his breath as Sorveno carefully turned off the key and closed the lid of the remote detonator.

AMT Compound
Hell's Canyon, Idaho
4:20 P.M. Mountain Time

WRAP-UP

Stiff with fatigue and anxiety, it was with unutterable relief that Steve heard Dan over the Comlink, "Command to all units. He's surrendering. Adams and his men are coming out!"

It had taken another hour of intense negotiations before the standoff was broken. Adams had to be convinced that the latest turn of events was not some trick designed to lure him out of his fort. Only after reams of legalese went back and forth between Washington and Idaho did the AMT leader agree to capitulate and allow the FBI to make an unopposed entry into his compound.

It was the most desirable of all possible outcomes to an armed confrontation: no shooting, no injuries, no deaths. As was true of any standoff, real success came with *not* having to pull the trigger.

"To Save Lives." That meant all lives from women and children to those of the suspected bad guys. As had been proved time and again, all the firepower in the world was best used when it remained unused.

Steve looked to the sky. "Thank you, God," he called out spontaneously. And for the first time in a long time, he truly *was* grateful. God had kept them all safe and prevented a lot of people from dying—maybe even Steve himself.

Murmurs of assent came from the other team members.

Thirty minutes later, at the gates of the fortress, the AMT men marched out with their hands laced behind their heads. Andrew Adams followed with his wife and two boys. Adams assured the FBI there was no one left inside and there were no booby traps.

When asked why he surrendered, he said, "Because I am innocent of the charges and a businessman as well as a soldier. And I have decided I will do whatever is needed to clear my name of any suspicion."

It was good enough for Steve, though he still had to reconnoiter the buildings. As the men searched the compound, room by room, cupboards and closets, Steve knew it would have been a nasty battle. Automatic weapons, shotguns, and pistols were everywhere.

Inside the building were barricades and shooting slits that not only opened to the outside but also covered from room to room. Fighting inside would have been difficult, even for the highly trained HRT. There was no doubt they would have overcome the AMT eventually, but not without heavy casualties.

When the Echo 1 Team reached the armory workshop, Steve found the walls lined with every assault rifle imaginable. There were probably a hundred—AR-15s, AR-10s, FN-FALs, HKs, and M1As. Upon examining them, Steve realized that all of them were missing trigger groups. He felt the furnace. It was still hot.

It seemed as though Adams had been working to clear his name, most likely melting down all of the parts that illegally converted guns to fully automatic weapons. Suspicion was one thing, but it would be awfully hard to prove that a pile of slag in the bottom of a furnace was a federal offense.

In light of the new evidence uncovered by Miles and Dr. Turnow, it was decided to withdraw Chapter 16 from Idaho. The remainder of the investigation there and the interrogation of Adams was left in the hands of Chuck and the FBI unit.

Every investigation involved exploring blind alleys and leads that went nowhere. But seldom had one come so close to starting a shooting war, only to be stopped at literally the last second.

TWELVE

Chapter 16 Forensics Lab
San Francisco
Sunday, 29 April
8:02 P.M. Pacific Time

WHERE DO WE GO FROM HERE?

The walls that weren't glass were a high-gloss white in Dr. Turnow's lab. Gas chromatographs and high-speed centrifuges shared space with more prosaic things like digital scales, rubber tubing, computers, and printers. The strong smell of disinfectant prevailed. A pair of minus-80 degree refrigerators hummed in the corner by the entrance.

In the center of the room was a high and wide lab table. At its head stood Senator Morrison, who was in charge of the meeting. Around the table Steve, Dr. Turnow, Teresa Bouche, Charles Downing, and Miles Miller all leaned over a detailed blueprint. It was a printout of the BART Red Line, from beginning to end, rendered in the size and shape of a high school wall map of the world, but much more intricately illustrated. Steve read some of the small details that had been sticky-taped to the map.

Morrison was busy summarizing the Idaho outcome. "Remember,

we're not ruling Adams out altogether. He could still be involved in the bombing, either directly or as a supplier. However, this connection between the bombing and the group Shaiton's Fire, made by Dr. Turnow and Miles, was an eleventh-hour, fifty-ninth-minute lifesaver, preventing what might have been a costly and terrible mistake. Well done."

Miles stuttered, unable to manage more than half a word.

"It's okay, Miles," Morrison said. "You need not speak." He cupped his hand to the side of his mouth and joked, "Better not. We don't want you to ruin the moment for yourself."

The team laughed.

Miles blushed, blinked, and stuttered. "A-all r-r-right."

The senator began delving deeply into the current considerations for the case. "We now believe Idaho was a false lead. We know that most terrorists want to claim responsibility for their acts, since that's essentially the point of committing the act: to gain some power by asserting their ability to create panic. So the first question is, why would they not take credit? Was planting a false lead the only consideration, or is there more to it than that?"

Steve had trouble believing that the trip to Idaho was all for nothing. He interjected with a raised hand, "How certain are we that AMT has nothing to do with the bombing?"

Downing suggested, "Aside from the fact that after the raid we found nothing to support such a connection, profile data suggests that a guy with a profile like Adams would never support or associate with a group such as Shaiton's Fire. Also, he's remarkably cooperative in naming contacts and candid about his group."

Satisfied, Steve sank down in his seat to listen without further comment.

"Accurately stated," Morrison agreed. "So why does a terrorist group carry out a violent and devastating attack and not take credit?"

The team quietly awaited the answer to his rhetorical question.

"Two reasons. Because they either want to throw us off their trail in order to carry out more plans . . ."

Steve took the opportunity to reassert himself. "Which supports the idea of Idaho being tactical misinformation."

"Yes," Morrison agreed, shaking his index finger. "And secondly, the bombing, which was an act of terrorism, may also have been the act of something else."

Teresa brushed blonde strands of hair from her face. "What else could that be?"

"Let's explore that in detail," replied Morrison as he turned to a white- board outline with the heading "The Many Faces of Terrorism." "There are various motivations, as you know, for committing a terrorist act. It could be blatant, such as taking lives to cause panic, or more focused. I just want to play devil's advocate here. Feel free to jump in." Removing the cap from a black marker, he underlined the phrase "Blatant Act of Terror." "The BART bombing was a horrible crime. We may not need to look any further for motive."

He tapped the next line of words with a dry-erase marker. "Second, the type of terrorism we are seeing more these days is economic terrorism. Attacking the World Trade Center is a good example. Besides the cost in human lives, it was a blatant attack on our economy as well. With BB, the target may have been the West Coast financial center."

Morrison clasped his hands together, bringing them to his chin. "The terrorists were not very effective in attaining that objective. However, to destroy the main feature of transportation in a financial area that is highly dependent on skilled workers is effective in its own respect. The city is crowded with white-collar workers making other arrangements, people who are afraid to go into work, businesses forced to make allowances which cost them. People lose money for time off. It costs the city vast sums of money to repair the extensive damage."

Teresa added, "The IRA does this in England."

"Precisely!" snapped Morrison. "But in every case they do it for a political reason. Terrorism 101. So again I stress, why did the group not take credit?"

Downing had, for once, slumped in his chair. Sleep deprivation had evidently taken its toll on him. He blinked quickly. "That is the million-dollar question."

Morrison slashed through another line on the board. "Moving to the next. This one is more uncommon, more unusual. A focused attack."

Steve understood. "Like an assassination?"

"Maybe," Morrison coaxed. "Why? Who? At the time of the attack, what was going on in the city?"

No one knew the answer to that question.

"We're not ruling anything out!" Morrison said. "Not yet! And as a result we are putting together comprehensive profiles for everyone on that train. I don't care if the victim was a newborn or an invalid. Whose grandmother was she? Whose nephew was he? Did he have a connection to the defense establishment, or fund pro-Israel rallies? Did she write novels about Middle Eastern history that someone may have disagreed with? When we finish this investigation, we'll know. In the meantime, I have a few assignments for Chapter 16."

Almost simultaneously the five team members opened notebooks and planners and electronic data organizers.

"Teresa," called Morrison, "we'll be holding a press conference today in relation to the Idaho situation."

"You mean the standoff," she corrected. "Thanks to a leak and CNN we can't deny our suspicions."

"Rumors," Morrison stated emphatically. "That's all they are. A special investigation team met with Andrew Adams because he has offered to assist us with the investigation."

Clarifying a related issue, Teresa asked, "So I'm not to mention Shaiton's Fire?"

Morrison nodded. "Correct. That name doesn't exist. And Dr. Turnow," Morrison continued, "please stand by to assist Teresa. Thereafter keep on with what you're doing. The forensic summaries are very helpful. Please take the liberty to follow what needs following. For everything that comes in, please highlight the pertinent, the critical, and the highly likely."

"Yes, Senator." Dr. Turnow returned to his notes and his coffee as Morrison angled on Downing.

"Charles, conversely, your job . . ."

Downing finished the sentence for him. ". . . is to get on the phone with my CIA friends and find out everything that I can about this group—where they are, who they are, what attacks they might have carried out before. . . ."

"The five *W*s and the *H*," Morrison furthered his statement. "Run the gamut on Shaiton's Fire. And Miles, you can assist him until we need you to process some more information into the database."

Steve doodled with his pen. What on earth could his job possibly be? He was a tactical consultant, not a hired researcher or a legman for running down unlikely leads. He dreaded the thought of what was coming.

Morrison cleared his throat and smiled. "Steve, well, relax. You've been the most under the gun . . . literally. The rest of the boys at HRT have tomorrow off. Get some rest. We'll see you here at 0900 Tuesday."

Steve was at a loss for words. *Did I ever luck out,* he realized as the eyes of the jealous foursome burned into him like lasers. "Thanks, Senator. I'd like to head down the coast to see my wife and kids tomorrow."

"Fine, fine, but keep your B-com handy. You never know when there may be a call in the middle of the night."

"Sure thing," Steve replied, remembering the two and a half years he had spent with HRT. Some days a guy slept with his pager clipped to his ear for fear of missing an emergency call.

Morrison wrapped up the meeting. "So far we have over 320 victims, and 44 names related to disappearances. So plug away. It may be a day or two before we get the rest of the other 10 unmatched victims' identities confirmed. Dismissed."

Hardly able to contain himself, Steve avoided eye contact with the rest of the team as he skipped out. He had been feeling desperate to visit his boys. It would be good to see Cindy too, he thought. At least, he hoped it would be.

The Alstead Condo
Morro Bay, California
8:56 P.M. Pacific Time

COMFORT FOOD

Cindy sent Matthew off with a shopping basket to cruise the dairy case for milk, cottage cheese, sour cream, and stuff for lunches, while she gathered the rest of the items on their list.

He returned with chocolate milk, three different kinds of ice cream, frozen corn dogs, raspberry tarts, Oreo cookies, and a big bag of M&Ms.

Comfort food.

This evening Cindy didn't make him put it back. One look told her how bad the kid felt. How much he missed his dad.

Well, Cindy missed Steve too. Since the breakup, she had found a new church, but the damage to Steve's faith and their relationship had already been done. Tonight she and the boys would go home, put away the groceries, and leave the junk food within easy reach. They would get their jammies on, microwave corn dogs, plug *Star Wars* into the VCR, and eat ice cream decorated with M&Ms. Tommy would mimic Yoda. Matthew would be Luke Skywalker for a night. Cindy would eat like she was Jabba the Hutt. They would forget for a while that they were on their own.

Their little condo on Morro Avenue was dark when they got home. It would take two trips to unload all the groceries from the back of the Yukon and carry them up the stairs to the kitchen. Arms full of bags, hearts heavy in spite of the loot, mother and sons ascended the steps.

"Phone's ringing," Tommy said.

Sure enough. Cindy juggled the load and tried to get the key into the lock. Inside, the answering machine picked up.

Cindy heard her own voice. "You've reached the Alstead residence. We're not able to come to the phone . . ."

"Hurry, Mom!" Matthew chided.

She dropped the house key. Quickly she set down the food and groped in the dark as Steve's voice came over the speaker.

"Hey, babe. Matthew? Tommy? You guys there?"

Matthew cried, "It's Dad! Hurry!"

"I'm trying!" Cindy fumbled it again. Then, victory! She recovered the key and found the lock!

Steve continued the message. "It's Dad. Okay, guess not . . . just wanted to tell you, Matthew, I got a break, time off for good behavior—so I'm coming to the game tomorrow."

The door flew open.

"Don't hang up!" Tommy shouted.

"Dad!" Matthew flung down ice cream, M&Ms, and chocolate milk. The plastic milk bottle burst open on the entryway tile.

Matthew sprinted up the stairs.

Steve signed off. "Okay, then. See you there. Love you guys . . . *all* of you."

Click.

After she cleaned up the chocolate milk, Cindy tried to reach Steve again. No answer. Why didn't he ever leave his answering machine on? She would talk to him about that.

Matthew replayed the message three times just to be sure he hadn't heard wrong. Dad would be at the game. It was good to have the promise recorded.

So the trio got their jammies on, cuddled together on the sofa, and watched *Star Wars.* They ate their corn dogs and devoured their junk food together. It was a wonderful evening.

Steve was coming home.

THIRTEEN

Bodega Bay, California
Monday, 30 April
8 A.M. Pacific Time

IT'S A SMALL WORLD AFTER ALL

The sea breeze whistled past the hilltop above Bodega Bay. Khalil pressed the GSP1600 satellite phone tighter to his ear. "The lab additions are satisfactory?" he inquired. "Your equipment is adequate and your assistants competent?"

"Da . . . yes," Oleg Petrov replied. "The new scanning force microscope was at first not functioning properly, but that has been remedied. Ten millions of American dollars purchases many fine toys."

The digitized voices of the two men bounced off a network of 36 Low Earth Orbit satellites circling 876 miles above the planet. The system, covering 80 percent of the earth's surface, could be accessed by a handset the size of a cell phone. The scrambled relay had a three-second delay. It made conversations difficult but not impossible, so long as neither party interrupted the other.

"And our North Korean friends continue to treat you well?"

"All things Korean agree with me except kimchee," Petrov retorted.

Persian and Russian both laughed. Seagulls swooped and screamed above the mud flats a few miles north of San Francisco.

Dr. Oleg Petrov was a brilliant physicist, trained in Moscow and at the Yerevan Physics Institute in Armenia. Rising in reputation during the depth of the Cold War for his work in purifying plutonium, he was cast adrift by the unraveling of the USSR.

In Petrov's thinking it was the best thing that ever happened to him. While a Communist loyalist to his core, his personal tastes ran toward capitalism in the extreme. Exchanging the musty-smelling, blank concrete corridors of the Russian Institute for State Engineering and Advanced Applied Physics for a completely new facility designed to his own specifications was merely a matter of finding the right patron.

Khalil was that patron.

Even better, Petrov was able to market his skills to other customers as well.

"And the tests were successful?" Khalil asked, setting aside pleasantries and getting down to business. Even though he'd paid a lot of money for a supposedly completely secure communications system, Khalil didn't entirely trust it. He suspected that the American military could intercept and decode his signals. For that reason he kept his calls under a minute and continued to speak in guarded terms.

"Entirely. It will selectively remove the . . . undesired material . . . from the volume required, in minutes. Also, I can provide sufficient product to treat any additional water that might be added until it is too late to prevent the . . . anticipated conclusion."

"Excellent!"

"However," Petrov cautioned, "the process still requires approximately five kilos of . . . salt."

Even after a relay of thousands of miles, Khalil's annoyance was apparent. *Salt* was code for Semtex explosive. "Negative. There are too many safeguards for that to be possible."

"I am working on it."

"Our time is limited! You know that since things are in motion they must be completed within—"

"Calm yourself, my friend," Petrov said reassuringly. "I will be bringing you a present in plenty of time for the celebration. A shiny new soccer ball."

"Fifty-five seconds," intoned the mechanical voice of the phone's built-in timer.

"Make it a baseball bat."

"Understood. Petrov, out."

Khalil also signed off. Shutting down his phone, he carefully folded the antenna blade and closed the case. He then placed the small leather-bound container into the trunk of his black Mercedes 600SEL and drove back to Sausalito.

Khalil never used the same location twice. Even if the Americans intercepted a satellite-bounced call and went to investigate, they would always be too many steps behind to succeed.

San Luis Obispo, California
3:45 P.M. Pacific Time

BATTER UP!
It was the first interdistrict baseball game of the season. The Old Mission Elementary School Bobcats against the Los Osos Grizzlies on the Old Mission field.

Eight- and nine-year-old boys in sparkling uniforms and unscuffed cleats lined up on the diamond to sing a soprano version of "The Star-Spangled Banner." These players could still reach the high notes.

The Old Mission team, however, was decidedly somber. Their head coach, Frank Daley, was missing from the ranks for the first time in 20 years. Paul Salim, new head coach, baseball cap over his heart, stood bravely warbling the anthem where Frank would have been. A handful of dads filled in as assistant coaches.

There was Aaron Daley, red hair gleaming in the sun, tears streaming down his cheeks. Michael Salim and Matthew flanked him. The whole scene was right out of an old Ronald Reagan movie, Cindy thought. *Win this one for the Gipper!*

The grim parents of Old Mission Elementary crowded the bleachers to watch as the battle unfolded. The Grizzlies were first at bat.

The Old Mission Bobcats took the field. Aaron was catcher. He donned his protective gear and squatted behind the plate. An almost audible groan of sorrow rose from the fans. The letters *D-A-L-E-Y* on the back of Aaron's jersey were a blunt reminder that this was the first year Frank would have coached his grandson.

Michael Salim, fierce and determined, went to the pitcher's mound. This was a surprise. Was he good enough to pitch against the Grizzlies? Cindy knew there would be grumbling about the lineup if Paul Salim's son didn't do well.

Matthew, taller than his teammates and usually the most vocal of the Bobcats, trotted silently out to first base. He raised his eyes briefly toward the stands. Cindy knew he was looking for Steve.

Steve. Late as usual! *Will he even show up for the game?* she wondered.

Little Tommy tugged her sleeve. "Is Daddy coming?"

"Yes," Cindy replied too fiercely.

The crowd was so quiet! Depressing. And the boys. Without Frank Daley the spunk was gone. Without his spark they were sure to lose! Okay, so the boys hadn't seen the Ronald Reagan classic, but the parents had.

Suddenly Mrs. O'Connor, principal of the school, leapt up on the bench and roared in a very un-ex-nunly way, "WIN THIS ONE FOR THE GIPPER, BOYS! WALLOP 'EM FOR COACH!"

Stunned silence followed as heads rotated to stare at the gray-haired administrator. The old woman glared back defensively.

Loudly Tommy asked Cindy, "What's a gipper, Mommy?"

Nearby a pigtailed girl of four replied, "Some kind of fish."

Someone snickered and repeated this bit of preschool instruction to someone else.

Then Cindy heard Steve's voice. "Hey, Matthew!" He was there, so handsome in his worn-out Levi's and blue polo shirt as he leaned against the backstop. He repeated Mrs. O'Connor's incomprehensible encouragement to Matthew. "You heard the lady! Win it for the Gipper!"

Twitters of laughter rippled through the surrounding crowd. Then a convulsive roar broke loose.

Relief!

Cindy jumped up and added her voice to Mrs. O'Connor's and Steve's. "GO, BOBCATS!"

At that, the crowd clamored to join them. The spell was broken.

"Right!"

"YES!"

"Bobcats, GO!"

"This one for the coach!"

They began to chant, "GO, BOBCATS, GO!"

Fists slammed expectantly into gloves. Caps were adjusted against the glare. Matthew took his position. Michael Salim pitched a few to Aaron, who pivoted and threw to Matthew, who tossed to chubby Bill Thorne at second, who missed it.

Steve, a crooked smile on his lips and his gaze fixed on Cindy, ascended the steps to take his place at her side.

Father Arul was a perfect choice for an umpire. One of Mother Teresa's first orphan converts, he was from India, a devotee of cricket, and thus extremely fair and dispassionate about the American game of baseball. Stepping behind Aaron, he pulled the mask over his nut-brown face and cried, "BAD-DEER UP!"

Buttonwillow, California
6:49 P.M. Pacific Time

THE HORSE TRADER

The deserted straight road bisected fields of almond and orange orchards as well as natural gas wells. Despite the springtime date, the valley heat was broiling as Shadir traveled down Seventh Standard Road in a borrowed, plain gray Toyota pickup, complete with camper shell. His arm hung out the window as he searched for the giant natural gas tanks. Twenty miles along, as he had been told, he saw three massive spherical tanks, the largest of which stood over 100 feet high.

Shadir slowed to examine the low chain-link fences and flimsy gates weakly securing the dirt road to a year's supply of natural gas for this half of California. He parked and turned off the engine, setting the ratchet foot brake.

Several cars blazed by. The vacuum created behind him rocked the little truck. Shadir's gaze was fixated on what lay beyond the gates: besides the giant golf balls, there was a forest of smaller but still house-sized propane and butane tanks.

Three dozen of them.

The throaty trumpet of the jake brakes on a big rig coming from behind caught his attention. The diesel squeaked to a stop in the middle of the highway, releasing a *whoosh* of air. Shadir could see a shaggy blond man in the cab leaning over.

Wiping the sweat from his face with a greasy paw and then on the shoulder of his grimy gray T-shirt, the man opened the door. "You lookin' to trade horses?" the wiry redneck asked over the clattering engine.

Shadir closed one eye, sheltering his view from the sun. "Are you the Horse Trader?"

"That'd be me!" the driver answered proudly.

"Then I am ready to trade."

The rough-and-tumble man smiled, proudly displaying the absent canine trophies he had given away in a bar fight at the infamous Trout's Biker Bar in Oildale, California, or up the street at the equally infamous Trap. Never had any other two bars brought so many unhappy couples together on a first date for a drink and a trip to Vegas to get married in the same night as the Trap and Trout's. "All right! Follow me up the road. I've got a good place."

Shadir started the engine and followed the Horse Trader a mile and a half up the road. The big rig slowed to a crawl alongside an orange orchard, then hooked a right turn down a dirt road. Clouds of dust choked out Shadir's view as he rolled up his window.

The truck circled around behind the bushes where they would be completely out of sight. Both men stepped out.

The Horse Trader brushed back his long locks. From the moment he opened his mouth, every other word was either slang or profane. "Hey, man," he said as he approached, "I forgot to ask if you was a cop or something."

Shadir pursed his lips in disbelief. "No."

"You ain't a cop? 'Cause I know if I ask and you is, you gotta say. Right?"

"No," responded Shadir, "I am not a cop. And the other way you should know is that I solicited you. Cops cannot do that."

"Oh, yeah! I seen that TV show *Cops.* I remember they said that when they busted some hookers in L.A."

Shadir smiled. For being lower than the lowest of the low, the guy was pretty entertaining to watch, like a gibbering ape. "Yes, I think that is where I learned it too."

The man studied him, as if to see if he was being truthful or mocking. Likely deciding Shadir was a straight shooter, he agreed. "I don't like cops. If there's two things I don't like, it's cops and minorities. No offense," he corrected himself. "I don't mind doin' business with a camel jockey once in a while. You people are smarter than you look. My name's David, by the way."

Shadir gladly took his hand, playing the part. "I am Ali."

"Cool!" David exclaimed, throwing some fake punches at Shadir's face. "Like the boxer? He's pretty cool for bein' a—"

Shadir cut him off. "So let us look at this horse, eh?"

"Sure, yeah. Come on around here." David led him to the back of the bobtailed, well-insulated, refrigerated trailer.

David opened the lock and flung the latch over. A wave of cool air poured off the tailgate. Condensation floated out, vanishing in the sweltering heat.

Shadir followed the Horse Trader into the van. Inside, as the cooler motors hummed, Dave pulled a light cord and shut the door, taking Shadir to see five round Styrofoam ice chests. "This is the dope, man! This stuff here . . ." He slid one over and lifted the lid. "This dynamite is good stuff too! We use it for—"

"Wait a minute!" Shadir cut him off. "I was told you had Semtex. Dynamite is no good for me!"

"Whoa, man! Don't go nuclear now. We'll get you sorted," David calmed Shadir. "I can give you some of each. No other exploration outfit even uses the stuff. Is that cool?"

Shadir paused.

"'Cause I don't wanna get in trouble, man. I told Joaquin, I ain't gonna pass my drug test next go-round, so it don't matter if a little goes missing. They're gonna fire me anyway when I tell 'em I ain't takin' no drug test. Ol' Sissy, my girlfriend, she about dropped a brick last time I did it. But they can't prove nothin' if they ain't got it on paper. And Greg my boss'll hire me back in another six months anyway."

Baffled by the twisted logic by which David, the Horse Trader, ran his life, Shadir listened. "You have done this before and they still give you the keys to the pyro lorry?"

"Lorry, man? What's a lorry?"

"A truck," Shadir informed him. "This thing is a lorry. It is a British word."

David nodded, clenching his jaw. "Lorry. Learn somethin' new every day."

Changing the subject, Shadir asked, "So shall we load this stuff?"

David jerked his chin in agreement. "Grab that one there." He pointed to a chest with the red detonating firecracker symbol for explosives painted on it.

The two carried the boxes back to the pickup. Shadir balanced the weighty chest on one knee while opening the hatch to the camper.

David gawked. "What do you got a mountain bike for, man? You a health freak or what?"

"You ask a lot of questions," Shadir said, annoyed.

David shrugged. "Yeah, well, so?"

"In case I am away from my car, so I do not have to walk," Shadir stated matter-of-factly.

"Like if you break down?"

"Something like that. It is a good idea in this heat, eh?"

"I guess. So where's your cash, man?" David inquired as he slid the second white foam carton into the bed of the truck.

Pulling the money from his pocket in a big wad, Shadir asked, "How much again?"

"Five," David replied.

Shadir began counting out twenties.

"Five bills, baby," David exulted. "Five hundred bucks!"

Shadir stopped counting and looked up. "Five hundred?" he questioned, knowing anywhere else the explosives would have cost many times that amount.

"Don't be tryin' to cheat me now, dude," David warned. "The raghead guy at 7-Eleven is always tryin' to do that."

Chuckling, Shadir replied, "No, I would never do that." He finished counting, handing 25 bills to David and stuffing the remainder of the large bundle back into his pocket.

David handled the money. "Cool, man. Now I can get this old '58 Chevy that I been wantin' to buy from this junkie who got his IROC-Z impounded. He wants eight, but I know if I offer him this stacka cash, he'll go for it."

Shadir awkwardly responded the way he thought David would. "That is cool, man."

Dave nodded. "But what I'm gonna do first, man, is have a smoke." He presented a pipe from his pocket. "You feel like it?"

Shadir hesitated, then accepted. "What could it hurt?"

"That's it, man!" David slapped him on the back, leading Shadir again into the cooler environment of the refrigerated trailer.

Once in the back, David lit up, passing the pipe to Shadir, who inhaled deeply.

From high in the back of the truck, Shadir could see the gas balls, towering above the orchard in the distance. "So what are those big things?"

David exhaled a burst of smoke, coughing. "Natural gas tanks. Round like that 'cause the pressure is so great if they wasn't, the gas would blow 'em apart. A lot of pressure that natural gas has. It's some of the only stuff that's ready to go, right outta the ground."

Shadir listened before passing back the implement.

"Believe me, I know!" David continued. "I was on a rig a few years ago out in Lost Hills, the one where that natural gas well blew up!" David swore. "Let me tell you, it was a hot mother. Burned up the truck, my tools. Check these out," he said, pulling a set of keys from his pocket. "These here is lucky."

Shadir examined them.

"That melted piece of metal there is what's left of a Craftsman half-inch box wrench. It was the only thing left of my tools. They wasn't exactly *my* tools, but you know what I mean?"

Shadir signaled that he understood.

David took the keys back. "Fire burned for months. They lost billions of gallons of natural gas and spent millions to put it out. The fire geyser shot 200 feet in the air. I could see it from my porch in the Dale."

"Oh, yes!" Shadir said, suddenly recollecting. "I remember seeing that from the I-5. Big flames, shooting into the air!"

"Yeah, man. It was somethin' all right." David returned to his smoke. The 10-story gas tanks caught his eye. He handed the pipe to Shadir. "That there though," he said, motioning, "them gas balls would make a big ol' fire."

Laughing, Shadir commented, "That they would. That they would."

"I'd like to blow 'em up," David joked.

Shadir's face grew serious. "So would I."

David stopped laughing. A sideways smirk rose on his face as he checked out Shadir. "I bet you would, you crazy A-rab."

Pretending to be amused, Shadir chuckled. "But seriously, what would it take?"

David studied him momentarily. "Funny you should ask. I was just talkin' to my supervisor about it yesterday."

Casually Shadir asked, "What did he say?"

"Wouldn't you like to know?" David bobbed his head, eyes half closed.

"Seriously."

The Horse Trader's speech was slower now as he explained. "Nothin' easier. You'd make a fat log outta that Semtex and wrap it like a tire right around the collar of the pipe as it comes out the bottom of the big tank. Then it's Fourth of July! When that blast goes off, it'd cut that pipe and a million gallons of natural gas would be tryin' to come out all at once. We figured that big ball would blast around ever' which way, probably knocking the other two off their cradles and *kaboom!* Fourth of July!" he repeated.

Shadir disagreed. "It could not happen."

David acted offended. "Now how would you know?" He swore at Shadir.

"Because security would catch you sneaking in."

"Oh no they wouldn't." David slurred his words. "My supe said the same thing, but I know different 'cause I worked on that joint."

"How would you do it?" Shadir questioned seriously.

"I'd go to the back side, with that big Semtex doughnut wrapped around my neck, right to where all the pipes—pipes as big as buses—come through the fence. There are holes. Then I'd keep real low and make my way down the conduit channel. It's like a trench, a canal, where all these really big pipes go. Anyway, it'll lead you right to the bottom of all three big balls."

Shadir didn't say a word as he studied the Horse Trader's plan.

David offered Shadir another hit on the pipe, but he refused.

The sky had gone purple by now.

David continued, "There's a service ladder. Now, they don't look that big, but when you get up to 'em, you realize that the top of the pipe bend, where it goes up into the collar, is about 12 or 15 feet off the ground. So you gotta use the ladder."

"The ladder?" Shadir questioned.

"Yeah, the ladder."

Shadir's words quickened. His face tightened. "Is there anything else I should know about?"

"No. That's about it. Just remember to get outta there, and don't stop before Fresno, 'cause it's gonna be a hot time in the ol' town tonight!"

"What about guards?" Shadir interrogated.

"What, are you really gonna do it, or what, man?"

"Maybe. What about guards?"

Shrugging with dope-induced fuzziness and disbelief, David said, "Naw, there ain't any real good ones. They got guns and stuff, don't get me wrong, but they're all lookin' for some crazy to run straight through the front gate and ram the thing. It wouldn't do nothing to it." David laughed. "I should know; I helped work on it."

Shadir interrupted now. "That is it?"

Again David offered the pipe to Shadir, who again refused, then said, "That's it, man, why . . ."

Shadir had moved behind David.

Pulling a small revolver from his pocket, he stuffed it into David's mouth, who grabbed it with his left hand. Shadir turned as he pulled the trigger. A muffled pop sounded and David, the great Horse Trader, fell lifelessly to the floor.

Shadir moved quickly. He grabbed the ice chests, loading the remaining three into his pickup. Then he carefully wiped the revolver off with his shirt and stuck it back in David's left hand. He laid his bike gently on top of David's legs and exited the back of the big rig, latching the doors.

There was a lot of work to be done before the night was over.

FOURTEEN

Avila Beach, California
7:04 P.M. Pacific Time

MAN OF THE HOUR

One of the things Steve had missed about Avila Beach was the summer get-togethers at the beach: the smoky smell of the campfire and the gentle washing of waves at sundown. He and Cindy had always come out on weekends, even before they had kids.

He closed his eyes and took it in as if he were home. In many ways, Steve felt reconnected just from being here. Though in many more, he felt alienated—especially from the peace of this lifestyle.

Perhaps it was because he didn't know most of the mothers of students and the teachers Cindy chatted with. And yet they seemed to know Cindy better than he did. What had happened over the years of their marriage? to their ability to share their thoughts and dreams together? Now it was as if he were on the outside, looking in at her world. And it was no longer *their* world.

And still so many of her friends seemed to live in that same world.

Most of the men were sports fanatics—jocks who had memorized statistics in their younger days and tonight played a sort of impromptu game of Trivial Pursuit: batting averages. World Series games and scores. These were the sort of topics that left Steve speechless.

Had the questions dealt with such trivia as the names of hijackers involved in the attack on the World Trade Center and the Pentagon, he could have won the game hands down. But tonight the crowd probably wanted to keep their thoughts far from the terrorist threats that had now encroached so violently on the East and West Coasts of America.

So Steve detached himself and simply listened quietly, as an outsider, while they chatted away. His thoughts focused on Cindy beside the bonfire. She was so beautiful, bundled up in a sweatshirt. Her eyes met his. He so badly wanted to put his arm around her and walk along the beach alone.

A loud, dominant man of at least six-foot-four addressed Steve. "So what line of work are you in, Alstead?"

"FBI," Steve replied flatly, realizing he had nothing in common with the guy.

The man was almost derisive in his response. "A lot of time spent looking at books and files, talking to people, huh?"

Steve smiled when he considered what he could say. *Actually, I'm an Echo Team leader for the HRT. I'm the guy with the machine gun who leads the raid into a tough spot, shoots the bad guy, and rescues the hostage.*

"We get our best leads from Tom Clancy novels," Steve quipped, resisting the urge to tell the truth.

The man laughed. "So you're doing all the things we dreamed about when we were kids. Before we grew up, that is."

"Yeah. Right." Steve kept it light. "I'm the guy who at 34 is still living the macho fantasy."

The man disengaged with a nod and joined a group of fathers with some insignificant conjecture about which National League team looked best in the early going.

Steve sipped his Coke and walked toward the water's edge. A child's cry caught his attention. Was it Matthew's voice? Steve squinted out to the railing of the pier, where most of the boys were fishing. What were they screaming about?

"Dad!" Matthew waved his arms broadly. "Dad! Help! Michael fell in!"

Steve raised his head, spotting the rippling water out near the railless end of the boardwalk. Someone was struggling hard to stay afloat!

Before anyone else on the beach had realized what was happening, Steve sprinted across the beach and up the stairs.

Shouts of panic echoed on the evening air.

Matthew yelled as he approached, "Michael fell in, Dad! He landed hard on his back! He went under! We can't see him!"

Steve searched for some sign of the child. It was difficult to see in the glare of the setting sun. But there was a flash of color! A red-and-white jersey. Kicking off his shoes, Steve dove in. Visibility was bad in the cold churning Pacific, but Steve had been trained for underwater search and rescue. He used all his senses to find his way to the now unconscious boy. Reaching out into the void where he had last seen the jersey, he grasped the limp body and thrust Michael to the surface.

Pulling Michael's face above water, Steve spotted a small ramp under the pier and made his way to it. The surf broke against the pilings. Steve positioned himself so he, not the child, took the force of the wave. His back was slammed against the support.

"Matt!" Steve called out as the boys scrambled down the ladder. "Call for help! Get an ambulance!"

Grabbing hold of the rising and falling dock, Steve thrust the boy from the ocean in a single motion. Then he crawled up beside him and began CPR. Steve turned Michael on his left side so the water would drain out of him.

Look. Listen. Feel. The boy was not breathing; there was no heartbeat either.

Emergency breathing. Rolling Michael on his back, Steve checked the boy's airway. The drumming waves made it hard to hear. The dimming light made it even harder to see.

Five thrusts a second apart.

Lifting the chin and pulling the mouth open with his left hand, Steve held the boy's forehead with his right. He placed his mouth over Michael's nose and mouth.

Two breaths. In one . . . in two.

Drops of water sprayed as the child exhaled. *Good.*

Chest thrusts, five.

One, one thousand, two, one thousand, three . . .

A man was at his elbow.

Steve did not look up.

"Save him!" the man's voice pleaded. "Save my son!"

Steve nodded, concentrating on the count, the rhythm. The man seemed helpless, unable to contribute to the effort.

Then Cindy was kneeling beside him. "An ambulance is on the way."

Breathing, chest compressions. *Don't stop. Never give up.*

He checked Michael's pulse.

Nothing.

Steve sensed despair sweep over the onlookers. He sensed rather than saw some of them turn away, giving up hope.

Another cycle. Five thrusts, two breaths.

Again . . . and again.

In the distance, a siren. A long way off; an eternity for it to approach.

Steve began to tire, felt out of breath himself. The siren stopped. Feet shuffled. *The paramedics must be coming,* Steve realized.

Another breath. Five compressions.

Then Michael coughed, choked, coughed again.

A ragged cheer from the crowd.

Turning Michael on his side, Steve held the boy's shoulders as he vomited seawater and then drew his first breath on his own. The boy was barely conscious and not in the clear yet. A high percentage of those receiving CPR still died after returning to breathing on their own.

But not this one, dear God! Steve pleaded silently. *Not this young boy.*

Steve had seen enough death for a lifetime. The photo of the two young boys killed in the BART bombing flashed into his mind again.

"They're coming," someone yelled.

Cradling the child in his arms, Steve commanded, "Move!" He carried Michael up the narrow flight of steps, the boy's trembling father following close behind.

The EMTs hustled toward them, the gurney bumping over the uneven timbers of the pier. Meeting the paramedics halfway, Steve laid Michael down at last. The boy was coming around.

"Relax," a red-haired attendant in a dark blue uniform said to the struggling Michael. "You'll be okay."

Ducking around Steve, the father pressed himself forward, grabbing Michael's hand. "Michael! I'm here, son," Paul Salim said.

"What happened?" the boy said weakly.

"You fell in. You'll be all right now."

The paramedics pushed the cart toward the ambulance. "Michael? Is that your name?" the red-haired one asked.

"Yes," the boy replied weakly.

"Well, we're gonna take you for a little ride, bud. Hospital. Check you out."

Michael lunged half upright. "Dad!" he said excitedly.

"I'm here."

"Dad, someone pushed me!"

Steve shot a glance at his son Matt, jogging wide-eyed alongside his friend. Matt shook his head, shrugged to indicate that he had seen nothing like that happen.

"Confused," the other EMT remarked. "Don't worry. Kids bounce back fast."

The gurney was loaded into the ambulance.

Paul Salim hurriedly grasped Steve's hand and pumped it. "My son . . . I owe his life to you. I . . . thank you!"

Then Salim was in beside Michael, the doors shut, and the emergency vehicle whisked away.

Steve felt people pat him on the back . . . heard murmured words of congratulations.

Unexpectedly the center of attention instead of an outsider, Steve wanted nothing more than to get away, hold his own boys, and change out of the sodden clothes he hadn't even noticed till now.

Matt joined his father.

Bending down, Steve placed his forehead against his son's. "Good work, Matt," he said.

"*You're* the hero, Dad," the boy corrected.

Steve shook his head. "You were quick enough calling out. You saved your friend's life."

Steve felt a tug on his arm, saw Cindy holding his elbow and smiling at him.

"Let's go home," he said.

Natural Gas Storage Facility
Buttonwillow, California
9:45 P.M. Pacific Time

FLAMING TUMBLEWEEDS

Shadir waited for dark before venturing back out on the highway. He had abandoned his little Toyota for the time being and set off driving the big rig in the direction he had come. It was only a couple minutes down the road to a gas station across from his chosen target. As he slowed down for the stop sign, a dark green Chevy Suburban charged toward him from the Exxon parking lot.

The decal on the side read *Golden State Oil Drilling Service.* Shadir took a deep breath, but before he could get across the intersection the Suburban swerved in front of him, forcing him to slam on the brakes.

The two men in the oil company truck were obviously looking for the long-overdue Horse Trader. Luckily for Shadir the pyro truck and trailer he had commandeered were unmarked. The driver peered across at Shadir, then shook his head.

Now that he had them convinced of their mistake, Shadir played the part of the outraged innocent party. Blasting the truck's air horn, he shook his fist out the window. The passenger in the oil service vehicle threw his hands into the air in frustration and the two Golden State employees sped off eastward.

Letting out a sigh of relief, Shadir wiped sweat from his face. He made a right turn, traveled north a mile or so, then flipped a U-turn in a vacant field and parked. Shadir leaned on the steering wheel. From his new position he had a perfect view of the extensive, barely lit gas-tank field and the giant white prizes that sat in the middle.

Having been careful of what he touched, Shadir still made sure to wipe down any surface where he might have left fingerprints. He removed his bike from the back of the big rig and locked the door again. With the jumbo Semtex putty sausage wound around his neck like a pet python, he hid the bike in tall, dry mesquite shrubs, a hundred yards or so from the trailer.

The walk across the field was longer than it appeared. The distance had been dwarfed by the sheer size of the natural gas containers. It took Shadir almost 20 minutes to traverse the tumbleweed-overgrown field. He kept looking back for cars or people who might have spotted the missing truck, but there was no traffic on the perfectly deserted dirt track. Parked as closely to ground zero as it was, if the vehicle wasn't spotted before detonation there would probably be nothing left.

Shadir arrived at the chain-link fence, heaving the bulky tire-shaped ring of explosives into the dry dirt.

It was completely dark on the back side of the gas plant. Massive pipes, taller than the diesel truck he had stolen, bisected the fence, leaving room beneath to crawl through. Shadir pushed the explosives under, then heaved himself through the gap.

He shinned down into the piping corridor. It was just as the talkative David had said: like an empty canal. The dry concrete bed made for a perfect place to duck along unobserved to a point right beside the tanks of natural gas.

The area was noisy with the growl and hum of giant pumps, all churning along. Making suspicious sounds was not something Shadir would have to worry about. As he neared the platform, the rumbling hiss coming from the lines was so intense that earplugs were needed.

It occurred to Shadir that he had significantly underestimated the amount of destruction that was possible. It wasn't just the tanks themselves. Hundreds of miles of pipe holding pressurized fuel would continue feeding the fire once blasted open, and they would continue to do so until someone, somewhere, managed to shut off the supply.

Shadir reached the access ladder.

It was amazing there was no one around, no security in evidence. Even very few lights and no surveillance cameras. Why had someone not done this before?

Shadir adjusted the load, shrugging it higher on his neck. Gently and slowly, he climbed the steps. At the top of the first platform, which was back at about ground level, Shadir could see men moving around. One man stood by the guardhouse and another inspected traffic.

Near the gate, a line of high-pressure tanker trucks awaited entry. A third individual came out of the office. Shadir froze. If he had missed a video eye, if someone had spotted him, this was when they would come after him.

Had he been too confident, too arrogant?

The third figure turned away from the lighted office, climbed into a passenger car, and drove out of the gate.

Shadir sighed and resumed his climb.

From the deck there was a ladder to the next level. Navigating it was more difficult as the Semtex sausage sagged and threatened to pull him backward. At the top was a small metal grate landing and a narrow catwalk. Shadir traversed this space, keeping to the shadows and out of the patches of light shining between the pipes.

He had reached the collar at the base of the northernmost of the three tanks. From underneath, the giant ball was so gigantic that the effect was like trying to gauge the shape of the world from its surface. The bottom of the container appeared flat.

Shadir continued upward, finally arriving beneath the middle tank. He examined the five-foot-diameter drain line. It dropped out of the bottom of the metal sphere, went straight down about eight feet, then curved out, paralleling the ground.

Shadir slung the gray snake of explosives over the railing while he studied the layout. The natural stickiness of the compound made it cling to the metal. The issue now was how to get the explosive doughnut wrapped next to the base of the tank in order to achieve maximum devastation.

Getting there with it was a challenge. The gap between catwalk and downpipe was too great for Shadir to lean across to place the charge.

He retrieved the Semtex and replaced it around his neck. Switching the detonating timer from his front to his back pocket, he climbed on the railing of the catwalk. Then he leaped for the pipe, intending to shinny up it to the connection collar.

As he flung his arms around the conduit, though, he realized he had underestimated something else: the diameter of the tubing was too great to reach around. With nothing to grab hold of, his body slid backward, dropping him onto the L-shaped bend of the outflow pipe. The steel framework supporting the pipe rang like a church bell with the impact. Despite all the other noise, Shadir had managed to cause enough of a disturbance to attract attention.

He knelt low, crouching like a cat as a security man aimed a flashlight in his direction. In his present position there was no concealment. He could even be spotted from below. Quickly he searched for a place to hide. Only one possibility suggested itself. Just above the bend of the pipe from horizontal to vertical there was a weld. Perhaps that joint in the tubing would provide a place for his toes and he could shinny around into the shadow of the enormous ball itself.

The inquisitive guard was coming.

Shadir leaped again, willing his fingers to dig into the metal long enough for his toes to find the half-inch-wide ledge.

The very tips of his shoes gained purchase on the welded ridge, and

Shadir slid around to his right, away from the catwalk. Pressing against the conduit in an embrace from ankles to whiskers, Shadir found that the bulk of the explosives kept pushing him away.

He reached the shelter of the greater darkness under the tank just as the guard arrived at the ladder. Peering out of his hiding spot with one eye, Shadir studied the enemy. The man probably wasn't more than 25 years old. His hair was short and his face clean-shaven. He turned his light upward and along the deck in search of something that could account for the disturbance.

Shadir turned his head away from the light, in order to avoid the possibility of reflections from his eyes. Facing downward, he could see a slight shadow cast off his body, mingled with the other shades of tubes and rails. Shadir wondered if the guard could sort out enough parts of an intruder from the jumble of puzzle pieces to make him call for assistance.

The sentry squinted, unmoving. He shined his light around again, apparently deciding whether to venture up to the catwalk.

Shadir didn't move. The air was still warm. Sweat beaded on his face. As he awaited discovery, his perspiration collected. Soon multiple beads of sweat dripped onto the pipe, gleaming trails pointing backward toward the trespasser. Shadir didn't dare move to wipe his face.

The guard lifted his radio to his lips. Static hissed. "Base, this is Tony. . . ."

A reply came. "Yeah, Tony. What did you find?"

"Uh, nothin', Base. I think too many night shifts may be gettin' to my eyes."

Base replied, "That's pretty much what I figured. Anyway, these trucks are backin' up here. Why don't you come on in?"

"On my way." Tony clicked off the radio and exited the area.

Shadir waited for at least a minute after Tony had left before resuming his task. By balancing on his toes, Shadir heaved the Semtex up the pipe to just below where it tied in with the tank. Then he had to make a tactical decision. The diameter of the conduit was so great that the explosive sausage would only wrap about halfway around. Should he thin it out so it stretched the length of the circumference? Could he get it around the back side? And if he could, would the charge be too light to cut through the heavy drain line? Shadir pondered a moment before securing the explosives as they were—to one side only.

Pressing and molding, he kneaded the putty into place on top of the collar before carefully removing the timer and detonator from his pocket. He pushed the blasting cap deep into the dough. Leaving the wires to hang out in the shadows, he turned on the timer and beeped it digitally upward till it read 20 minutes. Shadir considered the amount of time that would provide him to return to the fence and the distance across the field, then set the timer for 40 minutes.

He plugged in the wires.

Taking a deep breath, he paused with his index finger over the arming button. Shadir closed his eyes and pressed. A long beep sounded. He clenched his eyes tight until the beep stopped. The timer began to click down from 40:00 to 39:59 . . . 58 . . . 57 . . .

In haste Shadir scampered back around to the other side of the downpipe and jumped for the bar of the catwalk. Balancing on the skinny rail, he let himself down to the metal grate flooring, then retraced his path along to the edge of the pit.

At the back of the property, between Shadir and his exit, two men parked and uncoupled a tank trailer. Shadir waited on his belly in the dirt while seven or eight minutes ticked off. When they finally left, he sprinted for the fence.

No one saw him.

Once he was outside the chain-link fence, Shadir hustled across the field, reaching the roadside. He was out of breath when he found his bike. His face and chest were soaked with perspiration. As he lifted the bike, he spotted a plastic grocery sack and some roadside trash. He hurriedly threw two empty soda cans into the sack and hung it from his bicycle handlebar.

Looking like a migrant farmworker returning home from a long day in the fields, he was off and pedaling. A minute later Shadir passed the abandoned pyro truck containing the mortal remains of the Horse Trader. Evidently no one had yet noticed it.

As he rode onward toward the corner gas station, a smile crept across his face. He coasted across the parking lot to cut the corner. Two sheriff's cars were parked next to the Golden State Oil Suburban that had cut him off earlier. He glanced away as they eyed him, but no one tried to stop him as he pedaled onward.

Out on the dark highway the air had cooled down and the light of the stars shone brightly. Traffic was at a minimum—a car here and there. The ride was quite leisurely until Shadir glanced at his watch.

Nine minutes to go.

He pedaled faster, arriving at the Toyota pickup out of breath and peering over his shoulder as if the devil were after him. Shadir tossed his bike in the back, revved the motor, and sped away. Instead of turning left, which would take him west, back toward the natural gas-tank field, he made a right on Seventh Standard Road, heading toward Bakersfield and the 99 Freeway.

Again he checked the time. Less than a minute to go.

Shadir pulled off on the shoulder, probably five miles from the tanks, and watched the dark horizon in his mirror.

He visualized the timer counting down: 04 . . . 03 . . .

Suddenly the night lit up. The sky behind him turned a brilliant orange, increasing to an incandescent white glow. Then the shock wave hit. Shadir could see a bright orange cloud sweeping toward him like an ocean wave.

It rocked the little truck. He ducked, covering his ears as the whole earth shook. The small pickup was jolted up and down. The blast caused one of the tempered glass windows to crack and fragment into a spiderweb. The right front wheel was pushed sideways into a shallow ditch.

When the bouncing stopped, Shadir rose and turned around to look.

In the distance he saw that the center tank had ripped free from its scaffolding. Now it jetted over on its side, throwing fire like a flaming tumbleweed, and collided with its southern neighbor. The image of the separate gas storage spheres illuminated by the blast melted together. Another even brighter flash replaced the view with unbearable glare, as if it were daylight.

Shadir slammed the truck into gear and spun the tires as the second shock wave caught up with him. The whole pickup was lifted off the road like a toy picked up by a child. Both the driver- and passenger-side windows shattered and fell out. Shadir swerved violently to regain control as a tremor of dazzling light and furnacelike heat swept past him.

In his partially deafened state, the sound of the motor was barely a hum. It made Shadir aware of how overwhelming the inferno he had created must be since he could still hear its roar! It was a wonder the small truck even continued to run.

A minute later, one after another, two dozen fire trucks and emergency personnel vehicles sped past him toward the disaster. By the time Shadir had reached the 99 Freeway, heading north toward San Francisco, radio coverage of the event had already begun, warning drivers to stay out of the area.

Clouds of smoke created a reflective barrier on the sky, lighting up the night with an eerie orange glow. Shadir laughed as he looked on from the steadily increasing distance. "And that is only Satan's candle compared with what will be."

FIFTEEN

The Alstead Condo
Morro Bay, California
Tuesday, 1 May
12:45 A.M. Pacific Time

I WISH IT WASN'T . . .

So this was it. The way it was supposed to be.

Matthew and Tommy were asleep downstairs. Steve lay stretched out on the sofa with his head on Cindy's lap as *Forrest Gump* played on the television.

She stroked his hair and studied his face. There were so many things she didn't know about him. A thick scar followed the curve of his jawline for about two inches. She traced it with her fingertip. "Where did you get this one?" she asked.

He replied dreamily, "Shaving."

"Some razor," she replied.

"Yeah. You should have seen the barber after I finished with him."

"Uh-huh." She touched another beneath his eye. "How about this one?"

"Hockey."

"You never played hockey."

"Someone else's stick." He smiled at the TV screen as Forrest Gump sat beside Jenny's bed and Jenny saw him, really saw him, for the first time.

"You should've ducked."

"I did."

And then there was the scar at his hairline. The old one. She bent down and kissed it. "And this?"

"You did that. Don't you remember?"

"Never."

"Medicine cabinet. Our first apartment. You left it open when I was brushing my teeth and . . ."

Yes. She did remember that one. He had straightened up and almost knocked himself out. There was blood everywhere. She had held his head and cried. The hospital had confirmed it was a concussion. "You'll never let me forget."

"It was worth it. Doc put me to bed for three days. You felt so guilty you came to bed too. What a miraculous recovery! Matthew was born nine months later. Remember?"

She laughed. "Ummm. Remind me."

He reached up and pointed at his own mouth. "Here's an owie. Kiss it?"

The warmth of desire surged through her. She pressed her lips against his. He pulled her down to the sofa beside him. How long had it been?

"Better?" She smiled, wanting him.

"I dunno. Maybe try one more time." He kissed her again, not with rough urgency but with tender longing. "I . . . miss you, you know," he said softly.

Were those tears brimming in his eyes?

"Then stay, Steve." The agony of their separation welled up in her.

He cupped her cheek in his hand. "I wish I could."

"Then do. I die a little every time you leave us. I never know, Steve, if you'll be back. I can't say good-bye again."

She glanced, unseeing, at Gump tending the grave of his beloved. Mama always said death was part of living . . . I wish it wasn't.

Could she take living like this one more instant? *God,* she pleaded, *what should I do? What kind of decision is the right one? For me . . . Steve . . . and the boys?*

"Cindy?" Steve whispered her name.

Had she ever seen such agony in his expression? She sat up abruptly, the magic of the moment faded. She'd prayed for the right decision so many times that she wondered if God was tired of hearing it. "Don't talk to me about duty. Or sacrifice," she said heatedly.

"I haven't got any other explanation." He reached for the remote and snapped off the set.

"Your duty. My sacrifice. Me and the boys." She crossed her arms defiantly and moved away from him.

Silence. The clock ticked. There was always a clock ticking for Steve Alstead. Or was it a time bomb? She never knew.

"You know . . . Matthew's coach?" he said haltingly.

"What about him?" she retorted.

"It could have been anybody. He's just a guy who got up one morning and said good-bye to his family. Thought he'd see them again. Thought he'd be coaching his grandson's baseball team, you know? But there are people roaming around our country who don't care about ordinary guys. Don't care about our wives. Our kids. Don't care about our dreams. Our lives. Our freedom, our faith in God, or our hope. They don't care because they have no conscience, no relationship with God, and they don't value anyone's life—even their own. Cindy, they'd destroy everyone else in the world just to make a point. See?"

"And you're going to stop them?"

"I'm trained to . . . I believe, you know, that I was put here to try and stop those people before they tear our lives apart. A lot of innocent people are going to die unless . . ."

She nodded. The image of Steve pulling Michael Salim to safety came vividly to her mind. "Unless someone jumps into the water."

"I guess so."

"And it has to be you," she said slowly, sadly.

"If there's no one else handy who can swim, I guess so."

"We're talking in metaphors." She shrugged.

"We're talking about . . . you know, me loving you and Tommy and Matthew. About what I want for you. About what I want my country to be. A place where ordinary people have the right to expect that they can go to work or school in the morning and not be afraid of being blown up. Or afraid of getting their loved ones back in a body bag. Life is uncertain enough, isn't it? Without walking out our doors and into Armageddon."

"But you, Steve . . . every time you leave for work I have to live with the chance that I might never see you again, and . . ." She began to cry softly. "I can't do this anymore!"

He put his arms around her. "I need you to be strong, babe."

"Don't call me 'babe.' "

"Yeah," he soothed. "Talking pig, huh?"

"Don't—"

"You're a strong lady. I married you because you and I believed in the same things. You really believed in what I was doing. You knew. You used to pray for me when I left. And every time I came home, it was your victory too."

"I know," she said, "and I still pray for you. But it's so hard—and you're gone so much." She touched his face tenderly. "I was wrong to try and change you. I know that now. Selfish. I was wrong to listen to people who didn't have any right to tell me they knew what was best for our lives. But Steve, if you don't come back . . ."

He apologized too—sincerely—for what he'd done wrong in their relationship, but he didn't let her off the hook. "And you knew if I didn't come back . . . that somehow that would be okay too. That I would have done what I was born to do. And I would have done it because it was the right thing. Fighting the darkness."

"But the darkness seems so much stronger now. And I'm scared."

He lifted her chin and brushed his lips over her forehead. "What was it you used to say? Remember? 'Safety isn't the absence of danger. It's the presence of God.' I remember that every time I go to work."

"You love this more than us." Here was her final feeble accusation.

"No. I think you know . . . maybe I'm saving your life. Yours and Matthew's and Tommy's. Maybe by putting myself out there—"

She put a finger over his lips. "No more. Not tonight. Stay with me. Tonight. Don't leave me." She kissed him fiercely.

He returned her kisses, awakening a fire within her. "Whatever you want . . . whatever . . ."

"I want you, us, a life together. Starting tonight. Promise."

His breath was hot against her cheek. "When it's over, Cindy. I promise I'll come home."

Outside the Alstead Condo
Morro Bay, California
2:03 A.M. Pacific Time

I'M YOUR SHADOW

Condensation huffed from the exhaust pipe as the engine of Paul Salim's blue Ford Taurus idled in front of Cindy Alstead's Morro Bay condo. It was either very late or extremely early—which one, Paul was undecided. His eyes were heavy, his movements slow.

The hospital had sent him home. Apparently there was no lasting injury to his son, Michael. Steve Alstead's rescue had been so timely that virtually all the symptoms associated with post-CPR revival were nonexistent. But the boy would stay in the hospital one night for monitoring, just in case.

Paul's gratitude went far beyond words. In spite of the hour, he had come to thank Steve again. At least Paul had convinced himself that was the reason. Maybe too he would talk to Steve about the serious problem he was facing.

Paul sat there with the engine idling, not having the nerve to get out and knock, even though it looked like there were lights on. Just as he opened the car door, his cell phone rang. He answered it, figuring it was his wife. "Yes, honey."

"This is not your honey," said a harsh, intense voice on the other end.

The inflection seemed familiar, but Paul couldn't place it immediately. "Who is this?"

"I am your shadow!" the voice proclaimed. "I am with you wherever you go."

"Khalil. Is that you?" Paul asked, frightened.

"Yes. It is me."

"Khalil, it's the middle of the night. What is so urgent that you would wake me at this hour?"

"Do not lie to me!" Khalil shouted. "I know you are not asleep. I know you are not at home!"

Fear rushed through Paul. "What is it?"

"Do not even think about going to this man for help."

Paul pretended confusion, though the emotion he felt was closer to terror. "What? Who are you talking about, Khalil? I don't understand these games. I—"

"Do not toy with me! You know I mean the man who saved your son's life!"

"But how did you know?"

"Listen to me, Paul Salim. You will do everything Shaiton's Fire commands, or you and your family will pay with your lives. Was today not warning enough? Will it take standing over your son's corpse to convince you?"

Paul waited, speechless and motionless, with one foot out of his car.

"Get in and get home!" Khalil ordered.

Paul frantically began to look around. "Where are you?"

"I am your shadow. Whether it is day or night, I am right beside you. Go home and do not consider such foolish thoughts again, or next time I will kill him. Or your wife. You cannot protect them. Remember that!"

The phone went dead. Paul scrambled to shut his door as he continued to search around for Khalil. There was no way to respond, no way to reason. He slammed the Taurus in gear and sped away.

Khalil emerged from the alleyway between Morro Bay Liquors and the La Serena Motel in time to see him go.

Natural Gas Fire
Buttonwillow, California
6:47 A.M. Pacific Time

WHAT'S GOOD ABOUT IT?

It seemed the sun had failed to rise. The black smoke from the natural gas fires blotted out the morning sky. The smell of burned grass and petrochemicals caused Steve to sneeze. The combined effect made him feel more awake when he exited the southbound I-5 to head east on Seventh Standard. It was like driving under the ash cloud of an active volcano.

Steve reflected on his visit with Cindy and the kids, on saving the Salim boy's life and how that had impressed her. It was interesting how God could turn accidents into good things.

Sadly, though, Morrison's 4:00 A.M. wake-up call had made a mess of what would otherwise have been a perfect trip. The late-night talk with Cindy had been a great breakthrough in their relationship. Absence had made the heart grow fonder. After a quick shower, Steve had woken her at 4:20 to say good-bye, hoping her heart had grown fonder enough to cut him some slack. But she didn't agree and had flung a pillow at his head.

Which is the deeper reality? he wondered. *Last night's heart-to-heart connection or this morning's irritated parting?*

He wondered if it would have been better for him to stay in San Francisco. It would not have been better for Michael Salim—that much was certain.

Seventh Standard Road was barricaded off several miles from the freeway. The explosions had been so intense that Steve guessed whoever was in charge of disaster containment feared similar explosions might still occur.

A policeman on the roadblock checked his badge, eyeballed his Chapter 16 ID, and let him pass. It was another 10 minutes to the site. While driving Steve witnessed flaming torches that shot into the sky. Even from miles away the temperature grew significantly warmer. The growing column of smoke twisted upward like a giant black beanstalk in a horrifying fairy tale.

As he neared, Steve was shocked at the amount of destruction. Orchards were flattened and turned to heaps of charcoal. The place where the tanks once stood was a twisted pile of metal. Flames marking the spot of ground zero leapt at least 150 feet into the air. The whole place looked like film footage of Pearl Harbor shortly after the 1941 attack.

Steve's car was stopped again half a mile from the site. He was escorted to a trailer that was being used as a makeshift disaster-relief headquarters. It was there he met with a liaison from the Kern County sheriff's office and a rep from the local FBI, the Bakersfield satellite office.

"Good morning," he said, introducing himself. "Steve Alstead, Chapter 16, Counterterrorism Team of the San Francisco FBI." Steve extended his hand.

"Good mornin'! What's good about it?" retorted the loudmouthed, good ol' boy sheriff who was at first sight both overweight and overbearing.

"Good point," Steve agreed, even if the guy did come off abrasive and irritating.

The rotund man finally relented, reaching out with fat fingers. "Darren Hoffman, liaison from the Kern County sheriff's office. And this here is Bill Blanchard."

A middle-aged man with thinning dark brown hair reached out, introducing himself in a way that suggested he'd taken four or five Dale Carnegie courses but failed every one of them. "Agent Blanchard," he stuttered, "of the Bakersfield FBI satellite office. Your Director Morrison called me and mentioned that you guys might have some interest in this case."

Steve took Bill's hand. "Possibly. We're working on the BB."

"What's that?" Hoffman croaked.

"If I may?" Blanchard politely inquired. "The BART bombing. Their profile man thinks there may be a link between this explosion and that one."

"Now why would he think that? We haven't even gotten the fires out yet and you guys are forming opinions. Besides, we already know who did it and why."

Steve realized that if the explosion remained an isolated incident, Hoffman would keep jurisdiction. It quickly became clear that these guys, though on the same side, were potential rivals. "Would you care to fill me in?" Steve asked.

Hoffman explained. "Explosion ripped out the center of the complex first. Not an accident . . . deliberately set. Prelim suggests Semtex." Steve caught Blanchard giving him a surreptitiously raised eyebrow. He nodded in return. "Found a suspicious extra victim in an oil company service truck. The company uses explosives in oil exploration. This corpse was an Okie kid, David Metz. According to his boss, Metz was going to be fired for failing a previous drug test and bein' less than cooperative about a follow-up. When the foreman told him to take the pyro truck back to the base, he disappeared."

"They let a doper drive the pyro truck?" Steve asked, amazed.

"My thoughts exactly," Hoffman put in. "Anyway, we think when this kid got upset, he decided to steal the truck and blow up the gas plant. Go out in a blaze of glory. Sheriff's deputy Harold Minor, with the help of the company owner, discovered the truck and the body just minutes before the blast and radioed it in. Both of them were killed."

"Seems wrong." Steve voiced his thoughts. "Isn't usual for a disgruntled type to kill himself *before* the disaster he intends to create. Usually they want to witness the destruction they cause. Remorse or fear may lead to suicide *after.*"

Bill Blanchard hesitated to interject. "That's what I thought. My field office, based on reports that the guy was already dead when his boss arrived with the deputy, believe it may have been a robbery/ homicide."

Hoffman roared. "That's idiotic! When Minor called in, he said the guy had blown off the back of his head."

"If I may," Bill added, "that doesn't mean somebody didn't off him and make it look like suicide."

Hoffman was inflamed. "You tell me how that can be, Bill! This loser redneck disappears with the truck and shows up a few hours later. When he's found, there weren't any explosives left in the truck. And a minute later the bomb goes off. Now you tell me how that looks like a homicide. They even recovered the gun—right in his hand!"

Poor Bill Blanchard seemed to shrink away. He probably had to deal with Hoffman frequently.

"Where is it?" Steve questioned, realizing that the firearm might provide a big break.

Hoffman answered, "It's in the evidence collection truck. Just came in this mornin' after the natural gas lines drained out and things cooled off a bit."

"Do you mind if I look at it?"

Hoffman seemed annoyed. "Now what good would that do ya?"

Steve explained, "Chapter 16, a streamlined division of the FBI specially chartered by the president of the United States, was created so that counterterrorist operations can act more quickly and effectively by cutting a lot of the red tape and overlapping jurisdictions," he said significantly, bearing down on the last phrase. "I'd like to see it if you don't mind."

Hoffman rolled his eyes, then lifted the radio. "Berry, could you have someone run that little .38 Special found in the back of the truck over here?"

Moments later the skinny man named Berry arrived, carrying a white plastic tub. Steve lifted out a sealed plastic bag. In it was a slightly melted .38 Special, old enough that Steve was unfamiliar with the make. The handle had been burned off. The overall condition was pretty bad, but on a long shot, he asked, "Can I try to open the cylinder?"

"Don't be tamperin' with the evidence," scolded Hoffman, then grudgingly allowed Steve to proceed.

Steve spoke of what happens to oil from skin when it's exposed to indirect, high temperatures. "I've seen this once before, when I was a new field agent in Virginia." He slipped on gloves Berry had supplied from the tub and removed the gun from the plastic bag. Upon examination, Steve could see that the serial numbers had been ground off.

Bill commented, "Probably stolen."

"Did this guy Metz have any firearms registered in his name?"

Hoffman cleared his throat authoritatively. "Yep. We got records on ol' Mr. Metz. Says he got several. He must've stolen or got this one outside the system."

"Interesting," replied Steve, thinking what a terrific system it must be that let a drugged-up man handle explosives and own several firearms. But what he said as he struggled with the lump of revolver was, "It doesn't add up. A guy kills himself before he gets to witness his handiwork, using a gun that isn't even his?" He grunted with satisfaction as a piece of explosion-welded metal snapped. "Got it!"

Carefully he pressed the shell extractor rod outward. It too was stiff and gravelly feeling, but Steve managed to eject one of the shell casings. "See here." He held up the shell in gloved fingers, then pointed to a fingerprint burned into the nickel casing. "Just as I thought. Whoever loaded this gun left his fingerprints to be burned into the brass when the oils from his hands were cooked on."

"Well, I'll be," exclaimed Hoffman. "Three days in a lake eats up fingerprints, but 1000-degree heat doesn't."

Given the superior forensic equipment possessed by Chapter 16 and the shadows of doubt Steve had managed to cast over Hoffman's explanation of suspect and motive, the sheriff grudgingly allowed Steve to take one of the shell casings back for analysis.

Diablo Canyon Nuclear Power Plant
Avila Beach, California
10:15 A.M. Pacific Time

THE FIRST ANNUAL FRANK DALEY DAY

The Diablo Canyon Nuclear Power Plant was located at the end of seven miles of twisting private road, on the rocky shoreline between Morro Bay and Avila Beach. Despite opposition to its construction—a conflict reinforced by the discovery of an earthquake fault a few miles offshore—the facility had been operating successfully for more than 15 years and was a model of efficiency and safety. It produced 10 percent of the electricity for the entire state of California, generating thousands of megawatts for the energy-ravenous citizens of Los Angeles and elsewhere.

Since it employed hundreds of people out of the relatively small population of San Luis Obispo County, everyone was either related to someone who worked there, or lived next door or down the block from one.

Unlike the earlier days of nuclear energy, when movies such as *The China Syndrome* made everyone fearful of having atomic energy in their backyard, Diablo was now an accepted part of the community. The fact that warning sirens were occasionally tested was merely a nuisance or a way to tease newcomers. The nuclear accident evacuation plans listed in the front of every phone book were disquieting only if you *thought* about them.

Which mostly no one in San Luis Obispo did anymore.

It was hard for Cindy to concentrate on what Paul Salim was saying. It wasn't that she was uninterested in hearing his description of how a nuclear power plant operated. After all, if you have one in your backyard, how can you be totally disconnected?

But she had heard Frank Daley give this talk lots of times and besides, she couldn't help thinking about Steve's predawn departure, despite all his promises about being more reliable, more of a dad, more responsive to the needs of the kids.

The old anger bubbled up in Cindy again. A knot of irritation lodged just below her sternum, much like what happened when she ate jalapeño-topped enchiladas. Only if that was a forest fire, this was a nuclear meltdown.

And topping it off, she felt guilty, as if *her* thoughts were somehow betraying *Steve.* After all, wasn't it less than 24 hours since Cindy had glowed with pride at the way Steve first saved and then revived Michael Salim?

Her man had done that!

When everyone else had stood around and wailed and wrung their hands, it had been *her* husband who unhesitatingly risked his life to take action.

Nor had the excitement of the rescue blocked Cindy's radar. She had seen how the other women looked at Steve. Especially that Rhonda Sorenson! Shameless, brazen. . . . If Cindy had not bundled Steve away in short order, she swore Rhonda would have volunteered to . . . never mind what Rhonda would have volunteered!

Nor was Rhonda the only one waiting in the wings to happily rush in and pick up the pieces if Steve and Cindy's marriage crumbled.

If?

Two days ago, and again two minutes ago, she thought it *had* crumbled. And now she was jealous? Cindy shook her head and redirected her attention to Paul Salim, who wiped his forehead with the back of his hand. He pointed to a wall chart schematic of how an atomic power plant worked as he explained.

Nuclear power plants, like other electricity generating facilities, produced their energy by spinning turbines. A carefully controlled nuclear reaction heated the water in a closed loop, contained entirely within a concrete dome called a containment vessel. This water in turn imparted its heat to another loop of water, turning it to steam. The steam spun the turbines; the turbines produced electricity.

The steam in the second loop was cooled and recondensed by yet a third set of pipes containing seawater pumped into and back out of the plant for just that purpose. The saltwater was then returned to the Pacific Ocean, 20 degrees warmer but otherwise unchanged.

The three conduits were completely independent of each other so that radioactivity did not escape into the environment in either the steam or the seawater. Besides the fact that the radioactive material was surrounded by more than three feet of concrete, it was also rigorously restricted by radioactivity-absorbing control rods and radioactivity-absorbing water.

And the domes of Diablo's two reactors could, Paul Salim said, withstand direct hits by 747 jet aircraft. Before the World Trade Center destruction, that comment had merely seemed a phrase to dramatize the strength of the construction. Now it was a genuinely necessary reassurance.

The safety systems all had backups and the most crucial ones two. If the core began to overheat, for example, neutron-absorbing control rods would drop into place in two seconds, stopping the reaction. "But even if a rod got stuck for some reason, an enunciator light over there—" Salim pointed to the broad panel of warning indicators across the room from the gallery—"would instantly tell the operators what was wrong. And then do you know what would happen?"

"Blooey?" Cindy's son Matthew said. "Good-bye, Pismo Beach?"

Matthew's buddies snickered while class know-it-all Bill Thorne frowned his disapproval.

Attitude, Cindy thought grimly. Her kid really had an attitude. It had to be Steve's fault.

Paul Salim stuttered, then jumbled his words. "N-n-no, no! And not either meltdown. And radioactive steam does not go *gush* into the air! We flood containment with borated water, stopping everything, like that!" He snapped his fingers, then mopped his face again.

Joey Preston, whose father had worked as a temporary employee at Diablo's last overhaul, waved his hand. "My dad says you bring in new fuel but never take out the old. How's that work exactly?"

"Uh," Salim muttered distractedly.

The man is clearly struggling with something, Cindy thought. Maybe unwell? Worried about Michael?

"We replace part of the fuel rods every 18 months. The fuel pellets are—" Salim searched for a word—"weaker, but still dangerous. Soon there will be a place to bury them very deep underground forever, but now we store them under borated water in a big pool here, on site."

"Do you have the same sort of triple-safety things for that?" Bill Thorne asked.

Salim didn't reply.

"Control rods and stuff?" Bill prompted.

"Here's Ken Evans now," Paul Salim said, sounding relieved as he introduced one of Diablo's community relations employees who had just arrived. "He'll show you around. Through the plant and end at the marine biology lab?"

"Sure thing, boss," the tour guide concurred.

Salim blinked and ducked his head, as if made uncomfortable by the impromptu title.

As well he might be, Cindy mused. *Frank Daley's shoes must be extremely tough to fill.*

As the students filed out of the mock control room's observation deck, Matthew Alstead said to Evans, "The guards here have guns, huh? Real guns like Colt AR-15s and Glock 22s?"

Cindy rolled her eyes. Steve again!

On the way out the door she stopped to thank Paul Salim. "Maybe you need to go home," she said. "You're shivering. Are you coming down with something?"

"Yes, that's it," he said. "Touch of flu."

Monterey Bay Aquarium
Monterey, California
10:45 A.M. Pacific Time

SHARK FOOD

A trio of sea otters dove, swirled, and pounced on each other within their tank enclosure. Caring more about play than food, the three conducted a game of keep-away involving an empty clam shell. Whenever one of them surfaced in possession of the prize, the others would leap on him until he dropped it. Then the game would begin all over.

Their sport was interrupted by the arrival of a squadron of third graders. Nose-to-nose with the humans through the glass wall of the tank, the otters appeared more interested in the children than the reverse.

"Bor-ing!!" Shadir heard one of the eight-year-olds complain. "This is boring! Let's go watch 'em feed the sharks!"

And off they dashed.

At a more sedate pace, Shadir and Khalil likewise exited the otter exhibit and made their way to the outside terrace of the Monterey Bay Aquarium. Above a U-shaped pool open to the tides, where wild sea lions hauled out to rest on the rocks, the two men conferred.

"You have obtained what is necessary?" Khalil asked.

"For the moment," Shadir answered. "As the time approaches, Salim's reports will give me still greater direction as to the final requirements. But at least there is no doubt as to the quality or effectiveness of the material."

Khalil shaded his eyes with his right hand and turned away from Shadir. He pretended to watch a fishing trawler prowling the bay half a mile offshore. "What do you mean?" he demanded.

"You have," Shadir prompted, "doubtless seen the news of the explosion at the natural gas storage near Bakersfield?"

Khalil started, and the grip of his left hand on the guardrail tightened. "CNN called it an accident," he said coldly. "Do you know otherwise?"

"Indeed! It would be a most fortunate and dramatic accident in which the largest natural gas storage in the whole state went up in flames!"

Khalil stepped a pace sideways, nearer Shadir. Leaning toward the smaller man as if to offer congratulations, instead he clamped both hands over Shadir's fingers and crushed them into the cold steel railing. His smile fixed like a grinning skull, he hissed, "You would jeopardize everything for a bit of foolishness? for your own satisfaction? Have you forgotten so quickly the lesson of Rhamad?"

Since Shadir was trying to pull his hand free, he staggered when Khalil abruptly released the pressure. Hurriedly scanning the other visitors to the terrace, Shadir was relieved to find that none had noticed anything amiss. The rest of the tourists were watching the sea lions and paying no attention to the two men.

Shadir nodded toward a blue-painted telescope mounted on a pedestal. As he ducked his head toward the eyepiece, he muttered to Khalil, "You misjudge me! The fuel storage was a worthy target! Millions of dollars of gas, millions more in damage to the facility! And there is more than enough material left for the mission. But also, the American who sold it to me . . . he was not trustworthy and had to be eliminated. The method I chose accomplished this, while making it appear that he was the guilty one who afterward committed suicide. Given his character, my operation may even reinforce the belief that the attacks are the work of American paramilitary militias."

Khalil snorted. "It will not! The same news broadcast announced the 'peaceful resolution' of the standoff at AMT. Why would they do that unless they already knew they had been misled?"

Now it was Shadir's turn to look stunned. "So soon? But how?"

Khalil, not interested in speculation, pressed ahead with his new orders. "Paul Salim grows nervous. I gave him a brief lesson last night, but even after that I do not believe he will remain convinced . . . or quiet. We must move up the timetable of the attack."

"Of course," Shadir agreed. "At once."

Khalil's eyes bored into Shadir's. "No more sudden inspirations, Shadir. Unless you would like to assist the schoolboys in seeing how the sharks get fed."

SIXTEEN

Chapter 16 Forensics Lab
San Francisco
1:32 P.M. Pacific Time

A PERFECT MATCH

"I figured this would end up here eventually, so I just brought it myself." With a light blue windbreaker hung over his shoulder, Steve was out of breath. He entered the lab, flinging a plastic sandwich bag across the room to Dr. Turnow.

Turnow, who was settled back in a desk chair reading, practically dropped his book trying to catch it. "What's this?"

"One diamond of a fingerprint," Steve responded.

"From?"

"The gas fire. This came out of the gun that was found with the dead guy. The sheriff thinks the Okie blew up the thing." Steve paused. "The damage . . . man, it was overwhelming."

Turnow removed his spectacles to examine the contents of the bag.

"It was like nothing I've ever seen before," Steve added. "Makes the BART bomb look like a firecracker. If it's the same group, they have ratcheted up the stakes a country mile."

Turnow glanced up. He bit his lip, clenching his jaw. "I saw some of the photos that were e-mailed today. A regular war zone, huh?"

Steve's vision blurred as images of the sight returned to him. "If these are the same guys . . ." He shook his head at the thought.

Dr. Turnow slipped on a pair of gloves. "Very well could be. According to an interview done with the head of that oil exploration outfit—"

"Golden State," Steve acknowledged.

"According to them, some Semtex went missing three months ago." Turnow replaced his glasses as he searched for a report on the desk. He found it and continued, "The owner was afraid to report it, but now he's a victim of his own shortsightedness, and the foreman who knew about it is bending over backwards to be cooperative. According to the lab analysis, the signature specs of the explosives that went missing are the same as the bomb on the BART Red Line."

Steve blinked as a chill rolled down his back. The composition of explosives was as individual in its own way as fingerprints, and just as incriminating. "That would be a weird coincidence."

"Let's get this in the scanner." Turnow stood up, moving to a piece of equipment that resembled a kitchen microwave.

After gently placing the scorched shell casing inside and punching several buttons, a turntable began to rotate. Red laser beams scanned the shell as it rotated. On a nearby computer terminal, a message read "Building image." A moment later an exact high-resolution image of the nickel-plated casing remained on the screen.

Joking, Steve said, "Could you put some popcorn in there for me too, Doc?"

Leaning over a computer keyboard, Dr. Turnow pointed and clicked commands. By the time Steve finished a yawn, a blown-up version of the fingerprint had been lifted from the rest of the image and the curve of its impression on the casing flattened out.

"Wow!" Steve exclaimed. "You didn't even sit down."

"Wait till you see what else I can do with this thing," Dr. Turnow assured him.

Another message: "Transferring image."

"Very good," Turnow hummed to himself as he moved to another terminal. "I love it that things are so well integrated these days. It won't be long before I won't even have to come into the lab to do this sort of thing."

Positioned where he could see another monitor, Turnow waited. Images of thousands of prints flicked up. Various areas of the FBI's recorded fingerprints file were highlighted as the computer cross-checked points of reference. Flickering faster than the eye could follow, the image would change as print after print appeared, with about the same cadence as a stopwatch keeping track of an Olympic sprinter.

Crossing his arms as he rested his back against a cabinet, Turnow observed, "I can't believe they let you leave the scene with a piece of evidence like this."

"Well," Steve laughed, "you'd never believe a lot of things about that place, but after going there myself, I imagine they're all true."

Their laughs were interrupted by a metallic *gong* made by the computer. In the upper left-hand corner the enlargement of a single print was framed. Beside it appeared a photograph of a young, scraggly bearded man with long hair as well as a long personal history. The computer continued to search for other possible matches while Turnow read the profile aloud.

"Shadir al Mustafa. Arrested in 1992 in association with those who conspired to bomb the NYC World Trade Center. Convicted of possessing knowledge of criminal activities. Sentenced to three years, served 28 months in the federal penitentiary. Lay low after 9/11/01. No other history."

"I wonder where he's living now?" Steve inquired, examining the prints side by side. "It's a perfect match."

"It says here. Daly City, California."

Steve grabbed his B-com. "I'll bet he killed Metz to keep him quiet, took the explosives, lit off the gas tanks to cover his tracks and to point the blame at the Okie. And all that would mean . . ."

Turnow voiced the conclusion. "He now has more Semtex."

A voice answered the B-com. "Special Agent Brown."

"Anton!" Steve shouted. "Where are you?"

"I'm on 101, heading in with Agent Clearwater."

Steve felt agitated. If something wasn't done right away this no-longer-faceless terrorist would get away. "Listen! I need you to head for"—he read Shadir's address from the monitor— "Ingleside."

"I'm about one-five minutes away. What's up?"

"Big break, man!" Steve tore his fingers through his messy hair. "Big break. You're looking for a Middle Eastern guy named Shadir. I'll transfer a photo and the rest of the info to your car. I got a feeling if he isn't already there, he might show up real soon! Just get there, pronto!"

Turnow was already hacking away, sending the documents to Anton's mobile e-mail.

Steve pulled on his windbreaker and sprinted from the room.

Daly City, California
3:17 P.M. Pacific Time

CAN'T GO HOME AGAIN

Normally a trip from Monterey to Daly City would be a two-hour endeavor. Shadir, however, had other stops to make first. Instead of heading north on 101, directly home to the area of Ingleside in Daly City, he branched northeast on 880 to West Oakland. There he made a deposit in a small mini-storage, which he'd rented using the assumed identity of an unsuspecting college student.

The worker at Sal's U-Store-It told him, "You know, you're a good man. You're always on time." Shadir paid the bill in cash every six months to avoid a mailed invoice.

The man's statement was one of those momentous unconsciously ironic statements. If he only knew there were 10 pounds of high explosives in the little metal shed.

Shadir returned the gray Toyota pickup to a friend, Abdul, from a mosque in Oakland. Abdul, completely unaware of Shadir's real occupation and plans, had loaned him the vehicle in the belief that Shadir was headed south to visit a sick friend.

"Thank you," Shadir said to Abdul. "He is feeling much better."

"He?" questioned the elderly Abdul. "I thought you were going to visit a woman."

Shadir clucked his tongue, implying that Abdul was getting forgetful in his advancing years. Then he thanked the man again and split on his bike, riding through the seedy side of West Oakland to the BART station located there. A $2.70 fare would allow Shadir and the bike to ride the Blue Line home.

As he stood on the platform waiting for the train, something caught his eye on the graffiti-scarred wall. It was an orange flyer with a man's mug shot featured in the center. The face looked familiar. He squinted before realizing that it was a photo of Rhamad.

Shadir read the words: "Wanted: Any information regarding this man or any known associates, in connection with the April 20 bombing of the Red Line."

Shadir's olive skin grew pale as he stepped back, hastily searching the area for anyone who might have seen him staring at the poster. Above him he noticed a camera. Shadir quickly turned his face away and sweat broke out on his forehead.

A cool wind began to blow. He recognized the distant clatter of metal wheels on tracks and stepped up to the edge of the platform. The long car flashed by, squeaking before coming to a stop.

In a hurry to enter, Shadir almost ran into the doors with his bike before they had opened. He found a seat on a padded bench. The doors beeped and closed. The BART train sped away.

Shadir felt paranoid, as if all those aboard were staring at him. In an attempt to avoid eye contact, he read the overhead advertisements. But it was there too—the orange flyer. "Wanted: Any information . . . "

Shadir covered his face with his hands. Had he failed? Would someone discover him before he was able to carry out the final phase of the plan? Once the magnitude of his errors was known, would Khalil even let him live that long?

He sat bolt upright again when the train slowed to a crawl as it passed carefully through what was left of the Montgomery Street Station. The wheels clunked as they shifted to an alternate route. Through the window men could be seen moving materials around in wheelbarrows and shouldering lumber. A welder's torch arced. The intense blue light temporarily blinded Shadir.

Less than 12 days and already the line was passable, though with reduced and very slow service. Tunnel blackness refilled the view out the window. Shadir hung his head again and did not lift it for eight more stops.

"Daly City," a computerized female voice announced.

Shadir wheeled his bike to the escalator. More orange posters by the exit caught his eye. Escaping the subway was an obvious relief. He sighed as he climbed aboard his bike.

In Ingleside, Shadir noticed twice the usual number of police cars cruising the streets. Proceeding with caution, Shadir used all his instincts to alert him to trouble—very near, very real danger.

The gears of the bike ticked as he coasted, searching the side streets. Nearby there was a black Crown Vic. Two men sat in the front seat: an African-American and another unseen, hidden behind a newspaper. At the opposite end of his street, a dark blue Chevy Caprice was parked, also occupied by a watcher.

Did they know about his relationship with Rhamad? How could they? What had he failed to take into account? Were they there for him? Shadir's heart thumped intensely. His breathing was quick and shallow. Pretending to study a street sign, he unhurriedly and deliberately made a left-hand turn and rode away.

Pier 41
San Francisco
7:15 P.M. Pacific Time

PERSIA'S FLAME

There would be barely enough time for a shower and change of clothes before Steve and Anton would be off in another direction. North to Sausalito. After background intel revealed the name of Shadir al Mustafa's employer, several calls to the offices of Persia's Flame Shipping Company had turned up nothing.

Anton had convinced the Pier 39 gate guard that there was important FBI business there. One flick of his shiny black suit coat and a flash of his badge, and he and Steve had been allowed to pass through the gate by car during what were normally pedestrian-only hours.

"I'm around the other side now," Steve informed his friend.

Anton circled around the back side of Pier 39, where it fronted Pier 41. On the San Francisco waterfront, odd-numbered slips ran north from the ferry building just below the Bay Bridge. Even-numbered slips were south of it.

Besides Steve's battered boat where he was living now, there were very few other boats docked between Piers 39 and 41 except for commercial vessels and guest slips for boats in transit. And no other live-aboards.

Anton left the car running while Steve charged toward his boat for a change of clothes and his shaving kit. Rolling down the window, he noticed how much noisier and smellier 600 sea lions were from a few yards away instead of across the width of the commercial pier. They barked and honked, slapping their chests from atop floating platforms.

With a bundle of clean clothes in his arms, Steve saluted Anton as he exited his dock's metal security gate. "Won't be five minutes."

"Hey," Anton called after him. "what's up with you movin'? Last week the other side and this week here. And I know you haven't been on the boat. I checked."

Steve composed a case that would sound convincing. "Marina office did it for me. I like it over here. Fewer boats and it's quieter."

"Yeah, right!" Anton said in disbelief, motioning toward the obnoxiously jostling sea lions. "Must be cheaper. You cheapskate."

Steve should have known Anton would figure the move for what it was. What could he say? "I only sleep on it, and either way, I shower in the marina head. They let me have it for only 150 bucks a month."

Anton mumbled to himself as he watched Steve hurry off. "Cheap sucker. Livin' with all that noise and stink."

Five minutes later Steve returned with a pile of clothes rolled up in a wet towel and a patchy shave.

Anton cruised the Embarcadero to Taylor, then headed west again on Bay Street. Eventually the road tied in with Marina Boulevard and merged into 101 over the Golden Gate Bridge. Steve was busily reading up on Shadir.

"This guy may be dangerous," Steve asserted. "Based on the earlier charge and the fact that he's hooked up with some serious Middle Eastern money. The kind of dough that springs for Semtex."

"Just remember," Anton cautioned, "this shipping company owner, Khalil, is squeaky clean. No jacket on him at all, so don't go finding terrorists behind every Ali this or Baba that."

So far this call on Khalil was routine, an attempt to find out the current whereabouts of Shadir.

It was getting dark. The black Ford crossed the Golden Gate and exited into the town of Sausalito. The area was known to have some of the most expensive property in the country. A small condominium might run a couple million dollars or more. Khalil's residence was down the steep hill, located right on the water. From the gates Steve and Anton realized how expensive the half-acre property was, complete with tennis courts and an 8,000-plus-square-foot home.

Anton buzzed the gate.

A man with a deep, studiously nonaccented voice answered, "May I help you?"

"I hope so," Anton explained. "I am Agent Anton Brown from the San Francisco FBI and we need to speak with Mr. Khalil."

"What is this in regard to?"

"Can we come in?"

"No, sir. Please inform me what this is in regard to."

Anton looked at Steve. Both of them knew it wasn't going to be easy. "We are looking for Shadir al Mustafa."

"I know no one by that name."

"Oh?" Anton queried. "But we are aware that he works for Mr. Khalil's company."

The voice replied brusquely, "Mr. Khalil's firm employs several thousand people in 10 different countries. Perhaps you should try somewhere else . . . like Indonesia."

Anton jumped in. "We actually have some questions for Mr. Khalil. Is he in?"

There was a moment of silence before the answer came. "Mr. Brown, he is not available at this time. If you would like to speak with him, you may contact his secretary at the Persia's Flame office. They will make an appointment for you."

Steve figured they were wasting their time. "Stone wall. We need a search warrant to get in here."

It was clear from Anton's face that big iron gates and faceless voices over intercoms didn't sit well with him. They weren't neighborly; they weren't honest. "You know, it really would be a big help to the FBI if you and Mr. Khalil would cooperate."

The deep voice concluded, "I am afraid I can offer you nothing more. Good-bye."

The intercom clicked off.

For a second Anton was speechless. Then he muttered, "If it's a warrant they want, then it's a warrant they'll get! And I'm gonna personally serve it on that snotty-voiced so-and-so, whoever he is!"

Khalil's Residence
Sausalito, California
8:24 P.M. Pacific Time

WORMWOOD

Dressed in a long, striped robe, Khalil stared at the security monitor as the Ford turned around. He could see Steve, with his arm hanging out the window, make a gesture at the camera, as if he were going to shoot it. "Good work, Mehdi," Khalil said to his dark-skinned valet and bodyguard, who was formally dressed in a suit and tie. "You handled that well."

"Thank you, sir," replied the servant.

"American FBI pigs!" Khalil spat, turning away as the car drove off. "Shadir! You are an idiot. What have you done that would bring them looking for you?" Khalil faced Shadir as he walked up the steps of the wide, dome-ceilinged room, done in a modern Mediterranean decor of whites and turquoise.

"I don't know." Shadir acted baffled. "It is a mystery to me how they could make any assumptions about me."

"They are not assumptions, you fool!" Khalil scolded. "First Rhamad's body, which simple task you bungled, and then your reckless amusement with explosives! They have some evidence that points to you, and now you are wanted! If they catch you or come back, the entire plan may be jeopardized."

Shadir covered his face as he sighed. "I . . ." He could think of nothing to say. Nor was this the time to report the stakeout at his home.

"After all my expense and preparation, if you bungle this, you will share Rhamad's fate!" Khalil asserted. "You must go."

"Where?" Shadir worried aloud.

"South," Khalil informed him. "The time is near. I will say I have not seen you. 'Shadir has disappeared,' I will say. And you will be in San Luis, preparing for your ride into heaven. In the meantime, not a word of this to our visitor."

"I understand, Khalil."

The three men moved to a lower floor of the mansion. A tiled room displayed a brace of free-form bronzes, mostly images reminiscent of flames and spears, and an expansive acrylic painting of a flaming orange meteor striking a brilliantly blue-green Earth. Opposite the artwork a panoramic window provided a sweeping view of San Francisco Bay. Beside the window, hands clasped behind his back, stood Oleg Petrov.

"A thousand pardons," Khalil said, bowing to the Russian physicist. "Matters unrelated to our business detained me."

Petrov indicated the expanse of whitecapped bay and the pinnacles of San Francisco skyscrapers beyond. "No matter," he said. "This is restful after my journey. Always such a nuisance. Korea to Japan to Canada to here. Each leg, a different passport, a different name to remember."

As Petrov described his security precautions, Khalil was reassured. The operation had not been jeopardized in any way.

Thanking Petrov for all his trouble, Khalil shot Shadir a raised-eyebrow glance. Then he offered, "Please, sit. You will have tea?"

"That would be welcome," Petrov agreed.

Medhi bowed his way out of the room.

"You wish to see what you have purchased?" Petrov asked, nudging a padded duffel bag with his foot. Without waiting for Khalil's reply, Petrov unzipped the sack and removed a gleaming black baseball bat, bigger than regulation size in both barrel and length. Petrov extended it grip first. "With this we will make the entire West Coast of the United States uninhabitable."

"It is all right to touch?" Khalil inquired, hesitating for an instant.

"Of course." Petrov laughed. "It is only a special form of carbon."

"What's the joke?" Shadir demanded belligerently when Khalil passed him the bat. He had expected a fancy explosive device, a high-tech weapon. Moreover, Shadir had ties to the Afghan Mujahedin and hated Russians.

"Buckyballs," Petrov said, smiling broadly at Shadir's confusion. "This bat is made of a compound called *buckyballs.* Thanks to Khalil's generosity and my genius, this can do something nothing else on earth can do."

Petrov reviewed how a nuclear plant's spent fuel rods were stored under borated water for safekeeping.

"This I already know," Shadir asserted.

Khalil glared at him and he fell silent.

"Boron has two properties that make it ideal for such a task," Petrov continued pedantically. "In the storage pool it absorbs radiation so that particle collisions do not take place and the nuclear chain reaction does not occur. Secondly, boron forms an extremely strong chemical bond. It can scarcely be broken and therefore no known chemical agent can make it precipitate, that is, make it separate from the water in the tank."

The tea arrived, preceded by an intense aroma of mint and carried by Mehdi on a silver tray. After a sip of tea Petrov continued.

"No known agent . . . until now. In 1985 a compound called *buckminsterfullerene* was discovered. This structure of 60 linked carbon atoms was named for the architect who championed geodesic domes, because that is the shape of the molecules."

Shadir looked doubtful.

"Like a soccer ball," Khalil explained, using the metaphor by which Petrov had first explained the molecular structure to him.

"Like tiny mesh soccer balls," Petrov agreed. "Hence the name *buckyballs,* you see? These carbon molecules have the ability to trap other molecules inside. This is well known. But this is also where my genius comes in. I have primed my buckyball creation with small amounts of cesium and potassium. In their radioactive isotopes, of course."

At the word *radioactive,* Shadir fearfully placed the bat on the tile.

"Not dangerously so," Petrov said, laughing again. "But because of the radioactivity, each carbon molecule will attract the boron in the water to itself. Then the buckyball grabs the boron particle, pulling it out of the water solution and *shabash!* The boron is no longer there to prevent the nuclear-chain reaction from commencing. The radioactive fuel rods are suddenly covered only by plain water."

"That tank contains 7 million liters of borated water!" Shadir scoffed.

Petrov's smile froze on his face. He obviously didn't like to be challenged in his area of expertise. "This quantity of buckminsterfullerene is not only adequate to separate and remove all the boron from the water," he insisted, "it will continue to do so even if they add millions more liters to their tanks."

After another swallow of tea Petrov leaned forward on the black leather sofa and removed an Omega wristwatch from his forearm. "A present for you," he said, extending the timepiece to Shadir, who took it, eyeing it critically.

"Another bit of stupid Russian humor?" Shadir said. "It doesn't even run."

"No, and you had best not unscrew the stem and pull it outward until it's time," Petrov said. "Unless you want your children to be purple and have two heads each. The watchcase is lead-lined. The stem contains sufficient radioactive californium to start the nuclear reaction when you drop it into the water. You will not need to detonate an explosive device. No need to worry how to sneak a bomb past the security devices."

"Bravo!" Khalil exclaimed. "Tell me again what will happen then!" He listened eagerly to Petrov's discussion, like a child anxiously hanging on every word of a bedtime story.

"This is not just a suicide bombing at an Israeli bus stop. The reaction will proceed. The water in the pool will heat to boiling and radioactive steam will begin to escape. Hotter and faster will go the reaction as a jet of destruction plumes into the air. Soon all the water will be gone and the cladding will melt from the fuel rods. The fuel pellets will drop to the bottom."

"Will they go critical?" Khalil asked, as if inquiring whether the story would have a happy ending.

Petrov shrugged. "Perhaps," he said. "It depends on the proportion of older and newer fuel in the storage pool." Then he brightened. "If so, it will melt through concrete and steel until, upon reaching groundwater, an even more massive explosion happens, spewing radioactive steam high into the winds."

"Which are always from the northwest and blow toward Los Angeles," Shadir suggested, catching the apocalyptic vision. "The nearby area a wasteland forever. A wind-borne plague looming like the shadow of death!"

"Just like Chernobyl in Ukraine in 1986," Petrov concurred. "That facility was only running at 7 percent power. Just 7 percent! People forget that a nuclear plant is a controlled atomic bomb. *Controlled,* ha! They were merely testing the turbines, you see. A power surge caused explosions. The top of the reactor blew off. Poisonous steam shot 1000 meters into the atmosphere. Radioactivity spread hundreds of miles. Two hundred thousand people evacuated. Who knows how many killed, and more *still* dying of the radiation sickness. In any case, millions of Americans will be affected. The economy of California will be destroyed. Igniting Diablo will make Chernobyl look like the candle on a birthday cake."

The physicist sat back on the couch. "I have named my compound after that earlier event," he said with smug false modesty. "Chernobylene." Then he added, "Are you familiar with the Christian Bible?"

This was so unexpected that both Shadir and Khalil only stared.

"Revelation chapter 8, verses 10 and 11," Petrov intoned. His eyes were closed as if in prayerful devotion. "A prophecy of global catastrophe at the end of the world: 'The third angel sounded his trumpet, and a great star, blazing like a torch, fell from the sky on a third of the rivers and on the springs of water—the name of the star is Wormwood. A third of the waters turned bitter and many people died.' "

Khalil eyed Shadir, who shrugged.

"A pity you do not know Russian," Petrov suggested, "or you would catch the irony. In Russian, the word for Wormwood is *Chernobyl!*"

After Petrov's departure, Khalil took Shadir aside. "You see how all is in readiness," he said. "But I still have doubts about Salim's commitment. Perhaps a threat is not enough."

"Then what is to be done?"

"Mahmoud is shadowing Salim's wife and child. He will find a convenient time to kidnap one or both of them. Then we will have the leverage we need. Soon we will light Shaiton's Fire and the Americans will feel its heat!" Khalil scanned the bronzes and luxurious furnishings with a momentary expression of regret. Then his face hardened. "Giving it all up is a small sacrifice," he said. "By the way, are you certain no one can link you to the gas explosion, or you to me?" Fiercely he added, "Nothing can be allowed to go wrong now!"

His face revealing nothing but blind obedience and complete understanding, Shadir glibly lied, "Absolutely nothing!"

SEVENTEEN

San Francisco Waterfront
Wednesday, 2 May
6:40 P.M. Pacific Time

BETTER A MILLSTONE

Dr. Turnow's head throbbed as he walked along the waterfront of Fisherman's Wharf. He shoved his hands deeply into his jacket pockets and stared pensively over the rough seas as a ferryboat packed with commuters labored toward Vallejo.

A fresh, cold breeze swept down from the north, whipping the dark green waters into a froth. It would be a long, miserable crossing for tens of thousands of inland workers who had relied on BART to get them to and from San Francisco with ease.

Turnow had heard more than one nervous traveler mention the fact that if they weren't safe on a subway train, why should they think they were safe on a ferryboat? After all, look what happened to the World Trade Center. Because of box cutters in the hands of suicidal terrorists, thousands of innocent Americans lost their lives. What made a ferryboat in San Francisco Bay immune to the same twisted thinking?

Turnow made his way through the crowded arcade outside Alioto's Restaurant. Men and women pushed in to purchase shrimp cocktails and clam chowder in bread bowls. Acutely aware that the BART bomber was still at large, possibly hiding in plain sight, Turnow found himself scanning the hands and faces of strangers.

Was any place safe anymore?

Turnow knew well the grim answer to that question. No place in America was safe if a terrorist organization set its sights on destroying it.

The lion of fear and indiscriminate slaughter would burst again through the door of America. Before this, the horrific suicide bombings in Israel had been reported by U.S. news media something like the score of a boring baseball game: "Nineteen Israelis dead,105 wounded in the blast . . . one Palestinian activist killed . . ."

So terrorists had been labeled *activists,* as if they were trying to save the whales instead of murdering innocent children in a public restaurant. As small Jewish hands and heads and dismembered bodies were gathered up in black bags, the U.S. and the world had demanded "restraint" from the Israeli government!

Such idiotic political rhetoric was a green light for fanatics to strap on 40 pounds of nails and a handful of explosives and light the fuse in a crowded American restaurant, movie theater, or an open fish market on a waterfront.

Turnow knew that by tolerating and even excusing terrorism by any group, for any reason, anywhere, the United States was about to reap another bitter harvest of slaughter within its own borders. And Americans would watch it all on CNN as if it were a new made-for-TV movie. *Entertainment Tonight . . . Watch a four-year-old with nails in her eyes writhe with pain in the street beside her dead mother!*

Perhaps this was the *Brave New World* of which Aldous Huxley had written, or the only slightly delayed atrocities of Orwell's *1984:* Eliminate words like *right and wrong, moral, good,* and *truth.* Twist history to fit the times. Above all, seek entertainment!

The violent death of *others* was America's daily amusement. Turnow feared that only when terrorism took its toll on convenience would Americans get the real message of what political correctness and toleration of evil meant.

Like now.

The fleet of ferryboats would never keep up with the numbers of commuters. Traffic out of the city on the Golden Gate and Bay Bridges had slowed to a crawl. One stalled outbound automobile could virtually bring the entire city to a standstill. It would be weeks before BART was up and running at full capacity again. The terrorists had chosen their target well.

Turnow recalled the transportation strike of 1997 when BART had closed down for only a week. Some 270,000 daily commuters had been stranded; San Francisco had been crippled by gridlock.

As it was this afternoon.

Turnow was hungry. How long had it been since he had stopped to eat? He couldn't remember. The case had consumed every minute. Bitterness simmered slowly in his gut. Evil was descending like a thick cloud on this nation, and yet the public seemed more interested in the latest political sex scandal or what movie was coming out next week.

Suddenly he thought of Meg and wished she were here. In all the years he'd known her, his wife had always managed to help him walk through the dark reality of the world and find some ray of hope.

He bought a loaf of fresh sourdough bread and a Coke. This would be supper. His stomach couldn't take anything stronger. Breaking free from the teeming crowds, he strode down to the park outside the Maritime Museum and found a bench facing the Bay. Peaceful. But there was no comfort in the scene.

He remembered the quote, "Men say, 'peace, peace,' when there is no peace. . . ."

Tendrils of receding fog swirled around the arches of the Golden Gate Bridge. The tall masts of the sailing ship *Balclutha* brought to mind an era when Mark Twain had written that San Francisco had the best bad things any man could ever want. Corrupt with greed and violence, San Francisco had sprung up from a village to a great city. And it was still corrupt. Still violent. It was a microcosm of American culture. A logical target, really.

Tearing off a chunk of bread, Turnow put it in his mouth. He considered that there were no good old days. The battle between good and evil had been going on since the beginning of time. Every generation had turned from light to pursue darkness. Every man had raised his fist to God in defiance, in bitterness, in blame. How could a loving God allow such a thing?

This was the battle Turnow fought within himself now. The image of the dead children came vividly to mind. He couldn't swallow.

He plucked his cell phone from his pocket and dialed the number at Tahoe. Three rings. Would Meg answer? Was she outside putting bedding plants in the planter boxes?

"Is that you?" Her voice was cheerful.

"Meg." Of course she could hear the heaviness in his tone.

"Oh, Tim. I've been watching the news." Now she sounded sympathetic, grieved for him.

"It's not even close."

"I figured. Hon? I'm praying for you."

"Why is it always the innocent who suffer?"

"Darling, you remember what started this? Oklahoma City. All those kids."

Turnow recalled sitting out under the stars with her the night the first images of the Oklahoma City bombing flashed across the screen. The baby in the arms of the fireman had made her weep. She had sat with her head in her hands for a long time, unable to speak at first. And then the answers had come. Well, not answers, really, but truth sticking out like a snag in a raging river for a drowning man to grab on to.

She repeated her words to him now. "The battle has always raged, Tim. Evil is a real force, an entity, a being that exists in this world and directs the actions of willing men. And it lulls the apathetic into a stupor of acceptance! Apathy and evil. The two work hand in hand. They are the same, really. This is a war of cosmic proportions. It is the innocent who suffer. Evil wills it. Apathy allows it. Evil hates the innocent and the defenseless most of all. Apathy doesn't care as long as it's not personally inconvenienced. Most of the world fits into those two categories. If it wasn't true, there never would have been a Hitler. Or a Stalin. Or the leaders of al Qaeda who send young men in planes to blow up innocent civilians."

Turnow watched as the sunset changed the clouds from pink to deep purple. "There are some—political pundits—who will say the people who did this thing have their reasons. Political. Religious. That the cause they're fighting for somehow legitimizes the murder of innocent people. The madness of it, Meg! The world is upside down, and I feel like the guy who sees what's coming. I climb on a rooftop and shout the warning. But no one is listening and everything, every atrocity, is not only *allowed,* it's *forgiven* as long as it has a political label pinned to it. Finally, I looked at the face of a dead little boy and I . . . he never had a chance to live, Meg. And I made this child a promise that I wouldn't rest until we found the people who stole his life, but somewhere out there is the guy who did this. Still free. Content that he shut down a city at the cost of a few lives."

"And yet," Meg replied softly, "God said it would be better if a millstone were hung around the neck of anyone who hurts a child or who stands by and does nothing while a child is hurt. Read Proverbs, chapter 6: 'There are seven things the Lord hates . . . hands that shed innocent blood.' There is an eternal judgment coming, Tim. Until then, didn't the Lord say in Matthew chapter 18, verse 10, that the angels of children are always in God's presence? We have to believe it. God's love and mercy are alive and active. They are stronger than evil and apathy. Those little ones are in the Lord's arms now. But it's up to us to bring their killers to justice on earth if we can. I read something once: 'Mercy shown to an evil man is cruelty to the innocent.' God wants us to fight back! Some of us pray. Others—you —hunt killers. And since faith in what God has said about the innocent is all we have to stand on, we have to keep believing. The God of justice will direct your work to find whoever has done this thing. And to stop them from doing it again."

Turnow nodded, grateful for her, and her strong faith that could still believe when his own fell short. "Yes. Thanks."

"Are you eating?" she asked, turning to the practical matters which 30 years of caring for him brought to mind.

He looked morosely at the bag of bread on the park bench. "Yes."

"What? French bread and salami? I mean *eating.*"

"I miss you, Meg."

"I'll come down then. I didn't want to get in the way."

"You won't see much of me."

"Dinner at Neptune's Palace. I was thinking of steamed salmon in a clay pot. Sunset over the Golden Gate."

"The highways are gridlocked."

"So I've heard. I'll take the ferry in from Vallejo."

He frowned. "The killers. They're still out there. Maybe riding the cable cars up and down Powell Street. I don't know." Thoughts of the hole in the side of the *USS Cole* came to mind. "You're safe at home."

"I want to be with you, Tim. I won't ride the cable car."

"Sure. Yes. I want to see you too. Come on then. I'll think a bit more clearly if you're here."

Pier 41
San Francisco
10:12 P.M. Pacific Time

THINKING OF YOU

The day had been exhausting for Steve.

He reflected on the fact that it was more tiring to run into an unbroken succession of dead ends, blind alleys, and stone walls—every metaphor for failure in the book—than to literally run a 10K through soft sand.

Despite the irritating arrogance with which the FBI had been dismissed from Khalil's estate, it had not been as easy to go back with a search warrant as Anton predicted. Khalil, the shipping magnate, was not only wealthy, he was powerful, had powerful friends, and was squeaky clean. His family had been closely connected to Mohammad

Reza Pahlavi, the shah of Iran at a time when the monarch of the Peacock Throne had been among the few allies the U.S. had in the region. Besides that, Khalil had played a minor role in Colonel North's Iran/Contra machinations in the eighties. As such he was not easily tagged with the suspicion of aiding anti-U.S. terrorists.

Shadir's trail was also cold. Steve found it hard to believe that someone with a record as questionable as Shadir's could fall through the bureaucratic cracks, but apparently that was the case. And now the man, suspected of murder and terrorist bombings, had disappeared. An around-the-clock stakeout of Shadir's Daly City home turned up nothing; painstaking interviews of his neighbors revealed only that he was a quiet man who kept to himself.

Steve lay down on his bunk in his messy boat, resolving yet again to do something about fixing it up, even as he recognized the unlikelihood of fulfilling the vow.

Tourists usually left the Pier 39 area around nine in the evening. The sea lions were mostly quiet, with only the occasional growl or belch. The noises didn't matter to Steve. The fog rolled in, leaving a calm chill, a blanket of insulation between Steve and his frustration.

Except for one thing.

He sighed, realizing that he needed to call Cindy. "I hope she's not asleep yet," he said to himself as he dialed the number. It rang twice before she picked up.

"Hello," Cindy answered sweetly.

He wondered how she would react. Would she still be mad about his predawn departure the day before? "Cindy, this is Steve. Um, I was just thinking about you."

"Hi," she exclaimed. "I was hoping . . . I thought it might be you."

She sounded glad enough to hear from him, though he thought he'd better apologize before she changed her mind. "Listen, honey, I'm sorry for leaving so abruptly. It was a big emergency and . . ."

"It's really okay," she responded reasonably. "I saw the news. The big explosion out in the valley. Terrifying."

"It was pretty bad," Steve agreed.

"I understand. You had to go."

"Yep, I did, but I wanted you to know that I had a wonderful time with you and the kids. It seems like weeks have passed already. And I really did miss having breakfast with you and the boys."

"It was good to see you, Steve. We all missed you too, but you helped me see it differently. In some ways I think the boys already got it better than I did. People who do such things have to be stopped."

Her tone was so encouraging Steve wanted to ask her up to visit, but would she go for it? "I was just thinking . . . if you guys weren't too busy —"

"Yes?" she encouraged.

"What are you doing tomorrow and this weekend?"

"Oh, Steve." She sounded genuinely disappointed to have to refuse. "You know the school has that big Cinco de Mayo carnival Friday. In fact, I've been working all week on it. Is tomorrow Thursday already?"

"Yeah, Thursday," he replied as his hopeful spirit deflated.

She continued, "There's no escape. I have to get ready for it." A boy's voice sounded in the background. "Hang on . . . okay . . . Steve, somebody wants to talk to you."

"Is that Matt?"

"Here he is." She turned the phone over to their older son.

"Dad!" nine-year-old Matthew called out. "Did you go out to the big fire? Wow, I wish I could have seen it up close."

Steve was glad he hadn't. "Well, people died there, son. Some very bad men did that and hurt families they didn't even know."

"You'll catch 'em," Matt said confidently, then asked, "so when can we come up and stay with you?"

"You know, I was going to ask your mother, but you have the carnival."

"That old boring carnival. I'm tired of it." Matt dismissed it. "I'd rather be up there with you."

Steve had an idea. "If your mother wants to bring you halfway, I'd love to take you to a Giants game tomorrow night."

"Wow! Really? Cool! Mom, Dad's gonna take me to a Giants game tomorrow night!"

Steve heard Cindy say, "What?" Then, "Steven Alstead." Cindy was back on the line. "Did you tell your son he could go to a ball game with you tomorrow night?"

"I said maybe, if we asked you and . . ."

"That's as good as saying yes," she scolded him.

"I could meet you halfway. We could have lunch at the aquarium and the boys could play."

She thought about it. "The only thing is I have to be ready for the carnival on Friday. If I spend five hours up and back that doesn't leave me much time."

Steve overheard Matt urging her. "Oh, come on, Mom! It's not that far. You can take me and come back, then get up real early Friday!"

Steve teased her, "Late Thursday, early Friday sounds like fun to me, Mom."

It would be hard for her to get out of this one. The boys really hadn't spent much time with their father lately. "All right."

Steve was sure the neighbors could hear Matt's joyous shouts. "Yeah! I get to go see a ball game with Dad!"

After Matt had run down, Cindy remarked to Steve, "He really does miss you."

"I know," Steve replied. "What about my little guy? Does he want to come?"

"I'll ask him. Tommy, do you want to go to the baseball game with Daddy and Brother?"

Tommy's little voice was a higher, sweeter version of Matt's. "No b-ball. I wanna go to the carnival."

Steve melted when he heard it. Dear God, how he loved them all. A tear formed in his eye. *This is why I have to do what I do,* he vowed. *To keep them all as safe as possible in this evil world.*

"You heard him," Cindy added. "Carnival is more fun than a b-ball game, Dad. Guess you'll have to come down again."

"I'll do it," Steve assured her. "Soon."

Matt interrupted again. “Can I bring a friend? How about Michael?”

Cindy answered, “I don’t know if he’ll be up for it yet, Matt.”

“The boy I saved?” Steve asked. “How is he?”

“He’s doing well. Thanks to you,” she praised. “You made me proud. You made us all proud.”

Steve melted again and tried to think of something grateful to say without sounding too much like his old, cocky self. “Yeah, well, that’s what I do,” he offered awkwardly.

“All right, big head,” Cindy joked.

“Listen, if Matt wants to bring a friend, and Michael is up to it, it’s totally cool with me.”

Cindy considered. “I’ll ask his dad tomorrow and let you know about a meeting time.”

Suddenly a wave of dread washed over Steve. Now he’d have to clean his boat. What would the boys say when they found out he didn’t have power or TV? No video games, no videotapes. He’d have to make it fun, an adventure—something not easy with nine-year-olds these days. “Okay, babe. I’ll talk to you soon. I love you.”

“I love you too,” Cindy answered in a sleepy, affectionate voice. “Rest well.”

“You too,” Steve replied before getting off the phone.

Another idea came to him. It was a solution for his little nine-year-old problem. He would make the visit fun by taking the boys to the HRT Shoot House Friday evening for the simmunition drill. They would be doing a mock hostage rescue with real guns, firing paintballs. *I know the kids would think that’s a blast,* he decided.

All worries and frustrations temporarily set aside, he was soon carried off to sleep by the rocking of the boat in the surge.

EIGHTEEN

The Alstead Condo
Morro Bay, California
Thursday, 3 May
2:30 P.M. Pacific Time

GO FISH

The Morro Bay condo was littered with brown paper bags stuffed with prizes for the Cinco de Mayo carnival's Go Fish game. For three years running, this preschool money-raiser had been Cindy's domain. It wasn't as exciting as the Immerse Father Jerry pitching booth, but it beat ducking stray baseballs.

This year Cindy was also in charge of collecting donations from individuals and area merchants for the silent auction. Although almost everything had been delivered to Old Mission Elementary School, Cindy's garage was still jammed with stuff ranging from table lamps to an indoor/outdoor mahogany glider set.

So much yet to do and she still had to drive Matthew and Michael Salim up Highway 101 to Salinas. And where were Michael and his dad anyway? They were late.

Paul Salim had volunteered the use of a Diablo landscaping truck to transfer the remaining auction loot to Old Mission Plaza. He would drop off Michael and load the loot at the same time.

He arrived at last with Michael and a crew of three helpers.

Cindy, dressed in ragged denims and one of Steve's old sweatshirts, opened the door. Tommy joined her in the foyer.

Michael, backpack slung over his shoulder, grinned shyly at his teacher and jerked his thumb toward a new gas barbecue grill being unloaded from the truck. "What do you think, Mrs. Alstead?"

"Great," Cindy said enthusiastically. "But don't unload it. Take it on over to Old Mission."

Michael wagged his head. "No. This is for Mr. Alstead," he said seriously. "For what he did for me. Saving my life. And also, you know, inviting me to the Giants game."

Paul Salim did not meet her gaze. His brooding expression seemed more unhappy than usual. He added, "This is Michael's thanks to your husband. Saving Michael in the water. It was Michael's idea."

The father didn't seem pleased with his son's insistence on this gesture of gratitude. *Is he jealous of Steve?* Cindy wondered. No matter. She gushed over the gift.

At the sound of Michael's arrival, Matthew whooped and called down the stairwell. "Hey, Michael! Buddy! You ready? Come on up!"

Michael bounded past Cindy.

"Michael!" Salim called after his son. The boy seemed not to hear him.

"Excited, huh?" Cindy offered.

Salim nodded. "I want to wish him . . . farewell."

Cindy invited Paul Salim into the house. They ascended the steps and picked their way through the clutter to Matthew's bedroom.

Michael was instructing little Tommy. "You think I'd miss a Giants game? Over a stupid Cinco de Mayo carnival?"

"I'm helping Mom go fish," the preschooler explained. "I don't care about giants."

The place was a wreck. She had told Matthew he couldn't go unless the room was clean. She tried not to sound abrupt, though Matthew's disregard of her order irritated her. "Matthew! Do you remember what I said about this? We're not going if you don't clean this mess, and I mean now!"

Matthew glanced up at her in horror. She'd been pretty good at carrying out discipline in the past.

"I mean it!" she finished. "Five minutes, Matthew! And I mean clean."

"Okay, Mom." Matthew began to gather up toys and Legos.

Paul Salim cleared his throat, reminding Cindy he was in the room. His presence startled her.

He protested, "But the boys must go, Mrs. Alstead! Michael . . . he will be so disappointed if they cannot go."

Cindy winked broadly at Mr. Salim, giving him the thumbs-up-don't-worry-I-was-just-putting-the-fear-of-God-in-him look. "Five minutes to clean this pigpen and I've got to be on the road!" she said firmly. "If it isn't done . . ."

"We run laps," said Michael Salim. Having spent a year in her classroom, Michael believed her. He jumped in to help.

For the first time Paul Salim smiled. *There's more than amusement in his expression,* Cindy thought. *Is he relieved his son is going?*

"We'll get it done, Mrs. Alstead," Michael declared.

Paul Salim replied enthusiastically, "Yes, Michael! Clean it up, boys. And go. You and Matthew leave here and go have fun with Mr. Alstead. It was meant to be, I suppose, your going now. Yes! Indeed, that is an excellent idea. I very much want for you to go with Matthew to the Giants game!"

As the two boys completed their chore Paul Salim loaded the auction items into the Diablo truck. The task was accomplished quickly.

Then Salim called for his son and took him to one side. He embraced him fiercely, as if he would never see him again. *Is this some emotional residue from the loss of Frank Daley?* Cindy wondered. Everyone she knew had gained a sense that life was short and fragile, that each goodbye could be the last. But Salim, for a moment, seemed almost stricken by this parting with Michael. Salim whispered something quietly in the child's ear.

The boy, suddenly solemn, nodded and waved farewell. He stood at the curb and watched until the truck full of auction donations was out of sight.

Pacific Bell Stadium
San Francisco
7:37 P.M. Pacific Time

DODGING GIANTS

The trip south on the 101 had gone more quickly than Steve had expected. Late that afternoon he had met Cindy at a Denny's parking lot in Salinas, exactly halfway between San Francisco and San Luis Obispo.

She looked good. Steve wished he could take her back with him, but her dedication to the school carnival dictated otherwise. No matter. There had been, in the warmth of her embrace, the promise of a future reunion more than worth waiting for.

She'd headed back to prepare for the next day while Steve hurried the boys north for the 7:30 P.M. game—San Francisco Giants versus Los Angeles Dodgers.

Michael appeared none the worse for his unexpected dunking in the ocean. Cindy had whispered that the accident might have been good for him. He was a lot calmer, more serious, and respectful than he had been at school.

Michael seemed deeply grateful to Steve. His helpful, polite behavior made Matt jealous of Steve's approval, and as a result he tried harder. Both the boys were better for it.

Two hours of driving landed the three at the Pier 39 parking garage. There wasn't time to really see the boat. Instead they caught the F-line trolley east, changing to the N-line south at the ferry building. A couple stops later, the threesome arrived at the recently built Pacific Bell Stadium at the edge of the Bay.

Seeing the building was like taking a trip back in time. It was mostly red brick but had rectangular, black-tinted, latticed windows. The dark green steel girders, along with the rest of the architecture, made it appear genuinely old-timey.

They missed the national anthem but found their seats in the second tier before the first inning was half over.

The part Matt remarked as the coolest was that home plate faced a low wall on the waterside. "Every once in a while, if you're really lucky, you see a guy hit one out into the Bay."

Steve added with a wink, "And if you're outside the park when that happens, you get to see boats crashing into each other and people drowning themselves, trying to fish the balls out of the Bay."

Immediately after he'd said it, Steve remembered the other night when Michael had almost drowned. Steve wondered if there was any cure for habitually saying the wrong thing. Or was he just hopelessly socially inept?

Just when Steve felt the most stupid and incapable of recovery, Michael commented, "Yeah, and if they're *really* lucky, you'll be around to dive in and save them."

"There you go," Steve replied, grateful that a ten-year-old could put him at ease. He changed the subject. "Oh, no! We forgot something."

"What, Dad?" Matt replied, sounding worried.

"Food!" Steve joked.

Matt punched him in the biceps. "You scared me."

"Easy! You punch too hard, and I need that arm." He rubbed his shoulder. "How about I go get some Giant Dogs and drinks?"

"Yeah!" both boys exclaimed.

Steve smelled multicultural aromas as he walked the hall of the food arcade. Italian, Mexican. He wanted to stop for everything, but it was on to the American food for hot dogs, hamburgers, and garlic cheese fries.

"Watch it," Steve mumbled after a tall man in a white pullover sweatshirt slammed into the Glock 27 under his shirttail and kept on walking.

Steve slathered the dogs with mustard, ketchup, onions, and relish, and gathered up the goodies. His hands were full, though it was a good thing. If he'd had more carrying room, he might have stopped for ice cream, nachos, popcorn, and doughnuts as well. The food really was his favorite part about a baseball game. Who cares if your team won or lost so long as they didn't run out of food and you didn't run out of money?

Coming too often was begging for a heart attack, he knew. In Steve's mind a Viennese cardiologist with the voice of Arnold Schwarzenegger prescribed, *Keep away from PacBell Stadium if you want to live*. Indigestion was a given.

"What'd I miss?" Steve inquired, returning to his seat.

"Nothin'," Matt replied. "We're just waiting for the food."

Matt said he loved the game, but there was more of Steve in him than Steve had previously thought. Even for Matt it was all about the food, he realized. Second inning and they still hadn't seen the game. Their heads had been buried in the dogs.

Michael sucked the goo from his fingers. "That was good."

"Wait till you have the nachos!" Matt assured him. "Dad, can I have some money?"

"You gonna go this time?" Steve handed Matt some cash. "You and Michael stay together."

Matt accepted.

"And bring back some good stuff, you two. Nothin' lowfat, now."

"Like I would do that, Dad!" Matt joked in reply.

On the journey back to the concession stands, Matt discussed the relative merits of pizza and nachos. The pizza, he reasoned, could not possibly be as good as that from the Pizza Porte back in Morro Bay. On the other hand, since he didn't care for jalapeños, part of the cost of the nachos would be wasted. In the end Matt told Michael that his dad would certainly let them have both, so it really didn't matter which came first.

It was Michael who first spotted the bearded, sweatshirt-and-jeans-clad man staring at him from beside a water fountain. The figure gazed at him as if Michael were someone who knew him, but when he nudged Matt on the arm and pointed out the watcher, the man turned abruptly away. Matt shrugged and went back to debating between pepperoni and ham-and-pineapple pizza.

The line waiting to order food edged forward slowly.

Then suddenly the white sweatshirt was between Matt and Michael and Michael was being veered out of line, cut out of the flock like a sheep worked by a dog.

Looking around, Steve realized it was a packed-out crowd for the renewal of the traditional California north versus south rivalry.

The crowd cheered when a fly ball was hit toward center field. The noise tapered off, however, when the wind swirling off the Bay held up the ball's flight. It fell short of the wall and was caught.

Steve found himself staring out and thinking of Cindy. Boy, he missed her. She was so sweet, so interesting, and she looked more terrific than ever.

He still had a goofy grin on his face when the boys returned in a hurry, empty-handed. It took too many seconds for that incongruity to register.

"Mr. Alstead!" Michael called.

"Dad!" Matt yelled.

Steve was half startled out of his seat. "What?"

"Dad! Some guy tried to grab Michael."

Steve thought the boys were putting him on. Nothing like a practical joke, he knew. Then when he saw how shaken Michael was, he realized differently.

Steve jumped to his feet. "What happened?"

Michael tried to catch his breath. "I was in line and this guy started talking to me."

"What did he look like?" Steve was already moving toward the snack bar.

"He was wearing this white sweatshirt with a hood," Michael responded.

"And he had a real thin, long beard," Matt added.

Steve wondered if it was the same mangy-looking slug who had given him a bump. "Did he have on black jeans?"

Michael thought a moment. "Yes, he did. And he said, 'Come with me, Michael.' He knew my name."

"Truthfully?" Steve slowed. "Matt, did he say that?"

Matt wore a serious expression. "I don't know, Dad. I didn't hear what he said."

Steve stopped midway in the aisle. "This is not something you joke about, guys," he warned sternly.

"We're not," argued Michael. "He did . . ." Michael's expression took on a faraway look. He squinted, staring at a man who had just stepped out from behind a pillar.

"That's him!" Michael shouted, pointing.

The man, who looked as if he had copied his dress and facial hair from police sketches of the Unabomber, heard the cry and immediately ran.

Seeing this turned Steve into attack-dog mode. Running was the last thing a guy would do if he were completely innocent, he reasoned. Steve charged in pursuit.

A couple aisles around the bend of the stadium Steve's quarry crashed into a man with a box of food. He and it went flying. Nacho cheese and jalapeño rings went everywhere. Steve tried not to slip when he ran through it.

A second later the suspect darted toward an exit. From too far away to shout a warning, Steve witnessed the man grab a security guard by the arm and beg for help.

The uniformed black man, built like Anton, stepped out with another guard in front of Steve. "Stop!" the guard ordered, drawing his firearm to a low ready.

Steve skidded to a halt. His heart was beating in his ears as the suspect slipped out the exit. "I'm FBI," he pleaded. "That man tried to—"

"Put your hands in the air and turn around!" the guard ordered. "You carrying a gun?" he asked as a crowd formed.

The boys trotted up beside Steve.

Steve did as he was told. A defeated tone filled his voice. "Yes. Check my wallet. My FBI badge and ID are in there."

The second security officer lifted Steve's shirt and removed the billfold from his back pocket. After a quick inspection he said, "Put your gun away, man. He's a cop."

The first officer placed his firearm back in its holster and relaxed. He moved toward Steve, apologizing. "Look, I'm sorry. That guy seemed pretty scared. He said you were armed and I . . ."

Steve shook his head. The security men had fallen for one of the oldest tricks in the book. "Anybody ever teach you how to detain and assess?"

The men didn't reply.

The enormity of the error grew as Steve thought about it. Someone had harassed a kid and then was allowed to get away while the pursuer was held at gunpoint. Steve was hot by now. "Use your heads!"

Steve and the boys were led to the security office to make out a report. Steve was convinced that something had been narrowly averted. But what? He wasn't sure how much Michael had embellished the occurrence, maybe as a way of getting his attention. An aftereffect of the near drowning? Testing Steve's ability to rescue him again?

After 20 minutes of statements and note-taking, a senior park executive entered the room. He apologized as well, offering the three of them complimentary passes for another game.

Steve didn't let it go easily. "Do you know how reckless and unprofessional that was? I'm lucky I wasn't shot!"

"The officer in question will be dealt with, I assure you." The executive attempted to calm Steve down. "Tell you what. How about a season pass, good for the whole year?"

Since there was nothing further to be gained by additional discussion, Steve agreed and the three returned to their seats.

The shock had worn off the boys by then, at least enough to bum Matt out. "Ah, we missed mosta the game."

Steve felt bad. He wanted to put it all behind them, but there was now a new worry on the horizon. Cindy would be angry if she heard about it. What had he been thinking, letting the boys go to the snack bar alone? He also dreaded what Paul Salim would say. It was beginning to feel as though every time Steve was around, some near-tragedy happened.

Not good.

Oh, well. Now was not the time to worry about facing that particular music. What the boys needed was a diversion. "By the way," Steve said, "I've got something really cool for you guys for tomorrow."

"What is it?" Michael asked eagerly.

In a circus ringmaster's voice Steve answered, "Tomorrow night, for your viewing pleasure, I have two tickets for a training drill in the HRT Shoot House."

"Cool!" Matt exclaimed.

After he explained to Michael, the other boy replied with the same excited response. "What's going to happen?"

"You'll see," Steve assured him. "Tomorrow night."

The trolley ride back to the boat was quick since they left the stadium before the game ended. Grabbing their things from Steve's fastback, they headed for the Pier 41 side.

"What are you doing over here, Dad?" Matt asked, baffled that the boat had been moved.

Steve didn't want his son to think he was a cheapskate like Anton did, so he suggested, "I like this side better. It's quieter and I get to look at the sea lions."

Of course he knew that even to a nine- or ten-year-old any statement containing the words *quieter* and *sea lions* together was a contradiction in itself.

The boat smelled of old, wet wood. A little like rotting seaweed. For Matt and Michael, tucked into sleeping bags in the vee-berth, it was like roughing it on a pirate adventure or camping out on a floating tree house.

When they asked why there were no lights, Steve temporized, "You guys know how the power problems are in this state."

Michael agreed, showing off his knowledge of rotating grid outages. Steve grinned. Fortunately the boys were gullible enough to believe it, even though 20 yards away there was plenty of gleaming neon.

"I'm on a grid all by myself," Steve explained. Not wanting to seem unprepared, he kicked on the little gas-powered generator for a while and turned on the newly acquired 13-inch portable television.

The Headline News report that appeared onscreen confirmed Steve's claim. "California is preparing to be hit harder than ever this summer, with energy prices already soaring. . . ."

"That's enough for me, boys," Steve said, killing the generator. "I'll see you in the morning."

But they didn't reply. They were already asleep.

NINETEEN

HRT Shoot House
San Francisco
Friday, 4 May
1:35 P.M. Pacific Time

A DEADLY SERIOUS GAME

The perfect, blue-skied morning had been spent flying kites off the end of the pier. The hearty appetite that resulted was accommodated by equally hearty sandwiches: smoked Havarti and honey-roasted turkey on Boudin's extra sourdough rolls. The wind had picked up even further before the boys finished lunch, so they spent the next hour in the Pier 39 video arcade.

Matt couldn't believe it when Steve appeared, all decked out in his black Spec Ops FBI raid uniform, carrying a duffel bag. Kids in the arcade stared at Steve in awe as Matt swelled with pride.

The ride to the shoot house was filled with nonstop questions from the pair. Steve postponed answering most of them, wanting them to have the experience first. The boys would no doubt pick his brain clean later.

Steve drove the car down the ramp, pausing at the bottom for the armored security door to roll up. He was late. Fortunately he was already dressed, complete with a lightweight ballistic-level 1 bullet-proof vest under his shirt. Level 1 was barely enough protection for a powerful handgun round but would be plenty for the exercise to come.

Dan greeted Steve with the usual friendly banter. "Hey, buddy. You brought a couple new field agents with you?" Dan acknowledged the boys. He was always sharp and interested with kids, the mark of a good teacher.

Matt slapped him five. "What's up, Big Dan? You gonna do some shootin'?"

"Oh, not me, partner. But we're gonna watch your dad on the monitor and make fun of him when he misses." He gave a Groucho Marx wiggle of his bushy eyebrows.

Steve frowned back at him. "Not likely, big boy." He plopped his bag down next to a pile of gear that Dan had set out for him.

"We'll see about that," Dan joked. "So who's the other new agent?" he asked, extending a hand to Michael.

Michael was intrigued and showed it. "I'm Michael Salim, and I want to be an FBI man so I can save people like Steve does."

"I think we've got a serious recruit here, Steve."

"I know it," Steve responded, picking up a box of simmunition. "These are the sim rounds for me?"

"Yeah. I set out all of the gear for you there. Two boxes of 9mm simmunition paint rounds."

Steve began loading the stubby 9mm rounds into the 20-round capacity Colt 635 submachine gun magazines, used to simulate the AR-15s HRTs normally carried. This was a safety feature to reduce penetration, as even a paintball round in a rifle caliber was lethal. The bright blue, dedicated simmunition rifles felt pretty much the same as the real thing.

Simmunition was a lot more expensive than the real stuff—at two bucks a round, about double the price. Costly, though necessary, the sim rounds allowed the men to simulate a real firefight with virtually the same feel they were used to in an actual combat scenario.

Steve slid the mags into his tactical assault vest, tipped to his right so that when he removed one for a rapid mag change he wouldn't have to look which way it was facing to successfully load it into the firearm. He strapped on his helmet and connected some wires from a headset to a com-pack.

"Your dad looks ready to go," Dan said, lowering his ear protection. He adjusted a boom mic and clicked a remote switch to talk. "All right. It's Echo 1 against Echo 2. Everybody circle in by the cars."

Steve disappeared through a doorway. It led to the weapons locker. A moment later he returned with an AR and two other radio com-packs for the boys. "Slip these on. It's going to be real noisy in here, even behind the glass in the safety booth."

The four traveled through a set of doors that used to lead to the convention center floor of the defunct hotel. The simulated house Steve had watched being assaulted during his last visit had been moved away. In its place were 15 junk cars.

Dan stopped in the middle as the other men, all dressed like Steve, circled up and dropped to one knee around him. Those who were not already wearing a heavy-duty wraparound face shield and goggles pulled them on.

All of those present listened to Dan's instructions via the headsets. "Today we're reviewing outdoor urban scenarios," he explained. "This is, as you can tell, a parking lot scenario after a bank robbery. Just like the North Hollywood guys, Echo 2 is heavily armed and ready to blast any cop or HRT he sees. . . ."

Steve eyed the Echo 2 leader, Anton, kneeling across from him. He mouthed the words, *I'm gonna waste you, thug.*

We'll see, pig, was Anton's reply.

Dan continued to explain. "Now, Echo 1, just as you guys are about to make a forced entry, these guys are going to break out through those doors over there. Your No. 1 objective: to detain and contain. Capture them, take them out, whatever you got to do within policy parameters. Now if they get out that other set of double doors, they're safe. Losing team gets brass duty." Dan clapped his hands together, the sharp smack oddly muffled by the ear gear. "Be sharp, 'cause you got new evaluators here today." He put one hand on each of the boys' shoulders.

Steve was proud to have his son along, proud to have him watch his associates. These men were the best—dedicated and brave. Certainly Matt and Michael would remember this experience for the rest of their lives. "Wish me luck, boys," he called out, giving them a thumbs-up signal.

"Good luck," responded Michael.

Matt laughed. "No way, Dad. I'm rootin' for the bad guys."

"Dan, spank him for me, will you?"

Dan seemed equally entertained by Matthew's comment. He led the boys into a small room on wheels. It was low and narrow, constructed of plate steel and thick plate glass. Five television monitors lined the windowsill.

Dan pointed out the three aerial views that would reveal the action that took place behind the cars, then also showed them the other two ground-level, side-angle shots. "All of this stuff is recorded so we can play it back and find out what could have and should have been done differently."

The two Echo teams fell back to their respective starting locations. Bad guys behind the doors, good guys outside of the staged parking area.

Dan gave the order. "Move in, One!"

At the moment Echo 1 spread out across the parking area, Echo 2 burst through the doors with guns blazing. The confined space carried the shocking boom of a real gun battle. Paint bullets splattered on windshields and car bodies. Spent shell casings flew in every direction before falling on the ground.

Matt watched with fascination. He squinted at a monitor as his dad and partner hunkered down and double-teamed a guy on the other side of a car. This sort of drill was good for the men because few real-life bad-guy perpetrators had the skills and training that these simulated opponents had. So for the HRT to simulate bad guys in practice meant that the good guys were getting a lot tougher fight than they would in real life. At least, that was the intent of the training.

Steve motioned for the No. 2 man, Mooneyham, to go and then stood and fired a three-round burst at one of the perps, played by Willie. His weapon booming, Steve put two into his chest. However, Willie didn't go down. The rule of the game: never give up. "You play how you practice," Dan always said, and nobody needed practice dying.

Steve moved up to join his partner again.

On the opposite side of the court, Anton angled in between two junkers. He fired across the action, almost hitting Steve in the helmet. The round spattered off the auto's hood right next to Steve, who ducked, then assessed where the round had come from. Steve spotted Anton, kept low, and fired off a couple of shots. They punched into the car door behind which Anton was sheltered.

On the monitors, Dan and the boys witnessed a bad guy get taken out, followed by one more of each. Three to two, the good guys led.

Dan pointed to Anton on the monitor. "Watch this guy. He's got a surprise for your dad."

Anton disappeared from Steve's view. Steve raised his head slightly to see where Anton had gone. Crawling low along the ground, Anton slowly opened the door of a rusty orange Honda Civic. He slid behind the wheel, unnoticed.

The windshield was dirty and Steve couldn't see into it with the other two pieces of eye protection he had on.

Anton started the car and revved the motor.

Steve pivoted around to see where the new noise was coming from. The other two good guys, Chaz and Mooneyham, rose up and were struck down, one after another.

Popping off a round, Steve nailed "bad guy" Darjit.

Anton threw the car in gear and spun the tires. Steve spotted it immediately. Not expecting an operable vehicle, he dove out of the way. He hit the ground in a roll to the side as the vehicle wove through the maze of cars.

Raising his rifle, Steve took aim and fired through the open side window. It was a perfect shot, though Anton never felt it. The sim round struck him right in the side of the helmet just before he cleared the parking lot.

Steve laughed as he lay on the ground, out of breath and panting. A moment later he stood up.

Anton returned on foot, bragging. "Yeah, boy! Get some!"

Steve denied his victory speech. "Take off your helmet, bro. You got nailed."

Anton, in denial, was surprised. "No way, man. I was gone!"

"Check it out," Steve encouraged, wiping red paint from Anton's temple and displaying it in front of the black agent's vision.

"Dude!" exclaimed Anton. "So close."

Harassing him, Steve said, "Four words for you."

Anton finished the sentence. *"That's what you get!"*

Dan exited the observation house with the boys, who were wound up beyond belief.

"Nice shot, Dad!" exclaimed Matt. "You even caught the surprise."

Anton protested, "I thought you were voting for me, little man."

"Nope," Matt replied with a grin. "Got to go with the home team."

Steve complimented Dan for the bit of unexpected realism. "You didn't tell my crew one of these was the getaway car."

"Hey, man. Such is life." Dan didn't put up with much whining. "You've gotta be ready for a surprise at every turn."

Anton's team, as the losing effort, had to stay and sweep up the brass shell casings.

After all the gear was put away, Steve considered Dan's words on the way to McDonald's. Steve had been fortunate enough to make the shot, but Dan was right. You just never knew when some unforeseen circumstance might benefit the bad guy.

Steve bought the boys Value Meals. They munched French fries in the back of the Mustang on the way to the boat. He polished off his Big Mac, dribbling special sauce and shredded lettuce on his lap.

It was early when they arrived. The plan was to relax a bit before going out to see a movie. Still sweaty and unchanged, Steve elected to grab a nap while the boys played HRT on the dock.

Fat Cats Café
Avila Beach, California
5:35 P.M. Pacific Time

PAY THE PIPER

Fat Cats Café, a 24-four-hour eatery catering to fishermen and locals, was separated from the Diablo Nuclear Power Plant by a rocky headland and several miles of coastline.

Shadir's cryptic predawn phone call had alerted Paul Salim to the rendezvous. In an expressionless voice, Shadir told Salim that his obedience was required, then named the time and place.

Shadir scarcely needed to remind Salim of the threat to his family if he didn't cooperate fully. There was ample menace in the quiet comment. "We know where your boy is. Remember Disneyland? Someone is even closer to him now."

Shadir could almost hear Salim sweating.

Shadir arrived an hour before the appointed time. He left a rented Dodge Intrepid parked beside the Avila Beach children's playground and bicycled the remaining mile to the end of the road.

On the way he passed Diablo's entry checkpoint. It made him smile to see how quickly arriving employees were waved through without even a pretense at thorough security efforts. Shadir knew it would be a different story at the actual entrance to the power plant proper, but he was unruffled. His confidence sprang in part from the duffel bag slung over his shoulder from which a baseball bat protruded.

Shadir cycled nonchalantly past the restaurant, circling the parking lot as gulls wheeled overhead. Everything was as it should be. He noticed no unusual watchers, no agents staking out the café, no one whose presence set off his internal radar. He went inside the café, ordered a cup of tea, and waited.

Salim arrived alone. Shadir watched as the power plant's acting manager stood at the café's terrace, looking around uncertainly.

Tossing a five-dollar bill on the table, Shadir rose and walked past Salim. "Follow me."

Shadir didn't stop until the two men were out on the very end of the Port San Luis pier. "Your shift begins at nine o'clock tonight," he said. "Reactor 1 is down for fuel rod replacement, which is 90 percent complete. There will be only one operator monitoring the control room, because the core is cold." These were not questions but merely indications that Shaiton's Fire knew every detail of Salim's life and the workings of the plant.

Salim swallowed and nodded.

"I am your cousin Faroush," Shadir continued. "I am going with you to the plant tonight as your personal guest. You will call and tell security to expect me. You are the chief now. No one will argue if you want to show me around."

Shadir saw Salim eyeing the duffel bag apprehensively. "Nothing that will give your bomb sniffers or metal detectors a problem," he explained. Then he yanked the bat and an accompanying wooden bracket out of the canvas container. "See," he said, pointing to a brass plaque affixed to the bracket.

In honor of Frank Daley, it said. In gratitude for his service to the community.

"Touching, isn't it?" Shadir suggested.

Salim's raised, heavy brown eyebrows emphasized the haunted expression on his face.

"For the pool of fuel rods," Shadir said. "We have only to toss it in and wait a short time. When this dissolves, it will remove the protective boron from the water."

Salim spoke up for the first time. "The control room indicators will note the change. The operator will simply add more borated water to the mix."

Shadir sneered as he said, "Probably he will not believe the gauge. Why should the level fall? In any case, he cannot add enough to matter.

You do not understand the weapons we have at our command. The fuel rods will begin to heat, and I have what is needed to help the reaction along. Nothing can stop it."

A look of pure horror came over Salim. Shadir guessed the man was finally convinced this was real. He must be visualizing the cloud of radioactive poison that would sweep across the coastal cities on its way to Los Angeles. "You can't mean it!"

"Did you think we were playing a game here?" Shadir demanded harshly. "Did you think we only meant to switch off the lights and shout boo? The subway bombing was nothing! The gas storage fire was nothing! *This* is a blow that will be remembered to the end of time! And you, unworthy, ungrateful dog that you are, will have the honor of making it happen. Everything you are, everything you have, you owe to Shaiton's Fire. Tonight you will pay the debt."

"But my w-w-wife . . ."

"Martyrdom isn't yet required of your family," Shadir noted, "unless you disobey. Once the reaction is irreversible, there will still be time for you and your wife to escape . . . if you do exactly everything you are ordered. You will pick me up for my tour of your plant. Smile! You haven't seen me in a long time." Crisply Shadir gave instructions for Salim to travel a deserted stretch of Higuera Street that would be on Salim's route to work. "Eight-thirty sharp," he said.

After Salim nodded dumbly, Shadir gave him a shove toward his car. He waited until Diablo Canyon's Nuclear Power Plant manager drove away before retrieving his bicycle and pedaling leisurely back toward his waiting vehicle.

Pier 41
San Francisco
6:42 P.M. Pacific Time

I GOT YOU, MAN!

The sound of pretend shooting, followed by two sets of clunking feet on the deck, woke Steve. He rose and stretched, still wearing his drill clothing.

"I got you, man!" Matt yelled.

"No, I hit you first," Michael argued.

Steve remembered all too well playing army men with a brother or a friend and the arguments that came when someone didn't die honestly.

Even as an adult the problem bugged him, only now for a totally different reason. If a bad guy didn't stay down, more than an argument followed. Innocent people got hurt or killed.

His hair stood up as he climbed the steps. Partly it was because of the half-awake dread his brain put on childhood games . . . and half because he'd slept awkwardly on a lumpy pillow.

Emerging on deck, he cried, "Bang, bang! Got you both."

The boys were startled, but in fair play they both fell down.

Steve chuckled to himself. "I am a good shot. That was from the hip, too."

Matt was grinning as he got up, Michael smacking his gum with a big smile.

"Listen, guys," Steve told them. "You need to come in and get changed. I'm going up to take a shower." Sleeping with his black shirt over the tac vest had been a bad idea . . . he was royally sweaty. "We have to be out of here in 10 to 15 minutes if we're going to make the IMAX movie."

They agreed. There was of course more time than that, though Steve knew how boys this age were. He'd probably come back and find Matthew with one shoe off, yet in his old clothes, and telling mock war stories.

They stomped happily into the boat's cabin. Steve threw some clothes in a bundle and rolled them up in a green towel with his shaving kit. Suddenly he wondered what to do with his gun. There was nowhere to lock it up on board, he realized—he slept with it under his pillow—and he could never leave it accessible while the boys were present. He would have to take it with him, he decided, so he shoved it in the towel with the rest.

The hum of the generator began. Matt had gotten smarter already, Steve thought when he emerged from the cabin to find the pair in front of the TV.

He addressed them sternly. “Listen, you've got to be ready now.”

“All right.” Matt waved him off as the pair sat down to watch *Scooby- Doo* on the Cartoon Network.

Steve was about to leave when he heard a boat roar up alongside his. “That's strange,” he remarked to himself, looking through the main salon port.

A bright yellow cruiser idled into the slip adjacent to his. “Must be another cheapskate moving in,” he muttered. “If this side gets attractive enough, they'll raise the rates on me.” Thinking nothing further of it, he moved toward the cabin's sliding hatch. But the silhouette of a man blocked his view. “Wait right there,” the form commanded.

Steve stepped back, his head still fuzzy from the nap. He squinted. The olive-complexioned man had a beard and wore a gray suit. He looked familiar.

Unreasonable fear clogged Steve's mind when he recognized the accent as Middle Eastern. He remained calm, slowly reaching into the towel for his gun.

The intruder who had shouted at him also raised an elongated weapon, a handgun with a sound suppressor. “Don't move! Don't put your hand in there either.” The attacker quickly scanned the docks around him, then motioned with the pistol for Steve to back up.

Steve backed away, shooting a worried glance at the boys. Both of them turned with smiles on their faces, as if what they were watching was a scene on TV.

“Boys, don't move,” Steve cautioned, forcing his voice to remain more relaxed than he felt. “Stay put until we find out what this thing's all about.”

“I think you know what it's about,” the interloper corrected.

“Sir.” Steve attempted to stay cool and respectful since there was no time to go for his gun. He glanced at the barrel on his opponent's weapon. A Walther P-99. The silencer was illegal in California; even possessing one was a serious offense, which meant this guy was serious. "We can work this out."

"I'm sure we can," the man stated, forcing Steve backward with another wave of the muzzle.

"Boys. Just do whatever this guy says. Okay?"

"Sure, Dad."

"You got it, Mr. Alstead," Michael agreed, as if nothing were wrong.

Why were they not afraid? Steve wondered. His own bowels were churning, yet the boys acted like the threat was a game.

At last the unknown enemy began to talk. In words too low for the boys to hear over the still-blatting television he said, "And you thought you could hide him for that pathetic Paul Salim."

"I don't know what you are talking about."

"Shut up!" the man cried, grinding his face into an angry expression. Regaining his composure, he spoke again quietly. "You will not inhibit Allah's will."

Allah's will? Steve wondered. *What is he talking about?*

"It is Allah's will that Shaiton's Fire fulfill its destiny. Wormwood will be but a candle in comparison when the devil's inferno burns." The man raised the gun. "And the time is now."

The boys waited with great anticipation on their faces.

The man pulled the trigger. Steve lunged to the side, but the first round came too quickly.

Steve screamed out in pain when the bullet struck him in the chest. The sound of a sharp slap echoed in the room, followed by the tiny rattle of a spent casing on the wooden floor.

Steve agonized on the floor, gasping for breath.

The boys watched as if it were all planned, an HRT spectacle, another one of Dan's surprises.

Crack! Another shot split the air, striking Steve with the speed and sound of a mousetrap. He fell silent and lay still.

The casing was left spinning, like a silver top, on the teak and holly surface.

Turning to the pair of children, who were now more apprehensive at the way this drama was unfolding, the man said, "You will do everything I say, won't you?"

Matt spoke up clearly. "Yes sir."

Michael studied the man's face. He did not reply.

"Come with me, boys." The assassin motioned for them to come out on the deck. He stood behind them, watching Matt go first, then grabbed Michael's arm. "Do not try anything, little one. Your father wishes you alive."

Michael said not a word.

The boys were instructed to get on the idling speedboat. The kidnapper put the gun in his pocket and clicked the shifter into reverse.

Matt called out, "Good one, Dad. These surprises are getting better and better."

The bright yellow cigarette boat sped out of the tiny harbor into the dusky, choppy waters of San Francisco Bay.

TWENTY

San Luis Obispo, California
7:04 P.M. Pacific Time

AND THE MARIACHI BAND PLAYED ON

The mariachi band strolled among the carnival booths and long picnic tables set up in Old Mission Plaza. Smoke from enormous barbecue grills scented the air with tri-tip, chicken, and ribs, drawing several hundred newcomers to the festivities.

Cindy had spent the day behind a painted cardboard mural of swimming fish and an octopus holding a Barbie doll in one tentacle and a toy truck in another. These toys had been bait to draw hordes of preschoolers to the Go Fish game.

The skies above San Luis Obispo showed the tints of encroaching sunset. A beautiful day. Successful and glorious. There would be enough funds raised to give scholarships to dozens of kids and pay the salary of an additional teacher the next school year.

Cindy inhaled the mouthwatering aroma of food and glanced at her watch—7:04 P.M. Her Go Fish replacement, Michael Salim's mom, was four minutes late. For the first time Cindy felt twinges of exhaustion, hunger, and impatience.

Just as Cindy silently muttered complaints about Mrs. Salim's unreliability, the woman popped her head around the screen. Peggy Salim was an ordinary-looking, overweight woman of about 40 with gray-streaked black hair and deep brown eyes surrounded by smile lines. Yet she possessed what her husband, Paul, lacked in personality. An American by birth, she was bright and vivacious. Cindy had often seen her at school after hours tossing a few basketballs into the hoop with her son.

When asked, Mrs. Salim had been eager to take the last shift at the Go Fish booth and give Cindy a chance to eat. But tonight, Cindy's first sight of Mrs. Salim told her something must be terribly wrong. Her expressive eyes were red-rimmed and downcast. She had been crying.

"Hey," Cindy greeted her.

Peggy Salim pressed her trembling lips together. "The line for beef tri-tip sandwiches is long."

"You okay?" Cindy rose from the three-legged stool and snapped one last prize bag onto the clothespin at the end of the string.

"Smoke." Mrs. Salim turned away from her and pretended to survey the boxes of paper bags. But a single tear trickled down the woman's cheek.

"Mrs. Salim?" Cindy put a hand on the woman's shoulder. "What's wrong?"

The woman shuddered, holding back a sob. A broken sentence came in a whisper. "I don't know. It's my husband. For days now he's been . . . oh! Ever since Frank's murder, you know. I don't know what's happened to him. But . . . this afternoon he said he had a meeting with some plant official . . . then when he came home after . . . I . . . I . . . just have never seen him so . . . I don't know . . . shaken up. And when I asked, he got so angry at me! He wouldn't come with me tonight. Said he didn't want to see anyone. Not anyone. Said I should go." She wiped the tears on her sleeve, shook her head as though she had not meant to say so much.

So. A little quarrel. How many times had Cindy felt like breaking into tears while everyone else was oblivious to what was going on in her personal life?

"Maybe the responsibility," Cindy said. "Mr. Salim is Operations Manager at Diablo now. And Frank's death. It's all been such a blow."

Mrs. Salim nodded curtly. "Yes, I'm sure of it." She sniffed and plucked a prize bag out of the box as a line and clothespin snaked over the panel. "Go on. I'm okay. It's nothing. Go now. The line for ribs is growing by the minute. Chicken is not so bad."

Cindy gave her arm a squeeze. "I heard from Steve and the boys this morning," she said, trying to cheer the woman. "They're fine. Having a blast."

Mrs. Salim caught her in an unexpected hug. "Thanks," was all she could say.

"Sure." Cindy patted her back and then slipped out to find Tommy, who was at a table somewhere in the crowd with the principal, Mrs. O'Connor.

Diablo Canyon Nuclear Power Plant
Avila Beach, California
8:45 P.M. Pacific Time

BATTER UP, AGAIN

Shadir smiled as Paul Salim pulled his blue Ford Taurus into the reserved parking spot labeled "Operations Manager." "Cousin Faroush," he said, tapping himself on the chest. "Remember?"

Salim nodded.

Shadir thrust the duffel-wrapped baseball bat into Salim's hands. "You will carry this," he instructed.

"But they'll be suspicious!" Salim protested.

"Not when you take it out *before* they ask and show it off. Only keep your head, and your wife and son will keep theirs."

"Good evening, Mr. Salim," said the blue-uniformed security guard behind the counter.

Shadir noted the tactical rifle slung muzzle-downward behind the man's shoulder and the pistol at his waist.

"Brought a guest tonight?" the officer queried.

Salim could only manage a grunt, but the chubby, blond-haired guard took it as assent. "Sign in here, please," he said, reversing a clipboard on the counter. "Imagine you'll vouch for him personally, Mr. Salim."

Shadir had already signed, using his alias. He held the pen over the spot marked *Form of ID.*

The pause was a fraction of a second too long before Salim spoke up. "Yes, of course. My cousin, Faroush. I have always wanted to show him around. His visit this time is so brief he had to come tonight."

"Welcome, sir," the guard offered, handing over a plastic visitor ID tag on a plastic lanyard. "Hang this around your neck, please." He eyed the duffel bag curiously.

"Thank you," Shadir responded politely. He gave Salim's foot the slightest nudge with his shoe.

Salim started, then lifted the canvas sack onto the countertop. "I'm distracted," Salim apologized. "I've been thinking about where this should go." With that, he drew out the charcoal-gray baseball bat, placing the wooden shelf and brass plaque beside it.

"'In memory of . . .' Say, that's nice," the guard said. "Just right for old Frank. Where'd you get it?"

Salim froze. Blinking, he said, "Downtown merchants . . . you know, business sponsors of Little League teams."

The guard called toward a glass booth, "Hey, Captain, take a look at this."

A senior security officer emerged from his cubicle. Dark-haired and slimmer than his underling, he wore a pair of stars on his collar tab like an army general. He, too, carried a sidearm, but no rifle.

"Evening, Mr. Salim," he offered. Then to Shadir he nodded, "Sir." Admiring the bat, the captain commented, "Tributes coming in by the ton. Frank Daley was some kinda man. Guess you'll hang this out here in the lobby, or maybe up at the visitors' center."

"Perhaps," Salim said doubtfully. "I haven't decided yet. I'll just keep it in my office until I do, if that's all right."

Captain and guard exchanged quizzical looks. Shadir interpreted them to mean, *Since when does the top man ask permission over something so unimportant?* "Whatever you say, sir," the captain agreed.

"Shall we go now?" Shadir asked, taking Salim by the elbow. "I am most anxious to see where you work."

The two men passed single file through a bomb-sniffing device. Though Shadir thought Paul Salim visibly cringed, no alarms sounded and no lights flashed. This was followed by a metal detector. Salim stood to one side as the baseball bat, now back in its canvas covering, rolled unchallenged down the throat of an airport-terminal-style device.

Shadir had to nudge him forward. Again there was no danger signal.

Picking up his keys and wallet, Salim headed toward the racks of employee identification cards. He retrieved his, swiped it through the card reader, then paused before placing his hand into the connected palm-print scanner. In front of Salim was a turnstile whose revolving steel bars would only admit one person at a time. "I'll go first," he said over his shoulder.

Shadir didn't like what he saw in Paul Salim's eyes. He stared coldly back until Salim ducked his head. Salim mumbled, "Swipe your visitor's card. When the door clicks, you have 10 seconds to push through."

In less than 10 seconds both men were on the other side of the turnstile, successfully past the first security hurdle. "Be careful what you think," Shadir cautioned in a menacing whisper.

"What do you mean?"

"You thought you might go through the bars and then call out to the guards about me," Shadir said.

Salim's breath quickened.

"Don't try any such games with me," Shadir warned. "I am ready to die if I must. But your only hope is in doing exactly what I say."

Ghirardelli Square
San Francisco
9:01 P.M. Pacific Time

HOT FUDGE FRIDAY

Tim Turnow was happy that Meg had driven down from Tahoe for the weekend. He had missed her and he had missed Easter with the grandkids.

Since it looked like this investigation was going to drag on for some time, he leapt at the chance to say yes when Meg offered to skip a weekend of grandparenting in favor of their brief reunion. Besides, they had honeymooned in San Francisco 30 years before. As a matter of fact, they had sat together in this same ice-cream parlor, part of the famed Ghirardelli chocolate factory, three decades earlier.

Where have the years gone? Turnow mused.

Examining his waistline ruefully, he wondered if there was some formula by which years of happiness translated directly into that many extra pounds around the middle . . . as he spooned another bite of hot fudge sundae out of the oversized tulip glass.

As much as he was glad to stroll the waterfront with Meg, Turnow recognized that he had not been good company. While he stared out at the Golden Gate Bridge, his mind refused to relinquish the challenge of the present case.

What did a subway train explosion, a demolished natural gas storage facility, a body in the Bay, and the enigmatic Arabic phrase translated "Satan's Fire" have in common? What was the link binding them all together?

That there was an Arab terrorist group operating in California seemed clear. Miles had identified the cell as a radical splinter faction of Hezbollah. They were apparently handsomely bankrolled and eager to make a big splash in anti-American circles by outdoing even Osama bin Laden. Or so ran the international gossip.

So much for the big picture.

But the devil was in the details. What were their goals? Why no claim of responsibility for either the BART bombing or the Kern County gas facility? If the dead man in the Bay had been part of the group, who had killed him and why? Was there another target, and if so, what? Were they performing random acts of opportunistic terror? If so, their next atrocity would be that much harder to predict and defeat.

What was he missing?

God, help me think clearly, he pleaded. *So many lives could be at stake.*

It was days like this when he felt so small, so inadequate in the face of evil.

A melted lump of vanilla ice cream plopping onto the marble tabletop brought Turnow back to the present. He wondered how long he'd been sitting with the spoon halfway to his lips. He caught Meg regarding him with a mixture of pity and exasperation. "Did you say something?" he asked.

"I said, would you like me to put your coffee cup under your hand so at least the drips won't go to waste? Really, Tim, you haven't exactly been with me the past several minutes."

Recognizing the accuracy of the accusation, Turnow apologized and redirected his attention toward his wife.

"Can I help?" she asked kindly. "Sometimes a fresh perspective is exactly what's needed. Start over and look at things from a different angle."

The temptation to enlist Meg's assistance was enormous. Where Turnow's own specialty was thorough—sometimes plodding—analysis, Meg's incisive mind cut through layers of stagnation to make surprising and unexpected connections. But his pledge of confidentiality extended to his wife, and Turnow expected to honor it. Vows lost all meaning if they could be conveniently stretched according to circumstances.

"Thanks, anyway," he said, smiling. "Just have to puzzle it through. How about if I take 10 more minutes, tops, and then we go to a movie?"

"Fine," she agreed. "I'll be in the shop picking up some chocolate bars for the kids."

A different angle, she'd said, and rightly so. But where was it? The case had begun with the terrorist bombing of a subway.

Or had it?

Besides terrorism, what other reason was there to attack a train? To carry out an assassination but make it *look* like terrorism? Turnow's mind began to click, the same as when he was in the lab visualizing microscopic processes in a biochemical reaction.

Murder, rather than random killing, depended as much on the identity of the victim as on the killer. The list of the dead who had been in the actual car with the bomb had finally been identified. Turnow had seen names, ages, employment histories, political affiliations. . . . Was there a motive for murder in that mix?

The great Satan will be burned with Shaiton's Fire. The devil will be attacked by the devil.

What did it mean?

Had there been anyone on board BART who would constitute a target for a radical Muslim group? There had been no diplomats killed, no Israeli agents as far as Turnow could tell.

Turnow stared down at the paper menu now splattered with puddles of melted ice cream. Each time he and Meg came to Ghirardelli's they automatically picked up menus and then ordered the same hot fudge sundaes anyway. Maybe he was too much a creature of habit to think of fresh approaches and new angles. Too stuck in a rut to try something called *Strike It Rich* or *The Earthquake* or *Mount Diablo*.

Turnow blinked.

Mount Diablo.

Mount *devil.*

A concoction of ice cream, nuts, caramel, something, something . . . named for the sharp conical peak east of San Francisco Bay.

Satan's Fire.

Satan's mountain.

Furiously, Turnow turned over the facts in his head.

A man named Frank Daley had been on the destroyed subway car. Daley had been chief of operations for the Diablo Nuclear Power Plant.

Nuclear energy.

The attack on the natural gas facility.

Diablo . . . Satan.

Murder can be for revenge, money, or removal of someone as an obstacle. Who had replaced Daley as the head of Diablo operations?

Meg returned to the table. "I need some cash," she said. "I didn't bring my wallet."

Instead of removing bills from his money clip, Turnow simply nodded and, to Meg's evident surprise, handed her the whole thing.

Scrolling down his B-com's built-in address book, he hunted for Steve Alstead's number. Alstead's family lived in San Luis Obispo, within the danger zone of Diablo. If anyone could check Turnow's reasoning on this, it would be Alstead.

He let the phone ring 10 times, but no one answered.

TWENTY-ONE

Pier 41
San Francisco Bay, California
9:11 P.M. Pacific Time

HEARTBURN

It was dark and the floor was hard.

How did he get here? Where was here, anyway? What was that buzzing? Why did every part of him hurt so much?

A persistent beeping in his shirt pocket roused Steve. He groaned, trying not to move much at first. He could feel things grating together in his chest, as if someone was massaging his rib cage with a cross-cut saw.

He finally managed to answer his B-com, as much to silence the annoying buzz as out of any interest in the caller.

"This is . . ." Steve was short of breath. "Alstead."

"Steve, it's Tim Turnow." The doctor's voice greeted him with an apologetic tone.

"What's up, Doc?" Steve said, barely coherent.

"I'm sorry, Steve, I didn't mean to wake you. I just had a terrible hunch about the Nuclear Power Plant at Diablo Canyon and the Chief Operations Officer, Frank Daley, who was killed on the BART train. Anyway, I had some questions for you, but I guess I can ask you tomorrow."

It had seemed like a bad dream at first, like the worst hangover he'd ever had, like a trip to an Ensenada jail during a college road trip to Mexico.

Then his memory returned. "Oh, no!" he cried when his fingers felt a slug burrowed into the place on his Level 2 bulletproof vest, the spot from which the worst of the pain appeared to be coming. That's when he knew it wasn't a dream. The pain he felt wasn't just soreness from overtraining.

"Steve? Is everything all right?" Turnow sounded concerned. "Maybe I caught you at a bad time."

"Hang on, Doc." Steve bolted upright, stifling a cry of pain as his own ribs stabbed him. Where were the boys? Had they been taken? Then Steve remembered what the man said*: "Devil's inferno . . . Your father wants you alive . . ."* The Arab guy. He had taken the kids!

Devil's inferno . . . Diablo!

Grunting as he stood up, Steve exclaimed, "Doc, whatever you have realized about Diablo is probably true. My boy Matt has just been kidnapped!"

"What?" Turnow sounded confused. "Steve, slow down. Your boy?"

"Kidnapped, Doc." Steve searched the floor for his gun. There it was in the pile of clothes, concealed under the towel. "Yeah, but I'm certain of who did it and why."

"Who?" Turnow replied in a baffled tone. "Steve, are you all right?"

"I'm on my boat. I've been shot. Your call woke me up. My vest—luckily I still had it on—stopped the bullets, but I think a couple ribs are busted." He coughed. He knew everything was coming out jumbled and disjointed, but he couldn't make his mental processes go any smoother. The pain was excruciating.

"You need to see a doctor," instructed Dr. Turnow.

"No!" Steve gasped. "Listen to me. There's a guy, the new boss at

Diablo. His name is Paul Salim. I know him. Anyway, his kid was here with Matt and . . . " Steve rubbed his head, looking around the deck. He spotted a casing. "The guy who shot me took both boys. I'm sure I recognized the voice. . . . You've got to get down to Diablo tonight! This guy said something about the devil's fire. It all fits. You see?"

"That's what I was going to tell you," Turnow replied. "A thought occurred to me that someone, maybe this Shaiton's Fire, was going to blow it up. I need to make contact with the power plant immediately."

"No, you can't!" Steve replied in a panic. "They have my boy. Shaiton's Fire. They'll kill both boys. The guy said . . . ," His voice trailed off. "I need to get hold of Morrison, Doc. You and Downing should get down there as fast as you can. The whole West Coast may be at risk. But we've got to go carefully or my boy is dead!"

There was a pause. Steve knew Dr. Turnow was thinking it over. Now he couldn't just alert the people at Diablo. If the boss was in on the plot, who else might be? The last thing Chapter 16 wanted to do was to speed up the attack by giving the terrorists a warning.

"I'll get Downing," Turnow said. "You call me back after you talk to the senator. And Steve, if I don't hear from you again in five minutes, I'm calling an ambulance for you."

"Right, Doc." Steve ended the call to contact Morrison.

"Senator!" Steve exclaimed when Morrison answered.

"Is this Steve? You sound terrible."

"Never mind that." Steve explained the phone call from Turnow and the kidnapping. He pieced together the clues: the explosion, the dead man, the attack on the subway, which had actually been the assassination of Frank Daley hidden under a false lead pointing to Idaho's AMT. Shadir, Khalil, Shaiton's Fire.

It all tied together.

Steve convinced Morrison that Turnow had to get down to the nuclear plant that night. He also reasoned that HRT must make a rescue immediately or the boys would be killed. "If we can get to them in time—rescue Michael—maybe Paul Salim won't go through with it. But either way their lives are in jeopardy."

Morrison agreed to send Turnow and Downing on the Chapter 16 plane at once. "I'll send word to Anton to get the team ready. Meanwhile you go to the hospital."

Steve shook his head at the B-com. "No way, Senator. My boy is out there. I'm going in with the team."

"Steve," Morrison responded carefully, "I can guess at what you're feeling, but I can't let a wounded man who might not be thinking clearly jeopardize the op. Are you sure you're all right?"

"Got one bad case of heartburn, but I'm fine!" Steve argued. "Put HRT together. I still have the file on Khalil's Sausalito mansion. The guy who kidnapped the boys must have gone there. I've seen the grounds. I'm the logical choice to lead."

Morrison instructed him to wait a minute while he contacted Anton on the other line. Less than a minute later, he returned. "Anton is on his way. I'll get the HRT to meet at the pier with the SWAT van. I think I can get a couple Coast Guard cutters there for a waterside landing. In the meantime I'll see what intel we can pull together. If your hunch is right, it'll confirm the boys are there. Pull yourself together, Steve. Anton will be there in a few."

"Sure, okay," Steve replied, hanging up the phone as he collapsed on- to the couch. "Please, God! Let us pull this one off! Lord, for Matthew's sake . . ."

Before, they had held a nameless hostage; now it was his own flesh and blood. He had never felt so scared. Rising unsteadily to his feet, he took several careful breaths to stretch his chest. He spotted a bottle of Advil on the counter. With a half-empty can of warm soda, he took a handful of the pills.

Up to that point everything had gone so fast, he hadn't even thought of his wife. "Cindy!" he exclaimed, reaching for the phone again. He wanted to warn her to get Tommy and go to a safer place.

It rang and rang. She must be at the carnival. How would he get hold of her?

Surely there was no more sinister explanation than that. But not getting an answer made him shiver. He'd just come so close to death himself, and he could still feel the aftereffects of the shock. But he wasn't dead. And it would be only over his dead body that anyone would harm his wife or kids.

The answering machine at the condo picked up. Steve left a message. "Honey, listen. You gotta get out of there. Out of San Luis County, babe. I'm not messing around. As soon as you get this, you need to get Tommy and head north. I think that Diablo is going to be attacked." Steve considered telling her that Matt had been kidnapped, along with Michael, but decided it would be better to wait. What if he was in the middle of the rescue op when she got the message and she wasn't able to reach him on the phone? She'd be panicked enough, he decided, without knowing that Matt had been taken. "Get yourself in the car and head up here to the City, babe. I'll meet you on the boat . . . I love you, Cindy," Steve concluded, hanging up the phone.

The howl of a lone siren was approaching.

Diablo Canyon Nuclear Power Plant
Avila Beach, California
9:26 P.M. Pacific Time

BETWEEN THE DEVIL AND THE DEEP BLUE SEA

Diablo Canyon Nuclear Power Plant's offices were connected to the generator building only via a suspended fifth-floor walkway. To access the plant from the offices required Paul Salim to use his pass and tap in a numeric code three times.

The first gave them entry into the office building. The second swipe of the card admitted Paul and Shadir to the fifth-floor walkway. Glass-lined on both sides, the viaduct looked out at the crashing waves of the Pacific, white crests visible against the blackness on one side, and on the looming domes of the containment vessels on the other. The third use of ID and code would allow them to exit the viaduct. Salim, who had been moving slowly anyway, fumbled with the card reader.

Being 50 feet in the air, caught between two locked doors, with already innumerable barriers between himself and escape, made Shadir nervous. Despite his bravado about his readiness to die, Shadir did not actually intend to perish in this operation. It had been his expectation all along to live to gloat over the havoc for which he was partly responsible.

Shadir must have betrayed some apprehension—or perhaps being on familiar ground increased Salim's courage—because Salim dropped his hand away from the security device and turned to face Shadir.

"I've changed my mind," Salim said. "This has gone too far. You can't get out of this room without my help and I know you have no weapons. Before you can communicate to anyone something that would harm my family, you'll be in chains."

Shadir sneered. "If you were so certain of what you say, you already would have called the guards. No, I think you are testing me. Pathetic traitor! Did you think we would not anticipate that you would falter? At this very moment the knife is at your son's throat."

"You're lying!"

Smugly Shadir ticked off the points of his argument on his fingers. "He went to San Francisco with a friend. He was almost taken at a baseball game, but no matter, because by now his protector, Alstead, is dead, and Michael is ours."

"No!" Salim shrieked in agonized disbelief. "It's a trick."

"Is it?" queried Shadir coldly. "You *will* help me start a chain reaction. If the warning sirens from this plant are not sounded by midnight tonight, your boy will die." He stared through the glass-paneled top of the corridor exit. A Diablo employee was coming. "Decide quickly whether you wish to hazard your son's life or not," he said.

Salim visibly wilted. The plant maintenance worker barely glanced at the two men who passed him. Only two more security doors between Shadir and the spent fuel storage pool.

Old Mission Plaza
San Luis Obispo, California
9:30 P.M. Pacific Time

NEITHER PROTESTANT NOR CATHOLIC

Father Jerry, wrapped in a Scooby-Doo beach towel and looking for all the world like a drowned rat, padded around the empty stalls in the plaza. He had spent most of the day perched precariously in a sling suspended over a tank of water. Men and boys pitched baseballs at a target designed to dump him in—with more than moderate success.

His fair Irish skin was crimson from the cold. His teeth chattered as he grinned and thanked the workers while they took apart displays and game booths. Wet auburn hair stuck up in spikes as he approached Cindy, Peggy Salim, and Tommy, who were disassembling their station.

"Tanks, gurls. Tanks, Tomeen," he congratulated them in his Irish brogue. He eyed the painted octopus clutching the Barbie doll. "Next year—if Jesus doesn't come before Cinco de Mayo—you should paint me beside Barbie in the grip of this monster. Y'know, 42 dunks I counted! And all sober Protestants doin' the pitchin'! I heard last week, y'know, that the Methodists and the Baptists made a bet to see which congregation could drown the priest first! 'Twas Baptists hit the bull's-eye most."

Cindy laughed. "I never took you for a complainer, Father Jerry. There were three other guys getting dunked in turn as well."

"True! But there was no passion in the pitchin'! Tose Protestants! Wind up! I could almost hear their toughts! *Drown the priest! Drown the priest!* Well, a man would think he was in Belfast, now wouldn't he?"

"Okay, Father Jerry. So next year you clip prize bags on the fishing lines." Cindy humored the diminutive cleric. "I'll sit in the dunking booth."

"Nah! Your fifth-grade students would kill you, if you don't mind my sayin' so, Cindy." He tapped his head, trying to dislodge water from his ears. Then he addressed Peggy Salim. "And Peggy, I didn't see that husband of yours windin' up to pitch at me several times an hour. Where's Paul tonight?"

Her brow creased in a frown. "I don't know, Father. At Diablo, I suppose." She didn't look at him or join in the good-natured ribbing. Her tone was so melancholy that Father Jerry frowned and dried his face with a towel as if to wipe away his smile.

"Well then, Peggy—" his voice was suddenly serious—"it was good of you to come help us out. Tanks."

She nodded and commenced hammering the support plank loose.

Father Jerry bit his lower lip and eyed Cindy. Did she know what was up?

Well, yes, Cindy did, sort of, but she wasn't going to talk about it. Paul Salim was the only Muslim parent with a child enrolled in Old Mission Elementary School. Paul and Peggy may have needed Father Jerry's counsel, but they were not likely to seek him out.

Father Jerry sniffed and glanced toward the arbor. Now his serious expression became curious. Cindy followed his gaze to where a dark, thin figure of a man lingered in the shadow, staring openly toward Peggy Salim. His features were Middle Eastern. He was smoking a rank Turkish cigarette. In a suit and tie, he was decidedly overdressed for this event.

"Is that a parent of one of our kids?" Father Jerry whispered to Cindy.

She told Father Jerry as much as she knew. Cindy had caught glimpses of the stranger several times throughout the carnival. Always he had seemed to be watching Peggy Salim. Lurking. His presence had made Peggy more miserable by the hour.

Father Jerry's eyebrows arched in disapproval. "Well, then. You don't say. I'd guess he's neither Protestant nor Catholic, or I would have seen him in the pitchin' booth. So what's he doin' after hours starin' so boldly like at a couple ladies?" He drew the towel around him officially as though it were his vestment. He strode straight to where the fellow stood glowering.

"Are you a parent?" The priest's challenge carried across the plaza. "Well, you're botherin' the ladies here. Now if you're inclined, come help us out cleanin' up and all. But if you've no business here, then I'm tellin' you to be on your way. The party's over."

The stranger's brooding eyes narrowed threateningly. He tossed down his cigarette butt and, with one final glance at Peggy Salim, stalked from the plaza.

TWENTY-TWO

Diablo Canyon Nuclear Power Plant
Avila Beach, California
9:40 P.M. Pacific Time

STRIKE ONE

The fuel-handling building that housed the storage pool was built like a warehouse. Unlike the instantly recognizable concrete domes of the containment vessels to which it was adjacent, the steel girder and roof construction of the three-story-high structure was not remarkable.

Aside from the absence of windows, the only other noteworthy feature of the room was the stainless-steel-lined tank. Because the borated water so thoroughly prevented nuclear reactions from proceeding, there were no operators on duty inside the room and, unlike the reactor vessels, these tanks were not continuously monitored.

What could possibly happen there anyway? Even approaching the room was difficult, because there were so many layers of security doors and electronic passkeys. Besides, the only way to damage the storage facility would be with a bomb, and no explosives could possibly make it past the elaborate detection devices. Spent fuel storage posed no known hazard as long as the borated water covered the fuel rods.

Shadir peered over the edge into the 40-foot depths. Far below the surface he saw the honeycomb rack in which the fuel rods were standing. The pool was huge. He had heard that it contained seven million liters of water, but had given the number no particular thought.

For the first time a doubt about the success of this mission crept into his thoughts. How could the insignificant bat he was holding possibly transform this protective lake into a cauldron of radioactive steam? He was much more comfortable with Semtex and fuses, plungers and blasting caps. But it was too late to draw back.

Paul Salim, a pathetic, huddled shape, stood near the wheel that controlled the water flow into the reactor-containment dome.

Shadir decided to mask his own uncertainty by picking on the weakling, Salim. "You shall have the honor of starting the process," Shadir said, extending the baseball bat.

Salim shrunk back as if the graphite cylinder were poison. "No."

"I insist," Shadir sneered. "It is required. Hurry, unless you want the delay to cost the life of your son!"

With trembling fingers, Salim accepted the bat.

"Unscrew the plug in the end," Shadir instructed.

Salim did so, exposing a dull powder inside.

"The stuff of legends," Shadir remarked with evident appreciation of his own poetry. "Able to unleash a consuming fire. Throw it into the pool. You . . ."

Paul Salim glanced once more into Shadir's face, saw no pity, no remorse there, and so flipped the bat end-over-end into the tank.

"No!" Shadir said, shoving Salim roughly aside and staring after the sinking object. "You were supposed to cast the powder over the surface!"

"You didn't—"

"No matter!" Shadir interrupted harshly. "It's done. It will take longer perhaps to work, but it is already irreversible! *Allahu akhbar!*"

Embarcadero Station
San Francisco
9:52 P.M. Pacific Time

TAKE IT LIKE A MAN

With the exception of a few straggling tourists, a handful of die-hard human robot street performers, and a drunk doing a bad rendition of "I Left My Heart in San Francisco," the Embarcadero was empty and quiet.

There was a common civilian misconception that taking a bullet in the chest while wearing a bullet-resistant vest didn't hurt. That erroneous notion couldn't be further from the truth.

Steve's chest was deep purple in two places. The first shot had been low on his left side. He could feel the ribs bending freely when he breathed. The other bloody doughnut-shaped ring was right above his heart on the left side. That was probably the shot that had rendered him unconscious.

The process of getting shot while wearing light body armor was a bit like the desk toy that has five steel balls suspended from strings. If you raised and dropped one of the end balls, you couldn't see the movement in the middle ball, but from the bounce at the opposite end, clearly the energy was transferred *through* all five.

In this case there was no puncture wound, but there was most certainly a transfer of energy from the bullets to Steve's rib cage. Like the steelies suspended in the toy, bullet crashed into vest, vest into bone, bone into flesh.

Hydro-shock, a term used to describe the energy transferred through water molecules from a slug, was often enough to significantly damage the heart as well as other vital organs. The result at best with a small-caliber handgun was like being struck in the torso with a hammer in full swing. To take the hit and get up was not the average gentleman's Friday night parlor trick.

It was a credit to his exercise regimen—and the fact that God wasn't finished with him yet, he acknowledged—that he had survived. Steve was grateful to be alive.

In spite of all the blunt-force trauma he had experienced, Steve hardly noticed the pain from his injuries. Occasionally, while talking to the team, he drew in his breath too deeply. The rib flexed, like a spear point trying to escape from his midsection. But his mind was consumed with worry for Matthew, Cindy, and Tommy. Perhaps the most troubling aspect was that he couldn't be in two places at once.

Steve recognized himself as the type that had to be in control. He was the best man for the job and he knew it. Steve would never stand back and let someone else screw things up. In this case, he couldn't. As much as he wanted to be in San Luis, with Cindy and Tommy, he'd have to trust God on that end and pay attention to his trigger finger on this one.

"Hey, man!" Anton exclaimed as he trotted over to see him. "Morrison says you took a rod in the chest."

Conscious of the depth of his inhale, Steve nodded. "But it's the last thing on my mind right now."

Anton must have known what Steve was thinking; he had a baby girl of his own. He changed the subject. "You're guessing the boys were taken to the same place we went a couple days ago? Khalil's?"

On their brisk walk to the SWAT van, Steve told him, "The guy was Arab, Middle Eastern anyway. The rest all fits too. They just didn't expect me to live to figure it out."

"Well, you're right," Anton confirmed. "Morrison did some bouncin' around on the phone. Two field agents keeping watch on Khalil's mansion confirmed it. About 10 minutes after you took a plug, that same yellow Donzi cruised into the boathouse."

"Did they see the boys?"

"No," Anton answered seriously. "They rolled the door down behind them before anybody showed. But the good news is nobody has come or gone since."

That *was* good news, Steve realized. "How many guys do they think are in there?"

"Hard to tell, but maybe only a couple. I honestly don't think they counted on being caught so soon. I think they figured you were dead and they wouldn't have to worry."

"I was just playing dead," Steve said, gingerly touching his midsection. "Very convincing. At least I *think* that's what the boys thought. You should have seen the looks on their faces. It was like they thought it was a game."

Anton added optimistically, "Maybe a good thing. If they didn't resist, it means force wasn't required. We'll get 'em back safe."

Steve's heart rate increased. Tears swam in his eyes. Hatred, anger, and anguish surged through him all at once. He vowed, "I'm gonna get them back, God help me. It'll take a lot more than two nines to put me down for good. Not while my boy needs me."

"Steady, bro," Anton cautioned.

Their eyes met, and Steve's mind flashed to the loss of Anton's son. There was a brief but intense understanding between them before both averted their eyes.

"You don't need to be the Lone Ranger," Anton said softly. "You got lots of willing helpers!"

Morro Bay, California
10:13 P.M. Pacific Time

WOULDN'T IT BE LOVERLY

The last of her passengers dropped off, Cindy and Tommy headed west on Highway 1 toward Morro Bay and home. The main street of the tiny beach town had rolled up its sidewalks hours before. Antique stores, art galleries, and coffee shops had closed about the same time as the sun had set behind the gigantic volcanic rock that loomed over the Bay.

Cindy was exhausted. Mrs. O'Connor had cursed them all in the last five minutes of cleanup by dancing around Old Mission Plaza with a broom, singing Eliza Dolittle's song from *My Fair Lady.* For the past hour the words had played over and over in Cindy's fuddled brain:

All I want is a room somewhere,

far away from the cold night air . . .

"Shut up, Eliza!" Cindy muttered to herself. "All I want is a bed somewhere."

. . . wouldn't it be loverly?

No use. The tune and lyrics rewound and played again.

. . . warm face, warm 'ands, warm feet,

oh, wouldn't it be . . .

Cindy was tempted to telephone the old woman, wake her up, and sing in her ear when she got home.

Never mind.

Tommy was asleep in the backseat as Cindy rolled up in front of the condo. She stepped out of the SUV and inhaled deeply. The fresh, cool sea air filled her lungs. She imagined Steve and the boys being gently rocked to sleep on Steve's boat.

Someone's head restin' on my knee,

Warm and tender as he could be . . .

"Loverly," she said aloud.

She wished she was with them tonight. Lying beside Steve.

She consoled herself that perhaps they had a future after all. That the day would come when they would be together again as a family. Tonight her world seemed at peace. She could hear the clang of buoys and the pleasant drone of the foghorn beyond the harbor entrance.

She would sleep like a rock tonight.

"Tommy?" She tried to rouse the boy, but he would not open his eyes. She remembered being a little kid, going to a drive-in movie and pretending to fall asleep on the way home just so her daddy would carry her into the house.

Was Tommy faking it, looking for a free ride into the condo and up those steep stairs?

Never mind.

She hoisted him into her arms and kicked the car door shut. For moments such as this it would be good to have her man around. Eight steps to the front door. Why hadn't she left the porch light on?

Fumbling for her keys, she unlocked the door, plunged into the darkness of the house, and took the stairs leading up to the living room and her bedroom. From the corner of her eye she saw the red message light of the answering machine blinking.

Tommy groaned and shifted awkwardly in her arms. "Can I sleep in your bed, Mommy?"

"Sure."

Never mind the message. She'd get it in the morning.

Within three minutes Cindy had Tommy's shoes off and his jammies on.

. . . far away from the cold night air,
with one enor-mous chair,
oh! wouldn't it be loverly?

Thirty seconds after her head hit the pillow the foghorn blew mournfully across the waters.

"Good night, Eliza," Cindy whispered. "Good night, Steve."

That was the last thing she remembered.

HRT Tactical Deployment Van
San Francisco
10:45 P.M. Pacific Time

PLAN OF ATTACK

"Jiminy Christmas, boss!" Chaz Turner, Echo 1 medic, exclaimed as he carefully lifted Steve's vest. "Most guys who go for the Purple Heart just want a medal and a T-shirt, but you! You got the tattoos to go with it."

Steve held himself from swaying as the van lumbered along the 101 access route toward the Golden Gate Bridge. Every breath was grunted out.

Chaz shook his head, wincing almost as much as Steve at the sight of the wounds. "I don't think so, man. I'm advising you not to go."

This angered Steve. "I'm not asking. Shut up and tape it."

After a low whistle and another shake of his head to express disapproval, Chaz agreed. "I think what's best is just to wrap you with the level 2 on. Then you can throw a level 3 over it."

"You gotta be kidding me," Steve replied. "I won't be able to walk."

"That's what I'm sayin'! And the thing is, with your ribs busted this bad—" Chaz jabbed his thumb toward the higher of the two bruises—"you take another one and that rib'll turn like a spear and go right through your heart or lung or both!"

"That's my kid out there! Shut up and tape it!" Steve yelled.

The driver of the van turned around, then ducked his head before Steve's wrath landed on him too. Chaz began wrapping the lightweight vest tighter to Steve's body with Ace bandages, like preparing a mummy for a 1000-year burial.

It was more difficult to breathe than before. Though he did not and would not express it, Steve felt like a crumbling plaster pillar supported by wire and duct tape. Bits of him threatened to flake off and fall away, while the rest was bound up like a straitjacket.

Duffel bags and tactical assault vests hung in wire-mesh lockers along the sides of the transport. Resembling a black UPS truck, the vehicle was a full-service, mobile headquarters, complete with weapons lockers, benches, and a table. The only thing missing was a bathroom. That would have been a useful addition, since that particular need was the first thing every one of the guys remembered when they got nerved up.

Steve found a long-sleeve T-shirt in his duffel. He stretched it down over the level 2 vest, tucking it into his cargo pants. "Give me the other vest," he ordered.

Chaz paused, then inserted an extra ballistic plate in the chest pocket. "This will help."

But it wouldn't work and Steve knew it. The plate might keep him alive, but the extra weight would slow him down to the point of being an easy target. He might as well not have it. "Forget it," he said, slinging on his assault vest.

"You got to!" Chaz said, shocked.

"I can hardly walk as it is. Even with that stuff, if I take another shot, I'm done," Steve argued. "I'd rather be able to move."

The rest of the team looked on solemnly. There was no use arguing. No one could tell him not to go. Steve was the boss and it was his kid. If any of them thought he would be a burden or might endanger the mission, none of them expressed it.

"What have we got for intel?" Steve asked Sammy the Snake.

Sammy was a little guy, wiry and bouncy. He unrolled the plans on the table. They revealed perfectly the steep hill and the massive home, which was connected underground to the boathouse on the Bay. "Okay," Sammy said in his high-pitched voice. "Outer perimeter is already in place. We've got two Coast Guard cutters holding just around the bends in the shoreline, here and there, in case anyone should try to leave by water."

Steve knew they had better be on the ball. That yellow Donzi was prob-ably the fastest thing on the Bay. And it was really a dark night. "What do we know about these two roads?" Steve pointed to a short one from the gatehouse and another more winding road from the south side.

Sammy explained, "The gatehouse road is short, maybe 30 yards down to the garage and front entrance. The other is longer, about 50 to 60 yards. It runs alongside the steep hill. It's gravel—probably a service road."

Steve marked the fence to the side of the gatehouse. "Sammy, you and Brian throw your rubber mat over the wall spikes there. You wait in the bushes along the road until Chaz and I make it around the gatehouse. We can enter through the third story, upper-ground side on the front. Darjit," Steve called to the driver, "you serve the warrant at the gate. We'll cover you from the upper south side."

Steve radioed Anton in the Echo 2 van. "Echo 2 Actual. We've got two field agents covering the road. Why don't you split Team 2? Leave one guy to cover the service road. Two go along the shore from the north and two go along the shore from the south."

Anton replied. "Tory will cover the road. Me and Willie can cover the north bankside. Then we'll come up the path there to the lower-level deck. We'll enter there and work our way up through the house. Sorveno can go with Mooneyham along the south-side bank."

Steve interjected. "Two, can the four of you clear the boathouse first, then come up?"

"Looks good," Anton noted. "I'll see if I can disable the Donzi. Then we'll split. Sorveno and Mooney will enter through the second-story side deck and clear rooms for all of us to meet in the middle. Over."

Steve traced the plans on the map. It made perfect sense. Three levels, four sides. He wondered if there shouldn't be one more entry team, but the field agents would help. They would have level 3 vests and AR-15s in the trunk of their Taurus.

The repeated double-clunking sound from the tires made Steve aware that they were headed across the Golden Gate Bridge. For every 40 feet of roadway there was a new panel and a metal joint in the road that the tires crossed.

They were getting close. Less than five minutes now.

Just hang on, Matt, Steve thought. *I'm on the way.*

TWENTY-THREE

Pacific Skies
Between San Francisco and San Luis Obispo, California
11:01 P.M. Pacific Time

CRY HAVOC!

The flight time from San Francisco to the Central Coast county of San Luis Obispo was less than one hour in the FBI plane. In the mind of Dr. Turnow it was both way too long and not nearly long enough.

If there was an imminent terrorist threat to the nuclear power plant at Diablo Canyon, then every second counted. A nuclear power plant couldn't be made to explode like an atom bomb; the physics was all wrong.

But something almost as deadly was possible. If the core containing the radioactive fuel was caused to overheat past the protective ability of the chemical safeguards built into the system, then the incandescent mass could burn right through concrete and steel. Correction, *would* burn through concrete and steel. At that point it would be unstoppable.

The infamous meltdown.

So well-known had that phrase become that it was common slang for the total destruction of a plan or a relationship. Yet it was still little understood by the public.

When the fiery mass of molten uranium dioxide struck groundwater, it would explode in a fountain of radioactive steam, erupting with enough force to rupture what remained of the concrete containment vessel.

The direction and speed of the wind and the amount of warning time given would determine how many would die immediately and how many more would die of radiation sickness in the future. A hundred thousand, two hundred thousand . . . perhaps as many as millions of lives were at stake.

Like Chernobyl—*Wormwood* in English, as in the book of Revelation—Turnow mused, hundreds of square miles could be uninhabitable for decades . . . or longer. Arriving too late to prevent a radioactive holocaust was unthinkable.

But what if the tenuous connections drawn by Turnow and Steve Alstead were wrong? Was it certain that the death of Frank Daley had been the objective of the BART bombing? Were the same terrorists responsible for kidnapping the two children? And did that absolutely mean Diablo was the next target? If an assault was in progress, then shouldn't emergency evacuation plans be implemented at once?

Perhaps.

Turnow glanced down at the titanium band of his Omega wristwatch. The passage of time so registered in his head that he had no need to look at its dial.

Less than an hour till midnight.

How many injuries and deaths would ensue as a direct result of the panic a midnight evacuation would cause? And what if it was a false alarm? What if a tragedy could still be prevented? Was the countdown to Shaiton's Fire happening now?

If Paul Salim was part of a terrorist group, or being coerced by one, the last thing Chapter 16 wanted was to alert him that the secret was out. Because of Frank Daley's death, Salim was the boss at Diablo. How to check on him without telegraphing a warning? And what if others at the plant had been recruited by Shaiton's Fire as well?

There was scarcely enough time to think through all the ramifications; half the flight was already over.

Turnow shot a glance at Charles Downing, whose nose was buried in a file of material on Hezbollah splinter groups. It was no good asking the profiler's opinion of what should be done. Determining whether a nuclear threat existed was Turnow's call to make.

Connected by satellite link to Miles back at the FBI telecommunications center, Turnow was able to conference-call with the Nuclear Regulatory Commission, the president's National Security advisor, and Senator Morrison.

Professor Pennington was a high-ranking nuclear engineer with the NRC. It was his opinion that such a scenario as Turnow was depicting was impossible.

"One of the Diablo reactors is 'cold' right now anyway," Pennington argued. "New fuel cells haven't even been loaded yet. But the other core is surrounded by three feet of concrete, borated water, and control rods that can drop in less than two seconds. The whole thing is designed to withstand a massive earthquake, for crying out loud! Even a direct hit on the concrete dome by a 1000-pound bomb wouldn't make it go critical. To disrupt all the safety features someone would have to set off a bomb inside the containment vessel itself."

"Could they do that?" Morrison queried. "Is there access?"

"Not when the core is 'hot,'" Pennington explained. "It's completely sealed. And even when it's down, the core is serviced by a robot that's completely submerged under water at all times."

"How does the robot gain access?" Turnow asked.

"The whole system connects," Pennington replied. "New fuel cells go in and spent fuel rods come out in the same tank of borated water."

Alarm bells began to ring in Turnow's mind. "The old fuel is stored at Diablo?"

"Yes," Pennington grudgingly admitted. "Until the national underground storage site at Yucca Mountain is up and running, we keep the fuel cells in a million-gallon tank. The rods stand on end in a grid, far enough apart that there's very little nuclear reaction between them even if the borated water wasn't present. We've never had a problem in over 15 years."

That thought struck Turnow like a baseball bat. Fifteen years' worth of stored radioactive fuel? But maybe they were mostly inert, no longer harmful. "And how radioactively potent are the rods when retired—5 percent, 10?"

"No, about 50 percent," Pennington explained. "Using them longer is inefficient."

"Fifty!" Morrison interjected.

"That's not the worst," Turnow guessed. "The plant is in the middle of a turnaround. Not only are the rods that just came out still at their highest remaining potency, they are temporarily in the pool next to brand-new, 100 percent reactive fuel!"

"I'm getting on to the president right now," NSA Chief Seastrand said.

"Hold on!" Pennington argued. "Everything I just said is all routine! As long as there's borated water around the cells the reaction can't get started."

"Could someone bomb the storage tank?" Morrison demanded. "Empty the tank at a single blast?"

"How'd they get a bomb into the plant?" Pennington shot back. "Past the sniffers? Can't be done."

"How about making the borate stop working?" Morrison inquired.

"No," both Pennington and Turnow said simultaneously.

Turnow explained further. "Boron is such a highly reactive element that it bonds very tightly and is a terrific neutron-absorbing agent. There's no way to precipitate it out of solution, unless . . ." He snapped his fingers, and three men separated by thousands of miles all jumped. "Buckyballs. Dope them with something that captures the borate and the protection is gone!"

"Fullerene isn't water soluble," Pennington reminded him.

"Doesn't have to be," Turnow shot back. "Give it a molecular coating so that it acts as if it were soluble and the effect is the same."

"Wouldn't that stuff set off the bomb sniffers?" Seastrand asked.

"No," Pennington said. "It's just carbon . . . exotic, with amazing properties, but carbon." Then he snorted. "But it's too wild! Even with the borate gone, there'd still have to be a bomb to crush the fuel rods together and start the reaction. We're back to what I said before!"

With icy clarity Turnow asked, "How does a new core get up and running?"

"Well," Pennington offered, "we have to add starter catalyst . . . something highly radioactive, like californium . . . oh!"

"That decides it for us," Morrison said. "We can't delay any longer in contacting the chief of security at Diablo. You agree, Mr. Seastrand?"

"Absolutely, Senator! It's your show to run, but keep this connection open. At the first word that the threat is imminent, order the evacuation. I'll alert the president!"

Diablo Canyon Nuclear Power Plant
Avila Beach, California
11:15 P.M. Pacific Time

STRIKE TWO

Within the fuel-handling building the humidity above the great volume of water was almost stifling. Shadir's clothing clung to him in sticky clumps.

He stared morosely into the pool. There was no steam, no bubbles, nothing to indicate that anything was happening at all.

An hour and a half had passed! Where was the blow against the great Satan of the United States? Where was the pyre that would consume American vanity?

Nothing!

The Russian had lied! Petrov had cheated Khalil out of millions of dollars and Shadir out of immortality for nothing!

The terrorist punched the metal wall. It rang hollowly and hurt his knuckles but achieved no more. "You!" he said venomously to Paul Salim in his need to vent his anger. "What trick have you played?"

Blankly Salim stared without replying.

"Answer me! Why does it not work?"

"I don't know," Salim said at last. Imperceptibly he inched sideways until his body covered a recording thermometer, its pen inscribing a spidery line on a drum of paper.

Staring at the man, Shadir was suddenly suspicious. He shoved Salim out of the way and scowled at the unit. The tracing that crossed six tiny squares per hour showed an increase of barely half a degree in the water's temperature in the last hour. "What is this? Do not lie to me; you do not do it well."

"The water's heating up," Salim said dully. "That wouldn't happen if the borate were working properly. The reaction is starting. How do we report in, so my son is spared?"

Shadir caught the sideways glance Salim gave him. "You are not as beaten down as you seem," he said. "But you cannot trick me. You think we do not know everything?" He displayed the wristwatch. "We have the additional radioactivity needed to push the reaction into a meltdown. We will wait only a little longer. The Russian said there would be steam, and then it would be time."

Paul Salim didn't even bother to ask who Shadir meant. It was clear that what he had just heard explained everything. "You said nothing about an escape plan because there is none," Salim declared flatly.

Smirking, Shadir said, "You will have the blessing of martyrdom, even though you do not deserve it. Together we will be the first to feel the cleansing fire applied to America."

There was a spark in Paul Salim's eyes that had not been there before. "I don't care for myself," he said. "But my family. You lied about saving them?"

Shadir shrugged. "What you say proves your weakness. You have been corrupted by living in this country. But here is the truth: your wife will take her chances like the others. As for your son, he will be safe when the warning sirens sound . . . not before and not otherwise."

Diablo Canyon Nuclear Power Plant
Avila Beach, California
11:29 P.M. Pacific Time

WITH OPEN ARMS

The whole night, like much of the entire last two weeks, had been so packed with the unexpected and outrageous that landing a plane in a parking lot to thwart a nuclear attack really didn't seem that far from ordinary.

As the King Air circled the massive containment domes of Diablo Nuclear Power Plant, Turnow wished that in this case he were wrong. But the certainty was growing that every surmise was correct.

Turnow listened as Downing was enmeshed in the next round of weirdness. Speaking personally to Randall Goldbloom, chief of Diablo Security, Downing established his credentials then extracted a vow of secrecy from the man. Without revealing their suspicions, Downing inquired about Paul Salim's whereabouts.

On plant property, he was told, with a visiting relative, but apparently not in his office. Did Mr. Downing need them to page Mr. Salim?

Absolutely not! But for the record, had anything unusual about Mr. Salim's behavior been noted?

Not particularly, aside from the fact that he seemed embarrassed or uneasy carrying a commemorative bat in honor of his predecessor. Yes, it might be made of graphite. It clearly was neither wood nor metal.

Bingo!

So there had been no time to land at the San Luis Obispo Airport. Though only 30-minutes' drive away, even that delay might be too much!

Fortunately for Downing and Turnow, Diablo had an extensive parking lot. Massive, but mostly empty. This extravagance existed solely for the use of the 1000 or so workers who arrived every 19 to

21 months for routine plant maintenance. Even though it was during one of those regularly scheduled times, this refurbishment cycle was nearing completion, and at half past eleven, the parking lot was empty.

At least Turnow prayed it would be so.

There was no time to give better warning to Goldbloom. There simply was no time. The minutes were down to critical ones as far as Turnow could see. Even with a brief phone call from a man claiming to be Senator James Morrison, Special Investigations director for the FBI, there was no way Goldbloom could fathom what was in motion and no time for a better explanation while they were still in the air.

Turnow overheard the end of the conversation. "Mr. Goldbloom," Downing concluded, "please stand by. We'll be landing a plane in your parking lot in about three minutes."

Goldbloom's incredulous protest was cut off midsquawk.

The aircraft looped in from the sea south of the plant, rounded northwest into the prevailing wind, lined up with the windy road from Port San Luis, and came in as slowly as possible. There was only about half a mile of level field before the plane would either crash into the ocean or the reactor.

The wheels made smooth contact, and the captain hit the air brakes, applying full reverse pitch on the propellers. The vibration was unnerving, but the landing was successful. The King Air wound down its engines only 50 yards from the front entrance to the reactor.

Turnow was not disappointed with the response he received when the fuselage door opened. Men with light automatic weapons and shotguns ringed the plane. Turnow noticed one pointed at his feet. He placed his hands in the air.

Downing remarked, "Nice warm reception we've got here."

Turnow doubted this was the time for humor. If the guys with the machine guns weren't laughing, then Turnow opposed testing their sense of humor further.

A tall, heavyset blond man dressed in a black field uniform waved the muzzle of his weapon below the boarding door. "Step down, sir."

Turnow did as he was told but also opened his coat slowly. "I'm going to show you my badge. That way there will be no mistake." Stepping out, he carefully removed a leather wallet, containing his picture ID and FBI badge.

The SWAT member flicked it open. "With respect, sir, I've never heard of Chapter 16 before." He radioed the information in to Goldbloom at Security HQ. A second later he handed the wallet back. "If you'll follow me."

Leaving behind the plane to be guarded by sentries toting M-16s, moments later Turnow and Downing were in Goldbloom's office. Though the security chief was housed in an administrative building and not in the operating part of the plant, Turnow wondered how such an ostentatious arrival could possibly go unremarked by anyone.

Randall Goldbloom was a skinny man with tired-looking, unfriendly eyes. He extended a limp handshake to Turnow. "Now," he said in a nasally voice, "what in blazes is this all about?"

Turnow explained.

A minute later Goldbloom was not only tired-looking, he was perspiring and looking anxiously out his office window toward the only road leading away from the nuclear plant.

TWENTY-FOUR

Khalil's Residence
Sausalito, California
11:42 P.M. Pacific Time

GOOD GUYS AT THE GATES

As much as the bandages and the feeling of having been shrink-wrapped chafed Steve, the delay in launching the rescue of his son chafed him more.

It hadn't been Dan's fault, but a string of communication problems had seriously delayed the forced entry. The radio net center in the mobile command trailer wasn't working properly. The backup unit was, but it operated in VHF, which didn't have the scrambling capabilities of UHF and might leave the operatives vulnerable to having their moves intercepted by the enemy.

It was impossible to change the operating frequency on such short notice, so as a result, the Marin County SWAT reserves were called for a loan of equipment. By the time HRT received the unit as well as extra perimeter support, much time had been lost.

The mobile communications unit, when finally in operation, was positioned across Sausalito Bay for clear audio and visual recon of the mansion. On that side of things, two Observer-Sniper Teams, Sierra 1 and Sierra 2, were deployed into the backyard of a vacant residence. They each found hides in the lush hillside botanical garden of an avid amateur horticulturalist.

Their first concern was the neighbors who might see them and call the local deputy sheriff, who, because of the tight security, didn't know of the raid. The second concern was the extreme distance. At 350 yards across the narrowest place in the small bay, it would be a challenge for even the most accomplished marksman in urban combat conditions. However, with the assistance of Swarski 15 X 50 binoculars, they could see all the facing windows on the three-and-a-half-story house.

Sierra Teams were on the southwest side of the bay as well—three of them, in fact. Teams 3 and 4 were on either side of the house, just outside the property lines. Aside from a few trees and other minor obstacles, they would have much easier shots at only 50 to 75 yards, and any firing would be backstopped by the house, protecting bystanders from accidents.

Above the highway, nestled in the thick coastal brush of the rugged hillside, Sierra Team 5 could see it all. With a view of the entire estate and the bay, it would be the most valuable for observation. Unfortunately, due to the tight proximity of other properties, safe shots from their location would be limited to the direction of the house.

"This is Charlie," Dan announced, giving the call sign for Command. "Radio check. Sierra Teams 1 through 5, respond, please. Over."

Sierra 1 and Sierra 2, flanking the com trailer, both replied, "Reading you five by five."

Dan went down the list.

Steve was sweating it out in the back of the van, waiting for the communications net to go up. The pain and stiffness from his wounds had had time to set in a bit, along with the agonizing worry for the boys. He had never felt so relieved as when Dan called a radio check for Echo 1 and Echo 2.

After the communications channels were cleared, Echo Teams

deployed. The vans had been waiting a tenth of a mile south of Khalil's gates. With the interior lights blacked out, the rear doors swung open.

Sorveno and Mooneyham cut down to the water. Chaz followed Steve up the highway as the van sped up the road. Darjit was next. Anton and Willie deployed for the bay by the north gate service road. They were followed by Tory, who met field agents Brenden and Trent outside the gate.

Steve huffed with the load of his sound-suppressed Heckler & Koch MP-5 and rubber mat as he trotted ahead of Chaz. Every pebble underfoot was transferred to his chest as a jarring jolt, but he only grunted and kept moving. Chaz carried the med supplies as well as a Beretta 1201 lightweight, tactical-entry shotgun.

There was movement in the small stone guardhouse. Steve halted and presented his rifle in the ready position.

Darjit approached the front gate. Given the number of alienlike invaders wearing what might have been space suits, it was a strangely incongruous sight to have Darjit walk up to the intercom and push the buzzer.

Steve could see Khalil's security man stand and look out. Of course there was nothing to see, since Darjit was wearing black and faded instantly into the bushes outside the wall. There were no car headlights to give away any HRT operative.

Khalil's guard returned to his seat.

As if playing a game of doorbell ditching, Darjit rang again but didn't reply when the man spoke over the intercom. The idea was to draw the sentry out to the gate. Sierra 5 and others would be able to assess if he was armed. It would also limit the guard's ability to warn others once the warrant was served.

"Who's out there?" the guard called out angrily as he approached the highway. "You kids get out of here before I call the cops."

Darjit waited for him to reach the gate before he spoke. "FBI. You're surrounded and I have a warrant to enter. Don't move."

The man almost jumped out of his skin when he realized someone was standing right in front of him. He put his hand on his holstered sidearm while backing away.

"Sir," Darjit commanded, "remove your hand from your weapon, or I'll be forced to shoot you."

Instead of obeying, the guard attempted to present his pistol, apparently unaware his every action was clearly seen.

Steve held his breath. If the guard refused to cooperate, he would have to be taken out quietly or the surprise would be lost.

"Drop it!" Darjit ordered.

Khalil's sentry continued to raise his weapon.

Nearly silent rounds zipped in from two sides—Darjit and Steve. Neither missed. The guard crumpled where he stood. There was no time to dwell on it now. The Echo Teams had to move out immediately.

Steve heard a metallic pinging sound. Apparently Darjit had cut the power supply to the gate, which had then popped open.

Darjit moved to the body of the fallen sentry to check vital signs. The man was dead.

"Echo 1 Actual to command," Steve informed Dan. "Front yard has been cleared. Tango is down."

Dan replied, "Search Tango for keys, then hold entry until boathouse is cleared."

Darjit located the keys hanging from the dead guard's belt loop.

By clicking over to the command circuit, Steve could hear the progress of the other Echo Teams. Anton and Willie had reached the side of the boathouse opposite from Sorveno and Mooneyham. He heard them given the go-ahead to proceed.

Anton tried the side entrance to the pier-mounted structure. "Echo 2 Actual to Command. Boathouse is locked," he whispered.

Dan answered calmly, "Echo 2, have 2B pick the lock."

Willie was 2B, the second member of Echo Team 2. He was an expert with the tools of silent forced entry. He removed a small satchel from his tac vest, rolled it out on the ground, and began to work.

Steve was listening over the net. If they didn't do something quick, he knew Sorveno would be itching to blow the door.

"Command to 1 Actual," came Dan's voice. "We have traffic on the highway—a whole line of cars. See that the downed Tango is properly hidden."

Steve motioned for Sammy and Brian to drag the body away. The pair disappeared into the bushes. Steve and Chaz, Echo 1B, made themselves scarce in the shadows of the darkened gatehouse guard-shack.

Steve tried not to think of Matt, somewhere inside the sprawling mansion in front of him, tried not to think how many innocent people these terrorists had already ruthlessly killed. He forced himself to remain planted firmly under discipline and orders. Otherwise he might have thrown himself into Khalil's house through the closest window.

Khalil's Boathouse
Sausalito, California
11:48 P.M. Pacific Time

MIDNIGHT SWIM

"Ouch!" Willie exclaimed when his lock pick broke and stabbed him in the wrist. The bleeding was not severe, but the lock was permanently jammed, with the metal fragment of the pick burrowed deep into it.

Dan's voice addressed them. "Men, have we checked the boathouse roll-up gate? I know the water is deep there. Can't we swim under the roller door?"

The idea probably had not occurred to them. Even if it had, Anton hated the water and wouldn't admit it. Swimming in the murky bay with 40 pounds of gear was not his idea of a good time. "Echo 2 Actual to Command. Roger that."

Anton waded down the rocks. The path was slimy. He slipped, splashing into the bay. His whole body and head disappeared under the surface.

Willie made a jump after Anton's arm but missed and began to slide toward the drop-off himself. Grabbing onto a projecting timber, he steadied himself on the corner of the house.

A second later a watery gurgle came over the radio. The whisper was Anton's. "Command, I'm in. There may be a Tango inside."

"Proceed with caution," was Dan's reply.

Willie carefully submerged himself into the icy green waters. Blowing his cheeks up like a chipmunk's, he too swam under the gate. Mooneyham and Sorveno followed their orders to continue along the outside wall.

Inside the boathouse, Anton stayed in the water, edging his way along one side of the slip. He pulled himself by grasping a walkway's ledge. The Donzi was moored with its bow facing out, as if ready for a quick getaway.

Willie slipped along in the other direction. The dark room was simple, with white walls and an exposed beam ceiling. In the center of the front wall was an open corridor leading in the direction of the house.

Squeezing past a ladder, Anton caught a view up the tunnel. The walls were concrete. Three dim lights illuminated the enclosed path, which climbed to the mansion.

Anton informed Dan, "Command, this is 2 Actual. I see a ladder and a long hall to the main house. There are no Tangos visible."

"Again, 2, proceed with caution."

Anton climbed from the pool. Water gushed from his vest and equipment. The noise was not something anyone could miss, unless he was napping, as one of Khalil's security guards must have been, inside the powerboat.

When Anton heard a noise in the hull of the bright yellow cruiser, he crept up slowly, motioning for Willie to move back. Anton saw a man's head emerge from below deck. He was singing to himself. Anton froze in hopes that the man wouldn't see him. But as the careless guard turned around, spotting him, Anton pointed his shotgun and said, "FBI. Move and you're dead."

The slightly built, dark-skinned man looked afraid. In fractured English he agreed not to move or make a sound.

The guard's obvious apprehension increased with the shock of seeing Willie emerge from the dark water and climb the swim step onto the boat. "Please," the sentry pleaded, spreading his hands in supplication. "I don' wan' for to die."

"Shut up!" Anton replied in a sharp whisper. "And if you're thinking about warning somebody, forget it. His gun—" he motioned toward Willie—"is sound-suppressed. Nobody will hear a thing when we put you down. Got it?"

Apparently the sobbing had all been an act and the broken English too. "Okay," the man replied in an American accent.

"Tell me where the boys are," Anton directed.

"I don't know."

Willie smacked him on the back of the legs with the stock of his gun.

The sentry fell to the ground, now genuinely afraid. "They're on the second floor, center of the house. They haven't been hurt. I swear it!"

"Where are the guards?" demanded Anton. "How many and where?"

"There is one at the gate and one other inside, as well as Mr. Khalil's personal bodyguard."

Anton boarded the boat. "That's it?"

"That's it, I swear," the man vowed, cowering.

Anton instructed Willie to tie him up and gag him, while he relayed the news to Command.

Dan relayed the information out. "Command to all teams. We have unconfirmed intel stating that there are only three more Tangos. We have the heat signatures of two males moving about the second floor. That leaves one unaccounted for. All Echo members, move in slowly."

Willie would have to stay with the prisoner. Before starting for the house, Anton kicked the gearshift on the Donzi. He raised up several times before slamming all his weight down on the plastic handles. They cracked and broke.

With the gearshift hanging from its cables, the speedboat was disabled. Anton carefully returned to the dock and moved in to clear the long hallway.

Diablo Canyon Nuclear Power Plant
Avila Beach, California
11:51 P.M. Pacific Time

STRIKE THREE

Paul Salim's message box was empty. That meant he had taken his keys and was somewhere in a higher-security area than the administrative offices.

Randall Goldbloom summoned two of his guards. The woman was built like a man and held an M-16 like one. The male security member was slender, with a dark-eyed suspicion about him.

After what had felt like dangerously interminable delays, now Dr. Turnow and Charles Downing had to rush to keep up with the wiry Mr. Goldbloom. Out one set of one-way, revolving security bars that led them to an elevator. The security guards, their faces masks of cold-eyed competence, trailed behind.

On the fifth floor, Goldbloom coded in. An electric lock clicked. As soon as the entry was released, the procession charged along the narrow glass hallway, high above a maintenance road. The bridge led them to the massive, quarter-mile-long generator room. The churning noise was deafening.

"I'm sorry I didn't think to provide you with hearing protection," Goldbloom apologized.

"If we don't stop what I think is happening, a little deafness will be no concern at all," Turnow said dryly.

In the center of the spotless concrete floor were three huge blue-and-white cylindrical drums lying horizontally—Westinghouse generators. Collectively they stretched nearly a hundred feet. Giant pipes, wrapped with shiny, hardened insulation, protruded from the floor toward the ceiling and attached to the tops of the generators. At the opposite end of the long building was a mirrored set of equipment, identical in every way to the first, except painted white and orange.

Turnow remembered that Diablo had two reactors and that only one of them was shut down for maintenance. Would a meltdown of spent fuel rods ignite the adjacent reactor core? Would it make any difference to Southern California? Would you rather be shot in the head with one bullet or two?

Moving at an angle across the floor, the four men and one woman hustled toward the right wall. They exited the noisy room and clattered down three flights of metal grate stairs.

Turnow glanced at the name above a heavily armored door. It read "Control Room." The plate-glass window in the entry was two inches thick.

Around a final turn at the base of the stairs Goldbloom swiped his card through a security slot. A green diode illuminated and the entrance monitor beeped. The group entered the security surveillance room, where cameras tied into monitors from the whole plant.

Two men in black uniforms had their feet up.

"Gentlemen," Goldbloom snapped, startling them when he burst into the room. "Where is Paul Salim?"

Trying to look more alert, the men quickly sat up straight and exchanged a glance. "Saw him . . . about an hour ago," one ventured. "He's in the spent-fuel storage with a boration specialist."

"They're not on the monitor," Goldbloom said, pointing at a fixed view of the fuel-handling building. It appeared to be empty. "Redirect cameras 23 and 24."

The second guard punched a button and the views on two monitors revolved, delivering flickering images of the pool. "There they are."

Turnow studied the men. One was staring at a temperature gauge.

"That's Paul Salim," Goldbloom commented.

The other man paced in small circles.

Downing suggested, "They seem to be waiting for something."

The pacing man stopped to check his watch, then looked up at the camera. Turnow could see his face but not clearly.

Downing started to speak. "It looks like—"

The sudden realization of who the man was struck Dr. Turnow like a blow to the head. "Shadir! The terrorist we're looking for! How fast can security get in there?"

Goldbloom hesitated. "Are you sure of this?"

"The FBI has been looking for this man." Turnow stabbed his fingertip against the monitor. "He is partly responsible for the two most recent terrorist attacks!"

A phone buzzed. "Security," one of the guards said tersely. "It's the control room," he reported to Goldbloom.

"Put it on speaker," the security chief said, not taking his eyes off the monitor.

The voice of one of the operating engineers crackled over the speaker. "Where's the boss?" the disembodied voice floated down. "We got an unexplained rise in storage pool temperature. Need somebody in there pronto!"

Goldbloom's eyes widened. Spinning to the control board, he slammed his palm down on a red knob.

In that instant, red rotating lights activated. An unbearably loud honking siren went off. At Goldbloom's nod the armed guards hastened away.

On the monitor Dr. Turnow saw Paul Salim spin around. Shadir was fiddling with his wristwatch when Paul Salim tackled him from behind.

Turnow and Downing watched in confusion as Shadir struggled toward the containment pool on his belly, all the while his fingers fumbling with the clasp of his timepiece. Salim's grip slipped and Shadir climbed to all fours.

Though there was no sound with the video feed, Turnow could interpret the silent screams of Paul Salim. "Help me!"

A moment later Diablo's armed guards pointing rifles appeared on the monitors, bursting into the room.

Shadir didn't stop but continued fumbling with the watch. Scrambling to his feet, Shadir bounded toward the storage pool. As he moved, a second, more high-pitched, ear-piercing siren sounded.

Gaping up at a flashing light near the three-lobed symbol for radioactivity, Turnow's worst fears were confirmed. High levels of radiation had been detected in the air by the sensors.

The plant was in danger of a nuclear chain reaction.

Turnow could see the point man of the security detail shouting orders at Shadir, now within a few paces of the water. "The watch!" Turnow cried out. "He's going to jump in with it!"

The power plant SWAT team opened fire on Shadir. The bullets tore his clothing and he stumbled. Just behind him, Paul Salim was struck in the abdomen. He dropped to the yellow-striped floor.

One guard fired another burst and Shadir fell. Not on solid ground but into the bubbling storage pool.

Klaxon horns hooted and warning lights flashed. An automated voice intoned, "Dangerous levels of radioactivity detected in sector 23. Dangerous levels of radioactivity detected in sector 24." The recording sounded incongruously calm amid the unnerving tumult.

The SWAT team stared in bewilderment. They fell back. A few more seconds of the sirens and the team retreated through the exit doors.

Turnow grabbed the security chief. "Goldbloom! Get me into that room. I have to help him!"

Shaking his head violently, Goldbloom replied, "No, there's no going in there now. You heard the warning. High levels of radiation have been detected. You might die in a matter of hours or even minutes."

"But the pool water is heating! They've started a nuclear reaction. Who's here to stop it?"

Abrupt understanding flared across Goldbloom's face, followed by fear. "Maybe no one." He gestured helplessly toward the monitor. "The control-room operators can shut down the core, but not this! Paul Salim is the chief operating officer . . ." His words trailed away hopelessly.

"Get me a radiation suit now!" Turnow commanded. "I'll do what I can."

Galvanized into action at last, Goldbloom replied, "Come with me!"

Morro Bay, California
11:56 P.M. Pacific Time

THE DEVIL SCREAMS

Diablo!

One hundred and thirty-one sirens in 12 evacuation zones, from Nipomo to Cayucos, shrieked the warning of imminent destruction.

Cindy ran from the condo with Tommy in her arms. Ten miles to the south the devil had awakened, and he was seeking human flesh to devour. Fearfully she glanced toward the mountains.

When would the mushroom cloud appear? the plume of fire rising from behind the hills of Montana de Oro? How much time did she have before the hellish heat and brilliant glow would melt her eyes in their sockets and sear her flesh from her bones?

Cindy held Tommy closer against her as she dashed to the car and prayed for mercy! The scream of Diablo drowned out her prayers.

Darkness. The streetlights on the hills of Los Osos winked out as electricity from the plant was suddenly cut. In a rolling wave, blackness descended across the cities of San Luis Obispo County. Cindy moaned as the illuminated sign on Mid-State Bank across the street went black.

Neighbors clad in nightclothes stepped out onto the sidewalk in confusion. They gaped at one another. Cindy seemed to be the only one who knew what this meant! So this was it. The drills at school. The memorization of procedure in the event of a nuclear emergency at Diablo. The unthinkable had somehow become a reality!

What were the instructions in the phone book?

Stay put.

Turn your radio to AM 920 KVEC for information.

Don't use your phone.

"Oh, God, don't let this be happening!" she cried, her heart pounding as she unlocked the Yukon and shoved Tommy into the backseat. She would not stay put. In minutes, cars would clog the streets.

"What's going on?" shouted Mrs. Carver from her porch.

"I'm getting out!" Cindy cried the warning. The urgency in her voice told more than the wailing alarm that echoed in the valleys and swales for 100 miles.

Cindy had known instantly. Judgment day had come upon them. This was no drill.

Diablo sirens were tested once on the first day of each month only. And then only in broad daylight. Always there was plenty of public notification to avoid panic.

Panic!

Suddenly the terror of reality took hold on hundreds now milling in the streets. Screams of horror now accompanied the undulating wail of the dying nuclear plant. They had minutes to get out at best!

"Where do we go?" pleaded Mrs. Carver.

"North!" Cindy shouted, wiping tears from her blurred eyes.

Cindy revved the engine and tore out, leaving burned rubber on the street. She knew the evacuation plan for Morro Bay. If only she could make it out before everyone took to the highways! If!

"What's wrong, Mommy?" Tommy asked her.

"Get your seat belt on!" She pressed the accelerator and blew through a stop sign on her way to an on-ramp.

There were other cars now. Tens. Hundreds. Lights blazing. Grim-faced drivers hunched over steering wheels as they merged onto Highway 1.

Cindy recited the evacuation plan in her head. North to Route 41. Across the mountains to Atascadero. But everyone would go that way! The road was barely passable in the best of times.

She would take a different route. A year ago Steve had told her how to escape if something like this ever happened. She would go past Cayucos, almost to Cambria, where a twisting two-lane road snaked inland over the mountain to Paso Robles and then merged with Highway 101 to carry them away. North! As far as they could get before the radioactive cloud drifted down to envelop them!

How many had perished in Chernobyl? She tried to remember. How did it happen? How could it happen here? She thought about Frank Daley. And Paul Salim. If Frank Daley had not been killed . . .

What did it matter now? Everyone who knew and loved Frank was going to join him unless they could escape.

The siren seemed to grow louder as Cindy maneuvered the SUV and merged onto the four-lane road. The two northbound lanes were bumper to bumper. Everyone was trying to make it out. Yet the southbound lanes were totally deserted.

Too slow! A cacophony of automobile horns joined the blaring voice of Diablo!

A black pickup with its bed filled with eight passengers pulled out of line, crossed the center divider, and sped away going the wrong direction on the southbound lanes. Others joined him, crowding all four lanes in a mad dash away.

Where were the police?

There were no stoplights.

Cindy remembered she was supposed to tune in her radio. She fiddled with the switch. There was nothing but static where KVEC should have been.

Traffic slowed.

Brake lights blinked on.

And then all forward progress ground to a halt!

Cindy was hemmed in front, back, and on the driver's side. Could she make it out on the shoulder? There were dirt roads used by ranchers. Santa Rosa Creek led into the mountains. She'd heard a person could eventually get all the way to the central valley of California.

She rolled down her window just as someone called, "There's been a wreck up ahead!"

A woman near hysteria stepped out of a small white Toyota ahead of Cindy. She raised her arms heavenward and shrieked above the wailing sirens, "God! God help us! It's true! I just heard it! The radio! Diablo! An accident! Dear God! My children! My children!"

Gridlock. Cindy eyed the shoulder of the road. She could see the woman had three tiny youngsters in her car.

Cindy called to her. "Come on, lady! Come on! Get your kids and get in here!"

The woman stared blankly at Cindy for a second. Then in a flash of comprehension, she rushed to load her toddlers into the backseat of the Yukon.

No time for introductions. Three shivering tots crammed next to Tommy, who was disdainful. The mother, in the front passenger seat next to Cindy, was still sobbing.

"Knock it off," Cindy demanded. "I've got to drive!"

Cindy slammed her hand against the four-wheel-drive button and cranked the wheel hard to the right. She rammed the deserted white Toyota off the highway as she eased out of traffic and onto the dirt.

TWENTY-FIVE

Khalil's Residence
Sausalito, California
Saturday, 5 May
12:01 A.M. Pacific Time

HAVE A CIGAR

Khalil paced his elegant Mediterranean-style lounge. The 60-inch TV was on.

With an AK-47 machine gun strapped on his back, Mehdi, the bodyguard, scanned the news channels. "There is nothing yet, sir."

Khalil swore. "Where is that cursed Mahmoud? He should have called by now! He should have news for me."

Mehdi attempted to calm his master. "Maybe he is still following Salim's wife. Maybe she is out still. Maybe . . ."

"Maybe he is stupid like Rhamad and Shadir!" Khalil retorted. "Maybe all who work for me are stupid!"

Mehdi knew when to be quiet. He knew what happened to all of Khalil's servants who failed to measure up.

The satellite phone rang, and Khalil lunged for it. "Hello, Mahmoud!"

"It is I," replied an excited voice against a background of chaos.

"Tell me. What have you seen?"

"I am sorry it took me so long, Khalil, but the traffic is mad with people trying to flee this place. It is sheer panic. Can you hear the sirens?"

Khalil pressed the receiver to his ear. "Yes! Yes, I can!" he exclaimed. "Are those the early warning sirens?"

"Yes," replied Mahmoud, as if Diablo's screams were celebratory horns on New Year's Eve. "It is madness, I tell you. Whatever Shadir—"

Khalil stopped him before he said something foolish over the phone. "Enough for now, Mahmoud. Have you left her?"

"Once the sirens began, I believed that Salim had done his job. She is now swimming with the masses on this glorious night."

"Allahu akhbar," exclaimed Khalil, like a child getting the thing he always wanted. "Good work, then. Do not stay too long, Mahmoud, or when next we speak it will be in Paradise."

Slapping the cover closed on the sat-phone, Khalil was overjoyed at the news. "But now," he wondered aloud, "what shall we do with these two boys?"

"Have you not always said that no witnesses are best?" Mehdi suggested. "Why don't we kill them? Besides, Michael's family will all be dead. And so, too, will the other one's, now that I think of it."

Khalil hummed as he thought. "Usually I would agree. But what with California crumbling, why should we not take the boys? No one will miss them. You may keep them or sell them as slaves overseas. I will make it your bonus for being the last of my servants," offered Khalil.

Mehdi smiled. "I would be most grateful for that gift. Thank you."

"It is nothing. Go get us each a cigar and tell the children that is what you will do. But get out of my way! I want to see the news," demanded Khalil. "In 15 minutes we take the Donzi out to sea and meet one of my freighters for Singapore, so make ready!"

Proudly, Mehdi did just as he was told, careful to avoid blocking Khalil's view of the television. Taking the automatic rifle in hand, he opened a solid cedar door at the edge of the room. Mehdi closed it behind him. There was a second door only feet in front of him. It too was cedar, but lightly stained with moisture. Sharp tobacco and pungent cedar aromas stirred Mehdi's imagination with thoughts of returning to Iran as a wealthy man.

Mehdi entered the humidor, which would have been considered large even for a cigar shop. The walls were lined with wood paneling up to the low wooden roof. Floor-to-ceiling shelves spanned the entire circumference of the walls. In the center of the room were three chairs. Matthew and Michael were gagged and tied to two of the chairs.

With mocking pity Mehdi looked at them and remarked, "What is the matter, boys? Tonight is a night of celebration!" He examined their somber, frightened faces before studying the boxes of cigars on the shelves. "Shaiton's Fire is brewing at the reactor in your hometown. By tomorrow, there will be nothing left." He selected two 50-ring-gauge Cohiba cigars and smiled again.

Matthew glared at him defiantly.

Michael was afraid to look up.

"Do not stare at me like that, boy," Mehdi growled. "You are my slave now. And when we reach my homeland, you will do everything I say, or I will feed you to the jackals!"

Matthew did not flinch. He had the look of his father—brave and persistent. There was no doubt that if he was free he would attack the man, three times his size or not.

Mehdi leaned down. Grabbing Matthew's chin, he shoved the muzzle of his AK into the boy's face. "Maybe I should just blow your head off!"

The threat was overwhelming. Matthew's face weakened and tears filled his eyes.

"As I thought, boy." Mehdi scowled, pushing Matthew's face away.

The chair rocked a bit. Matthew closed his eyes as if praying. He stayed that way until Mehdi left the humidor.

Khalil's Residence
Sausalito, California
12:05 A.M. Pacific Time

QUIETLY, QUIETLY!

Steve was practically biting his nails with frustration. Standing by at the front door, adrenaline-charged and ready to roll, he was not allowed to proceed until the sub-ground-level room connecting house and boat mooring had been cleared.

He checked his watch. Though only minutes had passed, this felt like the slowest-moving domestic operation he had ever worked on. And some rational, unbiased part of him knew it could be no other way.

Hearing from Command that the captive guard reported the boys present and in good condition was the best possible news Steve could have received.

He so badly wanted to rush the halls until he found his son. But he knew better. When dealing with cold-blooded terrorists whose main objective was intimidation, he knew that often, when secrecy was lost, they would attempt to do as much harm as possible as things unraveled. They would certainly use Matt and Michael as human shields.

Steve shuddered at the thought. He took a shallow breath to steady himself, and winced at the pain in his ribs. Many a hostage was killed when rescue attempts were botched, as had happened at the Munich Olympics.

At the "move out" command, Steve had to restrain himself in the doorway to keep from rushing straight in, in search of the boys. HRT protocol required every room be cleared—that is, examined for occupants—before moving on to the next.

Chaz followed him in. As the pair moved down the steps, clearing the foyer and a small security office, Brian and Sammy, who both had MP-5s, cleared the adjacent rooms. The plan was to disable any sentries before any harm could come to Matt and Michael.

In this setting a shotgun would not be much use, due to its excessive noise and the unpredictability of its projectiles. Steve ordered Chaz to sling the Beretta and go with the high-capacity, sound-suppressed H&K pistol.

Steve searched the cavernous living room.

Nothing.

Dan clicked in. "One Actual. Sierra 3 reports movement in the living room."

Steve knew Dan and the Observer-Snipers were watching from across the bay. Fearful that any moment he and the other Entry Team members would be discovered and the advantage of surprise lost, he was almost afraid even to whisper to inform Dan that it was he and Chaz in the living room.

"That's 1A and 1B, Command," he hissed.

"Copy that." Dan's voice roared in his headset. "It appears we also have movement on the north side of that same level."

Anton cut in. "I am moving up the basement steps with Echo 2B."

Dan warned Steve to be careful.

Creeping carefully down the wide hall, Steve and Chaz listened at every door before opening each. Within every room was the potential of meeting an armed enemy, who was just waiting for a clear shot.

Losing his grip on a doorknob, Chaz accidentally banged a door against the wall. The jarring sound resonated through the corridor.

Not expecting the sharp noise, Steve reacted by spinning to face him. When he realized what had happened, he mouthed the words, *Quietly, quietly!*

In a flash Idaho came back to him. His greatest fear on the AMT standoff was facing off with or accidentally shooting a kid. That fear was escalated a hundredfold now as the kid who might be shot could be his own. Though part of him feared Matt might already be dead, Steve rejected the thought, pushing it away like a piece of rotten fruit. *I can't think that way!* he told himself. Thinking about failing was like a pitcher concentrating on the fear that he was going to deliver a hanging fastball to be swatted into a home run. The sheer amount of focused worry seemed able to cause the thing most dreaded to indeed happen.

"God help me," he breathed in prayer. Shaking the horror from his mind, he continued to move deliberately according to the plan, convinced he was going to succeed.

The other half of the Echo 1 Team called, "Command, this is 1C and 1D. We're on the second-story balcony but are unable to open the sliding door."

Dan replied, "Stay put, 1C and D. We are following the movements of Echo 1 Actual. He is nearing the stairwell to the second floor. Echo 2A, report position. Over."

Anton answered, "Echo 2A reporting. Level 3 nearly cleared. Once level 1 is clear, we will move to level 2, clear south-side rooms, and open sliding door for 1C and 1D."

"Roger that," agreed Dan.

Steve listened to the radio traffic in his headset. He didn't even have to be addressed in order to know where everyone was and what was going on. A three-dimensional vision of the home's interior was displayed in his head . . . with a giant question mark over the whereabouts of his son.

Just before he cleared the last room on the top floor a long beep tone sounded for about 30 seconds. It wasn't coming from the radio or any of his equipment. With a worried expression, he looked at Chaz.

Chaz shook his head. He didn't know what the beep was either.

It must be a silent alarm, Steve determined. *God, help everything not to fall apart now,* he silently pleaded.

Khalil's Residence
Sausalito, California
12:08 A.M. Pacific Time

YOUR WORST NIGHTMARE

Khalil, pausing from puffing his cigar, screamed over the blare of the television, "What is that incessant beeping?"

Mehdi stood to reply. "It is the alarm. That beep means that one of the guards has forgotten to make his hourly check-in with the computer. It is a way of holding them accountable."

"Fire him!" Khalil retorted.

Mehdi crushed the Cohiba into a square lead-crystal ashtray before moving toward the door. A hard *thump* from upstairs made him stop. "Master, I think someone is in the house."

Startled, Khalil muted the television in order to listen. He heard stealthy whispers. Dropping his cigar into an abalone shell, Khalil jumped to his feet. Gesturing for Mehdi to follow, he hurried toward the humidor, giving instructions as he went. "I want you to put me in with the boys. Tie me up and treat me very badly."

"But why?"

"Just do it!" Khalil almost screamed. "Hold the gun on the boys, and when the intruders come in, remain calm. We will confound them yet! I will tell you when to shoot."

Mehdi seemed baffled, as if he didn't know with what question to even begin.

"You must do this, Mehdi." Khalil shook him by the forearms. "Listen: we have already struck a blow that will never be forgotten. Even if we fall ourselves, is not your soul ready for Paradise? Is it not ready?" he repeated.

"I . . . I suppose it is, but . . ."

"Good. Then, Mehdi, you must do this for me. It is Allah's will."

Mehdi was overwhelmed and caught off guard. "If it is Allah's will."

"Do it!"

Mehdi shoved Khalil into the cedar room with the boys. Their heads were down. With gags in their mouths, neither made a sound.

Matthew glanced up at the strange sight: Mehdi, the big man, the kidnapper, who threatened death or slavery, bringing in an expensively dressed older man.

Khalil pretended to resist. "Get your hands off me, you radical pig!"

Mehdi responded on cue. "Do not speak to me that way, or I will feed you to the jackals as well! Sit down and shut up!"

As if Mehdi were in charge, Khalil did as he was ordered. Mehdi tied him up, pausing only briefly when he saw a small revolver in Khalil's hand.

Khalil pretended to be pained at the sight of the others. He gazed solemnly on the boys as if he were a fellow captive. *Take courage,* his look said. Michael's head lifted.

Mehdi studied the face of Khalil. Was he sure this was what he wanted?

Khalil nodded. Then . . .

With an unexpected crash, Steve burst through the door, his weapon trained on Mehdi. Steve spotted the boys and Mehdi's gun pointed at them. He froze, thinking he had blown it. In a millisecond the man before him would pull the trigger and all he'd be able to do was shoot the terrorist afterward.

"Don't shoot!" Steve pleaded. "We can settle this so no one gets hurt."

With his gun still aimed at Matt's head, Mehdi watched Steve to see what he would do. And in that instant, Khalil leaned to the side and aimed his revolver.

The world was in slow motion. Steve could feel his heart beating, but there was a roaring in his ears. He opened his mouth to scream, but no sound came out. Like the second hand on a clock. He could smell the room, the tobacco, the cedar, the sweat of the man before him.

And Matt. Steve recognized the scent of clean clothes that Cindy had washed. His eyes met his son's. Steve was already apologizing for having failed, though he wasn't sure what was going to happen.

Khalil pulled the trigger.

The muzzle flash reached out like a torch. The sound was deafening. Matt and Michael jerked away from it.

Mehdi stumbled back. His knees sagged and he fell forward, jerking his weapon around toward Steve and away from Matt. The moment his muzzle was pointed upward, Steve pressed the trigger. His MP-5 vibrated as fire flicked out the end. Empty casings showered the room.

Steve was uncertain who had shot whom. After firing several controlled bursts into Mehdi, he lowered the submachine gun to high-ready and assessed the scene.

The large-bodied man fell limply to the floor. Steve's eyes widened when he saw the pistol in Khalil's hand, moving again.

Anton broke in behind Steve.

Khalil's expression changed from one of a cat ready to pounce to that of a desperately frightened old man. He dropped the gun. "Oh, thank you! Thank you so much," he groveled. "I am but a businessman and this crazy who worked for me . . ."

Steve rushed to Matt, quickly assessing him for injuries. He pulled the gag from his son's mouth. Even then they didn't speak with their mouths but with their eyes.

Finally Matt broke the tableau. "Dad!" he cried. "They said you were dead! That man said you were dead!"

Tears streamed down Steve's face. "Thank God! Matt, I'm so glad you're all right."

Father and son hugged each other tight, while Khalil rambled on about Mehdi. "He was going to kill us or sell us off as slaves! A radical, a dangerously crazy man!"

Anton kicked Khalil's gun toward a far corner, then ignored him, moving first to Michael. "Are you okay there, Michael?"

Michael, who couldn't answer, nodded.

Chaz entered the room. "Command. House is clear," he reported.

After untying Michael, Anton retrieved the revolver from the corner. He stared at Khalil.

Steve gathered the crying Matthew up in his arms. In that moment he realized it would have taken just one stray bullet to end the boy's life, and he would have been powerless to stop it. Steve had never felt so grateful, so humbled, or so overwhelmed with God's goodness. After all, it had been God who had watched over both their lives and prevented Steve's worst nightmare from becoming real.

After a minute he managed to call Dan on his radio. "Command, this is Echo 1. Hostages are safe. I repeat. Hostages are safe." He left the room carrying Matt, the pair of them sobbing joyously.

TWENTY-SIX

Diablo Canyon Nuclear Power Plant
Fuel-Handling Building
Avila Beach, California
12:09 A.M. Pacific Time

NO OTHER CHOICE

High-pressure air jets blasted Dr. Turnow's orange radiation-hazard suit as he stepped between the two glass doors separating the fuel-handling building from the rest of the Diablo complex.

Beneath him a powerful vacuum collected the particulate matter that was dislodged from his suit by the jets and recycled the air through a micro- filter. The suit had been unused before he'd put it on. However, even the smallest unremoved particle could be commandeered by radioactivity and present contamination problems.

It didn't matter at this point, Turnow realized, if a few new particles were introduced *into* the controlled area. It was already highly contaminated by blood, lead particles, and gunpowder residue, among other things.

The air lock released him with a hiss.

He was thankful for the triplicate safety systems. Until a critical meltdown of the spent-fuel storage pond containing nearly two thousand fuel rods, the lock would provide security against the escape of 99.99 percent of all radioactive materials.

Turnow hurried around the pool to where Salim and Shadir had stood earlier.

In the depths, just on top of the vertical-standing fuel rods, all hell was breaking loose. From 20 feet below the surface, the water bubbled like someone had dropped baking soda in vinegar.

The incongruity of that homey, schoolboy image struck Turnow with the thought: *how many school children are in jeopardy of their lives at this exact instant?* How long did any of them have before it was too late?

In the cloudy turbulence below them he could see the body of Shadir, still bleeding into the water.

The blaring of the warning siren continued, making coherent thought difficult.

In front of Turnow, Paul Salim was struggling to strip out of his radiation suit. His breathing was heavy and labored. Turnow knelt beside him. "You mustn't take off your suit. Particles contaminated with radioactivity will latch onto your body."

Paul sighed, uncovering a puncture wound on the side of his abdomen. "I have no choice. I can't swim . . . in it."

Turnow turned him gently, seeing that the bullet had exited just above his kidney. Blood pooled beneath him. Was the man delirious?

Turnow very much wanted to save him, but Salim was right: until the nuclear process was stopped, neither of them could leave. Salim's chances for surviving weren't high. "We must put an end to this," Turnow insisted, "and get you to a hospital."

"Help me up," Paul instructed. "Got to . . . remove the thing . . . allowing the nuclear chain reaction." Not knowing who or what Turnow was, Paul Salim still acted grateful for the assistance. The man's speech rambled, as if he were speaking aloud to keep his own thoughts focused.

Turnow lifted him.

Salim was weak but managed to walk. "Borate . . . being removed from the water by a buckyball compound. The formula is water soluble, but . . . not fully dissolved. Remove it and . . . may be able to reborate the water."

"Can't we flood the pool without removing the bucky material?" Turnow asked.

Paul shook his head, cringing and doubling over as if he would vomit. "Compound . . . too strong. Must get the watch too . . . releasing californium."

Turnow recognized the significance of Salim's words. The nuclear reaction, enabled by the buckyball compound, was being urged along by a powerful additional source of radioactivity.

Turnow eased him down by the edge of the pool. A foul odor steamed off the water. He knew Paul Salim couldn't survive the ordeal. It was 20 feet to the bottom. How would the terribly wounded man ever hold his breath for the necessary amount of time? "You can't do this," Turnow argued. "Let me get someone else."

"No time," Salim said, "and my place. Dive gear," he added. "Go to the room—" he pointed to a closet door—"small tank of emergency air . . ."

Turnow was running toward it before Salim had finished. The booties he wore were slick. He almost fell but managed to regain his balance.

In the dark space his anticontamination gloves were no help in finding the light switch. "There!" he exclaimed as the illumination finally came on.

He jumped toward a rack holding four complete sets of dive gear. Attached to each buoyancy regulator vest was a small tank of air. *Spare Air*, the bottle read through a sealed bag. Turnow grabbed one and a mask before returning to Paul Salim.

"Good," Salim panted, accepting the equipment. "Need your help. Here's . . . what to do after I go in."

Instructing Turnow to move toward the manual controls, Salim said, "There in front of you . . ."

Turnow stared at an entire station of knobs and buttons, all foreign to him.

"Three things," Salim continued. He was short of breath and had to marshal his strength. When he spoke again his words were more forceful and clear. *"Reactor Gate* and *Storage Gate* knobs open tunnel between them. Be ready to dump all the water you can . . . but be careful not to go too low. Reactor dome is empty right now. The water will rush in. Go too far and the spent fuel rods will be uncovered. Meltdown could occur in seconds."

Only two dials, Turnow considered. Why then did it all seem so complicated?

Salim's next words were delivered through a scream of pain. "That wheel valve there!"

Which one? There were 20! Turnow tentatively touched one while Salim shook his head.

"No!" he corrected urgently. "Right one says 'Emergency BAD.'"

Turnow spotted a bright white sign with red lettering hanging from the indicated valve on a chain. "Emergency BAD," he read aloud.

"Boric Acid Dump!" Salim shouted. "As soon as the contaminants are removed from the pool, flood and reaction should stop."

"Should?" *Should* was a very open-ended word. "Will it?"

Paul had the look of defeat. He was fading fast. "Don't know. No control rods in spent fuel . . . don't know if the borated water will be enough."

A feeling of hopelessness flooded Turnow. If all of this wasn't going to work, then why was he still standing here? Why wasn't he running, evacuating with everyone else? Yet all he said was, "I understand."

"Thank you." Paul Salim pulled the mask over his face, inserted the mouthpiece of the breathing apparatus into his mouth, and plunged in.

Turnow hurried to the side of the pool.

The nuclear plant operator kicked his way down, one hand clutched tightly to his mask. The lower he went, the more obscured by the turbulent cloudy water he became. Visibility in the depths was reduced to murky swirls. . . . Turnow could only guess at the combined effects of the radioactivity and the gunshot wound on Salim's ability to function.

Turnow saw that Salim was hunting for the baseball bat by feel. He heard himself giving directions as if the diver could hear him. "No, more to the right . . . that's it! No, you're past it! There you go. Straight ahead. There in the corner."

Salim finally managed to find the black object. Grasping it, he turned upward, kicking as hard as he could. When he reached the surface he shrieked, "Ah! The water is so hot! The toxicity! It burns me!"

Flinging the bat upward he managed to toss it onto the concrete lip of the pool.

It rolled out of his hands, away from the edge.

A brown trail of blood streaked the water as he descended again.

Turnow watched the search for the body of the terrorist. Salim fumbled along blindly, feeling the metal tops of the fuel rods, then yanked his hand away as it was burned.

Despite Turnow's silent urging, it took a long minute of searching before Salim discovered Shadir's body. Salim ran his hand along Shadir's face, down the shoulder to the arm.

Turnow realized he was looking for the watch. "Not that arm. The other one!"

Almost at that instant Paul Salim came to the end of a watchless wrist. Turnow saw him swim closer, grabbing for the deceased's left arm.

"You got it!" Turnow exclaimed. He was ready to open the valves as soon as the other man surfaced and had started toward him, when Salim dropped the timepiece.

Turnow cringed and stared with horrified fascination at the drama in the pool.

Paul Salim dug his fingers into the metal grid, burned them badly, but swept the grid thoroughly anyway. A stray beam of light glinted off the watch crystal as Salim's hand struck it.

The watch was jarred. It slid toward a gap in the grid. If the watch slipped past the top, Turnow understood, it would fall 14 ½ feet to the bottom of the rack.

There would be no way to stop the reaction then.

Again Salim's fingertips bumped it. *The radioactivity must be getting to him,* Turnow realized. "Right in front of you . . . yes! You've got it!" Turnow exclaimed.

Salim placed the watch on his own wrist. Turnow started for the controls, expecting Salim to resurface in seconds.

Why didn't he? What was he doing?

Something had happened. He was acting strangely. Paul Salim began to thrash around in the water.

Turnow's heart stopped when he realized that the nuclear engineer had run out of air before he could ascend.

Salim kicked wildly, disoriented. He swam into the wall instead of upward before apparently realizing his mistake.

Fifteen feet to go . . . 10 feet . . .

Should he rush for another *Spare Air* tank?

Paul Salim's struggles grew feeble. He sank toward the bottom again. Squinting for a clear view, Turnow wondered if the man was still moving.

Then the figure rolled over, completely still, faceup, dead.

The contaminating watch was still on his wrist.

Turnow groaned, "What am I to do?"

For an instant he spun from side to side, started for the controls, then returned again. "He's dead," he told himself. "There's no way to save him. Go, you fool, go!"

In a sprint for the *Reactor Gate* valve, Turnow almost fell again. He skidded to a halt. Placing his hands on the dial, he cranked it counterclockwise to *Full Open.*

But what about the californium in the watch? he wondered. *If it isn't taken from the pool, will it perpetuate the reaction?*

No time left for any more questions. It might make no difference, but this was the last chance.

Turnow performed the same motion with the *Storage Pool* valve.

At the bottom, on the opposite side of the pool, a round butterfly gate, four feet in diameter, opened. In a second the water level of the entire pool dropped as if it were on an elevator, as if the bottom had fallen out of the storage pond. The contaminated water rushed into the void in the reactor- containment vessel.

Remembering what Salim had told him of the critical water level, Turnow grasped the BAD wheel. It was tight. He put his weight into it but couldn't budge it. The valve had obviously not been used in some time, if ever.

Fear-filled, he glanced over his shoulder to check the pool. The fluid level was nearing the top of the fuel rods. If they were exposed to the air . . .

Cranking as hard as he could, Turnow saw the bodies of Shadir and Paul Salim lift up. They floated toward the opening, swept by the current. Shadir's went through, headfirst. Paul Salim's corpse became hung up on the edge of the pipe, blocking the valve.

Turnow hoped that if he toggled the gate-control knobs, he might be able to knock the body free. In a few seconds, though, it wouldn't matter, for the water level would be too low for anything to do any good.

Good-bye, Southern California.

He spun the knob back and forth, open and closed. Salim's body moved at last, at first sliding imperceptibly. Then it slipped free all at once, disappearing into the black tunnel leading to the reactor-containment dome.

And with it, the watch and the radioactive catalyst.

Closing the valve with a vigorous wrenching motion, Turnow reached for the *Boric Acid Dump* again. He let out a groan and said a prayer, forcing the wheel with all his might. It gave a little. He backed up, checking the water level again, only to discover that there was a mere inch of coverage remaining!

Praying, he heaved again.

"Ahh!" he yelled, just before the valve broke free. A jet of borated water flooded the fuel-rod containment pool. The white foam distorted Turnow's view of the bottom.

"Thank you, Lord," he called out, slumping to his knees.

The pool continued to fill for several minutes. Turnow began to wonder, to hope. To his right, about eye level, he checked a Geiger counter monitoring the levels of radioactivity in the room. The RAD reading on the illuminated numbers had begun to drop from the hundreds.

He stared at them as the pool continued to fill.

The counter leveled out at last, finally fluctuating within "high normal" limits.

He had done it! He had stopped Shaiton's Fire before it burned the entire West Coast. Turnow sat on the floor, laughing and crying at the same time.

Two men in orange suits entered the air lock. Hurrying over to him, they inquired if he was all right.

The alarms were still blaring. One of the men leaned over the control board, smacking the siren override.

The soul-wrenching clamor stopped. Except for the churning waters, the room was silent.

Turnow leaned his head back against the wall. He and the team had come close to failure and disaster and yet . . . they had done it.

North San Luis Obispo County, California
12:22 A.M. Pacific Time

THE END OF THE ROAD

The headlights of Cindy's mud-spattered SUV shone down an embankment where the dirt road vanished into the depths of Santa Rosa Creek, then emerged on the other side. The waters were swollen with spring rains, making crossing impossible.

The children were sound asleep in the backseat, as though this midnight journey was as innocuous as a trip to the grocery store. The woman in the passenger seat stared straight ahead at the surging waters, as if hoping Cindy would forge ahead.

"Dead end." Exhausted, Cindy stopped the vehicle. What should she do now? To leave the shelter of the SUV and set out on foot was unthinkable with children in tow. Her cell phone blinked *No Service.* And who would she call anyway? Steve? She wished he were here and yet was grateful that he, Matt, and Michael Salim were so far away. Safe in San Francisco.

The odometer indicated that Cindy had traveled nearly 30 miles along the tortuous track into the heart of the coastal mountain range. It was not far enough. The distant blare of the warning sirens was carried on the night breeze.

And then, suddenly, they fell silent.

Terror flashed across the face of the stranger. As if expecting to see the brilliant flash of a nuclear explosion, the woman craned her neck to gape out the window.

There was only darkness. Peace. The rushing of the stream. Frogs croaking from the reeds.

"What does it mean?" the woman murmured.

Cindy fumbled with the dial of the radio, searching for news. But in the depths of the mountain canyon, reception was poor. Nothing from San Luis radio stations. The San Francisco channel was a buzz of interference. At last the faint signal of a news channel in faraway Salt Lake City hissed over the speakers.

"Meanwhile . . . central coast of California . . . threat of meltdown . . . sent tens of thousands of residents . . . fleeing . . . as warning sirens . . . moments ago officials of Diablo Power Plant . . . declared . . . the event . . . false alarm . . . internal accident claimed the life of an employee . . . will be fully contained and back on line in a matter of days . . . emphasize the public was never at risk . . ."

The woman laughed hysterically. "False alarm! Oh! Oh, thank God! All a mistake!"

Cindy covered her face with her hands and rested her head against the steering wheel. Tears of relief flowed down her cheeks. After a minute the passenger lapsed into exhausted silence.

Cindy turned up the volume and listened for a while as the news progressed to other, more important issues: the stock market. Unemployment figures. Latest violence in the Middle East. An FBI raid on the home of a smuggler in the San Francisco Bay Area. Baseball scores.

At last Cindy turned the car around and carefully drove toward home.

EPILOGUE

Cave Rock
Lake Tahoe, Nevada Side
Friday, 15 June
9:32 P.M. Pacific Time

So the threat of Shaiton's Fire ended in a whimper, not a bang. Though the truth of how near the world had come to disaster would never be fully known by the public, Steve shared the details with Cindy.

Her life changed forever in the moment of understanding. To see clearly that they had been at the brink of death suddenly awakened her to living. Love and life had been there all along, but she had taken everything for granted. She simply had not known what she'd had before she almost lost it. Now there was no time to waste in anger. Not a second for blame or recrimination. She knew she wouldn't always understand Steve or his job. But now she understood *why* he was so passionate about it. And she'd renewed her promise to love him and stick by him . . . the same promise he'd made when he'd brought Matthew home safely to her arms.

Tonight there were too many stars to count. The sky was a black velvet backdrop for a cosmic jewel case. Cindy looked up, as though seeing heaven for the first time. She had never felt so alive, so aware.

A brisk night breeze swept down from the snow-covered peaks that ringed Lake Tahoe, yet Cindy was warm in Steve's embrace as they stood at the water's edge.

Meg Turnow passed out cups of hot chocolate to the members of Chapter 16 who had come to celebrate their victory over darkness with a barbecue and a night of stargazing. Senator Morrison chatted quietly with Charles Downing, while Teresa Bouche shook her head as Miles shared yet another joke comprehensible only to another computer geek.

Dr. Turnow adjusted the focus of his enormous telescope, then stepped aside for young Matthew Alstead to have a peek at a compact mass of glistening pinpoints—the globular cluster known as M13.

The boy gave a low whistle of wonder, then lifted his head to peer with his naked eye at what appeared to be a single fuzzy star in the constellation Hercules. "There. I see it now. Kind of." Then he went back to the eyepiece. "Wow. But this is . . . wow!"

Steve gave Cindy a squeeze, obviously enjoying their son's pleasure at the sight.

Had there ever been such an evening? Of relief and gratefulness to God for saving their lives? Just looking at the stars reminded them all of how small they were and of how big God is.

Turnow instructed, "And we're just seeing the outside. The cluster may have a million stars in it."

Matthew invited Cindy, "Come see, Mom! You won't believe what's up there!" The boy stepped down and let Cindy take her turn.

Through the 35mm eyepiece, combined with the 12-inch scope, the miraculous view became clear and distinct. A glowing ball, three-dimensional in form and almost seeming to pulse with light, drew a gasp from Cindy. "Yes!" she exclaimed in awe at the vision. "I can see it!"

Meg Turnow, a cup of hot chocolate steaming in her hand, remarked softly, "You never get over it, you know, Cindy, or any of a hundred other wonders. God always brings something wonderful every season, year after year. After you see some of them through a scope for the first time, it's like suddenly falling in love with an old familiar friend . . . and understanding, you know, the amazement that it was there before time began . . . enormous! I thought it was only one star but it's so much more! So much beauty! This creation of God's love . . . only we often don't know where to look. Or, even more, we forget to look."

Dr. Turnow quoted a line from Shakespeare's *Hamlet:* " 'There are more things in heaven and earth, Horatio, than are dreamt of in your philosophy.' Miracles right under our noses. And right above our heads."

Cindy reached for Steve's hand and pulled him to the telescope. "Look! Hon, you've got to see this!"

Steve gasped, then whispered in awe at the sight. "Miracles *are* all around us. All the time. And all we have to do is look."

AUTHOR'S NOTE

WEEDS IN THE GARDEN OF EDEN

The real story behind this book began in 1993, when a close friend of mine, a geneticist (the inspiration for the Chapter 16 character of Dr. Turnow), visited the former Soviet Union. The country was in complete ruin. The entire population had been thrown into abject poverty. There were no jobs, no industry, and people were laid off by the thousands.

There was also little medical assistance and treatment. Children were dying for lack of common vaccines. On the outskirts of Moscow, "Dr. Turnow" (as I'll call him) witnessed a young boy being hit by a car. His ribs were crushed and his lungs punctured. The doctor attended to him, but his efforts were limited for lack of tools. No ambulance came, no fireman or paramedic. Local residents, who had heard the screams, came to help with the only things they had—iodine and cotton. Four hours later this twelve- year-old boy died from internal bleeding on the side of the road, while waiting for attention.

It seemed the country was dying too. In the vacuum of a crumbling government, the Russian Mafia took over.

Near Moscow, hidden in the trees of the countryside, was a secret Russian city, called Oblinsk. Inside the high steel walls, the country's top scientists had been working for years to perfect the most powerful strains of chemical and biological warfare agents. My friend had been escorted there by the Russians, in the hope that a place of death might be transformed into a fountain of youth, a pharmaceutical manufacturing plant. Critically needed, it would provide medical assistance for the ailing people and jobs for the most brilliant minds of the Eastern bloc.

Though Turnow was informed by former high-ranking KGB officials that all chemical and biological agents had been removed, many areas of Oblinsk remained quarantined and off limits to visitors. Many of his questions remained unanswered as well. Dr. Turnow dared not probe the armed men too deeply.

As he left Oblinsk he witnessed men dressed in soiled lab coats harvesting potatoes in the freezing fields. His escort informed him that the men were scientists who hadn't been paid in over a year. They were farming in order to keep themselves and their starving families alive.

In the final assessment, Oblinsk wouldn't be the medical savior of Russia. It had several design flaws, aside from the thousands of gallons of anthrax, plague, and other deadly cocktails still stored in the vats. The dying would go without medicine, and those with the power to poison the world would instead barely survive on potatoes, until necessity required many to sign on the Mafia's payroll.

When Dr. Turnow returned from his trip and shared this information with me, I was astounded. The very real and morbid tale intrigued me. For years I followed the story, plotting out the elements: *Starving scientist, hired by the Mafia, sells deadly secrets and other items on the black market to the highest bidder.*

But I never wrote that story; I was committed to other projects. Later, sadly, I watched it unfold as I imagined it would. In the spring of 1997, I received a fax from Dr. Turnow. The Associated Press article read, "Iraq Obtains Chem. & Bio. Weapons from Secret Russian City, Oblinsk."

My heart sank. Dr. Turnow's and my fears had become hard reality. I wondered what else was missing and where the weapons of mass destruction had gone. It was then, I realized, that ours had become a world where life would be traded for the right price.

That's when I became even more serious about retracing the seeds of recent history through the eyes of my friend, "Dr. Turnow." As I followed their growth, I was led to America, where the tendrils were taking hold. Anti- American sentiments had begun to sprout around the world. Terrorist cells were actually taking advantage of our American freedoms to raise money for terrorist acts—all in the name of charity. For a time the farmers of these strangling weeds were protected by our own freedoms and Constitution. They spread their roots under the protection of the American dream.

Our law enforcement agencies, though highly effective, weren't united enough to stop the course of what could eventually happen—an attack on America from within its own borders.

As Dr. Turnow and I talked, years before the events of September 11, 2001, I realized that it was time for our nation and government agencies to unify. It was time for the creation of Chapter 16—a streamlined, highly mobile, Domestic Counterterrorism Unit—a unit that could take advantage of all of America's elite security agencies. It was the story I had to write. And I did, finishing the first novel of the Chapter 16 series, *Shaiton's Fire,* two months before 9-11.

Then the tragedy of 9-11 hit. Immediately the face of our nation changed. In the minutes it took those four planes commandeered by terrorists to crash, Americans met the hard reality that even the land of liberty and dreams was not secure. Even with all the efforts of our domestic security forces to chop off the heads of the weeds before they spread—foiling many unknown attacks and apprehending hundreds of enemies within our borders—our safety cannot be guaranteed. That means we must all support the growth of America's law enforcement and domestic protection agencies. But we must also be vigilant *ourselves*, rather than complacent, about the values and the life we hold dear.

My hope is that this series will inspire a sense of patriotism in Americans and those abroad who believe in our way of life. That Americans will give gratitude to God for blessing the world with such a wonderful place as this country, our Garden of Eden. And, most of all, that each of us will learn to thank him for every day of life that is granted to us.

Jake Thoene
Jake@jakethoene.com

GLOSSARY

AFSOC Air Force Special Operations Command

BART Bay Area Rapid Transit

CSI Crime Scene Investigations
CT team Counterterrorism Team

H&K Heckler & Koch
HALO High Altitude Low Opening, a parachute maneuver
HRT Hostage Rescue Team

MRE Meals Ready to Eat

NAK North Aryan Knights
NCIC National Crime Information Center

Op Operation
OS teams Observer-Sniper Teams

PP Preliminary Profile

SatCom Satellite Communications System
SCOT Special Circumstances Operational Tactics
SOIC Strategic Operations Information Command
Spec Ops Special Operations
SWAT team Special Weapons and Tactics team

tac vest tactical assault vest

Read the following excerpt from *Firefly Blue,* the next exciting and timely suspense novel by Jake Thoene.

"Better sit down and strap yourselves in," Steve said. "There's been a change of plans."

Dr. Turnow appeared baffled. "Has there been another attack?"

Steve shut the fuselage door, wrenching the latch into place. The cabin became much quieter. Shaking his head, he replied, "A U.S. marshal and a Border Patrol agent were killed last night in Arizona. The marshal said he saw a Mexican Humvee."

Turnow clenched his jaw.

Teresa covered her mouth. "Federales helping drug runners—"

"Sounds like it. There's a standoff now. Hostages: a woman and two little kids. HRT is in the air, headed to a base there. Looks like you guys are going with me."

"I'll need to meet with the press." Teresa was stunned. "But I don't even have my things, a change of clothes. What will . . . how . . ." She stared at him. "Surely they don't need us."

Raising his head, Turnow disagreed. "I wouldn't bet on it, Teresa. You know they will probably need all the help they can get."

"Welcome to the world of Special Operations," Steve replied, reclining his seat. "Better get some sleep now, 'cause there isn't gonna be any until this crisis gets resolved."